Priestess Dreaming

An Otherworld Novel

YASMINE GALENORN

J

JOVE BOOKS, NEW YORK

THE BERKLEY PUBLISHING GROUP
Published by the Penguin Group
Penguin Group (USA) LLC
375 Hudson Street, New York, New York 10014

USA • Canada • UK • Ireland • Australia • New Zealand • India • South Africa • China

penguin.com

A Penguin Random House Company

PRIESTESS DREAMING

A Jove Book / published by arrangement with the author

Jove Books are published by The Berkley Publishing Group.
JOVE® is a registered trademark of Penguin Group (USA) LLC.
The "J" design is a trademark of Penguin Group (USA) LLC.

For information, address: The Berkley Publishing Group,
a division of Penguin Group (USA) LLC,
375 Hudson Street, New York, New York 10014.

ISBN: 978-0-515-15475-7

PUBLISHING HISTORY
Jove mass-market edition / October 2014

PRINTED IN THE UNITED STATES OF AMERICA

10 9 8 7 6 5 4 3 2 1

Cover art by Tony Mauro.
Cover design by Danielle Abbiate.
Map by Andrew Marshall, copyright © 2012 by Yasmine Galenorn.

Dedicated to:

Carol Padovan . . . dear friend, old soul, good times.

ACKNOWLEDGMENTS

Thank you to everyone who has helped me get to this point:

Samwise: my lover and consort. Meredith Bernstein: my agent. Kate Seaver: my editor. Tony Mauro: my cover artist. Marc Mullinex, Andria Holley, and Jenn Price: my assistants. My furry "Galenorn Gurlz": my feline brigade. Ukko, Rauni, Mielikki, and Tapio: my spiritual guardians.

Also, especially during the writing of this, Mandy Roth and Michelle Pillow, who listened a lot when I needed to talk and needed encouragement that my new plans *will* work out and that yes, I *can* accomplish the new goals I have set out for myself.

To my readers: Your support by buying my books helps keep my work continuing. You can find me on the net on my site: Galenorn.com. You can also find an Otherworld Wikipedia on my website.

If you write to me snail mail (see website for address or write via publisher), please enclose a self-addressed stamped envelope with your letter if you would like a reply.

The Painted Panther
Yasmine Galenorn

There are nights when the wolves are silent and only the moon howls.

GEORGE CARLIN

Mystery has its own mysteries, and there are gods above gods. We have ours, they have theirs. That is what's known as infinity.

JEAN COCTEAU

Chapter 1

I contemplated going back into the house, purse over my shoulder. Should I, or shouldn't I? Utter mayhem lay within. Absolute chaos in a kitchen, complete with spilled food, a huffy dragon, one very pissed-off house sprite, and my sister, the wide-eyed, *catch-da-giant-bird* turkey-chaser. Add to that the rest of the milling—and by now, thoroughly confused—throng that made up our extended family, and it was a no-brainer. *Not a chance. Nope. Not gonna happen.*

I was perfectly fine out here in the pouring rain, getting soaked. Let Smoky take his lumps from Iris. This was all *his* fault, not mine. The only part they could blame me for was that I had assigned him the chore of bringing home a twenty-five-pound turkey for tomorrow's Thanksgiving dinner. Was it really *my* responsibility to remind him to make certain it was already dead?

Not. My. Fault. And neither was the Three Stooges aftermath that followed. Now, with Iris and Hanna both on the warpath, I had no desire to go back in there and subject myself to their outrage.

As my gaze wandered over to the turkey pecking around

our backyard, it occurred to me that the bird was giving me
the evil eye. He reminded me of a big fat demon bird, gloating
like some demented vulture. The fat old Tom was closer to the
woods than our back door, and I wondered if he realized just
how lucky he was.

I stamped my foot in his direction. "Go on, you dumb
bird. Make a break for it while you can, before Smoky comes
looking for you." As if he understood me, the turkey turned
toward the tree line in back of the yard and slowly began to
waddle off into the sunset. Or as the case actually was, the
pitch darkness. It was only around five thirty, but by this
time of year, the Seattle area was swathed in night. Sunset
had come and gone about an hour ago.

I snorted. "Have a happy Thanksgiving, bird. You lucked
out, so say a prayer to the Great Turkey."

As I watched him vanish into the woods, I wondered where
the hell Smoky had found him. No doubt he'd stolen him from
some turkey farm or something. Wild turkeys generally didn't
go running around the streets of Seattle. But I wasn't going to
ask. After this fiasco, I had a feeling that my dragon-shifting
husband wouldn't be in any mood to discuss turkey-napping.

Thanks to sheer dumb luck, the bird had managed to
escape from the kitchen. He'd left behind a trail of walking
wounded, though—including me. That beak was nasty sharp
and I had the scratch to prove it, but at least I didn't have a
hole in my hand like Roz did. Yeah, in the great dinner war,
the bird deserved his freedom. He'd earned it. As the last of
his tail feathers vanished from sight on the path leading to
Birchwater Pond, I saluted him.

"You've got what it takes to make it, soldier. Carry on."

With one last look at the house, I straightened my shoulders and headed toward my car. We still needed a turkey for
Thanksgiving tomorrow, so I might as well head out to buy
one. On the up side, by the time I got back, things should
have smoothed over and the mess should be cleaned up.

Families. One thing was for certain: Mine was loopy,
batty, and all around, a freakshow crew. But I wouldn't trade
them for all the glitter and glitz in Otherworld *or* Earthside.

I slid into the driver's seat, but as I inserted the key into the ignition, a shiver ran down my back. A shadow passed through me, cold and dark and incredibly ancient.

Suddenly nervous, I hit the button to lock the doors. Maybe it was the wind that rattled the trees that had spooked me. Or maybe it was the driving rain. Or perhaps the darkness and perpetual gloom had finally managed to suck the smile off my face. Whatever the case, I glanced back at the house, anxious.

PTSD, maybe? We had recently come through a horrible stretch, what with the war raging in Otherworld and losing our father. We were all still a little shell-shocked. I had been coping with a lot of nightmares and flashbacks the past few weeks, but this didn't feel like it originated from the same place.

Trying to quiet my mind, I listened, breathing slowly.

Inhale.

Exhale.

Inhale.

Exhale.

Listen . . .

At first, I could sense only the wind and rain that lashed the yard, but then . . . below that . . . *There it was.* Something was on the move. Something *big.* I searched my feelings, examining the sensation. Was it fear? Yes, I was definitely afraid, but there was more to it than that. Anticipation? Anxiety? A tingling at the base of my neck told me that deep magic was afoot, and would soon be knocking on my door.

Magic rode the currents, on the wings of a flock of birds. They were there, in the astral, black as coal and shrieking warnings from an ancient wood filled with extraordinary beasts. The rolling mists of time poured past as the ravens cried, their song echoing with magic. Dark magic, deep woodland magic. *Death coming in on waves of flame and smoke.*

As if in synch with my thoughts, a shriek cut through the darkness, startling me out of my trance. I recognized the cry. *Raven.* Raven was calling. And where raven flew, Raven Mother couldn't be far behind.

And behind Raven Mother, chasing her, was a dragon. At first I flashed back to Hyto, but then caught hold of myself. Hyto was dead and gone. I forced myself to focus, to examine the energy that rushed past. This dragon was ancient—not a dragon from the Dragon Reaches, but even older. This creature rose from the depths of the earth, come awake after eons of time asleep in its lair.

As he roared to life, chasing the flock of ravens, he suddenly vanished from my sight.

I found myself sitting in the car, my hand on the keys.

What the hell was that all about?

Almost afraid to examine the vision, I shuddered and started the ignition. As the engine warmed up, I stared into the darkness, my thoughts far distant from Thanksgiving.

Something big was headed my way, and there was no use trying to avoid it. I might as well just open my arms and brace for whatever it was. Trying to hide from trouble had ceased to be an effective defense mechanism a few years ago when the demons had first shown up.

With a grimace, I pulled out my phone and texted Menolly that I was heading for the store to replace the turkey. As I eased out of the driveway, I whispered, "Bring it on, Raven Mother. Bring it on. I'm waiting for you."

A faint laughter echoed over the howling of the wind. She'd heard me. And she was waiting.

"Give me that!" Delilah's voice rang out, and I turned, scanning the mob for her face. Somebody was bound to get hurt in this mess. People were shoving in every direction, trying to push their way through the mass of churning bodies. To my left, a woman tripped and fell. I tried to maneuver through the crowd to reach her, but a man stopped to help her back to her feet and she dusted herself off, looking no worse for the wear, and then, a glint in her eye, she vanished into the seething throng.

Still unable to locate Delilah, I glanced over my shoulder. Smoky and Trillian were standing at attention, waiting for my orders, both looking resigned and rather frightened. Their arms full, they threaded their way through the chaos as they tried to follow me. With Delilah still nowhere to be seen, I made a unilateral decision. She'd just have to catch up to us later.

"Over to the pet section, pronto!"

Pointing toward the opposite end of the store, I began to

traverse the aisles. Wordlessly, they filed along behind me. I gauged the easiest, quickest route, then began to wind through the rows of merchandise, narrowly skirting a table of precariously stacked crystal dishes. Motioning for the guys to be cautious, I held my breath until we were past the display.

Once we were out of housewares, the crowd began to thin out as we maneuvered our way over to the pet toy aisle. Along the way, I caught sight of an insulated lunch bag in fuchsia, with a cat appliqué splashed across the front. It really was cute. Another woman was eyeing it and I had a split second to make up my mind.

"Nerissa would love that." I snatched it up seconds before my opponent could grab it and, once again, we were on the move, leaving her sputtering in the dust. A few moments later, we reached our destination: the pet care section. We had the department to ourselves. Most of the crowds were over in electronics and toys. Chase and Iris were forging their way through the latter and I silently wished them luck.

"Are we done yet?" Smoky grumbled. "Haven't you found enough loot? It's four thirty in the morning, woman." He didn't sound that angry, though. In fact, the twinkle in his eye told me he was putting on a show because he thought it was required. Just like a man.

Trillian, also my husband, snorted. "You really think that's going to work? Dude, you should *know* your wife and her sisters by now. We've got at least another hour to go. Remember last year?"

Trillian's obsidian skin glistened under the florescent lights. He'd braided his hair to keep it out of the way. The silver strands rested smooth against his back, shimmering with the faintest of cerulean highlights. He had worn a sleek black turtleneck and black jeans, but left his jacket in the car, claiming it made him more aerodynamic in the crowds. A Svartan, one of the Dark and Charming Fae, he usually managed to get what he wanted by smooth-talking whoever was in his way. But on Black Friday, all bets were off. My sisters and I overruled all opinions in the household.

Smoky, on the other hand, was attired in his usual get up: white jeans, V-neck pale blue sweater, and long white trench.

At six-four, my dragon towered over the crowds. Though I kept him near, even his imposing nature didn't offer us much protection during the early hours of the most terrifying shopping day of the year. He, too, had braided his hair, though it was ankle length instead of mid-shoulder like Trillian's. Luckily, his hair moved all on its lonesome. If it hadn't, his braid would have gotten trampled several times tonight.

"Don't remind me." Smoky rolled his eyes. "Last year was worse than this, I'll give you that."

"The others aren't done yet, so just hold your horses. Remember? Hanna promised leftover turkey soup along with fresh baked homemade bread if you guys play nice." I picked up a catnip mouse and shook it, frowning at the *squeaky-squeaky* sound. Delilah would love it.

Her toys were constantly ragged, she played with them so much. And then, the thought occurred to me that we should get her panther form a toy, too. One that could withstand a good mauling. Also—why not one for Nerissa? Her puma liked to play and, on occasion, Delilah and our sister-in-law went hunting together in the forest behind our house. They never really caught anything, but the big cats liked to prowl through the trees.

"After we're done here, we're heading over to the stuffed toys. So gird your loins, or whatever it is you boys do in order to stay sane."

Oblivious to their groans, I began tossing toy mice in my cart, before we pushed onward.

We had not only brought Delilah's Jeep, Menolly's Mustang, and my Lexus, but also Morio's SUV, which gave us room for everybody who had wanted to come, and all the packages as well.

Hanna had stayed home to watch Maggie, our baby calico gargoyle. Vanzir and Rozurial had begged off. They were planning some secret surprise and had shooed us out of the house, instructing us not to return till early morning. I wasn't sure what they were up to, but could only pray it wasn't something stupid like turning the house into a giant video game or something.

It was nearing 6 A.M. as we pulled into the driveway of our

lovely old three-story Victorian with basement. Menolly still had some time before she had to be in her lair to sleep. Vampires and sunrise? Not such a good mix, so we always made sure she was home in time to get to bed. But we still had nearly ninety minutes before the sun crawled over the horizon. Or up behind the clouds, as was more often the norm here in Seattle.

As we piled out of our cars, the men gathering all our loot for us, I glanced at Trillian and Smoky and wearily smiled. "You do realize how much I love the pair of you, don't you? And Morio, too." Morio was my third husband. I was one hell of a lucky woman.

His hands full, Smoky winked at me as a strand of his hair unbraided itself, slowly reaching over to caress my cheek. A smile creased his face. Dragon smiles were always a little sly, a little coy.

"You can show us just how much you love us after we haul all this stuff inside." His voice was husky, and I caught my breath as the touch of his hair sparked off an ache that rose between my legs. I wanted him and I wanted him *now*. It had been two days since I'd had sex—we'd all been busy. But that was two days too long.

Trillian brushed past me, arching an eyebrow. "That's the best idea I've heard all night."

"I wish." Shaking my head, I forced my attention away from my nether regions, which were now up in arms, demanding attention. "Go on, the pair of you. You know what waits for us inside there. An early morning brunch, and then Iris and Hanna are going to put us all to work. Except Menolly, of course. Honestly, how Iris manages to have as much energy as she does after having the twins, I have no clue. It's been less than a month and she's raring to go."

As much as the thought of an early A.M. tryst with my men appealed to me, the morning was given over to homely duties. Today we'd all be decking out the house for Yuletide, from bottom to top. With Iris and Hanna in charge, it meant we'd fill every nook and cranny with some sort of decoration. But I didn't begrudge the time spent, especially this year.

With Father dead and so much upheaval in our lives, it was important to keep our traditions alive. We needed these touchstones to ground us and keep us on track. My premonitions of the other night had faded, and I had put them down to skittishness. So far, nothing had happened, and I hadn't bothered telling anybody about them.

Trillian laughed. "Fine. We'll avoid facing the wrath of the house-maidens. But that means we're on for this evening, though frankly, I'm going to need a nap before then. The few hours we got after Thanksgiving dinner were helpful, but not enough."

But as we approached the porch I lost track of what he was saying, because the front door burst open and Vanzir came racing out, the look on his face somewhere between guilty and terrified. He scrambled down the stairs, leaping to take the last few.

"Run! Get out of the way!" The dream-chaser demon pushed past us looking like hell itself was on his heels.

Confused, I glanced back at the door. *Holy. Fuck.* It couldn't be—no, no . . . I couldn't be seeing what my brain thought it was seeing. Could I?

But there, on the porch, with gleaming yellow eyes, stood a very large, very burly creature with bluish-white fur covering its body. It was bipedal . . .

"*Yeti!* There's a freaking yeti on our porch!" I dropped my purse and backed away from the steps, never letting my gaze waver from the creature. Trillian and Smoky were doing the same.

Yetis were unpredictable. Like their cousins, the Sasquatch, they are large and muscular, but their hair runs from white to a dusky silvery-blue, compared to the deep brown of the Sasquatch's fur. Camouflage, no doubt. But what the hell was a yeti from the mountains of Tibet doing here, on our front porch? And more importantly—at least for the moment—what was it going to do?

The creatures were wild, almost alien in nature. In fact, back in Otherworld, there were rumors that the entire Sasquatch-Yeti family were originally from another planet, though nobody knew if this was true. It could have just been an urban legend. They belonged to the Crypto family, but they weren't found in Otherworld and they sure didn't mingle with the Cryptos over here, Earthside. Or with the

Fae. Pretty much everybody but monster-hunters gave the primate-like creatures a wide berth.

I searched my memory, trying to calculate our options. Attempting to communicate wouldn't do any good, not unless the creature was willing to talk. And so far, nobody I knew had gotten close enough to one to invite it to tea, at least not without getting mauled. Usually, approaching beyond a certain range triggered their defense mechanisms, and the creatures would attack. And an eight- to nine-foot-tall agitated primate who was feeling hemmed in wasn't the safest of critters to be around.

"Anybody have any suggestions about what we do with the big white giant on the porch?" I tried to keep my voice even and neutral. No use setting it off with any loud noises.

"My babies!" Heedless of the danger, Iris broke into a run, heading around the left side of the house. Her home was in back of ours, and her twins were there, waiting for her with their grandma and their daddy. I pitied any fool who tried to get between her and the babies, that was for sure. The house sprite might be a gorgeous, buxom hottie, milkmaid-pretty with golden hair down to her ankles and cornflower blue eyes, but she could turn a grown man inside out if she got mad enough. *Literally.*

"Astrid!" Chase followed Iris at a dead run. He and his daughter Astrid lived with Iris and Bruce. No doubt, he was just as freaked.

Startled by the sudden movement, the yeti let out a roar and bounded down the steps. My men moved immediately to intercept—Smoky, Trillian, and Morio dropped their parcels and darted to cut off the path so it couldn't follow Iris and Chase.

I backed up, looking at the sky. The clouds were thick. It was almost cold enough to snow, and there should be enough energy around to summon the lightning. I raised my arms and called on the Moon Mother. She was huge tonight—not quite full but nearly there, and I could feel her shining down even though she was obscured by the boiling clouds.

As I drew the energy into me, a crackle of silver racing through my arms, I began to feel giddy. What the hell? Her magic made me drunk at times, but never like this, and never this fast.

I wanted to dance, to spin and cackle and laugh. Trying to focus, I forced my attention back to the tingling moon-fire, but it was no use. The next moment, I heard music. Faint at first, the melody quickly swept up to surround me. Reverberating with a rhythm as deep as the soil, the singer enticed me to join the dance, his voice deep and guttural.

I began to whirl, laughing as I looked toward the sky. The Moon Mother, she was up there, and I could hear her singing along. But whatever the words were, I could not understand. Weaving in and out like a sinuous chain of dancers, the words sang of adventure.

The sky shimmered, a thin veil of sparkling lights flitting around me. Enchanted, I reached out, trying to capture the twinkles in my hands.

A low growl startled me. To my left, Delilah, in her panther form, bounded by, chasing a translucent figure with wings. Tiny, it was barely a foot tall. Oh hell! Some semblance of coherency broke through. I knew what that creature was! A *pixie*. A freaking pixie.

We were friends with a pixie, but the majority of them were annoying pests and worse. They liked to lead people astray, and they had it in for witches like myself. And this one was darting around, sprinkling dust right and left.

No wonder I wanted to dance. But then, reason escaped me as once again the music lured me in. I whirled, holding my arms out, and the energy I had drawn down from the Moon Mother suddenly cut loose in a volley of bolts as I became a spinning wheel of silver fire, sparks flying from my fingers.

Delilah snarled and lumbered out of reach. I heard Nerissa curse as I hit her with one of the mini-bolts. I wanted to stop, but my feet kept moving, I kept twirling, and the sparks kept flying.

"Stop me! Somebody stop me! Pixie dust!" I managed to shout between the violent fits of laughter that were erupting from my core. I had no clue what was so funny, but I couldn't stop that either.

By now, it occurred to me that if I had to be shooting out sparks, why not move to where they'd do some good? I tried to catch sight of the yeti in my dizzying spin and realized that if I shifted in a northwestern direction, I'd end up near the creature, who was now fully engaged with Smoky and the boys.

As I danced closer, still spinning like a crazed top, Smoky let out a shout, and then Trillian. The next thing I knew, the smell of burning fur filled my nostrils, and with each spin I found myself facing one very pissed-off and scorched yeti.

One circle around and I caught sight of him gazing at me with those glowing, angry, topaz eyes. A second circle, and a large fuzzy white arm came flying out. The third and I staggered to the ground as his big ole fist met my crazed body.

I landed on the frozen driveway. Apparently the temperature had dropped enough for frost to form. The fucking dirt was hard and cold. But even getting smacked by Mr. Abominable Snowman couldn't shake the pixie dust off me, because I began to struggle to my feet, still needing to dance. The next moment, Smoky had grabbed me under his arm, dragging me behind him as we raced through the yard toward the studio that had originally been a shed.

The minute we hit the door, he swept me up and barreled into the bathroom, where he shoved me—clothes and all— into the shower. One more second and he'd turned it on full blast. The water was cold, and shocked me into silence. As the spray warmed up, it began to wash off the pixie dust and my foggy thoughts began to lift. My body was still jazzed higher than a kite by all the energy I'd drawn in, but at least I didn't feel the need to go gallivanting in a crazed polka around the room. I stood there, mutely, under pounding water. *Yeah, this outfit is a goner.*

After a moment, Smoky turned off the spray. "Pixie dust gone?"

I searched for the dazed feelings brought on by the dust, but the only thing I felt was wired and bedraggled. After a moment, I nodded.

"Yeah, I think so. I'm pissed, but I'm thinking clearly and I don't feel quite so possessed to go frolicking with Mr. Yeti. *The yeti!* Where the hell did it come from, and more importantly, what are we going to do about it?"

"I don't know. When I saw it attack you, all I could think about was to get you out of the way. You were in no shape to protect yourself." He held out a towel. I stripped and, leaving my wet clothes in the shower stall, I stepped out and wrapped the thick terrycloth around me. The soft cloth against my skin felt good, and I suddenly realized that I was rapidly growing tired—another side effect of too much pixie dust.

"I need to find something to wear and then we have to get the hell back to the house. The fact that pixies are having a field day in our yard is bad enough, but a yeti bounding out of our front door? More than a little scary." A sudden thought hit me. "Maggie! We have to make sure Maggie is okay!" Pushing past him, I rushed out of the bathroom.

"You can't go racing out there in a bathrobe." Smoky motioned toward Rozurial's room. "Grab something from the incubus's closet and I'll go check on Maggie. I'll let you know the minute I find her and Hanna." And he was out the door before I could touch the knob.

Wanting to run after him, but realizing that dashing naked through the storm wasn't exactly the brightest idea, I hurried into Roz's room and tossed my way through his dresser. I found a tunic that fit over my Double-Ds, and a pair of drawstring pajama bottoms. Cinching them firmly, I realized I'd have to go barefoot. My shoes were ruined, and I couldn't wear any of Roz's boots—they were far too big. Sopping hair and all, I headed out of the studio, back toward the house, my feet freezing. The frozen soil and frosty grass made for a slippery mix, and I struggled to keep my footing as I jogged back toward the house.

All hell had broken loose. Trillian and Morio were still fighting the yeti and from what I could see, the damned thing seemed tougher than a dubba-troll. But that was only the half of it. Glimmers flickered from all over the yard— and every glimmer seemed to have some sort of creature attached to it.

The pixie was still flying around like a crazed maniac, and to my dismay, I spotted a couple more nearby. *Hell.* They were bad news, in general. Mistletoe was the exception to the rule and that's only because he was our friend.

Beneath a huckleberry bush near my herb garden, I could see some sort of frosty hedgehog-like creature. Not certain what it was, I decided I had better get dressed before investigating.

Trampled shopping bags were scattered all over the yard, and I scanned the area, trying to locate everyone. I finally spotted Nerissa, in her werepuma form, and Delilah, who was still in panther form. They'd treed something, and both big cats were standing up against the trunk staring at whatever it was they'd managed to trap in the branches.

Menolly was up on top of the roof. She was after—what the hell? It looked like some sort of gremlin. She was climbing along the shingles, but the creature scampered over the tiles as if it were running on flat ground.

Rozurial was nowhere in sight, and Iris and Chase had taken off for Iris's house. Vanzir was struggling with a figure beneath a cedar. They were rolling around on the ground, locked in a wrestling match, and I heard Vanzir utter a string of curses. Shade was chasing another glimmer around toward the backyard.

Motherfucking son of a bitch, what the hell was going on?

Just then, one of the Fae guards who patrolled our land ran over to my side, panting. "Camille—we're overrun. Four of the men are out back fighting a group of barbegazi. And two of the men are chasing a couple of ice wolves."

"*Barbegazi? Ice wolves?* What the hell are they?" I wasn't sure I wanted to know, but then again, there was a lot I'd learned the hard way that I wished I didn't have to know about.

"Barbegazi are creatures from the Northlands. They're very much like dwarves only smaller and hardier. Usually they're kindly natured but this batch appears to be a particularly surly lot. As for the ice wolves, they are also known as amaroks, at least to one Earthside tribal group. They're wolf demons, dangerous and hungry for human flesh." The guard glanced around, shaking his head. "I don't know what happened, or where all of these creatures came from. The wards suddenly went off and we were swarming with them."

"The rogue portal out back? Could they have come through there?" I motioned toward the porch steps, which were surprisingly clear. "I need to get dressed and get back out here."

He followed me up the stairs. "No, the portal hasn't been active at all. I—"

As we entered the house, he fell silent. First of all, the foyer was filled with snow. White, cold, sticky wet snow. And it was snowing up a storm. *Inside the house.* Second, a loud humming emanated from the living room.

"Well . . . this is a new look. Ice palace décor, for the win." But my sarcasm fell flat, even to my own ears, as I stared at snow on the floor. All twelve to fourteen inches of snow. My feet were beginning to freeze.

"Wait here, Lady Camille." The guard plowed his way into the living room, then within moments returned. "There's a portal in your living room. The snow's coming through there. Ten to one, that's where all of these creatures came from, too."

A portal? In the living room?

"Okay, then, well. I don't know what to say to that." I wanted to go prowling around, looking for Maggie, but Smoky had promised he would let me know the moment he found them and truth was, I was starting to chill. "Come with me, please. I need to change and I don't know what else might be rampaging through the house. I'd rather not be surprised while I'm getting dressed." I darted through the snow, wincing as the sting of the frozen water hit my feet. The guard— whose name was Dez—followed me, sword out and ready.

The snow was beginning to drift up the living room walls and out into the foyer and the parlor. But even more alarming, the room was also decked out in the most garish holiday décor I had ever seen. In one corner stood a ten-foot-tall tree, blazing with neon flashing blue and green lights that made my eyes hurt. The lights also ran the length of the room, following the ceiling around to form a terrifyingly bright border. Huge, ugly, acrylic ornaments bedecked the tree, catching and reflecting the lights like crazed prisms.

"What the fuck . . . It looks like Crack Santa and his methed-out elves descended on our living room."

"I don't know, Lady Camille." Sheepishly, he said, "I thought perhaps you decorated before you left for your shopping trip."

"Oh, hell no. *This mess?* I have better taste than that. And you know Iris . . . yeah . . ."

The thought of Iris allowing such a tawdry show in our living room almost made me laugh. Thoroughly confused, I turned to the portal, which was shimmering in the opposite corner near the window. It was swirling with icy blue sparkles. I had no clue to where it led, and I sure as hell wasn't going to dive through to find out.

"Okay, upstairs, to my rooms."

As we headed up to the second story, the chill followed. It was still snowing when we reached my suite of rooms and by the time we entered my bedroom, I could see my breath and my toes were numb.

Dez made a quick survey around the room and ascertained that nothing was amok—or at least, nothing was running amok.

I stripped down as he kept watch. The Fae—including half-Fae like myself—generally weren't modest or embarrassed by nudity, and he stood by the door, guarding me, without so much as blinking an eye.

Slipping into my ready-to-rumble catsuit that I wore when I knew we had a fight on our hands, I zipped it up and slid on a pair of kitten-heel granny boots. Then, slinging a belt around my hips, I fastened on the sheath containing my silver dagger.

After dressing, I made certain my unicorn horn was still safely hidden away in the secret compartment in my closet. For what we seemed to be facing, I didn't think we'd need to use it. I wasn't about to deplete its power this far from the new moon unless it was absolutely necessary.

Once I was finished, I slipped a capelet over my shoulders for extra warmth and quickly scrubbed the streaked makeup off my face. My eyeliner and mascara had survived—they were waterproof—but everything else was a lost cause. Less than ten minutes after we hit my bedroom, I was finished and ready to rock.

"Okay, back down to the first floor."

But as we reached the landing, I paused. Someone was coming up the steps. I pulled out my dagger as Dez held his sword at the ready.

As the sound of footsteps rounded the turn, I held my breath, but then let it out in one big exhale as I saw it was Smoky, looking grim. My heart skidded to a halt.

"Maggie—?"

"Maggie's safe and sound," he said before I could burst into tears. "Hanna took her down to Menolly's lair when the shit hit the fan. I told her to stay there for now. But that portal in the living room? I know where it goes. I hopped through to find out what the hell was going on."

"Where does it lead? And can you close it?" We followed him as he turned, heading back down the stairs.

Smoky shook his head, glancing over his shoulder. "No, I can't close it. The gate was opened by powerful magic, and I can't do anything about it. But as I said, I crossed over to see where it led. I'm not sure who the hell did this, but the portal? It leads into the Northlands, as far as I can tell."

My heart began to beat faster. The Northlands could be reached via Otherworld, and through perilous routes up in the higher reaches over here, Earthside. I had a lot of bad associations with the lands at the top of the world. A lot of harsh, volatile creatures made their homes there, including dragons like Smoky's father, who had imprisoned and tortured me.

"So the question is, who opened this portal, and why?"

"Right now, I think the more important question is: Just what all has come through so far? And what else can we expect before we manage to close it down?" Smoky's grim smile deepened. "Let's get back outside, woman. We need to do something to stop that yeti from trampling the yard."

I turned to the guard. "Dez, stay here, please, and guard the portal. Don't put your life in danger, but if something else comes through, do your best to stop it if you can. And if you can't, get the hell outside so we know what we're facing next."

With that, Smoky and I headed back outside, into the fray.

Chapter 2

So, yes, I'm Camille D'Artigo, and I'm a Witch and a Priestess in the service of the Moon Mother. Together, with my sisters and I, we run the Earthside division of the Otherworld Intelligence Agency—the OIA. We were originally sent over here because our track record with the agency leaves something to be desired. We weren't exactly the best agents in the world, though gods know, we tried. But our lineage kind of mucks up the works.

On our mother's side, we're half-human. And our father is full-blooded Fae, from Otherworld. Well, *was*. We're orphans now. Our mother died when we were young. Father died less than a month ago in the siege on Elqaneve, over in Otherworld. We miss them, dearly, but thank the gods we still have each other, though like all sisters, we have our tiffs and disagreements.

Anyway, I'm Camille, and I'm the oldest. Besides being a priestess and witch, I happen to be married to three gorgeous hunks of manflesh, which suits me just fine. I love sex, I love men, and I love good fashion and lots of caffeine. I also love magic, and above all, I love my lady, the Moon Mother.

Trillian, my alpha husband, is a Svartan—the dark cousins of the elves. He's from Svartalfheim. Smoky is a dragon—half white, half silver. And Morio? He's a youkai-kitsune, and Japanese. Together, we're all soul-bound, which means that we're connected on a soul-level. This can be both good and bad, and sometimes a little dicey, but it's never boring.

My sister Delilah's the middle child, though for a long time, she acted like the youngest. A twin at birth, her womb-mate Arial died before she could catch more than a breath or two. We never even knew about Arial's existence until the past couple of years. Delilah's a werecat, and turns into a long-haired golden tabby. She's actually what's known as a two-faced Were, which means she has a second shape—that of a black panther. And she's a Death Maiden, bound to the Autumn Lord, one of the Harvestmen, which means that she reaps the souls of the dead, a little like the Valkyries. She's engaged to Shade, a half-dragon, half-Stradolan.

Our youngest sister, Menolly, is a vampire. She was a jian-tu—an extreme acrobat/spy for the OIA, till she fell into a nest of vamps. *Literally* fell into their midst. Dredge, one of the worst scourges to walk the face of Otherworld, caught her. On the longest night of Menolly's life, Dredge tortured her and turned her, then sent her home to destroy her family. I managed to trap her in the safe room, and the OIA took over. After a long, hard year, she learned how to control her urges. Now, some fourteen Earthside years later, Menolly is happy. Married to a beautiful Amazon goddess of a werepuma, Nerissa, our sister is also the official consort of Roman, the son of Blood Wyne—the Vampire Queen. Oh, just for the record? Dredge? We killed him. Dust to dust. A satisfying end to that chapter in Menolly's life.

When we were sent Earthside by the OIA, we thought we'd been exiled. They wanted us out of the way, out of their hair. Instead of a lazy sabbatical, we ended up walking right into the front lines of a demonic war that nobody knew about until we showed up.

Shadow Wing, Demon Lord of the Subterranean Realms, is out to break through the portals and into Earthside and Otherworld. His goal? Raze both worlds to the ground and establish his own private playground. And he can do that through the spirit seals—which I'll get to later. One of his generals—a necromancer named Telazhar, is leading the war in Otherworld. They've already destroyed several cities with a massive sentient storm—so vast it makes any Category 5 hurricane look like a light breeze. Thank gods a group of sorcerers on our side have managed to dissipate the storm. But it's only a matter of time before they make the next push.

And we'll be right there to face them down. Because that's what we do.

By the time Smoky and I stepped back out on the porch, the lawn looked like Jack Frost had taken a paintbrush to it. Lacy white and beautiful, everywhere. One dead yeti was sprawled out on the lawn. Whatever else had been gallivanting around was long gone, except for the weird hedgehog-like creature that was belly up, unmoving, near one of the cedars.

Delilah and Nerissa were back in their regular forms, and Menolly looked like she needed a bath and new clothes. Her jacket was torn and dirty, and there was a hole in the crotch of her jeans. She looked more pissed than hurt.

"You have a hole in your crotch." I grinned at her, shrugging as she gave me a pointed look. "Just thought you'd want to know."

"Thanks a lot, genius. I figured that one out when I fell off the roof and landed on my butt in a puddle of water. Or should I say, ice-covered water. The ice was bad enough, but the water quickly found its way through the unapproved access panel." She let out a low growl. "I have no idea what that thing was, but it was fast and it was nasty. Had some damned sharp teeth and got me several times." Holding up her hand, she showed us the bite marks. They had almost healed over—vampires mended quickly—but they were still apparent. "It reminded me of a deranged porcupine."

"What's happened?" Delilah came running up. "Is Maggie okay?"

"Yeah, she and Hanna are safe. Did somebody go check on Iris and the others? I know she and Chase beat a quick path down there when they saw what was going down." I scanned the area.

"Yeah, actually. Shade went to check on Iris. Roz and Vanzir were chasing the pixies into the woods, last I saw. Morio and Trillian . . . I don't know where they went." Delilah brushed off her jeans, then let out a groan and pointed to the scattered shopping bags. "What a mess."

The bags and their contents were strewn everywhere, trampled and mangled. Some might have survived the rumble, but I wasn't betting on it. I grimaced, wondering just how much we were out in broken gifts.

Smoky cleared his throat. "We can't leave Dez alone with the portal for long. We have to figure out how to close that damned thing. I can't do it, and I doubt if you can, Camille."

I shook my head. "Oh, hell no. What about Iris? She might know what to do."

"Portal? What portal?" Delilah strode over to the figure stretched out by the cedar and wrinkled her nose. "And what the heck is this? Nerissa and I managed to get it out of the tree but it was taking some nasty potshots at us with some sort of magical zap."

"I have no clue what that thing is, and there's a portal in our living room. Which, by the way, is a mess. Not only does it look like Santa got stoned and freed a bunch of trailer-trash elves to decorate it, but it's snowing. *Inside our house.* We figure all these . . . things . . . came through the portal, and probably more are going to try unless we can get the damned thing closed down."

"I'll go get Iris." Smoky took off in a blur. Dragons were fast. Very fast.

"The rest of you—inside." I led the way. The temperature was holding around a chilly thirty degrees, and it was still snowing. The snow in the foyer was ankle deep, and there was at least two feet of the white stuff in the living room. Winter had come early and we were in a magical convergence zone. So much for any of our electronics—the moisture would have destroyed them by now.

Dez glanced over at us. "While you were outside, I managed to repel several creatures that look suspiciously like goblins. There's also something big and nasty and moth-like on the other side but so far, it's responded to my threats and stayed over there."

"Lovely. Just what we need. Mothman would *so* liven up this little party." The situation was going from bad to worse and we still had no idea what was going down.

Menolly shook her head. "How the hell did this happen?"

"That, we haven't figured out. Whatever the cause, we need to deal with the effects. We can worry about how it happened later." I turned as Iris entered the room, her eyes wide. Smoky was behind her.

"Everybody at my house is—what the hell happened here?" She stopped, staring at the portal. "Oh no, now I haven't seen one of these in years. A gate to the Northlands? Who on earth opened it?"

"We don't know, but we *do* know all those creatures came through it. Dez has been on guard since we found it. Wait—" The fact that she knew what it was offered a glimmer of hope. "Do you by any chance know how to close this? For one thing, we're getting snowed out of the house."

Iris frowned, tapping her foot as she stared at the magical gate. After a moment, she snapped her fingers. "I don't know if I can close it for you, but I think I can move it."

"Move it? A portal can be moved?" I'd never thought of portals as being moveable. Either they were there, or they weren't, in my experience.

"Some. The ones created by the spirit seals are fixed, but there are a lot of mutable vortexes in the world." Slowly, she approached it, motioning for Dez to guard her back. As she knelt, digging the snow away from the bottom of the opening, Delilah moved forward and began to help her. A moment later, and the floor was exposed. The rugs were doomed, that much I could already tell.

"Here's the thing. See these symbols?" She pointed to something that looked like a jumble of sparkles from where I was standing. I moved in to kneel beside her, and sure enough, on closer examination, I could just catch a glimpse of the faint outlines of runes glowing beneath the frosty exterior. But they were like no magical runes I'd ever seen.

"Definitely magical, but I don't recognize them. Sorcery?" I glanced over at Iris, who rubbed her chin, then shook her head.

"Possibly. I'm not sure, but they were cast by a powerful witch. They aren't demonic."

"No, they aren't demonic. I can tell that much." I could suss out Demonkin to a degree. "If they were cast by a powerful witch, wouldn't she . . . or he . . . need to be here?" I was one of the few witches we'd allowed in the house. Morio could work magic, but he wasn't a witch, per se. This was something beyond my capabilities.

At that moment, Trillian shoved Vanzir and Rozurial through the door. I glanced over my shoulder as they stumbled into the room, both talking at once. But as they took in the scene, they fell silent, the look on their faces a combination of fear and guilt.

"What are you two up to? Do you know anything about this?" I narrowed my eyes, standing. As I started in their direction, Vanzir took one look at Smoky and darted out of arm's reach.

"Tell them." Trillian reached out and twisted Roz's ear, which might normally be dangerous to do to an incubus, but Roz had a healthy respect for all of my men—especially Smoky, who had given him the beating of his life at one point.

"Ow, ow, ow! Okay, I'll tell them." He pulled away from Trillian's grasp and rubbed his head. "That hurt, dude." Turning to the rest of us, he cleared his throat. "We weren't trying to make a mess—honest. We were just trying to surprise you." The words tumbled out of Roz's mouth and he ducked his head, his expression guilty as sin. Vanzir gave him a scathing look, but then followed suit.

Smoky took one step toward them and they both cowered back.

Vanzir shoved his hands in his pockets. "We really are sorry." For one of the few times since we'd known him, the dream-chaser demon actually did sound apologetic. "We didn't know this was going to happen. We thought . . ."

"You thought *what*? What do you mean? What are you talking about?" I was starting to get nervous.

We called Roz and Vanzir the demon twins, not because they were both actually demons of a sort—although they were—but because the pair so easily got themselves in trouble, especially when they came up with some bright idea together.

Rozurial was practically a walking armory, his long duster always filled with weaponry of every sort you could hope to find, from wooden stakes to miniature Uzis. And he knew how to use all of them. Vanzir was a weapon in his own right. He also had a chaotic and unpredictable nature. But right now, the pair looked more sheepish than sinister.

Menolly stepped forward. "What did you do?" She bared her fangs, giving the boys a scare, although they knew she wouldn't go all bloodsucker on them.

Vanzir glanced at Roz. "We'd better tell them. This didn't go at all according to plan."

Iris had apparently had enough of their sidestepping, because she pushed me aside and stomped her way over to Roz. And when a house sprite is able to stomp through a foot of snow, it meant she was pissed as hell, especially since she was barely around four feet high.

"Rozurial, I swear if you don't tell me I'm going to put you on diaper duty for a year. You, too, Vanzir." As she shook her finger at them, they cringed. Hell, I would have cringed. Diaper duty didn't sound at all appealing to me.

"Okay, okay! Here's the thing . . ." Roz blushed. He had a crush on Iris, even though he could never commit to just one woman.

"We wanted to decorate the house for you, so we bought a spell. We bought a scroll, actually, from a magic shop. And . . . this is what happened." The words spilled out of Vanzir's mouth as he looked away.

We all stared at him. I wasn't even sure what to say, it was so out of left field. But apparently Iris had some ideas on an appropriate response.

"Are you *idiots*? Don't answer that, you've made it abundantly clear that yes, you do fall in that category. Okay, for one thing, there really isn't a spell to decorate a house and if you would have done your research, you might have figured that out. I can use my magic to clean but it's more directed

focus than a spell to make the broom zip around on its own."
She sighed, running out of steam, and looked at me.

"Hey, I got nothing. I have no clue what to say." Turning
to the boys, I asked a question that I knew I'd regret. "Do you
even know this witch? Have you dealt with her before?"

Again, the shifty-eyed looks between the two. Then, Roz
shook his head, looking even more sheepish.

"Actually, we bought the scroll from a store. We talked to
a witch we met at the Supe Community Action Council the
other evening. She mentioned you, and we thought you were
her friend. She recommended the store. I guess we should
have checked it out a little more but it wasn't like we were
looking for some sort of weapon or offensive spell—"

"You bought a scroll. Just like that. And did you ask the
particulars about this scroll?"

Vanzir pursed his lips, as if about to whistle, then shrugged.
"Um . . . no."

"Gee, ya think it might have been wise to check out the
history of the scroll a little better? Because I have a news
flash for you, boys. An offensive spell is what you ended up
with. Offensive to *us*." I stopped, a thought striking me. "Just
who was this witch? What did she say about me? You didn't
bring her here, did you, to use the scroll?" If they had
brought that woman here without permission and let her cast
a spell in our house, so help me, I'd flail them raw myself.
Smoky wouldn't even stand a chance of getting his licks in.

"No, of course not. We're not *stupid*." Vanzir glared at
me, then appeared to think better of it. "I guess . . . we
fucked up pretty bad."

Menolly, who had been watching the exchange silently,
shook off the snow that was clinging to her body. Snowflakes
didn't really melt on her skin easily—vampires were cold
enough that what body heat they had seldom managed to do
anything other than keep rain from freezing against them.

"Okay, let's get a handle on this. First, before anything,
Iris, you said you might be able to move this portal? Do you
think you can do so before we get snowed out of the living
room?"

Iris held out her hand. "Since it was created by use of a

scroll, it should be easier for me to do so. Rozurial, you get me the remains of that scroll right now. And don't dawdle."

He scampered off into the foyer.

Vanzir shifted uncomfortably from one foot to the other. "We really were just trying to help. We wanted to surprise you all after your shopping trip."

He looked so subdued, I was almost tempted to show pity. *Almost.* "Yeah, well, you accomplished that much, all right. Of all the fool tricks. Dude, why couldn't you just start putting up the decorations the normal way? You know we all enjoy helping. Having a head start would have been great."

Vanzir glanced over at Smoky, who looked ready to smack him. It didn't take much to set Smoky off, especially when it came to Vanzir. But I reached out and stroked my dragon's arm, and he pulled me through the snow, into his embrace, and kissed the top of my head.

"I won't kill him. I promise, my love."

"Good, because if anybody lays a hand on him and Roz, it's going to be Menolly, Delilah, and me." I kissed his hand, rubbing my face along his sleeve. My men all made me feel protected and safe, at least as much as that was possible with all that was going down in Otherworld.

Iris, however, had sputtered her temper out. She let out a loud sigh. "Honestly, the pair of you are more trouble than my babies. But I appreciate the sentiment."

He flashed her a grateful smile as Roz returned, scroll tube in hand. He opened it, and handed Iris the parchment. There was a faint acrid odor surrounding the paper—the magic within had been triggered and it was now useless as an actual spell. Iris gingerly took the sheet and unrolled it. I peeked over her shoulder. The writing didn't look familiar—though with runic script it was always harder to tell because runework needed to be precise.

Iris sniffed it. "Ice magic, as I thought. And . . . elf? Not quite . . . but not Fae either. Hmm, what was the witch's background, Roz?"

Roz cleared his throat. "She's actually Svartan."

Trillian whirled around. "Svartan? Not many Svartans come over here to Earthside."

He was right about that. In fact, Trillian was one of the few who had made more than a cursory appearance. Perhaps they visited more in the northern European countries—the legends of Svartalfheim had trickled down through Norse mythology over the years, and while they weren't all that accurate, at least the northerners had remembered the dark elves. Most people assumed the Svartans were Fae in nature, but they were the more seductive, shadowy cousins of the elves. It didn't help that their nickname was the *Dark and Charming Fae*.

For many years, Svartalfheim had made its home in the Subterranean Realms, but when Shadow Wing had taken over, they had packed up and moved, lock, stock, and barrel, back to Otherworld. Queen Asteria, the late Elfin Queen, had accepted their reemergence calmly, but the truth was that she and King Vodox had never gotten along. Now though, Vodox was doing his best to help Elqaneve—the Elfin capital—even though his own city had come under siege from the sentient storm that had destroyed the Elfin lands.

"So, a Svartan witch sold you this scroll. That's highly unusual." Trillian looked worried. Something had struck a chord, and I wanted to know what it was.

Vanzir shifted, glancing at Roz, then back at Trillian. "I thought as much. We seldom see your kind over here."

"True." Trillian frowned.

"Can you describe her?" I asked. "If she says she has met me and you tell me what she looks like, maybe I can remember something." But truth was, I'd met few female Svartans. I had never been to Svartalfheim, and Trillian was one of a limited number who traveled widely away from their city.

Warily, Roz shrugged. "She had long hair the color of Trillian's. I think . . . she was tall and thin. She had a scar above her left eye—for some reason that stood out. She said she met you at last month's Supe Community Action Council meeting."

Vanzir snapped his fingers. "Right! So, anyway, we always introduce ourselves to new members, and we got to talking. When we found out she was a witch and knew you, we asked her if she knew of any good magic shops in town. We told her what we were looking for and she recommended we go to Broom Stix. Do you have any clue who she is?" He glanced over at the portal.

The whole thing sounded bizarre. "She *couldn't* have met me there last month because I haven't been to a meeting since before September. Maybe she's mistaken. And I've never heard of the store." I turned to Trillian. "Any part of this ringing a bell?"

He shook his head. "I was afraid it might be my Aunt Seriana, but she doesn't have any such sort of scar, and she's short and plump. She's one of the family matriarchs." The look on his face was cold enough to freeze water. "She's always hated the fact that, even though he disowned me for a number of reasons, my father never did anything to punish me for what she considered grievous insults to the family name."

I caught a deep breath. Nobody else knew about Trillian's background, as far as I was aware. I only had a spotty sense of his history. I *did* know that his family had hated me from the beginning. And they had never approved of Trillian's gentler ways. He and his blood-oath brother Darynal were very much alike in that manner, both considered misfits in the Svartan society.

Trillian seldom discussed his family. My knowledge had come in dribs and drabs over the years. The Zanzera clan was composed of highly intelligent but harsh members. Cold and stern, with a disdain for anyone they perceived as weak, they didn't welcome new members easily. And I wasn't the daughter-in-law they had been hoping for.

Svartan society ran on a strong caste system, and Trillian's family was upper crust. That he had chosen someone from outside his race and stature to become involved with was his first sin. His second, that he had chosen to marry for love rather than prestige and connections. Svartans usually married to cement social standing, and they took multiple lovers for fun and play. Love didn't figure into their society all that much.

"So you bought the scroll from her?" I was trying to get things straight. The thought of a witch powerful enough to open a portal like this was fucking scary.

"No, we bought it at the store. She was there, reading cards for people, but the scroll was in their holiday section.

The name of it was . . . let me think. Oh, NORTHERN HOLI-DAY SURPRISE." Roz glanced at the portal then slapped his head. "Uh oh. If I remember right, the scroll was sitting near a pile of scrolls labeled GAG GIFTS. Maybe . . ."

"Maybe it just rolled into the wrong pile? Or maybe somebody moved it when they saw you come in. Think . . . where was she when you entered the shop?"

Roz bit his lip, then let out a slow breath. "She was near the counter—right in front of the table. And she's the one who pointed the scrolls out to us. She remembered us from the meeting."

"I'd say that's a strong coincidence."

"Before we go any further with this, can you move the portal, Iris?" Menolly broke in, sounding irate. "We have to stop this snow or pretty soon another yeti is going to march through into our living room."

Iris examined the scroll again. "I think I can move it, yes. It will shift it outside. *Somewhere.* I won't be able to pick the spot, but—and this is important—remember, what I do won't close down the portal. So you'll have to track where it went, so that we can shut it down once we figure out how."

I groaned. A rogue portal, open somewhere in the Seattle area, spewing out snow and winter creatures. "Recipe for disaster, but it's not going to be any better if we let the snow destroy our house."

"Somehow, I don't think we're going to have a problem with finding it. We'll just have to follow the snowstorm and mess of ice demons—or whatever those things are—that will be spreading out around the city." Delilah shrugged. "I vote to relocate it. Right now!"

There was a movement within the portal and we heard a low growl. I scrambled. "No more discussion. Iris—what do you need in order to move this sucker out of here? Maybe in the transfer, whatever it is will get stuck between dimensions."

Iris snorted. "We can hope. What do I need? My Aqualine crystal wand, a cup of sea salt, three holly leaves, and a few drops of Winter Solstice water—I have some in my house. I'll go get the water and my wand. Camille, would you gather the holly leaves and the sea salt?"

I nodded, heading toward the door. Hell, at this rate, it would be warmer outside than inside. Morio came with me. He was trying not to laugh, but the minute we cleared the porch, he cracked up.

"I can't believe those two. Yes, they were stupid, but they meant well." His eyes crinkled as he winked at me. "You can't blame them too much."

"Oh can't we? They've opened a rogue portal, unleashing dangerous creatures and swamping our house with snow. But it's not that I'm worried about. Not at the moment."

"The witch?" He sobered.

"Yes. She lied about meeting me, and seems to be trying to steer me to her shop—if it *is* her shop. And if she targeted Roz and Vanzir at the Supe Community Action Council, you know she had to have already done her research. She had to know that they're good friends of mine."

I didn't particularly believe in coincidence, and, while someone lying about knowing me wasn't necessarily indicative of any nefarious activity, the whole thing just felt off. Some events seemed too planned, too precise to be a quirky coincidence. This was one of those times.

"Is there a way to find out?" Morio pointed to the big holly nestled in our backyard. "Did you bring shears?"

"I have my dagger, that will do the trick. As far as discovering the hows of this . . . I suppose I could just go visit the shop and take the direct route. But first things first. Move the portal. Figure out the damage. And then, we cope with whoever fueled this mess."

I must have sounded ready to crack some skulls, because Morio turned to me. "They really didn't mean for this to happen, love."

Sighing, I shrugged. "Oh, I know Vanzir and Roz meant well. They wouldn't hurt us. It's just . . . so damned much has gone wrong and I'm tired of it. I'm tired of always feeling ten steps behind. I'm tired of everything leading to the hard road. For once, I want something to be easy, to go smooth without feeling like we're digging through a mountain of obstacles."

"I know." He kissed my forehead. "I understand."

"I don't like to whine, but after everything that's happened the past few months, I feel like I have the right. I just want to breathe for a moment, to rest and have some fun and not worry about who's going to die next, and who's out to kill us."

We came to the holly tree and I unsheathed my dagger. Since we were gathering leaves for magical purposes, I knelt on the frost-laden ground beside the outmost branches and dropped into a trance. I had the ability to commune with trees and plants to some degree—though it was harder over Earthside than back in Otherworld. As I drifted in that dreamy state that bordered full consciousness, I reached out to the tree and connected with its spirit.

"We need some of your leaves for a spell. Do you mind?"

The tree shifted—or rather, its essence did. And then, quietly, a murmured whisper brushed past my mind, kissing me gently with winter's embrace. "Take what you need, Priestess."

As I began to cleanly sever the leaves from the bough, a keening broke the stillness. I forced myself to focus on my task—magical work required focus, whether it was gathering the components for a spell or actually casting it. But Morio jumped up, turning to see what might be coming our way.

As I finished my harvest and tucked the leaves in the small basket I'd brought with me, Morio gasped. Quickly, I turned to see what the matter was.

"Look—over there."

The air was shimmering a few yards away. Another portal? But it couldn't be. No, this had to be something else. We slowly began to edge forward. I thought maybe we'd be wise to go summon backup, but the truth was, by the time we reached the door, whatever it was would already be here. We might as well wait to find out what was coming our way.

Morio pulled out his own dagger, and I kept mine at the ready. The air shifted and moved, rippling like pleated plastic. And then, a hole in the fabric of space opened—a black abyss, with sparkling gold and silver lights darting through it. And out of that hole stepped a tall man.

He towered at least eight feet tall, with burly muscles to match, and he wore a long dusky green velvet cloak trimmed with dark fur. Around his head, a wreath of holly encircled the wild tangle of brown hair streaked with gray that cascaded down his back. His beard, an anarchistic tangle of curls, was so long it reached his chest. The cloak he wore reached the ground, but beneath the edge, he was wearing brown leather boots—tied with a leather thong. And in one hand, he held a tall spear. In the other, he carried a lamp filled with sparkling lights.

The Holly King. Oh shit. Santa in the flesh. Only Santa wasn't the gentle kindly soul he was in Earthside legends. No, the Holly King could be ruthless, and he ruled over the darker half of the year, bringing frost and cold and death to the land. One of the Immortals, he was one of the primary Elemental Lords, like the Autumn Lord.

As he stood there, staring down at us, I flashed back to when I was a little girl. I'd met this man once, long, long ago when I was very young. I'd gone hunting for him through the city, and when I found him, he was actually quite gentle with me, compared to his usual nature.

Mother had still been alive and when she found out what I'd done—one of the neighbors had spotted me in the tavern at the Holly King's table where he was resting and taken me home—she'd blistered my butt. I couldn't sit down for hours.

Now, he stared down at us, and then let out a rich belly laugh. "Well, well. Camille Sepharial te Maria. I haven't seen you in a long time. You were knee high to a jackrabbit when last we met."

I managed to stammer out a squeaky "You remember me?"

He snorted. "Remember you? Oh, I remember all the girls I meet. And you, my dear, were a brave and foolish little witch. So, why have you summoned me? What do you want?"

And with that, I realized we were rapidly writing ourselves onto Santa's naughty list. Because summoning an Elemental Lord for no reason? So not a good idea. I glanced at Morio, who looked as frightened as I was, and scrambled for something to say.

Chapter 3

❧❧❧

"We didn't realize we had summoned you." Morio spoke up, saving me the trouble.

The Holly King's eyes narrowed as he glanced around the yard. "Where is your snow? This puny covering? Nothing to speak of. You're not having much of a winter."

"This is what winter is here, thank you." I didn't want him getting any bright ideas and gifting us with a blizzard. "But we have more than enough inside our house. I don't know how we summoned you, my lord, but it was unintentional and I beg your forgiveness."

Always best to apologize when you disturbed someone more powerful than a god. And the Elemental Lords? *So* much more powerful. Only they, along with the Harvestmen and Hags of Fate, were the true Immortals. Even gods could die. But the Elemental Lords were beyond the scope of life and death. They simply *were*.

Morio coughed. "We were just cutting some holly for a spell . . ."

"That wasn't what brought me here. I saw the beacon shining and followed the path." He stroked his whiskers, staring at us. "You opened a door into my realm. I'd like to know why."

"Your realm?" Oh hell—the portal! The Holly King must

live in the Northlands! It made sense, and if the portal was, indeed, acting as a beacon, we were in deep trouble until we figured out a way to shut the door.

But before I could say another world, Smoky came racing across the yard. "You need to get the leaves and salt to Iris, pronto. We have a situation on our hands." He skidded to a halt, staring at the Holly King.

"We kind of have a situation going on out here, too." I turned back to the Holly King. "I'm sorry, but I have to run. We're kind of in an emergency-sort-of-thing, because of the portal that accidentally opened. The door into your realm. I have to get back inside. Please, with no disrespect intended, as we said, summoning you was an accident. Don't feel you have to stay on our account."

But the Holly King wasn't ready to be dismissed. He chuckled. "You have aroused my curiosity, Camille. I think . . . I think that I shall stay for a while to catch up on what's going on in your world. Yes, now that I think of it, I could use a vacation and some time to play." And with that, he vanished, but I had the feeling he hadn't gone far.

"Fuck." I stared at the spot where he'd been standing. "Okay, well, no time to speculate. Let's get these leaves back to Iris. What's going on?" Morio and I began jogging alongside Smoky back to the house.

"Snow imps. A whole band of them rushed through and out the front door. They're loose now, and more are attempting to push their way into the world. Even when we move the portal, the city is going to be hopping with them." He let out a grumble.

"I know next to nothing about the creatures. What are they?"

"The damnedest little freaks—snow imps are . . . think malicious gremlins who aren't deadly like goblins or snow demons, but who love to stir up trouble." He spat on the ground as we neared the house. "They're vermin—a pestilence in the Northlands and Dragon Reaches."

"Oh great. So we have yeti and barbegazi and amaroks running around, as well as snow imps and snow demons and pixies and other creatures we don't even recognize, and there's nothing we can do at the moment to keep them out of the city. This is just getting better and better."

"That about sums it up." Morio reached the porch first, with Smoky following and me behind him.

As we burst into the kitchen, I pushed past them and, grabbing the box of sea salt on my way, skidded into the living room with the holly leaves. "Here, leaves and salt," I said, thrusting them at Iris, who was standing there, in her blue gown and white fur cloak, with her Aqualine crystal wand.

She said nothing, just took them and laid the holly leaves on the snow in front of the portal. Dez and Shade were standing on either side of her, keeping an eye out for any wandering monsters who might take it into their heads to crash our little party.

She motioned for us to move back and then, kneeling in the snow, circled the holly leaves with a ring of salt. After that, she sprinkled the solstice water over them. Then, holding her Aqualine crystal wand over the runes, she began to whisper softly. A flurry of snow rose from inside the ring of salt and it carried the holly leaves aloft, buoying them up and sending them spiraling into the air. The next moment, the mouth of the portal rippled as the leaves were swept through it, into the shimmer of energy, and a loud explosion rocked the house, sending me tumbling sideways.

Frantic memories of the sentient storm in Elqaneve crowded in and my first thought was to scramble for shelter—duck and cover. But a moment later, it was as if some giant vacuum sucked the portal out of the room, leaving us and the snow and the remnants of the singing energy.

"Where did it go?" Delilah asked in a hushed voice.

"I have no idea." Iris slowly stood, shaking the snow off her dress and cloak. "That's our next task, after we get rid of this mess in here." She stared at the drifts lining the room, and the gaudy decorations, and mutely shook her head.

Vanzir and Roz pushed their way forward. They'd been whispering.

"We'll take care of this," Roz said. "We'll clean up everything. Just go get some rest and we'll clear out the living room and do whatever it takes to dry it out." The look on his face softened my heart. He was so upset that he looked like a whipped puppy. He knelt by Iris. "I'm so sorry, Iris—we never meant for this to happen."

I wanted to remind him that this was *our* house we were talking about, *our* house that he and Vanzir had made a mess of, but the fact that he had a raging crush on Iris made me relent.

"You do know the Holly King is now wandering around Seattle? This whole mess summoned him, too, and boy did we have a fun time trying to explain why we'd called him here. So we have a rogue portal to find, an Elemental Lord who's decided to take a holiday here, and a bunch of critters racing around looking to cause havoc." Exhausted, I wanted nothing more than to drop into the rocking chair, but the rocker was buried under a mound of snow.

So instead, I slogged back through the white stuff, into the kitchen, which was clear of the winter storm if still icy cold. There was a rocking chair there, too. Somebody needed to go downstairs and tell Hanna that it was safe, but it wasn't going to be me.

Vanzir wandered into the kitchen behind me, Menolly behind him. She opened the steel door leading down to her lair and vanished. Vanzir swung a chair around and strad-dled the seat, leaning on the back of it as he stared at me.

"We really were trying to help."

"Nothing about the situation struck you as odd? Not the fact that she was Svartan and said she had talked to me?" But even as I asked the question, I realized that there was no reason it should—not unless you understood Svartan culture enough to know that they seldom visited Earthside.

"No, I can't say that it did. We thought we were helping out." He let out a snort. "Last time I ever try to do a good deed. Now you're all pissed as hell at us and look what happened."

I let out a sigh, feeling resentful. Why was it, when some-body fucked up, it was always up to *me* to soothe their fears and egos, even when they screwed me over in the process? That uncharitable thought ran through my head for about five seconds before I reached out and patted his arm, push-ing the feeling away.

"Dude, we all make mistakes. Just . . . go help Roz. We'll sort it all out."

As he flashed me a grateful smile and headed back into the living room, Hanna opened the door, Maggie hanging on around her neck. She kissed the little gargoyle and then passed her to me.

"Heaven help me, I dread seeing what those two got themselves up to." She glanced at me. "Is it so terribly bad?"

"They were trying to surprise us. They succeeded. It's not good." I rolled my eyes and nodded toward the living room. "Be prepared."

Grimacing, she vanished into the hallway, leaving me holding Maggie. A baby woodland gargoyle, Maggie was adorable and snuggly and also dangerous, if you didn't understand gargoyle nature. We had to keep her away from children and small animals, but she was our baby and we loved her. I'd rescued her from a harpy's lunch bag up on the Space Needle when we'd gotten into a fight, and when I brought her home, Delilah and Menolly hadn't argued a single word against adopting her.

The size of a large stuffed animal, she was brown with calico coloring, with wings that were still a little too big for her body. A pointed tail whipped around from her rear end, and she had long claws on her hands and feet. Her eyes were wide and golden, and she let out a soft *mooph* as I gazed down at her. Gargoyles were all very intelligent, sentient Cryptos. But she would take decades—if not longer—to reach the teenager stage, and so we had a long time to look forward to in baby- and toddlerhood.

Now, she reached up and clumsily stroked my cheek. "Cam-ey. Camey?"

"Yes, Maggie. It's me, Camille. How's our girl today?" She couldn't understand most of what we said yet, and could say even less, but she knew what *no* meant, and *yes*, and *food*, and *eat*, and *snuggle*, and *toy*, and a scattering of other words. Her mother was dead, we knew that much—her ghost had come visiting once or twice to make sure Maggie was okay.

"C-c-c-old." She shivered and snuggled closer.

"Yes, Maggie, it's cold." I wrapped my arms around her and leaned back in the rocking chair, gently rocking her as Trillian wandered in. He let out a soft laugh.

"Our girl awake?" All of the guys loved Maggie, too. She was a real little heartbreaker, that was for certain.

"Yeah, no doubt all the excitement is keeping her awake. But I think she's starting to nod off." I glanced down at her.

Maggie's eyes were closed and she was resting against my breast, breathing softly.

"You want me to put her to bed in Hanna's room?" Trillian reached for her.

"Sure, just make certain none of those critters got into the closet or under the bed or anything. In fact, we should scour the house from top to bottom, just in case we have to evict any squatters." I passed Maggie off to him, then stood and stretched. "I'll grab Morio and Shade and start on that. You stay with Maggie to make certain she's okay until we know the coast is clear."

"Start on what?" Morio was standing at the kitchen door.

"We need to search the house from top to bottom, make certain nothing unwelcome has taken up residence."

"Good idea. I'll go get Shade. You check out the first floor, and we'll start upstairs." He vanished back toward the living room.

After Trillian and I made our way to Hanna's room and tucked Maggie in, I began searching through the closets and under beds and behind anything large enough to hide even a pixie, looking to make certain nothing had decided to hide and surprise us later. Twenty minutes later, we all met in the kitchen. Well, all but Roz, Vanzir, and Hanna, who were cleaning up the living room.

Menolly glanced at the clock. "I have to get downstairs and sleep." She shivered. "The pull of sunrise comes no matter how thick the cloud cover."

Nerissa kissed her. "Sleep well, love. We'll keep watch out here."

"I hope you find that portal." As she headed down the steps, Menolly mumbled something under her breath that I wasn't sure I wanted to hear. It sounded vaguely like "Idiotic demons . . ." but I decided not to ask.

"Nothing in the house that we can figure out—" I paused as another noise erupted from the living room. "For fuck's sake, *what now*?"

"Camille?" Roz's voice echoed from the living room. "You'd better—"

But before he could finish a towering figure came striding into the kitchen, her robes swirling behind her. Derisa was

six-five, and she was the High Priestess who ran the Coterie of
the Moon Mother. She had been the voice of the goddess for longer than I could remember—for far longer than I had been alive.

With a plum tunic over a pair of form-fitting leather
pants, and an indigo robe covered with silver moons and
stars, she was striking with her pale skin and black hair and
eyes as blue as the morning sky.

I hurried over to her, dropping to kneel at her feet. If there
was one person I wanted the respect of—besides my sisters—
it was this woman. She was the voice of my goddess. She had
taken me into the Moon Mother's service, had heard my oath,
witnessed my vows as I entered the Coterie as a Witch. And
Derisa also had given me my priestess robes when I earned
them by sacrificing the Black Unicorn. Derisa was the one
who had informed me that—one day, when I was fully
trained—I would become the High Priestess of the Moon
Mother over here, Earthside.

"Lady . . . I knew you were due for a visit, but didn't know
when to expect you—"

"I come and go as the need arises. Do not worry yourself.
Although I think the winter storm had a detrimental effect
on your furnishings." But she was grinning and I knew she
was making a joke.

"Yes, Lady. It wasn't exactly planned." I wondered briefly if
I could get some advice from her on our unexpected portal, but
decided to shelve the question until I found out why she was
here. Derisa didn't usually make house calls. When I'd found
out a few weeks ago that she needed to see me, I had been worried, but as the days went on, I started to think maybe it wasn't
all that important. Now, the butterflies were back.

"We must talk." The way she said it made me nervous.
For one thing, Derisa didn't make small talk. For another,
every time that phrase had been used on me, it had been
attached to something I didn't want to hear.

I started to ask if there was something wrong, but that would
be about as helpful as a dull-bladed sword. Obviously, something was up, or she wouldn't be here. "Do you need to speak to
me alone, or can you talk in front of the others?"

Derisa glanced around the room. "They'll know eventually,

so we might as well talk here. I don't fancy sitting in your living room at this moment."

Morio grabbed a chair for her and motioned for her to sit down. Delilah brought over a plate of cookies—grabbing a couple before offering them to the priestess. And, anticipating trouble, I found a notepad and pen. Inevitably conversations like this led to the need for copious notes, and right now, I didn't trust my memory.

"I didn't expect to find you up at this hour—or rather, I did, but not so ill-rested." Derisa repressed a grin, the corner of her lip curling up ever-so-slightly. "You obviously haven't gone to bed yet."

"We had . . . an incident of sorts. We were out shopping—oh, never mind. Long story, ending in the aftermath you witnessed in the living room. A mishap we still need to fix." I returned to my seat with the notepad and pen, wishing only for bed. It wasn't that I didn't want to talk to Derisa, but I was bone-weary. "What brings you Earthside? Trenyth said you wanted to talk to me."

"First, I must reset the rogue portal on your land."

For a moment, I thought she meant the ice portal—the one that had just opened up, but then I realized she knew nothing about that. No, she was talking about the random portal that had appeared out of nowhere in our backyard. It led to Otherworld, and we had to constantly have guards standing watch to keep out goblins and other creepy crawlies.

"Where are you going to direct it?" Delilah frowned, snatching another cookie off the plate.

"You're not going to like this but, with Telazhar on the move, it's safer to set every rogue portal that has appeared over Earthside to a different destination. We're going to recalibrate it to point toward the realm of the Elder Fae." She grinned as my jaw dropped wide. "I knew you'd feel that way—you don't even have to say a word. Don't bother arguing because there's a secondary reason for my decision."

I had been to the realm of the Elder Fae several times. In addition to being a massively huge place, it was also filled with powerful and dangerous creatures who thought nothing of eating people for lunch and their pets for dessert. The

Elder Fae were a breed apart. They were the predecessors of OW and ES Fae, ancient and mostly unique. Seldom were there more than one of each type. They paid no attention to the laws of any land—be it human or Fae—and lived by their rules and their rules alone.

Regardless of how nervous it made me, Derisa was right. Having the Elder Fae as neighbors was far less dangerous than should Telazhar discover the portal and bring through the Demonkin and goblin hordes. But, that didn't mean we would be able to let up our guard. In fact, if something decided to meander through, chances were the creature would be far more powerful, on an individual level, than anything from OW, but it wouldn't necessarily be out to kill us.

"Lovely. How are you going to reset the destination point?"

"That's one of my talents. I was trained over the past few years in how to adjust the magical settings of the vortexes. I'd show you how but I don't think your magic would be well-suited for it." She winked at me, and I finally managed a smile.

"Right. Well, then, do you want to go do that now? It's nearing daylight."

"Resetting the portal isn't the only thing I came for—it is simply one facet of what we need to discuss. There is far more." She regarded me silently for a moment and then, quietly, reached in one pocket and pulled out something. When she set it in front of me, I shivered.

A raven feather.

"No," I whispered. "No . . . I hoped it was just my imagination."

"I'm sorry, but no. I can feel your thoughts . . . what you saw was not an illusion." Derisa shifted in her chair.

She knew. She knew about my vision.

"There's a journey you must undertake, Camille. You must walk under the raven's wing." Derisa gave me a faint smile, and I knew there was no getting out of this one. When my High Priestess gave me orders, I obeyed without question, regardless of what they might be.

"Take me to the dragon," I said, not even sure who I was talking to. My voice reverberated through the kitchen, coming to rest in silence.

All eyes were on us and the fear from my vision came sweeping through again as the image of the giant dragon roared to life in my mind. I slowly reached out, picked up the feather, falling into trance swiftly, as if I were being sucked down a deep well.

At first, I could hear the flutter of wings. Ravens, again. Then something came through, sweeping the air into great currents. The presence of an ancient force, rising out of the depths, filled my senses and I caught my breath as the stench of sulfur and molten stone engulfed me. Choking on the acrid fumes, I coughed, but fear froze the tickle in my throat as two giant eyes glowed out of the darkness at me—round and brilliant, black orbs in a field of white—sparkling with life and cunning.

"Who are you?" The voice echoed in my head. "Who are you . . . ? *What* are you?" And then, the voice became a questioning tendril, probing my thoughts, reaching out to test, to discover, to seek answers. "I smell the Raven on you, and the Black Beast."

I pulled back, but didn't break contact. I wanted to know what this was, and why we were connecting. Dragon he was, definitely, but like no dragon I'd met. This wasn't a dragon from Smoky's realm, from the Dragon Reaches, but something old and crafty, alien to the nature of dragons as I knew them. He swirled in an abyss, a creature of fire, clinging to what appeared to be some sort of orb. Obsidian, perhaps, or jet, or onyx.

I circled him, wary, trying to keep out of his peripheral vision. As I scoped out the creature, I sought for any tidbits of information I might be able to glean—for any clues that might come in handy when I . . . when I what?

"Cunning creature you are." The dragon spoke again, interrupting my thoughts. "Bring the Raven to me and I might let you live."

The feel of the raven feather in my fingers made me leery. The dragon wanted it too much. And where there was that much greed and lust, danger wouldn't be far behind.

I let out a slow whistle of breath. No chance in hell would I get its name, dragons didn't offer their names up without a fight. Hell, I *still* didn't know Smoky's real name. That he was called Iampaatar in the Dragon Reaches was common knowledge, but his true name? No one but he and his mother knew. So I didn't expect to find out anything useful by asking. But if I could gain some sort of reference, then we might be able to trace its origins and discover what we were facing.

"Tell me who you are and I might tell you where I'm hiding the Raven." I had no clue what the whole "hiding raven" thing was about, but I might as well use it to my advantage.

A pause, then a long, low chuckle. "*Ohhhh. I see now.* You are one of the Fae—though I smell human in the mix. And you are magical as well. And crafty and as ready with your false promises as I am. Girl, you know I would never give you my name, but you may call me Yvarr. Not that it will do you any good, but when I wake and escape this prison, we will meet. And girl . . . you will need a name to cry out when I devour you. Because unless you hand over the Raven to me, then I shall, indeed, eat you, skin and bones."

I gazed at the piercing eyes, and my fear began to drain away. He was frightening, yes, and terribly powerful with a keen sense of magic, but his arrogance was strong. As I'd discovered before, ego often led to a downfall.

Another moment, and the abyss into which I'd tumbled vanished, along with the dragon and his fire. I opened my eyes, still clutching the raven feather, and inhaled sharply, letting out my breath in a slow stream. Derisa gazed at me, waiting.

"Fucking hell." Shade was shaking. "I have *no* desire to be anywhere near his vicinity."

"Neither do I." Smoky paled. "I never thought we'd encounter one of them. Did you?"

Shade gave a quick shake of the head. "I knew they weren't myth but . . . I thought they had all fallen into history, into sleep forever."

"Well, obviously one of them has woken. I pray he never gets free from his prison. For all our sakes." Smoky actually looked afraid—not a good sign.

So both Smoky and Shade knew what this was? And whatever the strange dragon was, it scared the hell out of both of them. That didn't bode well. "Explain, please?"

"Allow me." Derisa leaned back and crossed one leg over

the other, a stark look on her face. "Well this pair should know what you are facing, given their backgrounds. An ancient power is waking in the depths, one the great Fae Lords thought they'd imprisoned long ago." She seemed to be considering her words cautiously, as I did when I was trying to figure out how much to tell someone.

"This has nothing to do with Shadow Wing, does it? This is something different. Something indifferent to the Demon Lord." Given the reaction of the two dragons and my own, I had the feeling I would rather have been facing a demon general.

Derisa nodded and pinched her brow, squinting as if she had a headache. "Correct. What you met—Yvarr—is an ancient wyrm—he's a dragon, yes, but not of the Dragon Realms." She glanced over at Smoky.

"The wyrms are our ancestors." Smoky's hair was coiling wildly. "They are the predecessors of the dragons. They lived before my race evolved from them. They are our Titans, so to speak."

Fuck. Titans were the fathers of the gods. We knew a demon who was half-Titan. There was no telling how much power he had—we were on his good side, but we all knew he was far more powerful than he let on. The dragons were incredibly strong and powerful. If *they* had their own Titans, then we were all in trouble.

"He seemed to be under the assumption that I am in league with the 'Raven,' and he wants me to hand her over. He also mentioned the Black Beast. And the other night, as I was about to head out to buy the turkey, I had a vision of an ancient dragon, and a flock of ravens . . ." I told them all about my prescience in the car. "I was hoping it was just the jitters from all that's gone on, but apparently not."

Derisa shook her head. "No, the wyrm is awake and attempting to break free from his prison. He was a danger in the times before the Great Divide, and he is a danger once more. Aeval contacted me and we agree. There is only one in existence who can wield the power to stop him should he escape."

"There's somebody still alive who knows how to combat him? I take it, then, it's not just a matter of run in and hit hard." Trillian leaned back in his chair. "We have plenty of ancient horrors in Otherworld but it's far easier to evade them over there unless they are focused directly on you."

"Yes, there is one who fought him long ago, before Yvarr was imprisoned and cast into sleep. Who still knows the one spell that can bring the wyrm under some semblance of control." Derisa didn't exactly fidget in her chair—she'd been High Priestess for so many years she probably wouldn't even know how to fidget—but there was an evasive tone to her voice. She'd tell us when she was good and ready.

"Why is he waking up? Did we do something? Is our war against Shadow Wing bringing all these ancient critters to life? Don't tell me Cthulhu is next."

She smiled softly. "No, Lovecraft did visit Otherworld and saw plenty of creatures to base his books on, but Cthulhu himself is pure imagination. Well, at least the actual god. There are sleeping giants, and Yvarr was one of them till recently."

Wanting her to just get to the point, I pressed. "What woke him up?"

Derisa bit her lip. "There are many factors, but among them: Aeval waking, woke him up. Titania coming out of her stupor woke him up. Bran crossing over to Earthside woke him up. Camille, you woke him up—killing the Black Unicorn stirred many sleeping cauldrons."

Soberly, I put down my pen. Sacrificing the Black Unicorn had been an act that had forever changed my life, and one that I would never forget. I hadn't wanted to do it, but the Black Unicorn himself had chosen me to be the instrument of his rebirth and when one of the Elementals invites you to play in their sandbox, you don't decline the invitation.

"Aeval . . . Titania . . . Bran . . . and me. There's a theme here but I'm not quite following it." Or maybe I just didn't want to follow it. I didn't mind working with Aeval or Titania, but Bran gave me the creeps.

Smoky let out a slow breath. "I think I know where this is leading. This journey you want Camille to go on? You are sending her to locate this . . . person . . . who went up against the wyrm long ago." He turned to me. "The wyrms of the earth cannot shift form like we can. They are alien even to those of us who sit in the Dragon Realms. Most have slumbered so long they will never wake, but others . . ."

"Others will waken as time goes on, Iampaatar, and you know this. Even if we could defeat Yvarr without . . . his help . . . our luck can't hold out forever."

Smoky slammed the table with one fist. "Yes, but you know Camille cannot face this wyrm. Yet you seek to send my wife off to get mixed up in this—"

Derisa stood, towering over everyone in the room. She was even taller than Smoky. "Camille is *already* mixed up in this, like it or not. We must seek out the one person who knows how to handle the ancient wyrms and dark denizens from the battles during the Great Divide. You know he is the only sorcerer who has lived even longer than many of the Great Fae Lords. He comes from a noble line, an arcane family tree. His powers were renowned among the ancient Druids, and he led them with fortitude and might."

I dropped the cookie I'd picked up, and it crumbled on the table. A wave of panic began to rise. She couldn't mean who I thought she meant. "You mean you're sending me in search of *him*? I thought he was lost in the mists of time, imprisoned at the same time Aeval and Titania were shackled into submission." During the time of the Great Divide, those who disagreed that the worlds should be separated—into Otherworld, Earthside, and the Subterranean Realms—were either cast into servitude, killed, or stripped of their powers.

Aeval had been imprisoned in a crystal cave and I had helped free her. Titania had been stripped of most of her powers until she remembered who she was and woke from a drunken stupor that had lasted for millennia. While not alive during the Great Divide, Morgaine had come seeking my help, and ended up aligning herself with the two Fae Queens, to become the third member of what I now called the Triple Threat.

Together, the Court of the Three Queens created the new sovereign Fae nation—Talamh Lonrach Oll. Loosely translated, it meant the Land of Shining Apples. They now ruled as a trio, and they had forged treaties with the government for a five-thousand-acre compound.

Derisa gave me a gentle smile and reached out, touching my shoulder. Once again, the cold swath of panic raced over me. She was asking me to go in search of a legend.

And then I realized why she had talked about resetting the portal. "That's why you want to redirect the portal to the realm of the Elder Fae. That's where he is, isn't he? That's where you're sending me." And *that* thought was even more frightening.

She let out a soft laugh. "Yes, you understand now. We need you to do this Camille, and we are sending Bran, Morgaine, Mordred, and Arturo with you. You may choose three of your own people to go as well."

"Bran! But I . . ." I stopped. It was no use arguing. The quest was set and nothing I could say would change their minds. No, I'd have to join forces with four people I didn't trust, on what could well be a wild-goose chase. The best I could do was gather as much information as would help me.

"Why does Yvarr want the Raven so much, and who is he talking about? What's Raven Mother got to do with this?"

"This, I'm not certain of. But her allegiance with the Black Unicorn has exposed her to danger and the Moon Mother has ordered me to help. I know she's an Elemental and they are Immortal, but the wyrm must not be allowed entrance into this realm. If he goes on the hunt, he'll destroy everything in his path to get to her. That's where you come in. Stop him before he has a chance. And the only way to stop him is to waken the one who knows the Spell of Naming."

"The Spell of Naming . . ." I had heard of it, but only vaguely. What it was, didn't matter at this point. I stared at the window. The morning light filtered through, and by the looks of things, we might have a bit of clear sky on the way.

After a moment, I turned back to the High Priestess. "So, that's it. I'm going in search of the Merlin."

Derisa laughed then. "Oh, yes, Camille. You're going in search of the Merlin, and we can only hope that you find him before the wyrm is free from his icy cage and comes after you and Talamh Lonrach Oll. Because once he shakes off his shackles, he will rampage and destroy, and he's convinced you hold the key to Raven Mother. Not all evils are Demonkin, you know."

Chapter 4
❧❦❧

Smoky sputtered. "This is madness. You don't even know if the Druid still lives, do you? The Merlin is a chaotic force. One who is far too dangerous to bring back into the picture. What are you thinking?"

Derisa stared at him, contemplating her answer. When she spoke, it was in a way I'd never heard a non-dragon speak to a dragon before. "I am thinking—and the Moon Mother agrees with me—that to protect this world you *claim* to love so much, along with the people in it, the Merlin is your best hope. He's a wizard—he is the Father Druid and his powers go far beyond the faerie tales and stories of Camelot."

"I will not allow my wife to set off on a suicide mission!" Smoky leaped to his feet so quickly he tipped over his chair. He swung around to grab it up from the floor, but his expression was hostile. I hadn't seen him this angry in a long time.

"Love, I don't think I have a choice—"

"You can say no. You can refuse." He turned to Derisa, who slowly stood, staring him down. I wouldn't want to be in the middle between them, that was for sure, though in a way, I was.

She rested her hands on her hips and glared him down.

"Dragon, do you realize just how powerful the wyrms are? You sat in your Dragon Reaches while they helped scorch the world during the Great Divide and you *did nothing*!"

"It was not our fight!" Smoky's voice thundered through the room and his nostrils pinched in. His eyes were frozen over, and I realized he was dangerously angry—I'd only seen him this furious a few times before. I had a feeling this time it stemmed back to his guilt over not protecting me from being kidnapped by his father, but that was ridiculous. It hadn't been his fault, but he hadn't been able to let it go.

"Not your fight? But now you seek to interfere? Would you be so quick to help if you weren't married to Camille? If you didn't know her, would you be so concerned if she went off traipsing after the Merlin? Or would you just fly back to the Dragon Reaches and ignore the whole situation?" Derisa could be pretty daunting herself when she was angry.

I had to do something. "Stop it, both of you."

"Camille, keep out of this." Smoky cast a dark look my way, and his order made me bristle.

"Excuse me? I'm directly involved in this. You don't get to tell me to shut up and mind my own business." I let out a low sigh, already tired of the whole mess. "I'll make my own decisions, thank you."

Smoky growled. "And you'll never let me in, will you? Never let me have a say in what you do. You'll put yourself in danger with no thought to your sisters or your husbands."

I stared at him. "Smoky, you're being ridiculous. We're *all* in danger. My sisters as much as I am. We have no choice. We never have, not since the day we were sent over here." Exasperated, wanting to smack some sense into his thick dragon skull, I just stood there, wishing somebody would back me up.

A moment later, Derisa seemed to realize that there was some serious smoothing over needed. "Smoky, your wife . . . she has a place to play in this drama. Destiny calls for her presence. Duty . . . calls her."

That was a word that Smoky seemed to respond to. He bit back a retort and slammed into a chair, staring at the table.

I turned to Derisa, all too aware that the storm wasn't over yet. "You think the Merlin can help contain Yvarr?"

"The post of the Merlin is that of High Priest to the Hunter. Chaotic? Yes, but the forces of the earth are chaotic. He can help you contain Yvarr; he and others like him who wake to these turbulent times. And after taking on the wyrm, the Merlin might just be able to help you counter Telazhar. His powers are grounded deep in the earth."

I closed my eyes. Legends had come to life before and left me disappointed. Morgaine—one of the supposed greatest sorceresses—was also a distant ancestral cousin, but she was corrupted with greed and I found it hard to trust her. Would the Merlin be different? I could only cling to a faint hope that he would. Whatever the case, we had no choice. With a creature like Yvarr on the loose, the world would be a far more dangerous place. If there was any way to contain him, we had to attempt it. Plus, the lingering thought that the Merlin might be able to take on Telazhar tantalized like the proverbial carrot and horse.

I cleared my throat. "There's no question about it. I'll go. Even though I have to take Bran and Morgaine with me. We need his help."

The room fell silent as I stared at the table. The thought of traipsing off into the realm of the Elder Fae again was terrifying and gave me the cold sweats, but it was probably safer than Otherworld right now.

Don't bet on it, a tiny voice inside whispered. *Telazhar has nothing on the Elder Fae. Remember Yannie Fin Diver?*

Another shudder raced through me. The freakazoid Elder Fae had chased Delilah and me down, determined to prove that we were his lunch.

"I have a question, and maybe it's stupid but I don't understand something." Delilah broke the silence. "Why do you keep saying *the* Merlin? Isn't his name just Merlin?"

Derisa cracked a grin. "No, my child. The *Merlin* is actually the title of a post—the post of the High Priest to the Hunter. The Father of the Druids is the son of the Earth Mother's consort. Whoever holds the post, holds the title. But the men who wear that mantle are neither human nor Fae. For when they take the post, they are reborn into what they become. The men who are born to this post are groomed for it, a lot like the Dalai Lama—the boy is chosen when young and trained, when the reigning Merlin knows he's nearing the end of his time."

Delilah finished her cookie and reached for another one. I shook my head. My sister was a sugar freak and a junk food junkie. If she'd been fully human, the amount of crap she ate would probably have done her in. "So, was he human when he took the post?"

"When he was chosen to be the new Merlin, yes. But they undergo a dark and treacherous rite and this changes them. The Merlins live for thousands of years, although they can be killed. They are not kindly old men, they are not Gandalf of the *Lord of the Rings*, nor the wizard portrayed by *The Sword in the Stone*. Never, ever underestimate him."

I turned to Delilah. "Think of the human pope—he takes a new name when he's chosen to office. The world has been without the Merlin for so long, it will be interesting to see what changes when I find him and bring him back. *If* we manage the task. His presence gives the planet a strength . . . it's hard to describe, but think of it this way. If Derisa here vanished from Otherworld for a couple of thousands of years, the Coterie of the Moon Mother would fall into shambles."

"So the return of the Merlin could mean major shifts in the human pagan movement." Delilah cocked her head. "That's going to be interesting to see."

"Yeah, providing he hasn't jumped the shark. All we need is a crazed Druid sorcerer running around loose." Even as I said it, I felt sick to my stomach. Unleashing old energies could be dangerous. But again—we didn't seem to have much choice. Somehow, Yvarr had woken, and the Merlin was one of the few who could fight him.

"What do we call him when you find him?"

"His last known name was Myrddin and at one point, he was pretty much categorized as a crazed legend—a madman prophet. But we know how history goes." I grinned. "It's always written by the victors."

"So, not only do we have a rogue portal open to the Northlands, but you're going traipsing off into the realm of the Elder Fae to look for the Merlin." Trillian drummed his fingers on the table. "And I'm still worried about Darynal."

His blood-oath brother, along with another compatriot, was lost somewhere in the Shadow Lands, a region in Otherworld that separated the Southern Wastes from the eastern side of the major continent. There were ghosts there, volatile and angry, of thousands of people who had fled from the Scorching Wars. They had been hunted down and murdered, their bodies rotting into the land and fens. Restless spirits had taken hold in the Shadow Lands—giving rise to the name. They lingered there even now. And once again, Telazhar was leading an army across the land. This time, their rampage threatened to be far worse than the Scorching Wars.

"I know you want to go looking for him, but we . . ." I stopped. The danger was everywhere. We needed Trillian here, but Darynal was his blood brother. We had been arguing about this for almost three weeks, and it had gotten pretty loud and there had been several times when one of us had stormed out, slamming doors and the whole shebang. But now, how could I encourage him to stay here with me running off in search of the Merlin? And should I even try? He had a blood-oath debt to Darynal that preceded our connection.

A knot formed in the pit of my stomach, and, from somewhere far away, I heard myself say, "Go then. Go find him. But damn it, if you die I'm going to kick your balls till they're blue." I stared at him.

Trillian pressed his lips together, but the look in his eyes said everything.

"Are you sure?" Smoky turned to me. He seemed determined to put me on the spot today. "You are willing to allow this?"

With a sense of defeat, yet knowing that I was doing what was right, I shrugged. "What else can I do? This war in Otherworld isn't going to end tomorrow. I have to go find a living legend. We have a portal leading to the Northlands cranking out monsters by the minute and we have no clue where it is right now. Chase still has bad guys he has to catch right here. Life is happening all around us. It won't wait for the perfect time to spring things like this—nature is unfettered, and Fate weaves her own path without regard to our comfort. I hate that Trillian will be risking his life, but the fact is—Darynal? He would do the same for Trillian or for me. We owe him that much."

Trillian swept around the table and gathered me in his arms. "My love, this means so much to me."

"I know," I whispered. "That's why I'm telling you to go. Go find him. But damn you, come home to me. You understand? No dying. No getting hurt."

"Understood." He gave me another kiss, then straightened up. "I promise you, if I haven't found him in two weeks, I'll return. If I can't find Darynal in that time, then chances are he's dead. The Shadow Lands claim their victims without regard to the good in their heart." Frowning, he crossed his arms over his chest. "I won't go alone, either. I'll find someone to take with me."

"I'll go." Rozurial stepped forward. "I know Otherworld inside out. I have been in the Shadow Lands before, when I was hunting Dredge. And I have several . . . acquaintances in OW that owe me favors. I'll call one or two of them in— they are trackers and bounty hunters. We'll do best traveling with others used to the open road."

Grateful to Roz, I beamed at him and he gave me a quiet wink. He knew how terrified I was at the thought of Trillian trekking off down to the Shadow Lands, and he knew just how dangerous that area was.

Trillian leaned over and clapped him on the shoulder. "I'm glad to have you with me. Honestly, if it were anybody but Darynal—well, anybody outside of this room—you wouldn't catch me anywhere near that place."

"When will you leave?" I reached out, took his hand and rubbed it gently against my cheek.

"Tonight, love. We'll take the portal in the basement of the Wayfarer—that one's pointed to Y'Elestrial."

The Wayfarer, Menolly's bar, had been torched and burned to the ground shortly before Samhain, killing a number of people in the process. We'd found out who did it and put an end to them, but now the bar was undergoing a total rebuild. Not *renovation*, there hadn't been enough of it left to renovate. The basement had managed to stand intact, and part of the floor, but the bar had been destroyed. The workmen had gutted out all the burnt timbers and had started the new construction. Menolly was spending a lot of evenings talking to the architect about the new plans.

The portal in the basement had fared much better than the main floor, as had the safe room. Neither had been damaged and we'd managed to keep the fire marshal and his men from tripping through into Otherworld. Portals were common knowledge, though their exact locations were not.

The construction company promised that by the beginning of the year, Menolly would have a brand-new bar. She'd decided to nix the bed-and-breakfast angle and just go for a bigger, brighter kitchen and a new dance floor. Tavah—the guardian Menolly hired to keep watch over the portal at night—was still stationed there, only now there were two other guards on duty with her. And three during the day when Tavah slept. We'd begun to realize solo gigs were likely to end badly.

I let out a long breath. "So you leave tonight. Derisa, when do you want me to go?"

"Tomorrow afternoon, if you can. The sooner you find the Merlin, the better. We still have to convince him to work with us, though. Iampaatar is correct that Myrddin is . . . or was . . . capricious at best. The legends are filled with his tumultuous status." She smoothed her cloak. "I will return tomorrow afternoon, late. Be ready. I will visit Talamh Lonrach Oll and bring Aeval and the others with me. Neither Bran nor Morgaine and her crew know about the journey yet."

"They're going to be *ever so overjoyed*, no doubt." I had no illusions about the pair's reaction to the news. Neither one of them liked me—Morgaine because I would not throw my allegiance in with her, and Bran because . . . well, I'd killed his father. Even though it had been at the Black Unicorn's decree—and even though he had been reborn and was now running free and growing strong again—my sacrifice of the father of the Dahns Unicorns hadn't gone down well. Bran was an ally only so far as it met his agenda.

"Then I will take my leave. On the way out, I'll recalibrate the portal out in your backyard. And I will warn your guards."

Suddenly so tired I could barely think, I stood and curt-seyed deep. She brushed my forehead with a kiss and then vanished out the back door.

Turning to the others, I shook my head. "Can't we even go on a shopping trip without drama of some sort?"

"Speaking of shopping, I've sorted the bags in the parlor room. Some things were ruined, others look like they made it through without wear and tear." Nerissa entered the kitchen. "I'm afraid I missed everything that was going on. Bring me up to speed, somebody?" Menolly's wife was a gorgeous Amazon of a woman. As Iris began to run down what had happened with Derisa, I pushed myself to my feet.

Making my way upstairs, I passed by Vanzir and Hanna, who were finishing the cleanup of the living room. The heat was turned up, and the place was a mess, but overall, I thought most everything but the electronics would make it through okay.

Trillian, Smoky, and Morio followed me to our suite. I wanted to shout at Trillian for taking me up on my offer that he go find Darynal, but I knew all too well: If you tell some-one it's okay if they do something, don't whine when they accept the challenge.

As we silently filed into our bedroom, I turned to them. "I don't want to talk about Trillian's trip. I don't want to talk about going to find the Merlin." Then, after a pause, I added, "This might be . . . Trillian's going to be gone for a while. I want to spend some time with him alone." As I gazed at Smoky and Morio, they quietly nodded and withdrew. The sofas in my study were comfortable and they could rest there for a while. Grateful they understood, I waited till they left, closing the door behind them.

Trillian moved silently toward me. "Thank you—for want-ing time alone. For wanting to be with me before I go." He nodded toward the bed and I crawled on it with him. I usually was with all of my husbands, I preferred it that way—but this time . . . just in case, I needed to be with Trillian before he left for the Shadow Lands. The thought that he might not return weighed too heavy in my mind.

I slipped out of my clothes and into a loose, sheer nightgown. Trillian undressed. He was fine. As he stripped off his turtleneck, his strong, dark pecs rippled, and my gaze followed his chest down to the six-pack abs that were lean and tight, then to that smooth V that disappeared beneath the front of his jeans.

He reached back, loosened his hair out of the braid and it fell to his elbows, the silvery-cerulean strands smooth and glossy. His ice blue eyes glistened, such a contrast to his gleaming obsidian skin. Trillian seemed aloof if you didn't know him, but beneath that cool exterior, his nature seethed with passion and a fierce intensity that could easily overpower anyone who had a weak nature.

The passion between Svartan and Fae could reach critical mass very quickly. Both races possessed intensely sexual natures; the chemistry was like electroshock at times—high-voltage sex. And even though I was only half-Fae, I took after my father's people. Sex was as necessary as breathing was for me.

Slowly, I moved into his arms, and he pulled me close. "It's been awhile since it's just been us," he whispered, encircling my waist and pulling me close.

"I know." I closed my eyes, feeling his breath, smelling the toasty cinnamon fragrance of his cologne. He was familiar—we had been together back in Otherworld before fear had driven me away from him. The Svartans were not known for sticking with partners . . . and while I didn't ask for monogamy, neither had I been prepared to be cast aside. So even though Trillian and I'd undergone a ritual that bound us together—the Eleshinar ritual—I'd run away, leaving him behind. He'd pursued me, but it was only when we came over to Earthside that he finally managed to catch up with me.

When we met again and I dared to kiss him, my heart was as good as gone. He would always be my alpha lover, though if pressed, there was no way I could pick one husband over another. They all complemented me. We were bound together, with each of them occupying an important space in my heart.

Trillian called me on my bullshit. He was blunt and honest, and while he was arrogant as all get-out, he earned the right. I always knew where I stood with him.

Now, he gazed into my eyes, his forehead pressed against mine. "And here we are. So very far from where we first met at the Collequia. Remember, love? Remember I told you that you could do anything you set your mind to?"

I remembered, all right. He'd caught me right from the start, his silken voice wrapping around me. "I remember."

"I still believe it. Look at you. Look at what you've done, and what you're becoming. Look at how much we've gone through, and yet here you are, calmly facing a journey that would send lesser women screaming their heads off. I'm so proud of you, Camille." As he sought my lips, I sank into his kiss. It was warm and luxurious. *Opulent and lush and reeking of sex.*

Moaning slightly, I shifted under the weight of his embrace, and he caught me up in his arms, carried me to the bed, and tumbled me onto the comforter, covering me with his body, pressing against me as the warmth of his skin melted through the sheer lace nightgown. I could feel him, through his jeans, hard and rigid, and straining for release.

Gasping, I pushed against him. "Pants. Off."

He laughed, throaty and dark, and rolled over, unzipping his jeans and sliding out of them in one smooth motion. As he sat up, I feasted my sight on him. He was glorious, with a few scars from battle here and there, but his muscles and skin gleamed in the dim lamplight, and I wanted nothing more than to lean over and run my tongue along the faint beads of perspiration that rose along his stomach.

I followed the trickle of sweat as it rolled down his chest, down to his groin, following the curve of the V leading to his cock. Rigid, hard, and throbbing, it gleamed as black as the rest of him—jet black, not coffee brown like Shade. Trillian was the color of glassy obsidian, and I moaned, suddenly so hungry for him that my stomach hurt.

He laughed then, seeing my desire, and leaned back against the pillows, his arms beneath his head. I knelt by his side, bending to press my lips to the head of his cock, fitting them tightly over the strength and girth that I knew so well.

Trillian had been inside of me more times than I could count, filling every part of me that could be filled—he'd fucked my mouth, my ass, my cunt, driven me into a frenzy of orgasm till I was giddy.

Getting serious, I slid my lips along his length, and Trillian let out a garbled moan. Grinning—I knew how to work my tongue—I stroked him with my mouth, pressing my lips firmly around his shaft as I swallowed him deep, relaxing my throat muscles so I could almost take him to the hilt. His pre-cum tasted like salted caramel, warm and sweet, and the pulse of his veins throbbed through his cock as I slid up and down, working him over, tightening my lips around him so that the suction was strong.

He pulsed, growing harder under my tongue. All I could think about was how much I wanted him to dive deep inside my cunt, to stretch me out, to thrust again and again until I was out of my mind with desire.

Coiling around him, my tongue playing the snake, I covered every inch, then broke off and moved down, gently sliding my mouth over one of his balls, As I sucked, not hard enough to hurt, but hard enough to make him groan, the smell of his sweat filtered through me and his neatly trimmed pubic hair brushed against my cheek, tickling. The smell of his arousal urged me on.

A moment later he tensed, and I thought he was about to come, but instead, he propped up on his elbows. "Enough for now. Come up here. Let me taste you." The grin on his face said everything. He was Coyote, taunting me, cajoling me.

I flipped around to reverse cowgirl position, and back up, straddling his body on my hands and knees. As I lowered myself inches above his face, Trillian leaned up and I felt his tongue begin to slide around my clit, circling, teasing me as he darted around the bud, tickling lightly and then stronger.

I bit my lip and let out a whimper. His teeth caught a light hold then, sucking me, as one hand reached up to caress my butt, smoothly sliding over the curve. The next moment, he inserted a lubed finger up my ass, twisting as he slowly drove his way deeper. The next moment, he sucked on my clit, hard, and then gave a little nip—hard enough to smart.

The pain combined with the grinding pleasure going on in my backside sent me into a tailspin and I let out a sharp cry. Trillian yanked his finger out and the next thing I knew, he had rolled out from under me and pushed me onto my stomach on the bed. I spread my legs and he lay flat on top of me, sliding his cock deep in my pussy, resting his hands on either side. As he thrust against me, my pussy tightened, squeezing him each time he plunged into me.

One moment, he was deep inside me, then he was on his knees, grabbing me up to flip me over and pull me to my feet. As he walked me back to the wall, bracing me against it, I raised my legs, wrapping them around his waist, as he once again rammed his cock deep in my cunt. Caught in the sex haze, I held him tight, my arms embracing his back, clutching those broad shoulder muscles, as he pounded me against the wall, driving deeper with each thrust.

My lips tingling, I leaned back, gazing into his eyes, and watched as the smile on his face turned to dark intensity, and then—before I was ready—the sudden rush of orgasm washed over me as I came, screaming out his name. Trillian gave one final thrust, and then he let out a low roar as he climaxed, filling me full with his cum, awash in the breaking light as morning began to unfold.

I woke around noon, not refreshed but alert enough to get up. Trillian was still asleep beside me, and I left him in bed, silently padding over to the bathroom, where I took a long, hot shower. I didn't want him leaving here tired—better he was fully rested and able to cope with whatever Otherworld might choose to throw his direction.

After drying my hair and putting on my makeup, I dressed in a warm gunmetal skirt that reached my ankles, but had a slit up the side to my thigh. I added a black PVC corset over the top, then slipped into a plum bolero jacket to keep myself warm. As I slid into a pair of stiletto pumps, and headed out the door, closing it softly behind me, I heard noise coming from downstairs. Somebody was making a racket.

The kitchen was a flurry of activity. Iris and Hanna were

in full cookie-making mode. Delilah was tapping away on her laptop at the table with Maggie by her feet. Morio and Smoky were outside, doing something to the side of the house. I slipped out the door and motioned to Smoky. He was in white jeans and a T-shirt that was sticking to his back, and he was carrying a hammer from where he'd been nailing a board back onto the house.

I slipped my arm through his elbow and walked him away from Morio. "So . . . where was the temper tantrum coming from yesterday? What's going on?"

He was silent for a moment, then a strand of his hair rose up to wrap around my shoulder. "I have a lot on my mind, Camille. I love you and am worried sick about the chance of losing you."

I was used to him being overly concerned, but this was a bit much even for Smoky. "What's going on? You're not going to lose me. I'm not going anywhere."

The clouds broke overhead and a new round of rain began. I shivered, wondering how he could stay so warm without a coat.

Smoky cocked his head to the side. "A year ago, I almost lost you to my father. He just about destroyed you and that would have destroyed me. Two months ago, I almost lost you to a storm that devastated Elqaneve. That would have devastated me. I can't stand the thought of finding your body, broken and bruised . . ." He winced, and his hair thrashed around him, reflecting his feelings.

"This is *who I am*, Smoky. You've known that since the beginning. I didn't hide my life from you." I couldn't figure out what to say to calm his fears. I understood them, but I also had a better hold on my emotions than my beloved dragon.

He shrugged. "I've never felt this way about anyone. I'd never loved anyone before I met you. Not any of the women I'd met. Not Hotlips. No one. I share you because that is who you are, and I've grown to accept it—I actually . . . admire the Fox and the Svartan. I even like them, but don't you dare tell them that." He allowed himself a faint smile, but then it vanished before I could say a word. "I love you with all of my heart, and the thought of what you go through . . . what your destiny has laid out for you . . . it tears me up."

I let out a long sigh. "I can't stop fighting. I can't just walk away and pretend everything will be okay because it won't. The demons are at the door, Smoky, and this is my home. So is Otherworld. I can't just ride off into the sunset and let them take over."

"I know that, and it makes me love you that much more." He groaned, pulling me into his embrace. He wrapped his arms around my waist. "I will find a peace with this. I promise you that. Somehow." Leaning down, he nuzzled my neck and I caught my breath, his musk filling me with desire and hunger for him, his tall body engulfing me in a protective haze that allowed me to feel safe for even just the moment we were standing there.

"I hope you do," I whispered. "Because I can't have you getting angry at Derisa . . . or Aeval or any of the others. Do you understand? My duties to the Moon Mother come before anyone or anything in my life. That's just the way it is for a priestess." Pressing my hand against his chest, I looked up into his eyes, willing him to say yes, willing him to accept what our lives were.

After a moment, he kissed my forehead, gazing beyond me. I had a feeling his thoughts had suddenly shifted elsewhere, but for some reason, I didn't want to ask why.

He kissed me again, then—still not answering my question—picked up his hammer and returned to his work. I stared at him for a moment before turning back to the kitchen.

Nerissa was nowhere to be seen, but I knew she wasn't working on Black Friday. Shaking off my concern over Smoky—there was nothing I could do about it until he was ready to open up—I thought about Black Friday and the mess that had been made of our bags. How much had been trashed? Whatever the case, I wasn't about to go shopping today, not with Trillian leaving tonight.

"Where is . . . well, whatever's left from our shopping trip?" I glanced around the room. Nothing in here, except a whole lot of cookie dough, and a pot of something that smelled fantastic bubbling on the stove.

Iris motioned toward the living room. "In there. Go sort

through and find out what survived. Eighty percent of what I bought? Nothing more than rubbish now."

She sounded growly. No wonder Vanzir and Roz had vanished. If I were either of them, I'd give both Iris and Hanna a wide berth for a while. It might be *our* house, but those two ruled the roost and everybody knew it. In fact, I expected that for the next few days we'd be seeing very little of Vanzir. Rozurial, of course, would be leaving with Trillian tonight.

Tonight. Again, a pang of fear stabbed me in the gut. But I wasn't going to back out now. Darynal deserved to have his oath-brother looking out for him.

Returning my attention to Iris, I gave her a quick hug. "You okay? Where are the babies?"

She flashed me a warning look. But all she said was, "They're home with the Duchess. She's leaving at the beginning of the year, so I'm making the most of her stay. Babies are wonderful, but twins are double the trouble."

Even with the lightness she forced into her voice, I realized Iris might have miscalculated just how much effort children of her own might take. It was one thing looking after somebody else's kids, but your own? A lot harder. And *that* was a problem I wasn't about to take on. The more we went along, the more I had decided that the position of *Auntie* suited me just fine.

Touching her lightly on the arm, I said, "If you need to, after your mother-in-law leaves, we can help you find a nanny."

She ducked her head, a flutter of a smile crossing her lips. "Thanks, Camille. I appreciate that."

Heading into the living room, I quickly realized that it was roasting. Several space heaters were scattered around, and it must have been eighty degrees. The room was starting to dry out. Twine had been rigged to run around the ceiling and there must have been sixty pieces of paper clothespinned to it. The books had been taken off the shelves and were scattered everywhere. It made me cringe to see them open, in some cases propped open, but if we didn't make certain they were dry then we'd have a nasty mold problem on our hands. And the thought of losing all our books made me queasy. They'd never be quite the same, but I hoped we could save them all.

The shopping bags that had survived were lined up on the sofa. I quickly found mine and peeked inside. Three out of the five bags were here, which meant two had bit the dust. As I sorted through the gifts I'd picked out, I realized that about sixty percent of the actual gifts had made it through. But two of the most expensive—for my sisters—had vanished. Considering both had been small jewelry boxes, I wondered if they had just gotten lost out in the yard. Which meant high-tailing my ass out there to look around. I was about to slip into my coat and go look when the phone rang.

"I've got it!" I picked up the phone. It was Chase. He had to work today.

"Camille—we have a problem."

Lovely. Just what I wanted to hear. "Okay, spill it dude. What is it this time? Zombies in the cemetery? Ghosts in the Greenbelt Park District?"

"Not exactly. There's . . . well . . . there's a pack of crazed pixies yukking it up in downtown Seattle. They're harassing a group of people trying to watch the parade. Turn on the TV."

Uh oh. If it was on television, it was bad. "I can't right now—we need to let it dry out or it will short circuit, if it even still works. The snowstorm in our living room last night, remember?"

"Right—how could I forget. Okay, well, here's the deal. The Black Friday parade? Sponsored by Engrams Department Store? It started at noon and no sooner did the first floats hit the streets when a group of pixies decided to have a field day. They're out there dive-bombing the people along the street with pixie dust, and most of the people are getting stoned. I have a free-for-all going on. Streakers, brawlers, it's worse than the St. Paddy's parade. I need you to corral the pixies while our men corral the afflicted."

Great. Just great. A bunch of pixies were going all frat-boy Animal House on the parade. Just what we needed. With a long sigh, I told Chase we'd be right there, and hung up.

Chapter 5

"All hands on deck, we have to hit the road." I rushed back into the kitchen, only to be met by a series of hostile stares. Nobody wanted to hear this. Hell, *I* didn't even want to hear this. "Well, not all hands. We're going into this personnel-light."

"Right. Menolly's down for the day. Trillian and Roz should rest before they leave, Vanzir and Nerissa are out somewhere." Delilah pushed herself to her feet. "That leaves you, me, Morio, Smoky, and Shade."

"We'll have to make do, then. Somebody has to watch over the house. Smoky can stay with Iris and Hanna. You get Shade, I'll get Morio. There's a group of pixies waging war on pedestrians out watching the Engrams Black Friday parade. We're talking pixie dust, which, apparently, means nekkid FBHs and punch-drunk brawlers."

Even as I said it, the situation sounded ludicrous. Pixies tended to be nasty. Most of them were little thieves and they liked to cause havoc, but they seldom deliberately caused death. Mayhem, however? They thrived on it. We'd tangled with groups of them before.

Delilah stared at me. "Pixie dust, huh? Um, remember,

you've been doused with it a couple of times before, so you're extra susceptible. Last night, then back when we first met Mistletoe."

"I *miss* him, and Feddrah-Dahns. I wonder what they're up to." Feddrah-Dahns was heir to the throne in Dahnsburg, the Crypto city run by the Dahns Unicorns. His best buddy was Mistletoe, one of the least objectionable pixies we'd met. Actually, I *liked* Mistletoe, though it kind of irked me to say so, given my general distaste for the creatures.

"Probably coordinating the armies. They sent help to Elqaneve, remember?" She fell silent, then shook her head and headed out of the room, toward the staircase.

The thought of Feddrah-Dahns and Mistletoe being swept into the war made me unaccountably sad. Unicorns were dangerous creatures, and they could be deadly foes. Logically, Feddrah-Dahns was probably more apt to stick it to the enemy rather than be harmed, but that didn't change the fact that he was a friend who was in the line of fire.

Hanna was watching me as Iris opened the oven and pulled out another batch of cookies. The Northlands woman gave me a soft smile.

"Your friends are strong. They will weather through. Now find Morio, and go help the people who need you."

Grateful for her innate understanding, I gave the stoic woman a smile. Hanna was pragmatic, and she was a good foil against fear. She'd helped me escape one of the worst situations I'd ever been in, and she'd done so at a great cost. We had developed an odd bond because of that.

"Right." I scooted over to the window facing the front of the house and opened it. Smoky and Morio were still outside; now they were clearing the gutters. They'd probably gotten clogged with the last of the leaves blowing off the trees during the storm of the other night. Western Washington was prone to nasty windstorms.

"Morio, get your ass in here. Chase needs us. Smoky, please stay here and watch over the house. We don't want to wake Roz or Trillian just yet, not until it's time for them to leave for Otherworld."

As both men traipsed in the back door, I quickly ran down

what was going on. By then, Delilah and Shade were back in the kitchen and, after I changed out my stilettos for a pair of ankle boots with kitten heels, we headed out.

"Let's take my car." I held up my keys as we clattered down the porch steps. "There are only four of us." Glancing up at the sky, I shivered. The clouds were banked up, and had an odd sheen to them. The smell of ozone was in the air and I groaned. "Ten to one, snow's on the way. It's cold enough for it."

"Don't say that." Delilah sighed. "I'm riding shotgun."

We headed over to my Lexus. The men jumped in the back. As she climbed into the passenger seat, Delilah tossed me my dagger over the roof of the car. I caught it and, pulling back the slit of my dress, strapped the sheath to my thigh. Easy access. I usually changed clothes before going out on a mission, but we were chasing down a group of pixies in a parade. This wasn't likely to turn into a knock-down drag-out fight. I grinned at her as I started the ignition.

"You ready to rumble?"

She let out a burp. "Well, apparently my stomach is."

"Too many cookies." I laughed. "Okay then, let's go kick us some pixie ass."

Sure enough, as I pulled out of the driveway and maneuvered onto the street, a fine layer of snow began to fall. Wondering if it were due to the rogue portal Iris had managed to banish, I guided the car down the road as we headed out to save the parade.

The streets of Belles-Faire were a mess—throngs of people out shopping for the holidays as well as the noontide crowd of business people, scurrying off to lunch. If it were this bad in Belles-Faire, then Seattle proper would be even worse.

The mixture of traffic, falling snow, and people jaywalking always made for treacherous conditions in the Pacific Northwest. Yes, the sudden snow was always an upset. No, we usually didn't get much most years, though the past few, it seemed like we'd gotten slammed by storms. But in general, enough snow fell that one would think Seattleites would realize that, no, it *wasn't* a good idea to barrel through the steep streets in their giant SUVs like it was any other overcast day. Drivers either were overconfident, or they panicked and traffic slowed to a crawl. Either way, both extremes caused snarls and accidents.

As we neared the Belles-Faire strip mall, I cautiously skirted a small mini that had swerved off the road. The tiny car had slid into a ditch. I slowed down and Delilah opened her window to make certain the driver was okay, but the guy inside held up his cell phone and waved us on.

"Those clown cars are dangerous." Morio leaned forward. "They don't have enough weight or traction to keep them on the road."

"I dunno about that, but if driving in this weather? Best to slow down. The skid marks behind that car pretty much say he was zooming along. At least he doesn't seem hurt." Delilah rolled up her window again. "Look on the bright side. Maybe the snow will drown the enthusiasm of the pixies."

"Well, it may stop traffic but I doubt it will stop the parade." I flashed her a grin. "Around here, not much stops for anything but a full-scale West Coaster." There really wasn't a comparable term to Nor'easter, but we got our fair share of violent windstorms and floodwater rainstorms. When they had to close the 520 Evergreen Point Floating Bridge to sustained winds of over fifty miles an hour, *that's* when people tended to slow down and stay home.

As we entered the northern edge of Seattle proper, I asked Delilah to consult the Seattle Traffic app on her phone. Not only did it show major blockages, but it showed alerts as to streets that were closed and detours—a good thing considering the parade would undoubtedly have caused major route changes.

"We're on Aurora, right? Follow it down and turn onto Seventh Avenue, then continue till we get to Lenora Street. Turn right, and then follow the route down to Alaskan Way and Pike Place Market. The parade is being held in that area, so we'll have to park in the Pike Place Market parking garage and go from there. Where did Chase say to meet him?"

"The pixies are congregating around Western Avenue, in back of the market."

Oh joy, that was going to make for a lovely trip. "It figures.

Okay, let's keep alert. You know traffic's going to be a bitch."
As I pulled into the chaos of the Seattle city streets, I sucked
in a deep breath. Driving in the city—so not fun. But then
again, neither was hunting pixies.

By the time we had navigated to Pike Place Market through
the maze of two-way streets that suddenly turned into one-
way streets, down the slippery hills that gave Seattle its nickname of "Little San Francisco," and through the pedestrians
that believed in their right of way regardless of the oncoming
cars, I was about ready to pull my hair out. There were some
seriously self-entitled people in this city, and I wanted to
throttle a good dozen of them who had cut me off in their rush
to evade the snowflakes now steadily drifting down.

This was no blinding whiteout, or even a heavy snowfall, but
a steady skiff was building up on the grassy areas and around
the base of the trees. I eased into the parking garage and wound
my way up to level four before we managed to find one single
parking spot. As we hustled out of the car, the rush of holiday
shoppers wove a steady tapestry of motion around us. I let out a
little sigh. I thought I was done with my shopping, but here we
were, on Black Friday proper, ready to dive into the crowds.

Hurry up—they're going nuts out here! The text from
Chase might be words only, but I could imagine the panic
rising.

I texted back, We're on the way—we're heading over
from the parking garage.

We sped up to a jog, threading our way through the milling
throng of bad holiday sweaters. People were chattering about
the snow, and all around us I heard the ever-present complaints about how many people were out on Black Friday.

I had the desire to shout out, "If you didn't want to deal with
the crowds, why the fuck are you here?" but decided that sometimes, keeping my mouth shut was the better choice.

We made our way to the elevator and hit the button
labeled WESTERN AVENUE. Unlike most elevators, the ones
here didn't use numbers, but instead place names to identify
the destination. The elevator was crowded, but our fellow
riders seemed leery, and they left a little ring of open space
around us, crowding to the back. I glanced around, and one

woman gave me a bright smile, after the startled look that
said she didn't think we'd deign to notice her.

"Are you . . . are you from *Otherworld*?" Her question
was hesitant, but friendly.

I chuckled. "Yes, we are. Well, my sister and I are." I
didn't want to hit her up with the fact that Shade was half-
dragon, or that Morio was anything but a mesmerizingly
cute Japanese guy. I didn't think she'd be able to handle it.

"You look so . . . so human and yet, you don't." She
seemed to be thinking out loud, but unless she started insult-
ing us, I didn't care. In the past few years since our arrival,
we'd gone from being novelty superstars, to being not *routine* but part of the landscape.

"Well, Delilah and I are half-human, so you're half right."
I flashed her a smile in return. "So, how goes your holiday
shopping?"

At that, the whole elevator crew seemed to exhale a
pent-up breath and people started talking about the crazi-
ness of the holidays and the struggles to find just the right
gift, and by that time, we were at our destination. As we filed
off the elevator, Delilah and I gave them a little wave.

"Happy holidays!" I called out as the doors closed. A little good PR never hurt anybody.

As we headed out into the street, crossing a brick courtyard
leading to Western Avenue, the sounds of the parade assaulted
us with all the fury of a deranged high school marching band.
Sure enough, the West Sound High School was out there, but
instead of playing whatever it was they had been scheduled to
play, the marching band was making a raucous cacophony
loud enough to wake the dead, and nobody was playing the
same song. As the street came fully into sight, I stopped cold.

The band was out there all right, running around with
their instruments, in their skivvies. That's right—the entire
fifty-piece marching band had stripped down to their underwear and were having a high old time. Pixie dust sparkled in
the air. But a bunch of half-naked high school students were
the least of our worries. Over on the other side of the street, a
major tussle was underway and I could see Chase's men trying to calm the multiplayer action.

At the center of the group, Santa—not the Holly King but a department store special—was holding his own. I had the disconcerted feeling that he'd been the one to start the whole mess. Kids were crying as they watched Santa throw punches right and left, and he, himself, had one hell of a shiner. He was joined by one of his elves—again, the holiday type, not an elf from Elqaneve, and inexplicably, Batman plunged into the fray. Oh wait! Not just Batman, but Chewbacca along with him.

Well, weren't we just the happy united-league-of-freaks here?

It wasn't clear just who anybody was fighting. For all I knew, they were beating up on whoever came within reach. Mothers were crying, screaming about their kids, and at least one leather-clad woman had shoved her two-year-old into his father's arms and was joining the pileup.

At that moment, a loud siren whooped and the marching band scattered as a crazed float came careening—as fast as any float can careen—down the middle of the street. Oh, for the love of . . . it was a cartoon float, but it had been commandeered by a group of the famed Seattle Pirate Boys—a performance group who ran around cosplaying pirates and winning the hearts of little boys and grown women. The float was also sparkling—more pixie dust, no doubt.

"Fuck, those damned little pests have been busy since Chase called us."

"It took us over a half hour to get here. A lot can happen in thirty minutes." Morio stared at the mayhem, looking mildly dazed. "What the hell are we supposed to do about this?"

"Find the pixies and put a stop to them. Somehow, I don't think we're going to have much luck rounding up all the players, so let's concentrate on finding the supporting cast. The engineers of this debacle, so to speak."

I looked around. The pixies couldn't have gone far, not having caused all this chaos. For one thing, even for a pixie, it took a lot of time to sprinkle enough dust to bring down a parade. For another, pixies tend to like to watch the results of their interference.

"Now, if I were pixie, where would I hide myself . . ." Hmm, they were small, so chances are they'd be higher up in

order to view the goings-on. Which meant . . . I glanced up.
Sure enough. Atop of the market across the street, I caught a
glimmer of something—just a flash, but enough to tell me
that whatever it was, it was magical.

"There—let's go, get across the street. But be cautious of
the pixie dust—it's heavy in the air and you know we're all
susceptible to it." The last thing we needed was for Delilah
to go sprinting down the street in panther form, or for me to
start shooting energy bolts around.

Shade grunted. "I'm immune to it. Take my hands, you
two, and I can rein you in if you start to misbehave."

Delilah stuck her tongue out at him but offered her hand.
I took his right hand, and Morio took mine. We crossed the
street on a dead run, trying to avoid the thickest patches of
dust. But the pixie dust was settling into the snow now, and
the snow was starting to stick to the street, and before I knew
it, Delilah had tripped over something and went face-first
down on the pavement.

"Oh, fucking . . ." Delilah didn't swear as much as I did,
but the fall took her by surprise. As Shade dragged her to her
feet, her chin was trickling a little blood. She'd managed to
pop herself a good one.

At that moment, I began to feel a little light-headed.
"Dude . . . it's starting to get to me. Better get us out of here,
pronto."

Shade didn't have to be told twice. Once again, he broke
into a run, dragging us behind him, and we were across the
street. One of the wayward clowns took a stab at Morio with a
pointy umbrella, but Morio just let out a growl and the clown
backed away, his red nose bobbing. I shuddered. FBH clowns
gave me the creeps. They were a far cry from the jesters and
harlequins of the courts over in Otherworld.

We pushed through the crowds on the other side, toward the
building. The brawl had now reached epic proportions, and
was spreading rapidly. I sneezed, light-headed. For a moment,
everything shimmered and I wondered why the hell we were
rushing. There was a party going on and it felt like playtime!

Shade must have sensed my impending defection because
he tightened his grip on my hand and yanked me harder

toward the door. "Don't you go AWOL on us now, Camille."
He was usually soft-spoken, but now his dragon heritage
reared up and the authority in his voice shook me out of the
borderline haze I had entered.

Blinking, I nodded. "Right. Sorry about that. I have a
strong sensitivity to pixie dust and it's everywhere right now."

We maneuvered around a group of men who were playing
football, using what looked like a ham for a ball, before
reaching the door. I glanced back at the game. The ham
made a weird sort of sense, it had once been close to a pig,
after all. As we made it to the building and rushed into the
hallway, Shade slammed the door shut behind us, cutting off
the clouds of pixie dust in the air.

I leaned against the wall, trying to clear my rapidly cloud-
ing head. After a moment, my thoughts started to sort themselves out. I inhaled slowly, filling my lungs with the canned
air of the building, a welcome relief to the fresh air that had
been clogged with joy dust.

"How many pixies does it take to create that much mayhem?" Shade sounded vexed, and looked like he was about
ready to bite the head off anybody who crossed him. "They're
nasty little buggers, aren't they?"

"Most of them, yes, to be honest. They delight in causing
chaos, and frankly, except for Mistletoe, I prefer to steer
clear of the entire lot of them." I let out a long breath and
shook my head, feeling back to myself.

"Mistletoe is nice, though." Delilah flashed me a smile.
"But even I have to agree, we're better off without them
around."

I caught sight of the staircase. We had four flights to the top
of the building and I didn't want to chance hunting down an
elevator. If the pixies caught wind we were on their tail, their
dust could affect things like cars, elevators, electronics. The
thought of being locked inside an elevator with a bunch of
laughing pixies outside didn't set well with me.

"Stairs—up to the roof." I opened the heavy metal door
and headed for the steps, the others following suit. Concrete
stairs and shoes meant that anybody who happened to be in
the stairwell would hear us coming, but too bad. Chances

were, most of the pixies were up top, watching the chaos they had caused in the streets.

We wound our way to the fourth floor, then up the last flight to the roof. The door was locked. I stepped aside and motioned to Delilah. One of her skills she had first developed for her private eye business—the Cat's Eye Investigations Agency, as she'd recently renamed it—was that of picking locks. She pulled out her picks and fiddled with the lock for a moment, then stepped back, a satisfied smile on her face.

"I did it. We're in."

"Let me go first, since I'm not affected by their magic." Shade took the front, Morio going second. Delilah was third, and I brought up the rear since I seemed to be the most susceptible.

As we burst out onto the roof, I scanned the area. The roof was covered with snow, and there were four pixies in sight—but I knew there had to be more. Sure enough, as we made our appearance, another five popped out from behind what was probably an air-conditioning unit for the building or a heating unit or some such machine.

"Nine of them, looks like."

They were about a foot long at the biggest, with long, silvery wings that shimmered with frost. Their skin wasn't as dark as Trillian's, but they were a glowing coffee color, and they wore ivory-colored loincloths. They didn't look like the pixies I was used to, but considering they came from the realm of the Northland Fae, I wasn't surprised.

"Try to avoid killing them—they aren't really *evil*." I frowned. This was going to be harder than attacking a monster or demon. Killing pixies wasn't high on my list of things to be proud of.

Shade stopped in his tracks, glancing over his shoulder at me. "Then what do you suggest we *do* with them?"

That was a good question and one we obviously hadn't thought out. We were so used to being in seek-and-destroy mode that, until this moment, I'd forgotten that we really shouldn't be killing these creatures.

"Talk to them?" Morio suggested, but then shifted nervously as the nearest three pixies moved toward us, looking for all intents and purposes like they were ready for some action.

I thought fast, but Delilah was faster. She shifted— transforming into her panther self in a blur of motion. A moment later there was a big black panther on the prowl and she bounded toward them, startling the little freaks.

The pixies chattered, darting out of the way, their attention off of us and onto the big black kitty who looked all too willing to play chase. Delilah took another leap and reached up with her massive paw, swatting the nearest one out of the air. Her swat was gentle enough to not actually *hurt* it, but hard enough to send it careening back across the roof.

I snorted. Sometimes my sister was pretty damned bright, that was for sure. Then, before the pixies could shift their focus to us, I summoned a bolt of energy from the Moon Mother, praying it wouldn't backfire, and sent it into their midst, trying to aim so that it hit none of them. The energy raced through my body, into my arms, but suddenly, I felt a strange surge as it neared my fingers. Oh fuck, what was happening? Maybe the pixie dust I'd inhaled had managed to affect me after all?

I gulped, trying desperately to pull back the energy, but it was too late. The bolt shot out of my hands, into the air. Watching it shoot up, rather than toward the pixies like I'd intended, I prayed that it wouldn't sweep back on us.

While the death magic I was learning with Morio tended to be spot on, my Moon Magic had always been a little off-kilter. Since I'd discovered that I was meant to be a Dark Moon Witch rather than the Bright Moon Witch for which I'd been trained, I'd been trying to re-learn my spells but it was going to take quite a while. My half-human heritage didn't help matters much when it came to my spellcraft.

The energy bolt rose into the air, high overhead. Below in the streets, people were shouting and pointing. Oh good gods, they probably thought it was some sort of fireworks display. Maybe I'd luck out and that's all it would be, but I had a feeling in the pit of my stomach that whatever I'd just done would be something I'd live to regret. Hopefully, we'd *all* live to regret it.

The next moment, the situation got worse. The energy I'd

sent up collided with a thick cloud of pixie dust. *Oh fuck, fuck, fuck.*

As we all watched—the pixies were also aware that something was happening and their gazes were as riveted as ours to my faux pas—a large cloud began to form out of what was rapidly becoming an energy convergence zone.

The next moment, a hail of slugs and frogs began raining down on us and the street below. People started to scream as hundreds of the critters pelted the sidewalk, stirring up the snow. I groaned as a slug hit me, sticking to my arm. It barely moved. The current temperature wasn't conducive to slug activity.

A frog was next, and it managed to use me as a launching pad—bouncing off and hitting the ground alive, a fate sadly not shared by many of its fellow base jumpers. It looked as startled as we were, and I wondered how long it would last in this frigid temperature.

Morio let out a shout—he and the others were as surprised as I was by the sudden rain—and he yelped as a frog bounced off his nose. Shade looked bewildered, and Delilah—in panther form—was suddenly taken by her feline nature and went bounding after a frog that landed near her and tried to hop away.

Frogs, slugs, snow, pixies. Yep. That about summed it up.

As I stood there, rooted by sheer confusion, the snow softly fell around me. The rain of creatures stopped as quickly as it had started. The cloud vanished, and all I could hear were screams echoing up from the street, and the tinkling laughter of the pixies. They were near the rooftop's edge, cracking up, pointing at me as if I had just slipped on a banana peel. With one spell, I'd managed to magnify any chaos they'd done by tenfold.

Silently, I walked to the nearest edge of the roof and peeked down. People were scrambling in the streets. Not only was the pixie dust still thick down there, but now kids were running after what frogs had managed to survive, and the slugs were freaking people out. One of the naked revelers was having a screaming fit—from what I could tell a giant banana slug had affixed itself to his penis. All in all, the scene belonged to some surreal Dalí painting.

I turned back, staring at the pixies. The little freaks. If they hadn't started it, all this wouldn't have happened. Before I realized what I was doing, I charged toward them, sliding a bit on the snow, uttering a string of curses.

"You fucking little freakshow perverts—get the hell out of here! Go home to where you belong—"

As I drew near, they began to look worried. I must have sounded like a harpy straight out of the Sub-Realms, because their laughter turned to anxious chatter and the next thing I knew, they disappeared, vanishing in a puff of sparkling dust. I skidded to a halt before I ran into the cloud of pixie dust, and glanced around.

Nope, there was no sign of them. Maybe they'd gotten their jollies off enough, or maybe they thought I was going to kill them. Back in OW, pixies steered clear of witches because there were a number of my kind who trapped them to steal their pixie dust, an act that was frowned on but still prevalent. It didn't kill the pixies, but it wasn't pleasant for them by any means. Kind of like milking spiders and snakes for antivenin.

I turned back to the others. Delilah had changed back into her normal shape, and we all just stood there a moment, silent, staring at one another. After a pause, Morio cleared his throat.

"Well, that was special." But his eyes were twinkling. He let out a hiccup that sounded suspiciously like a laugh.

Delilah wrinkled her nose. "Sort of a *This is Camille's magic. This is Camille's magic on pixie dust* moment?" She snickered, and Morio cracked up. The two of them began to laugh. Shade just shook his head, but he was smiling.

"That's not fair! I had no idea that was going to happen!" I swatted at Morio, smacking his arm. "If you guys want to act so smart, then what now?"

Shade struggled to restrain his laughter. "Well, we've chased off the pixies. I guess we're done here?"

"What about the chaos going on down in the streets?" Delilah glanced over the side of the roof. "It's like bedlam down there." She scooped up a frog that was struggling in the snow. "Poor little guy. He's going to freeze."

I frowned. There were at least ten frogs that were still alive that I could see. I felt bad. I hadn't *intended* for this to happen, but intentions didn't matter to the freezing amphibians.

"Oh, for fuck's sake. Pick up the frogs and we'll . . . we'll put them in Iris's greenhouse. They can eat any bugs that happen to get in there."

"That's a great idea." Delilah began scooping up the frogs, a goofy smile on her face. She had always had a soft spot for stray animals, and as a child, we'd had more bunnies, birds, and stray dogs than we knew what to do with. As a cat, she'd been territorial and not once had she brought home what I wanted—a kitten. She was mellowing, though, and I had a suspicion I might be able to get away with bringing a kitten into the house at some point. After all, Delilah had given me Misty—my ghost kitty—a year ago at Yule. I loved the fluff-brained spirit, but I still longed to have a flesh-and-blood cat that wasn't my sister.

"But what about all of those people down there?" She finished picking up the last of the live frogs she could find.

"Chase and his men can handle them. The pixie dust will wear off. There's not much more we can do here." I sighed. "I suggest we stop somewhere and buy a box for those frogs, then I want a mocha. A very large, very caffeinated, mocha. And then, I suppose, we'd better try to track down the place where the portal landed. Iris sent it somewhere, and by the appearance of the pixies, I have a feeling we aren't too far from where it ended up."

Morio wrapped his arm around my shoulders. "Sounds good. Starbucks, here we come."

As we headed back to the rooftop door, I wanted nothing more than to go home. Trillian should be up and packing by now, but finding the portal took precedence over saying good-bye to him. The pixies may not be out to harm anybody, but they could have easily done so.

And there were other, bigger, nastier things that were capable of coming through that portal. The yeti, for one, and the barbegazi and the amaroks and who knew what else. And *those* creatures were out for blood. With a sigh, I straightened my shoulders, and led the way back down to the street.

Chapter 6

The nearest Starbucks was just down the street, but we decided to drive to the one located on Blackthorn. For one thing, when the parade ended, the traffic would be even more of a nightmare. For another, I just wanted out of the area.

Seattle was home to the mega-coffee chain and the people were as divided about it as they were about politics. We were on the pro-Starbucks side. I loved their coffee, loved the atmosphere. Small, independent coffee shops vied for the java trade here, too, but there was room enough for both. The coffee fixation in Seattle and the surrounding area was on par with religious fervor.

On the way back to the parking garage, I texted Chase. He responded with a rather sarcastic thank you—the result of the frogs and slugs, no doubt—and said his men would get things under control.

As we seat belted ourselves in, I glanced at Delilah. "You know, if those frogs get loose while I'm driving, I'm not going to be very happy. How do you plan on containing them?"

The frogs had been relatively silent but with the warmth in the car, I could easily see them coming out of their

cold-induced comas to bounce around the car. I had no clue
where she had put them, but I was assuming she'd stuck
them in her pockets.

She grinned and turned around to look at Shade in the
backseat. "Might want to make sure your pockets are but-
toned, sweetie."

I glanced at Shade's expression through the rearview mirror. He didn't look very happy, but he'd learned the lessons
of a relationship well. He just nodded. The pockets on his
duster were deep and I knew exactly what had gone down.
Delilah had convinced him to store the frogs inside his coat.

"Whatever you say, Pussycat." Shade's voice was like
smooth honey, and he humored her with a smile while
checking to make certain his pockets were closed.

"I just . . ." I started to say something snarky but then
relented. Delilah truly loved animals of all sorts, and as
rough as we'd had it lately, if saving a few frogs made her
happy, then we'd save the frogs.

She glanced at me. "What?"

"Nothing, hon. Nothing." I paid the parking garage fee
and we were off. Traffic going back toward the Belles-Faire
district was lighter than coming into the city proper, and it
didn't take us long to emerge from the main congestion.

As we turned onto a side street that would lead us directly
to the Blackthorn Starbucks, I spied a drugstore and eased
into the parking lot. "Wait here. I'll go get a container for the
frogs."

Within under five minutes I was back, a plastic tub with a
very secure lid in hand. I used the tip of my dagger to poke a
few holes in the lid and then Shade carefully transferred the
frogs into it. I'd also picked up a bottle of water, a plastic
soap dish that would serve for a trough, and tissue paper. I
figured we could crinkle it inside the tub and give the frogs
some extra warmth. Delilah rigged it all up, then fastened
the lid on. When she was ready, we took off again.

Another five minutes and we reached the Blackthorn
Starbucks. Leaving the frog brigade in the car, we wandered
into the coffee shop. I was ready for caffeine. A lot of it. The
afternoon had worn me out. While my thoughts were preoc-

cupied with finding the portal, I longed to be home to say good-bye to Trillian. I ordered a quad shot peppermint mocha and a brownie, and—leaving the others to order— looked around the room.

There, at a table in the corner, was a familiar face. Tanne Baum, one of the Fae from the Black Forest in Germany. He was from the Hunter's Glen Clan, a group of demon hunters originating in Europe. Tanne had decided to migrate to the United States. We had saved his girlfriend, Violet, from an unscrupulous sex slave operation run by a local businessman who turned out to be a daemon, but that was a whole 'nother kettle of fish. Catching his eye, I waved and he gestured for us to join him at his table.

"Hey, Tanne." I slid into a seat at the long table. Starbucks had recently changed their décor to include communal seating and I wasn't sure just how I felt about it, but a chair was a chair was a chair.

"Camille, hello." His accent gave him away. Tanne spoke in precise sentences, his words overlaid with an odd European accent. It wouldn't be found in any country per se, at least not among FBHs, since he was full Fae. He pushed his book away and leaned back in his chair. "You were at the parade?"

"Not exactly. We were fighting pixies at the parade. A group of them decided to raise havoc there. It was a barrel of laughs."

He took one look at my face and burst into laughter. "That good?"

Ducking my head, I shrugged and smiled. "Pixie dust makes me giddy. My magic conflicted with theirs. It was . . ."

"Breaking news: Raining frogs and slugs in downtown Seattle. You were responsible? I saw it on Twitter." Again, the sparkling glint in his eye.

I couldn't help but smile in return. "Yes, that was me, all right. Lovely, huh? We got rid of the pixies but . . . it's hard when your opponents aren't ones you can just look at and say, *'attack and destroy,'* you know?"

Tanne sobered. "I know. In the Old Country, when my clan would go out hunting, we sought for beasts of destruction. We had no qualms about killing them—they were dangerous and had to be stopped. It's much harder when your opponent is more . . . innocuous?"

"You understand then." Sighing, I looked up to see Morio. He had my order in hand and I gratefully accepted the drink and food, relishing the rush as the caffeine begin to work its way through my system. "Oh, I need this so much."

Morio returned to the counter for his own order and then, with Delilah and Shade in tow, joined us. "So, Tanne, what brings you out on this snowy day?"

Tanne saluted him with two fingers. "I needed to get out of the house." Then, after a beat, "Violet and I broke up. She needs her space. I think the imprisonment cost her too much on an emotional level. She isn't capable of sustaining a relationship right now. At least, that's what she told me. So, I am stepping back. I will not pursue a woman who doesn't want me. She quit her job and is moving back to the forest with her mother."

I bit my lip. I'd undergone torture far greater than Violet at the hands of Smoky's father. On one level, I understood what she was going through. But for me, the thought of running away from the memories and my family and lovers held no promise of healing. But everyone had to find their own recovery from assault, and Violet was doing what she needed to do.

"I'm sorry." Reaching out, I placed my hand over Tanne's. His skin was warm, and sparks flowed between our hands. Not sexual sparks, though I could easily find him attractive, but more—magical. He glanced at me, startled, as a surge of strength and power rushed from me into his fingers. Surprised by the energy rush, I slowly withdrew my hand. Tanne kept hold of my gaze with those piercing eyes of his, like glacial pools from high in the Alps they were. They matched the tousled mop of platinum hair carefully styled to look fresh out of bed.

"Thank you for your concern." He studied me for a moment, his fingers stroking the side of his cup, then he glanced at Morio and back at me. "Violet . . . I will miss her, but I would never stop her from following her heart. And her heart is no longer focused on me." He paused for a moment. "I am looking for a task to take my mind off her departure. If you need any help, I'm available. I'm adept, as you know, and have faced danger."

I caught my breath. Beneath the table, Morio reached out and put a hand on my knee, squeezing gently. I wasn't sure if it was a warning, or a love tap. But I just smiled.

"We'll remember that. We have your number. It can be helpful to keep busy, can't it?" I sipped at my mocha when a thought crossed my mind. "Hey, we *do* have something you can do today if you want. We are looking for a runaway portal and need all eyes on deck."

Tanne blinked. "Runaway portal?"

"Yeah, it kind of . . . got away from us." I ran down what had happened with Vanzir, Roz, and the misguided spell. "So, we have an open portal to the realm of the Northlands. That's pretty much like putting up a bright neon sign saying, COME FUCK WITH US! Not only that, but it's spewing out snow. Which means—well, I don't know how that will affect the environment, but it sure as hell fucked up our living room."

Tanne glanced at Shade, laughter dancing in his eyes. "Living in the house with the three of them? Must be one hell of a ride. Okay, then—and yes, the Northlands creatures can be temperamental. The pixies must be from the Snow Fields branch."

"Their wings were frosty white and they were dark as night in skin."

"That's right. You're lucky they only wanted to fuck with the parade. They tend to be nastier-tempered than regular pixies. *Everybody* up in the Northlands seems to be more stoic, harsher edged." Tanne finished his coffee, draining the cup.

I thought of Hanna. "They have reason to be. It's a harsh place. When Hyto kidnapped me and took me there, it didn't take me long to develop a sense that it's eat or be eaten. Survive or die. When the winters are long and brutal, when the snow muffles the world, there's no time or place for fancy parties or delicate sensibilities. Even within Howl's clan, there are few barriers to privacy."

"You've met Howl?" Tanne leaned forward. "Is he like the legends say he is?"

"Howl is . . . He's Howl. There's no other way to put it."

Howl was an Elemental Lord, one of the Immortals. He was a wolf spirit—not a werewolf, but a true shifter. Together with his wife, Kitää, he ruled over the Katabas Wolf People—the Wind Wolves. They had helped me when Hanna and I escaped from Hyto's cave and made our way down the glacial mountain to their home.

"I've always wanted to meet him. He has a huge following in the Black Forest among the Supe groups. Our werewolf clans there tend to pay him homage." Tanne leaned forward, his stare focused on me. "You should come to the forest someday. Our lands are ancient and the magic runs deep. The woodlands reek with it. You would find the moon brighter there."

I smiled softly. Magic blood recognized magic blood. Whatever kind of woodland Fae Tanne was, his heritage was steeped in magic. He might be a demon hunter, but his spellcrafting roots ran deep as the trees out of which he had come. That much I could sense about him.

"Maybe someday I will. Meanwhile . . . will you help us find the portal?"

"Why not? I don't have much else on my plate today. I've got a good sense for ice and snow magic, so I'll head out and see what I can dig up. I'm good at tracking, you know that." He pushed back his chair. "I'll call you later, regardless of what I find." And with that, he slipped on his black leather jacket and headed out the door.

I watched him go. "I have a feeling he's going to become very useful to us in the future."

"Plus, he has a charm that's hard to ignore." Delilah winked at me.

"You might want to try a little harder to ignore it." Morio scowled at me, but then laughed and shrugged. "He's sincere. That much I can tell. I have a feeling he's blunt and to the point."

"I like that. He doesn't mince words." I watched him exit the shop and turn to the right. "I'm sorry about Violet, though. They seemed well matched."

Delilah shrugged. "You of all people know what trauma

like she went through can do to you. She may not have been tortured or . . . " Her voice drifted off.

"You can say it." I looked at her. "Hyto *raped* me. In every way he could. And he beat me black and blue. I live with that every day and it actually helps to talk about it—I don't feel like I'm hiding some dirty little secret then. And . . . it's difficult to be blunt about it around Smoky because, as much as I love him, let's face it—he still feels like he was responsible and to hear me discuss what his father did to me? Even though Hyto's dead, it sends him into a fury."

And *that* was a Catch-22. I was the victim, yes, but Smoky had been targeted by his father as well and Hyto had done a good job of wounding both of us.

Morio slid his arm around my waist. "He tries—but he's a dragon. He'll never feel like he exacted enough revenge on Hyto for you."

"I know. As long as I can talk to you guys about it, things will work out." I had to believe they would. It had been over a year, but I was learning that some wounds took a little longer to heal, even when they weren't visible on the body. I knew that logically, and from watching Menolly, but now I knew what it was like to carry baggage on an entirely different level than I had ever had to before.

"Back to Violet," I said, clearing my throat. "Regardless of whether or not they tortured her, they still kidnapped her, imprisoned her, and were going to sell her off. She has every right to feel what she's feeling. She was in quite a state of shock when we found her." I gathered my purse and finished my drink. "Well, the portal's not going to walk up and say, 'Here I am.' I guess we'd better get a move on."

"So head out now?" Delilah asked, finishing off her peanut butter cookie.

I sighed. "Right. The problem is: Where the hell *should* we look for it? We can drive up and down the streets keeping an eye out for a yeti, but none of us is all that skilled at tracking down magical signatures, especially when there isn't a person involved. Morio and I can sense them, but picking one up without a place to start looking? Not so easy."

"I think we just should go home and ask Chase to call us when the next mess happens. Because you know it's going to happen. And you can say good-bye to Trillian." Shade reached over to rub Delilah's hand with his own. "If I were him, I'd want Delilah there to kiss me good-bye." The look on his face said too much. Even Shade was dubious about Trillian making it out of the Shadow Lands alive.

"Yeah," I whispered. "I suppose that's our best bet." I stared at my shoes, not wanting to discuss Trillian's chances. I didn't want to talk about the odds because they weren't good—they weren't in our favor at all. The Shadow Lands were fucked up and deadly, and if Darynal had gone missing there, chances were good he'd never see the light of day again.

The mood dampened, we silently returned to the car. I turned the ignition, and we headed home, the only sound that of the frogs croaking in their plastic prison.

By 4 P.M., Trillian and Roz were ready. They were outfitted for the road—the OW road, that is. Trousers, tunics, heavy cloaks, backpacks, and bedrolls. Weapons, of course. Roz wore his duster-cum-armory. As I watched the two of them standing there, once again a feeling of foreboding swept over me. Whether it was premonition or just nerves, I didn't know, but a chill raced down my spine.

Even though I wanted to cry, I didn't. I was raised to be a soldier's daughter. I understood duty, and I had learned early to keep my tears inside every time Father left for a mission. My mother had had a harder time—but she had respected Sephreh's wishes and taught us girls to respect the solemnity that went with the departure of a loved one, whether to war or to a rescue mission.

We all gathered in the living room—everyone was there, except Menolly. Trillian walked over to me. He reached out to stroke my cheek gently.

"I will miss you. Keep it together. Keep up the good fight. Be cautious in the realm of the Elder Fae and don't you dare get hurt. You are my wife, and we are bound by two rituals. Know that I love you, and whatever you choose to do, I stand behind your choices." He leaned in, kissing me so lightly I barely felt it. Yet the kiss buried deep in my core, raced pounding to my center, like a wild stallion at full speed.

"Come back to me. Find Darynal, and return." I pressed my fingers to his heart. "I am here, in your heart, and I will never leave."

Trillian turned to Smoky and Morio. "Take care of our woman. See to her needs. Keep my space on the bed warm and waiting."

For once, there was no snarking, no snide comments or joking. Smoky held out his hand, then pulled Trillian into a man-brace—the kind where they clap each other on the back and then pretend they didn't actually hug. Morio did the same.

"We'll keep her safe. And she'll keep us in line." Morio winked at Trillian, breaking the tension that was building.

"Roz, you be safe. Watch over each other. You can travel through the Ionyc Seas. If things get bad, you guys hop into the currents and get the fuck out of there." Even though I knew they could do this, I also knew how quickly things could escalate. One mistake was all it took to find yourself six feet under.

Roz nodded. "I promise."

I could barely stand it and just wanted it over by now, like ripping off a bandage. And then, it was too soon, because Roz put his arm around Trillian's waist, and they were gone. In the blink of an eye, Roz and Trillian vanished into the Ionyc Seas. Roz knew how to get to the portal in the Wayfarer that way, and it would save us the trouble of driving them to the bar. It also meant that my alpha husband and first great love was gone, and who knew when he'd be coming back?

I stared at the empty spot on the floor. Trillian and I had been parted too many times. It never got easier, and I never got used to it. But I had promised him no tears. And I knew that promise would last as long as it took me to get upstairs and into a hot shower. There, I would break my vow and cry as hard as I wanted to, until the worry and pain eased up enough to let me breathe again.

As I finished drying my hair and putting on my makeup for the evening, I heard noise coming from the bedroom. I slipped on my robe and padded across the hallway. It was 5 P.M. by now and dark as sin outside but the room was lit with the glow of Christmas lights. They sparkled through the room and, with the glittering green garland we had strung, turned my bedroom into a faerie land.

The music was on—In Strict Confidence was throbbing out of the stereo, a Germanic band heavily influenced by darkwave and goth industrial. I loved the reverberating thunder of their music, and it always turned me on as the beat pulsed its way through my body.

I glanced over at the bed. There, Morio and Smoky were waiting for me, both naked and both obviously ready and able to make me forget my cares.

"Trillian told us to keep you happy." Smoky laughed. "He made us promise to keep you satisfied till he came home, so we're just doing our duty." He reached out and I let my robe slide away. "Bring those beautiful boobs over here, lovely."

Morio arched his eyebrows. "What he said."

I slowly moved to them, my hips swaying lightly in the glow of the lights. Trillian's leave-taking was still painful in my heart, and their open arms looked comforting. As I knelt on the bed, crawling slowly up the mattress to them, Smoky's hair reached out, coiling around my wrists and ankles.

"You're hurting, and you're afraid for him," he whispered.

"Take away my fear. Take me out of my head." I closed my eyes as they pulled me between them and then, some-how, I was beneath the covers with their musky bodies flanking each side. Their skin was warm against mine.

Morio reached out to brush his fingers over my shoulder as I leaned back against him. I closed my eyes, sinking into the feel of his touch, the smell of my dragon and fox, the feel of Smoky's hair binding my wrists.

I liked to be restrained. The ties helped me quiet the rush of thoughts in my mind. Some days it was the only thing that would silence my mind—being tied up and blindfolded, letting them play my body like a harp. Letting them do what they would to me while trusting them never, ever to take me places I could not go. There was a freedom in sexual submission that allowed me to surrender my control, surrender all the responsibilities placed on my shoulders. I could give myself over to sensation, knowing my men were there to catch me if I fell too far.

I regulated my breath. Doing so deepened the sensations, helped me slide into that twilight trance between waking and sleeping where everything was cast in shades of purple and indigo and sparkling silver. I closed my eyes as Smoky stroked his fingers along my arms. Morio leaned down and began kissing below my breasts, following the center of my torso down, slowly working his lips along the gentle curve of my belly.

A low fire began to burn between my thighs, catching hold to sizzle its way to my clit, where the sudden ache of need flared up, roaring to life. I moaned gently, catching my breath as the flames worked their way up to meet Morio's lips, and then past, into my nipples as they stiffened, hard and firm, erect against the globes of my breasts.

Smoky's hair drew my arms taut, out to the side. His fingers caught my right nipple between thumb and forefinger, squeezing hard enough to make me jump, hard enough to hurt, but the pain lasted only a few seconds, fading into desire and hunger. He squeezed again and then leaned down, his lips catching hold as he worried me with his tongue, coiling around the nipple like the draco serpent he was. He licked it, then roughly mouthed my breast, sucking hard.

I forced my attention to my breath. *Breathe in, breathe out. In . . . out . . . space the breaths evenly. Don't pant, don't let yourself slide out of control just yet. Let them build the fire within.*

Morio reached my pubic hair—what there was of it that I didn't shave—and he slid along over it, nestling his face against my mound. The next moment, I felt him spread me with his fingers, and then—a pause as he watched me, murmuring softly.

"I want to eat you out, to taste your dark honey." He pressed his lips against my clit, his tongue darting out in long strokes against me. It was almost sandpaper-like, at first rough and startling, then he circled the nub and began to alternate between sucking and licking. As I began to rise on the sensation, he edged his teeth along me, nipping ever so slightly—just enough to make me cry out. I whimpered, wanting to come, but I wasn't there yet.

Smoky's hair held my arms tight against the bed and now he loomed over me, his lips meeting mine, his tongue probing my mouth, as the kiss went on and on. The tendril holding my right hand suddenly yanked it forward, plastering my fingers against his rigid cock, forcing me to take hold of him. He was big—wide and round, long and rock hard in my hand, and I squeezed, forcing enough pre-cum out of the tip to lubricate my fingers. Working them up and down his shaft, I focused on seeing how hard I could make him.

But Morio's tongue recaptured my attention and I lost track of everything except the spiraling in my stomach, my breasts, as he licked harder and faster. He swirled my clit, not letting me rest.

I began to pant in earnest, letting out cries as a series of jolts began to race through my body, ripples forcing me along with the current, and there was no stopping it. If anyone had opened the door, if the world would have come tumbling down, I couldn't have shaken out of the orgasm. The intensity of his strokes increased and I suddenly screamed, sharp and harsh as my pussy contracted and I came, hard and fast and without mercy.

I wanted to rest, to float for a moment, but Smoky yanked me up, turned me over on my hands and knees. He slid behind me, his cock forcing deep into my cunt as he grabbed my hips and drove himself into me, pounding against my ass. Morio swung around in front, on his knees, so that he hovered in front of my face, thick and pulsing. I opened my mouth as he took hold of my head, fisting my hair, and thrust into me. His cock slid back in my throat and he laughed, low and lusty.

"Blow me, suck me dry."

I murmured around his shaft, sucking hard, bobbing my head as I licked and nibbled. Smoky rammed into me from behind, laughing as his hair reached around to play with my breasts, squeezing them together.

"You want to tit-fuck her?" he asked Morio. "I'll hold her for you."

I felt my cheeks burning as they talked about me over my head, but it wasn't unpleasant. We were each others' play-toys and I felt dirty, raunchy, and I wanted more.

Morio growled. "Thanks, and yes." He pulled out of my mouth, then slid beneath me, his face near my clit as his cock nestled between my breasts. Smoky's hair squeezed them tight, forming a channel in which Morio could thrust. As he began to rub his cock between my breasts, his lips found my clit again and I was back on fire, burning so bright it felt like I might go up in a flash of light, leaving only ash and dust behind.

Behind me, Smoky had hold of my waist as he drove deep into my core, unrelenting. He twisted to the right, changing his aim, and I let out a sharp cry as his balls pressed against my ass and he ground against me. My cunt was so full, my pussy so engorged as he possessed me with his cock, making me his.

Morio reached up and pinched my nipples as Smoky's hair squeezed my boobs tighter. Morio's cock was slick from being in my mouth, and he rubbed against the space between my breasts as his tongue roughly stroked my clit. The pace became frenzied, and I lost track of what was going on—there was only sensation, only the feel of their bodies against mine, their bodies inside mine. We were color, we were movement, we were song in motion.

As the momentum built, my stomach flipped again and all thought fled from mind. Smoky let out a loud cry as he came, pumping his hot cum into my pussy. Morio was next, soaking my breasts as he arched, his cock rigid against me, and then—with one last tongue stroke, I came again, long, and hard, and crying, my last thought before release that of Trillian and how I wished he could be here with us.

Shower number two and I was once again clean of sweat and cum and smelling like sweet vanilla. I leisurely dressed. Smoky and Morio had gone downstairs to help with dinner, after a quick rinse off, and I lingered by the bed, smelling the sex that wafted off our sheets. I felt thoroughly wrung out, satiated, and my tears for Trillian had dried in the release of orgasm.

As I stripped the sheet off the bed and deftly replaced it with a clean one—we didn't change them every time but it had been four days, and with our sex play, we definitely changed the sheets frequently—I glanced out the window. Six P.M. and the clouds were thick. It was snowing just lightly enough to skiff against the ground. We only had a few inches, and chances are it would change to rain over the next week and melt away, but right now the yard looked calm and peaceful in its blanket of white.

I pushed the window up, leaning my arms on the sill as the chill night air hit me full force. It was icy and cold, and tiny snowflakes landed on the arm of my robe, but I didn't care. I inhaled deeply, then slowly exhaled, clearing my body and mind with the crystalline air. As it rushed through the room, I felt calm and peaceful in a way I hadn't for a long time. There was something about winter nights that called me to slow down, to pause and rest for a moment.

From our window, we could see the roof of Iris's house, and the warm lights coming from within. It hit me that we still needed to decorate. Our usual tradition had been trashed by Vanzir and Roz's well-meaning stunt.

Brushing my hair back into a ponytail, I decided that we were going to fix that little matter. And we were going to fix it before I had to set out in search of the Merlin tomorrow. I was still in my robe, so I hurried to finish the bed, then I quickly fastened my bra and slipped into a pair of bikinis. I crossed to my closet and pulled out my black spidersilk skirt and a warm V-neck sweater in vivid plum. Once I was dressed, I tied up my kitten heel leather granny boots, and bounded downstairs.

Smoky was in the kitchen, along with Delilah, Nerissa, and Menolly. I kissed Menolly good evening—or good morning, depending on how you looked at it—and then sauntered over to Smoky.

"Love, I want something." I leaned down and planted a kiss on his nose.

He glanced over at Delilah. "Should I be scared, do you think?"

She laughed. "I probably would be."

"Oh shush, you two. I want us to head down to Birchwater Pond and find a beautiful tree for Yule. We're going to chop it down and bring it back and decorate tonight, because I'll be damned if I traipse off to the realm of the Elder Fae without leaving a pretty, sparkly, home waiting for me to return to." I wrapped my arms around Smoky. "You have no choice, you know that."

He laughed, patting my hand and placing a kiss on my cheek. "I never do. But don't you think we should go buy a tree instead? The trees on our land are too beautiful to cut."

I frowned. He had a point. The trees in the lot had been bred and grown for this—they hadn't lived their lives free range, so to speak. "Fine, we'll go to a tree lot, but either way, we're heading out. Delilah and Menolly, you're coming too. We're a family, and we're going to pick out a tree as a family."

The look on Delilah's face made it all worth it. Our Kitten loved trees and ornaments—sometimes too much—and she had counted on me to make the Winter Solstice shine ever since Mother had died. Father certainly hadn't gone out of his way to help.

She jumped up and grabbed her coat. "Should I go get Iris and Bruce? They may want to come with us and get a tree, too."

"Sure. Is Chase home yet?" I glanced over at Nerissa, who wrinkled her nose and nodded.

"Yes, and he sure had plenty to say about that little incident downtown today. He was not amused." She leaned over Menolly's shoulder to plant a big, fat kiss on my sister's cheek. They made one hell of a cute couple, and so clearly loved each other. I was grateful she'd come along to show Menolly that, yes, she, too, could have love, even though she was a vampire. Even though she'd lost everything else.

"Hey, it wasn't our fault. Blame the damned pixies. Blame Vanzir and Roz—"

"Blame Vanzir and Roz for what?" Vanzir meandered into the room.

"The pixie attack. By the way, before I have to leave tomorrow, I want you to show me where you found that witch. I want to get a good look at her and figure out if I ever met her and just forgot, or if she's lying." Sometimes, things were random. Sometimes, things didn't link up, and I'd learned the hard way not to make assumptions.

"Sure thing. Hey, Camille, can I ask you something in private?"

"Why do you want to talk to my wife privately?" Smoky grumbled, but Vanzir let out a snort and waved off his protest.

"Calm yourself, you big lizard. I'm not going to cop a feel or anything." With that, Vanzir caught my eye and motioned me into the living room. Once we were there, he lowered his voice. "I didn't want to say anything in front of them, but I thought you might want to know. Aeval summoned me to Talamh Lonrach Oll. I'm to go there tomorrow night, right after you leave. She told me that she might have a job for me to do. I have no clue what she's talking about, but I thought I'd just run that little fact by you. So if anybody tells you I've been out there, that's why."

I nodded, thinking on the fly. So much had happened. I knew that the Fae Queens were doing something with Vanzir but had very little clue what—they hadn't taken me into their confidence, and it wasn't my place to ask.

"Okay . . . thanks for telling me. I have no idea what's going on, either." As we headed back into the kitchen, a dozen possible reasons sprang up in my thoughts but I brushed them away. Life was hard enough without borrowing trouble, and every single scenario I envisioned did just that.

Chapter 7

~~~

By seven thirty, we'd found our tree and were fastening it onto the roof of Morio's SUV. Smoky, Morio, Delilah, and I had scoured three tree lots to find the perfect one. Bruce and Iris had also tagged along, though they had brought Bruce's limo and now there was a tree being tied to the top of their car, too. As Morio and Smoky finished lashing the trees to the roofs, my phone rang.

I glanced at it, grimacing. *Chase.* Normally I was happy to talk to the dude but I couldn't help but wonder just what the hell was going down now. If it was another pixie fight, I was going to strip the wings of every one of the little buggers. Hoping to hell it wasn't anything earthshaking, I answered.

"What's up?" My phone-side manner wasn't exactly up to par lately. I'd taken one too many bad news calls.

"Hanna wants to know if you can stop and pick up some sugar before you come home. And baking cocoa. She's out." He laughed, his voice easy and far more relaxed than it had been that morning. "You think I was calling with more pixie action?"

Feeling vaguely guilty, I let out a long breath and closed

my eyes for a moment. "Something like that. Tell her sure, we'll do that. Chase, how are you doing? We've had so little time to sit and talk lately."

He snorted, but I could tell he was laughing, not being sarcastic. "Little heart-to-heart, huh?" Sobering, he continued. "Honestly? All my attention has been focused on Astrid and my job. When I'm at work, I feel like I should be here with her. When I'm home, I feel like I should be at work. I've never been so torn in my life. And I'm worried about Sharah, and what's happening over in Otherworld. I wish I could see her—it's been a month, and she hasn't seen Astrid once in that time. I know they've got her penned in, but honestly, I worry that my baby girl won't know her mother at all."

I scowled. Chase was right to be worried, and the way things were going, I wasn't sure exactly when Sharah would be able to get away. While the sentient storm was either off to other parts or had been dissipated—which, I wasn't sure—the fact was they were now dealing with the aftermath. The attacking goblin hordes had been driven off for the time being, but the danger was far from over, and they hadn't even begun to clean up after the havoc wreaked on the city of Elqaneve and the entire kingdom of Kelvashan. The dead were more numerous than the living. The Elfin race had been decimated and their lands torched by the fires of war.

"I'll ask Trenyth what he can do next time I talk to him via the Whispering Mirror." I wasn't hopeful, but it was the least I could promise.

Chase let out a soft sound. "Thanks. I don't expect anything—I know what's going on over there. I've heard enough about it from you and Delilah . . . but I appreciate the effort. Meanwhile, I'm damned grateful Iris and Bruce invited me into their home. It's odd, living in somebody else's house, but it's best for both Astrid and me at this point. I know she's loved and taken care of when I'm out, and I can be there to help out Iris and Bruce when need be. Speaking of which, I'd like to get them something to show my appreciation. I haven't picked up their Yule gift yet. What do you think Iris would like?"

I groaned. I hated it when people asked me what other

people wanted. I seemed to be the go-to font of information, though I'd never set myself up as a purveyor of knowledge.

"I don't know but I'll see what I can find out. Okay, signing off. We've got the trees and we'll stop by the store for Hanna on the way home." I said good-bye and hung up.

Before we got back in our cars, I pulled Iris off to the side. I wasn't going to bother with pussyfooting around. "Hey, Chase wants to know what you'd like for Yule. He wants to buy you something special so no blenders or anything mundane like that, unless it's über cool." I grinned at her.

"Does he now? Well, then." She frowned. "I'd tell him not to bother but I know he feels like he's imposing, even though he isn't. All right, tell him you found out that I'd really love a print of the aurora borealis—something spectacular."

I started to ask why she didn't just pick one out she liked, but stopped myself. Bruce could afford to give Iris anything she wanted. He was a leprechaun, from a very wealthy family. But she was thinking of Chase, of something that would make him feel good to give her—something that wouldn't cost him a fortune. Iris liked nice things, but she wasn't focused on accumulating stuff.

"I'll tell him. That sounds beautiful." I leaned down to brush her cheek with a kiss. "He sure appreciates your help."

She grinned. "Astrid is a little doll. I've got this fantasy going that she and my Maria and Ukkonen will grow up to be best friends. I wonder what Astrid will be like—she's half-elf, half-human. And, if the council in Elqaneve pulls their heads out of their butts, she'll be heir to the throne."

I stared at her. That thought hadn't even occurred to me, but Iris was right. Provided that Sharah could change the laws, her daughter would one day inherit the throne of Elqaneve. But the elves would never allow a half-breed to sit at their helm. Even with Trenyth's help, that wasn't likely to happen. You could only push tradition so far before it pushed back. Which meant that Sharah would be expected to produce a full-blood heir. Which meant she and Chase faced rocky times ahead. I hoped that hadn't run through his mind yet. He needed that worry like he needed another hole in his head.

"I just hope they change their minds about it," I murmured.

Iris nodded. "Let's not borrow trouble. I haven't said a word to Chase about it and don't you either."

"Trust me, I'm not planning on it." And with that, we got back in our cars and headed for home. Along the way, I asked Morio to stop at the Save-and-Go and ran in to buy a big bag of sugar and a couple boxes of baking cocoa. With the holiday season, I didn't bother with the small size— Hanna and Iris were in full cookie-baking-mode, and with the amount of sweets and breads they were making, you'd think we were expecting an army for Yule. But then again, given how many people belonged to our extended family, and how many friends we had drop over, they knew what they were doing. Plus, we had the upcoming holiday party at the Supe Community Action Council on the calendar. And we were down for refreshment duty.

When we arrived home, Hanna was beaming as we handed her the groceries. An excited shout from the living room caught my attention and I scooted in there pronto. Delilah was clapping her hands and I looked around, amazed by the transformation in less than two hours.

While we'd been out buying the tree, Menolly, Shade, and Vanzir had begun decorating. All the ornaments were out and sorted. The garland and lights were up in both the living room and parlor. And as soon as the men brought in the tree, they began making quick work of setting it up, guywires and all. We always anchored our trees to the ceiling since Delilah had a propensity, in kitten form, for climbing the branches. The tree nearly reached the ceiling and made our rather bedraggled living room look beautiful.

"We thought we'd get a start on things." Menolly gave us a fangy grin.

I wrapped my arm around Smoky's waist as we gazed at the soft glow of the lights wrapped around the garland.

Smoky winked at her. "Menolly, you're a good sister-in-law. Why don't you girls decorate the tree while Vanzir, Morio, and I tackle the lights outside?" His crinkling eyes smiled as he leaned down and kissed me on the forehead. "We'll get them up tonight, no worries."

"Thank you, love." I kissed him back, softly. "Maybe you could run down and set up Iris's tree for her first?"

Iris laughed. "That would be a great help, if you could, Master Dragon. Bruce and I will decorate later but that would give us a leg up on the task. And while you are there, ask my husband and Chase to bring the young ones over. I'd like them to be here as we decorate your tree—time to start them in on family traditions, you know."

I loved that Iris considered us her family, and while I had no desire to have children of my own, I had fun playing with Ukkonen, Maria, and Astrid. I could give them back when they started crying. "Oh yes, please do!"

"You'll have to make certain that Maggie's safely in her playpen." A sad look crossed Iris's face and I patted her arm.

Maggie was a Crypto, through and through. She had no comprehension that she could hurt the babies if she were allowed to play with them. She was rough on her dolls and stuffed animals—not out of malice, but because she had sharp claws even at her age, and she was a strong little dickens. She was in no way human—she didn't understand enough to know *how* to be gentle with weaker creatures. Delilah was able to fend her off when in cat form, but we never let her loose near small animals or children.

"We can put her in the playpen over in the corner. And *I* can sit with her while the rest of you decorate. That should take care of matters." Delilah wrinkled her nose, shrugging. "Will that work?"

Iris nodded. "That should be good. I just don't want her getting too curious, so make sure she has her dollies and toys with her."

While Delilah pulled the playpen in, Smoky and Vanzir followed Morio outside to go help unload Iris's tree, which was considerably smaller than ours. It was only about six feet tall. But then, neither Bruce nor Iris had a lot of excess energy, considering the twins were barely a month old.

Menolly and I sorted through the ornaments as Hanna brought in a tray with hot cocoa and cookies—chocolate chip, sugar cookies, cinnamon sprinkles, homemade maca-roons, and thick gingerbread men. Everything was tinged with the flavors of the season: peppermint and chocolate, cinnamon and orange and spice. She brought in Maggie next, and settled her with all her toys into the playpen.

"I'm going to make fudge. You girls call me if you need help." She winked at us, then headed back to the kitchen.

Menolly stared at the food. "Damn, I wish I could eat. The smell's enough to drive me nuts, and before you ask, yes, Morio's been making me dessert-flavored blood, but you know what? I'd give just about anything for a bite of one of those gingerbread men."

"Where's Nerissa?" I glanced around. The blond bomb-shell was nowhere to be seen.

"My wife decided to brave the mall. She left me with strict orders to stay home and not follow her, which means she's off buying my gift. Camille . . . what should I get her?" Menolly's braids clicked—the beads threaded in the thin cornrows shimmered, a brilliant blue and silver. Nerissa had been buying her different colored beads for every season and occasion possible.

Not again. I grumbled, "I have no idea what your wife wants for Yule. Have you tried asking her?" I finished off a piece of chocolate shortbread and licked my fingers before beginning to break out the special ornaments that always went on the tree first.

Our mother had bought us each an ornament every year until she'd died, and then Aunt Rythwar kept up the tradition until we left Otherworld for Earthside. Because we aged far slower than FBHs, we had each accrued over fifty ornaments each—I had a couple more than my sisters. And every year, they went on the tree first.

"Yes, and she told me to figure it out." Menolly set her lips in a pout, and I broke into a loud snort. "What?"

"You and pouting? Not so good a combo. You look more like you're getting ready to put the fang into somebody. Honestly, you're better off rethinking the puppy dog eyes and opt for something a bit less . . ."

"Bambi?" She grinned at me, the tips of her fangs gleaming.

"Yeah. Bambi's more your dinner than your role model." With that, I went back to hanging ornaments. Delilah sat by

Maggie, playing with her. We wouldn't allow her to help us trim the tree—we had banned her from that years ago because she couldn't keep her paws off of the shiny ornaments—literally. She almost always turned into her tabby form during the decorating phase and had to be corralled from causing mischief. That's one reason we bought such a tall tree to begin with—it made fixing it to the hook on the ceiling that much easier, and our tree stand was a heavy steel one that made it harder for a twelve-pound tabby cat to tip over.

Chase and Bruce came into the room, carrying the babies. Chase was carrying Astrid and Maria, Bruce was carrying Ukkonen. Morio followed with one big-ass playpen and Hanna hurried in behind him to set it up—well across the room from Maggie—and fill it with blankets. They laid the babies in the playpen and Bruce pulled a chair over beside it. He shook his head as Delilah stood.

"You go ahead and stay with Maggie. We don't want her jealous of your attention." The leprechaun looked tired. Bruce looked a lot like Elijah Woods from the Lord of the Rings films, only his hair was darker and he was cuter. But there, the resemblance ended. Bruce wore a tweed jacket with leather-patched elbows, and a pair of black jeans. He was a few inches taller than Iris—I'd put him around four-four. He yawned, leaning back in the chair, watching the babies as they fussed a little. But with a tuck of the blanket here and there, all three of them fell back asleep and Bruce wearily smiled.

I meandered over to peek in their cage. They were cute—as far as babies went. Astrid was bigger than the other two, of course. She wasn't a sprite or leprechaun, but size notwithstanding, all babies looked about the same to me. They gurgled—or rather, one of them gurgled. It was Ukkonen. I knew because Iris had wrapped him in blue, while Maria was always wrapped in a violet blanket. Astrid was cloaked in green. Ukkonen blinked, his tiny arms waving around in some sort of attempt to communicate his thoughts, and then he hiccupped and closed his eyes. Within seconds he was back asleep. I stared at them for another moment, then—not knowing what else to do with them—went back to the tree.

As Menolly floated up to the ceiling—the levitation thing vampires had going on was pretty damned handy—Morio set up the ladder. Chase climbed halfway up, and I handed him ornaments and he passed them on to Menolly to hang near the top of the tree. We were about a third of the way through—we'd worked our way down to the center of the tree—when a crash startled me. The silver ball I had in my hand shattered as I whirled, sending it across the room in my surprise.

Maggie had tipped over her playpen and Delilah was nowhere in sight.

"Oh, hell! Delilah! Where are you?" Frantically, I scanned the room.

Maggie had managed to reach over the top just enough to get hold of the heavy wooden lamp pole next to her. Instead of sending the lamp to the ground, it was heavy enough that she'd used it to tip her playpen over on its side. She was walking better now, still wavering a bit, but she was on her way across the room toward Bruce and the babies. Bruce had jumped to his feet and was standing guard.

Delilah came running back in the room. She took in the situation with one glance and scooped Maggie up, righting the playpen with her other hand. She plopped our girl back inside, then dropped into the chair beside her.

"Damn, I just ran to the bathroom."

"She's strong." I let out a sigh of relief. Nobody was hurt, including Maggie, but we had to be more careful. "I think we should ask the guys to build a better pen, one that's taller and stronger. Maggie is big enough to want to go wandering around by herself, but she's still a toddler. And she will be for a long time. We need to protect her from her curiosity."

"She's over her growth spurt for now, at least." Delilah stroked Maggie's head and ears. "I was reading the other day in the *Care and Feeding of Woodland Gargoyles* that Maggie's about ready to go into a plateau phase for a while. Her next growth spurt will probably be in about five years. She'll learn new words, and slowly get a clearer sight of what's going on, but she won't grow much between now and then. And then, we better be prepared for the equivalent of a five-year-old who has very sharp claws and who will be a solid fifty to sixty pounds by the time her next growth spurt is done."

"Lovely. Well, we'll deal with that when it comes. Can someone sweep up the ornament I broke?" I went back to hanging balls.

At that point, Nerissa swept in, bags in hand. Iris set to breast-feeding the babies—all three of them. She was acting as Astrid's wet nurse since Sharah had had to go back to Otherworld. And damn, her breasts had grown huge. They'd always been nice but she could put me to shame easily now.

Fueled by more cookies and hot cocoa, and a plate of grilled cheese sandwiches and side dishes of olives and pickles, cherry tomatoes, and fruit salad, we worked on into the evening. By the time it was 11 P.M., the entire bottom floor was decorated and the men had hung lights and garland on all floors, including down in Menolly's lair.

We cleared up the boxes and then gathered in the living room, Bruce and Iris joining us. Menolly was sitting on the floor and Nerissa was sitting behind her on the sofa, her legs flanking Menolly. I curled up with Smoky on the other end of the sofa, with Morio sprawled on the floor beside me. Across the room, Shade and Delilah snuggled in the oversized chair and Bruce and Iris sat cross-legged on the floor next to their babies. Chase sat in the rocking chair, slowly rocking Astrid. Vanzir and Hanna joined us, comfortably sharing the loveseat.

By the soft glow of the lights, Menolly started to sing. I remembered the song from Otherworld, from when we lived in Y'Elestrial. Every winter, the city-state would hold an official Winter Solstice ritual. Every Yule we would all gather by the shores of Lake Y'Leveshan, where the priestesses from the Coterie of the Moon Mother—my grove—would lead the massive ritual. We would reenact the rise of the Oak King, and the fall of the Holly King, and there would be singing and dancing and feasting—the city provided a massive feast.

As Menolly sang, I softly joined in, along with Delilah. Menolly's voice was beautiful, but Delilah and I managed to keep on key, at least.

> *Do you feel the north wind blow,*
> *Does the chill run through your blood,*
> *Can you hear the Winter calling,*
> *Would you answer if you could,*
> *Does the ice groan as it shifts,*
> *Do the snow banks drift so high,*
> *The heart of Winter beckons,*
> *As the Solstice, it draws nigh.*
> *The Oak King rises softly,*
> *The Holly draws his sword,*
> *The brothers meet in battle,*
> *Twins set to spill their blood,*
> *For today the Holly falls,*
> *And the Oak will take the crown,*
> *Until the summer's zenith,*
> *When the Oak will tumble down.*

As our voices faded away, the flames crackled and popped from the fireplace, and once again, I realized that—even though our father and mother were dead—we were a family, we were strong together, and our lives and traditions would live on. Menolly started up singing again, and as we joined in, the evening faded into night, and we pushed aside our worries for a while as we sought a little respite from our duties and cares.

I managed to greet the crack of dawn thanks to Tanne. He texted me at five thirty, and for once, I didn't mind waking up to the *ding* of my phone. I kept it on the headboard shelf above me, because with Smoky on one side, and Morio on the other, it would have been too hard to crawl over either one in order to reach it. Blurry-eyed, I pulled it down and squinted, trying to read the text:

Found portal, I think. Check out the area behind the grove of trees in Yagur Park. But how did the pixies get downtown Seattle, if it's over on the Eastside? Something to think about.

Yagur Park? Tanne was right, that was across Lake Washington, over on the Eastside. But pixies could fly and travel in the blink of an eye. They must have found out about the commotion in Seattle and decided to check it out.

Yagur Park was a secluded park in Kirkland, leading into Woodinville. It was more rural, and definitely not on a main thoroughfare. The only reason I knew where it was, was because Trillian and I'd taken a tour of the wineries in the area during the summer. On the way home, we saw a turnoff for the park and drove in to explore. It was a tangled patch of woods and walking trails, with a spacious meadow for picnicking. A small pond served as a swimming hole.

I frowned, leaning back on the pillow. Neither Smoky nor Morio had woken up. We had to take care of this before I left this afternoon.

The smell of musky dragon and fox surrounded me like a snuggly blanket. Their smooth, taut, bodies were warm beneath the coverings. Usually Trillian slept in Morio's place, because Morio preferred sleeping in his fox form at the bottom of the bed. But with Trillian gone, it made me feel more secure to be flanked on both sides. The days of a luxurious king-size bed to myself were long gone, but when I thought about it, I didn't really miss them. I would never be domesticated, but I enjoyed knowing they were there for me and I was there for them.

Pushing back the instinct to go back to sleep, I forced myself to sit up, pulling the comforter up to cover my breasts. My hair tickled my back as I poked first Smoky, then Morio, in the side.

"Wake up, sleepyheads. We're needed." It took me three times, but I finally managed to rouse them. While I waited for them to blink their way to consciousness, I had a quick peek under the covers. Oh yes, they were aroused all right—both firm and hard in their morning salutes. Hit by a sudden fit of giggles, I considered taking a few licks, but then decided that I wouldn't start something I couldn't finish. And, like it or not, Tanne's text meant we needed to get out there and figure out what was going on.

A moment later, Morio dragged his ass to a sitting position, and Smoky followed suit. They were both cross-legged under the covers with me.

"Woman, why are you waking us up at this infernal hour?" Smoky was grumbly—he seldom got that way with me, but he liked his sleep.

"Because Tanne found the portal that Iris zapped out of the living room. Or at least, he thinks he did. And we'd better get over there and check it out. It's in Yagur Park—on the Eastside."

"Yeah, I guess we'd better." Morio yawned, his goatee twitching as he stretched. "Okay, out of bed."

I slipped out of bed and wandered over to the window. In the darkness of the winter morning, both Smoky and Morio cut fine figures, honed, chiseled muscles . . . and yet, they had their scars from battles past. They weren't perfect, which suited me fine. Perfection was an illusion—a myth.

"I think a shower is in order." Smoky pushed me toward the door. "Go. I'll take one downstairs. Morio, you share with Camille this morning. But no play. Camille is right, we don't have time. There are far deadlier foes in the Northlands than you can imagine—ones that make those we've already fought off look like playful kittens."

I shuddered. "I don't doubt it."

Smoky pressed his lips together for a moment, then, with a slow sigh, shrugged on a bathrobe. "Camille, be cautious. This wyrm . . . he is dangerous."

"I know."

Shaking his head, he caught me by the shoulders, a worried look in his eye. "No, you *don't* know. You don't realize just how dreadful these creatures are. The ancient wyrms are chaotic and rapacious. They will not be denied. They have no sense of right or wrong, they act solely on whim. They are far more grasping than Hyto was."

The seriousness of his tone nixed any good mood I had going for me. "I'll remember," I promised.

Hyto had left me scarred with nightmares, as well as a few physical marks that hadn't faded away. There were lashes on my back that would never vanish, but thankfully I didn't have to see them. If the wyrms were more dangerous than he was, we were in for one hell of a fight.

"Are they psycho like he was?"

Smoky shook his head. "Not in the way you think of it, but the ancient wyrms tend to be greedy beyond all human scope, and they have no consciences."

Morio headed toward the door. "So get a move on. Lather up and rinse off. I'll ask Hanna to wake Delilah when I go downstairs."

"Ask her to contact Iris, too. I think we should take her with us, if she's willing to go." Since Iris had been the one to move the portal in the first place, she might be able to pick up on anything we should know.

As Morio and I hit the shower, the hot water massaging my back, I tried not to think about what might have already come through the portal. The possibilities were not the stuff warm, fuzzy feelings were made from. As I rinsed off and gave Morio a light kiss, I could only hope that the portal had remained unused since the pixies bolted through. But somehow, in the pit of my stomach, I had the feeling that wasn't the case.

Chapter 8
⤜⟡⤛

We were out the door half an hour later, Delilah, Shade, and Iris with us. Nobody was in a good mood being up so early. Well, Iris was used to it, but that didn't mean she liked it any more than the rest of us. Hanna had quickly pulled together breakfast sandwiches for us to eat on the go—English muffins, sausage patties, and cheese. Along with peanut butter cookies, they were waiting for us when we trooped downstairs, dressed and ready to go.

"Thanks, Hanna. You're wonderful." I scooped up the brown paper bag full of food and we headed toward the door.

"Miss Menolly went to bed just a few minutes ago. Sunrise won't be for another hour but she wanted to spend some time with Miss Nerissa—her workday starts early." Hanna was already frying up bacon. A moment later, Chase appeared through the kitchen door. He and Nerissa had taken to carpooling into work together, except when one or the other had errands to do after work.

"I smell bacon," he said. "You guys want me to go with you? Iris told me what you found out."

"No, you go on to work with Nerissa. We'll take care of this and let you know what we find out." I walked over to Chase, placing my hand on his shoulder. "I have to leave before you get back. I'm taking Delilah and Morio with me. Help Smoky watch over all of them for us, would you?"

I had a feeling this journey was going to take me a long way into the mists, and even though I'd have my sister and Morio with me, a cloud had settled over my mood. The Merlin was unpredictable. Even when—*if*—we found him, there was no guarantee he'd agree to help us.

"I'll watch over them. Everything will be all right, Camille. Trillian will be fine, too." As if he were looking into my heart, rather than hearing my words, Chase pulled me close and gave me a hug. We'd started out at odds when we first met, but now we were good friends, and I was fond of the detective.

"Thanks, dude. Just take care of yourself and your daughter, too."

"I hate to break this up, but we better get our butts to Yagur Park and see what we can find out." Delilah leaned over my shoulder, grinning at Chase. "Have a good day, and tell Nerissa we said hi."

Chase winked at her. "Aye, aye, Pussycat." He and Delilah had been lovers for a while, but it hadn't worked out. Now, they were just good friends.

We took two cars—Delilah's Jeep and my Lexus. Smoky rode with Morio and me. Iris and Vanzir, who had opted to come instead of Shade, were with Delilah. Shade would stay with Hanna. Before we left, I texted Tanne to meet us at the park.

The morning commute was starting, but we were still early enough to miss the worst of it. Half an hour later and we'd be stuck in gridlock.

The Eastside—part of the Greater Seattle Metropolitan area—consisted of a number of cities ranging from thirty thousand to well over one hundred thousand people. All were on the east side of Lake Washington, and included Bellevue, Redmond, Kirkland, Issaquah, Mercer Island, Woodinville, and several other cities. Altogether, the GSMA—including Seattle—contained a population of over three and a half million people.

The land was rich and lush, thick with trees and moss and fern, with deep ravines leading into a tangle of detritus at their bottom. Streams, from full-blown whitewater rapids to trickling brooks ran through narrow channels everywhere. Seattle and its sister-cities were bordered to the east by the Cascade Mountain Range. High glacial peaks, the chain of mountains was still highly volcanic, and very much alive and awake. Old, deep magic inhabited the mountains, trickling down into the cities and infiltrating the woodlands and parks.

On the west, Seattle buttressed up against Puget Sound, a long, wide inlet of water coming in from the Pacific Ocean via the Strait of Juan de Fuca. A complex series of channels, the Sound was considered an estuary and had long ago been carved by the glaciers that covered the land. The same glaciers, during their retreat, had left large swaths of boulders in the mountains known as alluvial deposits. We'd encountered several in our adventures.

There were several ways to get over to Woodinville, and we opted to go around the northern tip of Lake Washington rather than drive all the way down to the 520 Floating Bridge. We eventually ended up on Woodinville Drive and then, on State Route 522, which took us right into Woodinville.

The town itself wasn't very big, and we navigated through the downtown area, then out into the suburbs, which were much more rural. With the GPS directing me, we wound our way through the trees and neighborhoods, which were now sparser and interspersed with patches of undeveloped land.

172nd turned into 165th and we continued along the two-lane road, past thick swatches of woodland and what now appeared to be farmhouses. To the right, power lines ran along the road, and very little shoulder meant that if we had to pull off, we'd have to find a driveway or turnoff.

We finally reached the intersection of 165th and Avondale Road NE. I idled at the red light, grimacing as the traffic on the opposite—going south—began to build up. Rush hour, definitely. Thank gods we were going against it. Turning onto

Avondale, we continued along, turning on several more streets, until we came to the sign for Yagur Park. We eased our way along the drive, which was hidden between large, sprawling homes that surrounded Cottage Lake. As we pulled into the parking lot, I noticed it was snowing lightly.

There were other parks around the lake, but this was the most secluded. Sixty-three acres in size, the lake was four miles east of Woodinville. Yagur Park was heavily wooded, with a play area for children, and a roped-off swimming site. As we stepped out of the car, I noticed another car nearby. It was a small Volkswagen. A moment later, Tanne opened the driver's door and stepped out.

He gave me a quick salute. "I think it's over there, beyond that stand of trees." I shaded my eyes against the powdery snow and squinted at the stand of cedar and fir that were lining the lake. In truth, the snow looked heavier over in that direction. Considering that the portal had caused a snowstorm in our living room, it made sense that it was lowering the temperature and turning the morning drizzle into snowflakes.

"Let's go." Smoky swung into the lead, and Morio and I followed behind him. Iris came next, and Delilah and Vanzir brought up the rear. As we crossed the picnic area, a sense of desolation fell over me. Yagur Park wasn't well known, and while it was maintained by the city, winter kept most parks in the Seattle area vacant and silent. Even when we didn't have snow, the rain drove people indoors. As we neared the stand of trees, the snow grew more intense and the temperature began to drop.

"This is magical cold." Smoky turned around. "I can feel the energy of the Northlands from here."

Iris concurred. "He's right. The portal must be through here. I'm just not sure what we're going to do once we find it. I can move it again but that isn't going to do us any good. However, maybe we'll be able to figure something out that we couldn't before. We were just in a hurry to get it out of the living room. Maybe we overlooked something."

"I wonder if the Triple Threat can help. Aeval used to be the Winter Queen before the Courts split away from Summer and Winter. I can always ask her before we leave tonight." I didn't want to think about the fact that she'd be bringing Bran and Morgaine with her, or that I'd be stuck with them on my journey. Which brought me to another point. "Delilah, are you sure you want to go with me? Morio's going, but there's nothing that says you have to come."

"Of course I am. I was there when Yannie Fin Diver attacked us. So, I'm sure as hell not about to let you traipse off with Morgaine and Bran without me along. I don't trust either one of them farther than I can throw them. Especially not around you. Morgaine is jealous of your connection with Aeval, and Bran . . . well, he's just a freak. And I don't care who knows that I think so." She shivered. "Geez, it feels like somebody turned down the heat."

She was right. The temperature had dropped at least thirty degrees in the past three minutes that we'd been approaching the portal. It felt as though we'd stepped into a refrigerator. As we rounded the nearest cedar, Smoky stopped short and held out his hand. I peeked around him, and sure enough, there was the portal, between two trees, spewing out snow and cold. I didn't see anything else in the general vicinity, but there was plenty of foliage behind which creatures could hide, so that didn't necessarily mean squat. There could be anything hiding out, waiting to pounce.

Iris stepped forward, eyeing the polar vortex. This close up, we were icy cold, and the temperature was rapidly dropping. Iris had thought ahead and brought her long coat. I wish I'd been that smart. My own coat was warm enough, but for typical Seattle weather, not the lower extremes.

We stood guard while she examined the edges. Now that we weren't frantic to get it out of the living room, we were able to take a closer look. After a moment she stood back. "I really wish we could figure out who created the scroll."

"That's it!" I swung around to face Vanzir. "Do you remember where the shop is?"

"Yeah, real hole in the wall." Vanzir blinked, then shook his head. "No . . . you aren't thinking seriously . . ."

"I *am* thinking seriously. But I doubt if the store is open yet. Iris, are you sure there's nothing you can do?"

Tanne stepped forward. "Let me have a look. I've dealt with a number of portals and vortexes before."

Iris stepped back as he moved in. Tanne was a spell singer. He was also from a long line of demon hunters—the Hunter's Glen Clan—and he had a number of odd powers that I wanted to know more about. He knew old spells, from far back in ES Fae history. Spells that were rooted in the world around us.

He knelt by the edge of the portal and placed his hand on the energy flowing between the brilliant blue gates. The portal looked like a rip in the air, the borders of which were crackling blue—thin bands of the energy radiating outward. The threads formed a braided ellipse that was at least eight feet high and four feet wide. The center was misted over—a swirl of cold air pouring out from the foggy center. Somehow the snowfall was related to the portal, but I wasn't sure how. If I were to pop my head through, I'd see another world. But I'd *been* in the Northlands and had no intention of peeking through there.

Tanne knelt down and put both his hands on the ground, directly in front of the portal. He began singing in a low voice, and I strained to catch the words, but it sounded like an ancient Germanic tongue. Energy built around him.

He inhaled slowly, exhaled even slower, keeping an even pace so the cadence of his song never changed. Mournful, it was, and haunting. I closed my eyes, trying to follow the thread of energy. It reminded me of a vine, tendrils creeping out from his voice. The words probed the energy of the portal, testing the edges, tapping them, looking for a place to burrow in.

I wanted to join Tanne, to lend my strength to his, and I could feel Morio itching to do the same. But our magic was different and we'd most likely be an interference rather than a help. So we stood vigil, watching the progression.

The tendrils of Tanne's spell worked in a widdershins fashion—counterclockwise—around the vortex's opening. Every few inches, the thread would stop, probe, then move on. I could see it clearly now. Anyone who worked magic couldn't possibly miss it as Tanne's focus strengthened.

And then, he found whatever it was he was looking for. The current of energy paused, tapping against one area of the portal's edge. Like a snake, it struck, burrowing into the neon blue, penetrating it with a forceful thrust. A moment later, the tendril swept into the swirling vortex and began infusing it with its own energy.

And then, the fun began.

There was a crackle as the two forces met. As Tanne's magic wove into the portal, a deep resonance echoed through the air, like thunder rumbling below the surface. Every hair left on my body stood to attention and I turned to run.

"Get out of the way, it's gonna blow!"

Morio scooped me up, racing away from the area. He'd shifted within the blink of an eye and an eight-foot youkai met very little resistance. Smoky snatched Iris up and he and Delilah were bounding away from the portal. Vanzir was hot on their heels. Tanne caught up with us, his eyes wide.

"I didn't expect this to happen so quickly," he said, just as an explosion rippled through the air. The force sent us sprawling to the snow-covered ground. Unfortunately, the snow wasn't deep enough to provide much of a cushion, so when I hit, I landed face-first in a low-growing fern. The fronds weren't sharp, but they were strong and tough enough to scratch me a good one. Luckily, my face didn't land center, but to the side, in the snow.

I lay there for a second, trying to ascertain if anything was hurt more than the usual bruises and scrapes. *Ankles? Check. Knees? Check. Arms? Check. No sensation of bleeding out anywhere.* Warily, I rolled into a sitting position. Everything seemed to be in one piece. Shaking my head to clear it from the shockwaves that were still reverberating through my body, I looked over at the portal. It was still there, but the opening had frozen over, and was a tangle of vines interlaced with the ice.

"Cripes. What the fuck happened?" Whatever Tanne had been attempting, I had the feeling it wasn't this.

Tanne shaded his hand against the still-blowing snow. "I'm not sure, to be honest. I was trying to unravel it with the

Song of Unraveling. Apparently, it didn't work quite like I'd planned."

"Maybe not, but that was pretty impressive." I frowned, noticing something. "At least it's getting warmer." That much was true. The wind was still blowing but the temperature felt like it was starting to rise. Without the Northlands polar air, maybe we'd be able to ease off on the snow shoveling. Sure enough, by the time we'd all picked ourselves up off the ground, the snow had turned to sleet. It would probably shift over to rain in a few minutes.

"Well, at least nothing can get through, right?" Delilah cautiously edged toward the portal, staring at it suspiciously.

"I don't think so." Tanne paused, then added, "The truth is, I have no idea. Something strong enough can probably break through. Unfortunately, to put it to a test, we'd have to find something big enough to crack the ice and that would undo what . . . whatever it is I did." He looked as confused as he sounded.

"Do you think the block will hold?" I joined Delilah, holding my hand up a few inches away from the frozen swirl covering the center of the portal. The energy still thrummed from within, but felt muffled, the way snow muffled sound.

Tanne shrugged. "I have no clue. As I said, I don't even know what I did. I was trying to unravel the spell that opened the portal but . . . instead, my magic seems to have infused itself with the magic inherent within the runes."

Iris pulled her coat tighter around her and joined me. "I think I know what might have happened. Or at least, I have a theory. I've seen spells backfire like this before. Only it's not so much of a backfire as a mismatch of energies. For example, Camille—you know how you don't dare touch a Corpse Talker?"

I nodded. If I were to touch one of the magical beings we used to talk to the dead, an implosion would happen. Our energies were so off-kilter that they wouldn't cancel each other out, but they'd conflict, a lot like an inadvertent magical battle.

"Right. You think that's what happened?"

"I think Tanne's energy conflicted with the energy of the

witch who created the scroll. The nature of their magic must be fundamentally different enough to cause a disruptive episode when they meet. When Tanne tried to unravel the spell, the energies grappled and, instead of burning each other out, they solidified." She reached up and—before we could stop her—ran her fingers over the surface.

"Iris! Don't do that." I grabbed her hand and pulled her away, but not before she could slam her palm against the ice. A moment later and another layer of water rippled across the surface of the block, freezing as it went.

"Don't interfere, girl. I was just strengthening the blockade. Why didn't I think of that? I could have frozen over the opening, albeit in a different way." She shook me off and returned to the portal. I let her go. I had an instinctive reaction to protect her, but babies or not, Iris could turn me inside out if she was mad enough.

She motioned to Tanne. "You are Black Forest Fae. I am Finnish. We aren't that far off in our roots, although my kind are crazier than most. But I am thinking, if we tried together, we might be able to shatter the portal now that it's frozen shut. I cannot perform your magic, but I can make ice shatter, and if you tried the spell of unraveling again, perhaps we could shake things up a bit."

At that, I took a step back and so did Delilah.

Smoky just frowned. "Are you sure? Experimentation doesn't always bode well. Not for our group."

"I'm not Camille," Iris said, winking at me.

I wasn't sure whether or not to be insulted, so I kept my mouth shut.

"But you're right," she continued. "We are experimenting. Until—and unless—you first find the witch who created the scroll, and second, make her remove the spell, then our doorway to the playground of the north is going to remain open. Because the block won't last. It's already weakening. The ice won't hold for long."

Tanne took his place beside her. "The Lady Iris is right. We need to close it down. Together, we might be able to do so."

I glanced at Smoky and he nodded. Turning back to the

house sprite, I motioned to the portal. "Have at it, you two. Just be careful, all right?"

The rest of us stepped back—lesson learned from take one of *Let's Destroy This Portal*. Tanne and Iris consulted. After a moment, he pressed his hands against the left side of the vortex, right on the frozen rings of energy. Iris stepped back about five feet and pointed her palms toward the center of the portal. Tanne began to sing again.

Iris also took up a tune, her voice countering his dusky tone.

I blinked. I'd heard her sing before—we all had—but for some reason, I'd never paid that much attention. She'd sang lullabies to Maggie and had joined in our songs during ritual, but now, her voice rang out rich and throaty and sultry. She could be a siren with that voice.

Another moment, and their voices blended together, weaving around each other like a braided rope, and the portal began to vibrate. I watched, fascinated, as the ice began to fracture. Spiderweb cracks raced through the block, then along the outer rim of the vortex, their rift a deep blue as they rippled in waves.

Tanne kept his hands on the portal, even as the ground began to shake. I grabbed hold of Morio's arm for stability. But neither Iris nor Tanne moved.

A high-pitched hum filled the area as the cracks grew more pronounced. Iris suddenly stopped, her voice hovering over a single note. Tanne did the same, his voice a good octave lower, underpinning the magic they wove.

The vibrations of their voices thrust into the cracks, racing along the channels. As they infused the grooves with energy, the portal began to phase in and out. I could barely stand the cacophony—between their voices and the humming and the groaning of the portal, the noise was rapidly rising to an unbearable level.

Then, in a fraction of a second, Iris and Tanne fell silent.

The last rush of energy poured into the fractures lining the vortex, and it broke into a thousand pieces, flying every which way. With one last shriek, the portal shattered, and it vanished in a swirl of light. The area was clear. The portal was gone.

Iris dropped to her knees, as did Tanne. She held up her hand when we started to rush forward, and we were smart enough to hang back. Sometimes, residue energy could produce a nasty jolt when you touched someone who had just been working magic. We waited as it dissipated, and only when Iris motioned to us, did we approach her side.

"I can't believe it. We did it." She was smiling, although she looked worn out.

Tanne burst out with a goofy grin that softened the stoic look I was used to seeing. "We did at that, my lady. We did at that."

Smoky swept Iris up in his arms. "I will carry you back to the car. No protests. You worked harder than you should have to, little mother."

Iris shook her head. "Times being what they are, we all have to work harder than we should. You'll hear no complaints from me.

I sighed. "You know, as much as I don't want to, I think we'd better go check out that store. And if she's there, the witch who supposedly knows me."

Iris nodded. "Please take Morio and Vanzir with you. I'll go home with Delilah and Smoky. Tanne, will you tag along with Camille?"

Tanne nodded. "Of course."

I didn't want to go. I didn't want to deal with it, but Iris was right. Better to take care of matters now and know the truth of what was going on. And Morio was a better choice for the job because, in a magical situation, he and I could work it a lot harder.

"Okay then. Looks like we're going for a ride." I glanced at the others. "The rest of you, go home. We'll see you in a while." I shoved Vanzir in front of me and he grumbled, but with one look at Morio, he quieted down and led the way.

We were on our way within less than five minutes. Tanne sat in the back with Vanzir. Morio punched the street address that Vanzir gave him into the GPS and I was surprised to find out that we didn't have all that far to go. The shop wasn't in Seattle proper, but up in the Lake Forest Park area.

We ended up in a deserted neighborhood of hole-in-the-wall shops, most looking either empty or like they were waiting for the after-eleven crowd. That is, the after 11 P.M. *waiting for the hookers and pushers to come out* crowd. Vanzir pointed to a little shop up ahead that was called Broom Stix.

I groaned. Cutesy names were not my thing, and I had the feeling the shop made its money on the wishes of poor people—you know, the "win the lottery if you buy this spell" or "we'll get your husband back for you if you pay us enough" types. Witches who owned shops like this were usually FBH scam artists, but now and then, one of the Fae set up shops such as this one, and they were trouble, too. They preyed on people's insecurities and their desperation.

As I parked in front of the shop, I mentally steeled myself for a confrontation with the owner. I wasn't looking forward to getting into it, but I would if I had to. While I was a live-and-let-live type of woman, scammers and moochers drove me up the wall, and I detested those who took advantage of other peoples' pain and fears.

I nodded for Morio, Tanne, and Vanzir to follow me in. I wasn't in the mood for subtle, and we needed as much information as we could get, as fast as we could get it.

The shop was dark, decked out in postmodern goth, with fake ravens perched on the tops of the shelves, dripping cobwebs—all black and sparkly—hanging from the ceiling, and the requisite resin skull candleholder sitting on the counter. Jars of herbs lined one wall and candles in all colors, another. At least they had something useful in stock. But dozens of what looked like homemade spell kits stocked one set of shelves, and some of their names made me cringe. HOO-DOO JUSTICE CROSS, LOVE-SLAVE, and GIVE ME YOUR MONEY were three examples of why I had a sudden urge to shut the place down. Then I saw the piles for the holidays—and it was clear to see how some of the scrolls could easily have rolled into the wrong section. They were separated by about an inch of space with little in the way of dividers. *Or it could have been deliberate.* The thought just wouldn't leave, but niggled in the back of my mind.

The woman behind the counter looked all of seventeen and she was FBH. I was surprised to see she wasn't decked out like Elvira, but instead, she was wearing what looked like an anime schoolgirl's outfit, and her hair was tied high in two ponytails. She took one look at us and her smile turned to fear.

"How . . . what can I help you with?"

I rested my hands on the counter and leaned toward her, giving her a big smile. She was wearing a nametag that read JENNY. "Well, Jenny, here's what you can do for us. First—you can make certain those stacks of scrolls over there are in the correct pile. Somebody caused us one hell of a mess and cost us quite a bit of money. Second, I hear there's a card reader here? A Svartan from Otherworld? I'd like to talk to her."

"She'll be in soon. And . . . I'm sure that whoever bought the scroll just picked up one from the wrong pile. We never . . . they never . . . We don't let them get mixed up." Jenny stumbled over her words and I could tell she was lying.

"Don't fib and you won't get in trouble. Trust me, we have no beef with you, but I suggest finding a better-quality shop to work in. And if you have any leanings toward magic or witchcraft, steer clear of whoever threw this shop together. This is a dive, and reputation is everything." I wasn't in any mood to dick around. "Now tell me about the woman, and don't lie."

Her eyes grew even wider and I swear, if she was animated, she could have stepped right out of a show like *Full Metal Alchemist* or *InuYasha.* A moment later, she cleared her throat. "My stepmom owns this shop. I only work here for extra money. I'd rather work at the mall."

Now we were getting somewhere. I detected a note of dislike in her voice. "That's rough. Maybe you should look into changing jobs. How old are you?"

"Seventeen. But the minute I hit eighteen, I'm out of here. Anyway, yah, there is a card reader that comes here. She's from Otherworld. I don't know what a Svartan is, though."

"Does she have jet black skin, silvery hair?"

Jenny nodded. "Yah. She scares me. I don't know where she lives, but she's been around for a while. She doesn't like anybody, but Maddy—my stepmom—makes good money off the percentage the woman pays her."

"What does she do besides read the cards? What's her name?"

Frowning, the girl shook her head. "I don't know. Her name is Iyonah. I don't know if that's her real name or not."

It was my turn to frown. The name rang no alarms. I had no clue. I had met few Svartan women and I was sure that I hadn't met any over Earthside—not that I remembered talking to for any significant time. But, if she was targeting us, would she have openly asked about me? Then again, what better way to get to know someone than ingratiate yourself with their friends?

"You said she's due in soon?"

"Yeah." Jenny glanced at the clock. "Any minute now."

At that moment, the door opened and my Spidey-Sense tingled. Without even looking around, I knew that Iyonah had entered the room. And I knew that she was trouble, without even saying hello.

Chapter 9

༄ སྲིན ༄

Iyonah was Svartan, all right. She glanced at Vanzir and her eyes widened. Well, she recognized him, all right. She slowly set down her bag—a black leather affair that looked more expensive than one of my corsets—and crossed her arms, a coy smile on her face.

"Hello. Vanzir said we'd met, but I didn't remember you so thought I'd stop in and say hello to refresh my memory."

She cocked her head. "I must have been mistaken. My pardon." She was lying through her teeth. "But now that you're here, won't you have a seat?"

Curious, and suspicious, I sat opposite her. She was eying me up and down as if she were searching for something, and a puzzled look flashed through her eyes. "Would you like your cards read?" She handed the deck to me and I stared at it. Then, it hit me. She wanted me to touch it. For some reason, she wanted my energy signature on it.

"Thanks, I'll pass." I couldn't pin down what the hell she was up to, but I didn't like this cat and mouse game. "I read my own cards."

I stood and nodded to the guys. "We should get moving."

Turning back to Iyonah, I cocked my head. "You know, Earth-side can be a dangerous place. You might want to keep an eye on your back while you're here. Just a little friendly advice."

She glared at me, but set the cards back down in front of her. Turning on my heels, I headed back over to Jenny.

Lowering my voice, I asked, "Is your stepmother around today? I'd like to know why she hired her."

"I know why—and my stepmom won't be in till late this afternoon. We needed someone to bring in new customers. Iyonah promised our sales would go up if we let her set up shop in the corner. And they did—the past two weeks have been fantastic for business." Jenny bit her lip.

"Do me a favor. Don't say anything about me being here? Please? And have as little to do with that woman as possible. She's trouble." I glanced over at the spell kits. "By any chance, did Iyonah make those?"

Jenny nodded.

"Destroy them. They'll only bring angry customers in. Trust me on this one. You sell many of those and your shop will be ruined for good. Think of some excuse. Here, I'll give you some money and you tell your stepmother you sold them. Don't let Iyonah see you get rid of them, though." I tucked a couple hundred dollars in Jenny's hand and she nodded, looking nervous but willing.

I turned back to Iyonah. I'd have a talk with Aeval, have her look into things. She might be able to ensure that Iyonah didn't cause any more trouble than she already had.

With Vanzir on one side, Tanne the other, and Morio behind me, we headed out to the car. Shoppers on the street stared at us, but at my GTF out of the way look, they gave us a wide berth. That was just fine with me. Better to intimidate than get picked on. And right now, I was irritated. Something with Iyonah sat wrong—just really wrong. And I didn't have time to look into it.

I glanced at the guys. "We only have a couple hours till Aeval comes out to the house. Let's go home."

Vanzir cleared his throat. "Do we get a pardon for the chaos we caused?"

I grumbled but then flashed him a smile through the

rearview mirror. "Oh why the fuck not? It's not like you set out to raise havoc, and the fact is that a spell was involved and you guys aren't stupid. Let's call it good and let it go at that."

As we trundled into the kitchen, Delilah came bouncing into the room. "Trenyth is on the Whispering Mirror. He was just asking if you were around."

I hurried into the living room, remembering my promise to Chase. Trenyth—the elf who had been Queen Asteria's advisor from the time she first took the throne until the day she died—was there, waiting patiently. He looked tired, but then again, war made everybody tired.

"Hey, how goes it?" I slid onto the bench in front of the mirror. We used to keep it in my study until war broke out in Otherworld. Now it was easier to keep it down in the living room, where we could easily hear it.

He actually smiled. "It goes . . . as it goes, Camille. I have a few updates for you. First, Trillian and Rozurial are in Otherworld, the grapevine tells me?"

I blinked. They'd gone through to Y'Elestrial. The fact that Trenyth, in war-stricken Elqaneve, knew they were there, well . . . that meant that anybody might know. We had enemies far and wide, and I could only hope that they were harder to track than the information that they'd arrived there.

"Yes, they are. They're going in search of Darynal. And before you say a word—they know how dangerous the mission is. Darynal is Trillian's blood-oath brother, his *lavoyda*. I couldn't deny him the chance." Darynal had gotten lost while on a mission for the elves. With their resources stretched so far beyond their limits, none of us expected the elves to send out a search party when the scouts had disappeared.

"I see." Trenyth pressed his lips together, then gazed at me with eyes that had seen the eons come and go. "I wish them safety, Camille. I wish we could help." He was a handsome man, regardless of his age, but stern and regal. And he had been in love with the queen for many years. That kind of unrequited love would never die, especially now that she was gone and he'd never had a chance to tell her how he felt.

"What did you want to tell us? And then, before I forget, I have a question for you."

Trenyth sighed. "I know Menolly can't be there, but is Delilah? Gather as many of your company as possible."

I whistled, loud enough to make him grimace. "Yo, Trenyth wants to talk to us. Get your butts in here pronto."

"I swear, Camille, if we ever need someone to lead a war cry, I'm calling on you." The elf smiled and I let out a little laugh. He regarded me for a moment before asking, "How are you doing, girl? I know your father's death was a blow for all of you."

"That it was, but we move on. What else can we do? We have his ashes in an urn. We'll return it to Otherworld as soon as we know that our house is safe. Have you heard from Aunt Rythwar lately? Is she all right? Is Y'Elestrial under siege?" Our aunt had returned to Y'Elestrial to look after our home when our father was killed.

He shook his head. "She is doing well and so is your father's house—your house now. Y'Elestrial fights off goblin hordes, but they are still strong enough to withstand the siege. As far as the storm, the Goldunsan took heavy damage from it. Their city was not spared. Then it began to move southeast toward Y'Elestrial, but before it could reach there, the seers of Aladril came to the rescue. They sent several of their powerful mages, who were able to disrupt it before it ever reached your city-state. Aladril is officially on our side. As is Ceredream, but they've been overrun with the grunts of the enemy and are not faring well."

By that time, everyone had gathered around. I counted heads. Delilah, Morio, Smoky, Vanzir, Shade, Nerissa, Chase, and even Iris was here. Hanna held Maggie, standing in the back.

I turned back to the mirror. "We're all here, Trenyth, except Menolly, who is still asleep."

Trenyth shuffled several papers on his desk. "All right. Here's the latest news. As I told Camille, Aladril has joined the fight—the seers disrupted the sentient storm and kept it from reaching Y'Elestrial. Ceredream has joined our side but they are under siege. The enemy's hordes are thick, and numerous. They're attacking Y'Elestrial, but your city-state is holding them off. They're also attacking Ceredream. Alas, the

City of the East is not faring well. There are a number of bands roving around Kelvashan but there's not much left to fight over here. We took the brunt of the damage because it was so unexpected."

Smoky stepped forward. "Have you ascertained your full damages, Lord Trenyth?" He always accorded the advisor his full title, even though my sisters and I had fallen into a more intimate nature of addressing him. It would feel odd for me to call him "Lord" now, though it was his proper title.

Trenyth leaned back in his chair, his expression pained. "We'll never know the full extent of what was destroyed. We do know that we have over fifteen thousand dead accounted for. There are six thousand missing, at least that have been reported. Three villages escaped destruction, the rest of our infrastructure has been all but obliterated. The food stores are gone. We're relying on outside help for just about everything at this point."

The numbers were staggering. Even Earthside, where cities numbered in the millions, that kind of destruction would have been horrific. Over in Otherworld, where the cities were smaller and the population lighter? It was unthinkable.

Chase cleared his throat and moved forward, standing behind me. "Lord Trenyth, do you have any news about Sharah?" His voice quivered and I could tell he was scared.

But Trenyth gave him a wide, if tired, smile. "Hello, Chase. Your love is healthy, and safe. She's doing well. She misses you and Astrid. While it would be too dangerous for you to come here, and we cannot allow her to leave at this time, we can let you talk to her through the Whispering Mirror for a couple of hours. We can do that tonight, if you like."

Chase brightened. "Really? I miss her so much." He faltered, and for a moment looked like he was going to cry, but then he steeled his back, and I was proud of him. He already knew how to conduct himself as an officer, now he was learning what it meant to be a soldier.

"Yes, really. We will set it to eight P.M. your time? Sharah has been run ragged, though she's holding up well. The demands on her have been great, but I think it would do both of you a world of good to talk. Until then." And with that, Trenyth signed off.

Chase turned to me, beaming. "I'll bring Astrid here, so Sharah can see her and talk to her."

I rested one hand on his arm. "I'm so glad, Chase. I wish things were different for the two of you. Sharah never expected to end up on the throne. That much we all know. If the storm hadn't hit exactly when it did, she would still be here. Things don't always work out the way we want them to, though."

He wrapped his arm around my shoulders. "Yeah, I know. Thanks, Camille. You've been great during this. *All* of you have. I never expected to fall in love with Sharah. When we first went out, I was interested but wary. But . . . I guess when it's right, you just figure it out."

Delilah was listening in and she grinned at him. "True, that, dude. I'm glad you guys got together. I'm lucky I found Shade. I just hope that we can get out of this war and settle down and all be one big, happy family."

"Amen to that." Chase glanced at his watch. "Okay, I promised Iris I'd watch the babies while she and Bruce go out for the afternoon. The Duchess is off shopping. She's headed home after the holidays, and while I know Iris will be happy, she's going to be working her fingers to the bone with Astrid and her own two."

I glanced over at Delilah. "We should hire someone to help her. Or at least, tell Bruce to get on it. He's smart and funny, but he's not always that observant. Typical absent-minded professor."

"I'll make a note of it." Delilah waved at Chase as he left the living room.

"You'll have to set him up at the Whispering Mirror tonight. I'm not going to be here." I frowned, then told her about Iyonah. "I don't know what her game is, but she's trouble."

"You should have just conked her over the head and brought her back here so we could interrogate her." She blinked, her eyes wide and all too happy with her suggestion.

I snorted. "Kitten, how the fuck could I justify that? She hasn't actively done anything to us."

"Maybe not but . . . well, it was just an idea. We wouldn't have any place to keep her, anyway. I wish the Wayfarer was fully rebuilt. We have the safe room there. No magic will work in it." Delilah snapped her fingers.

"What now?" I was almost afraid to ask.

"I have a brilliant thought. We should build a safe room *here*, just like at the bar. That way, we could cage anybody we needed to. Catch a demon on the property? Cage him until we figure out what to do. A crazy witch? Same thing."

As she spoke, I stared at her. Delilah really was gorgeous, and her short spiky golden hair only set off the color of her eyes, their brilliant green the color of leaves in the forest. She was also a loon at times, but now? What she said made sense. It had been a safe room back in Otherworld that had kept Menolly from killing me when she was turned.

"Good thinking. Let's get Smoky and Shade on that before we leave. Meanwhile . . ." I paused.

"What? I know that look, it means you've thought of an idea that's probably going to be more trouble than it's worth." She wrinkled her nose and I resisted the impulse to ruffle her hair. She hated it when I did that. Even though Kitten had matured a lot over the past couple of years, she had the ability to Bambi us into submission, with her wide, curious eyes and impish smile.

The thought had first come to me out in the park, and while I still wasn't sure, it was worth running past Delilah.

"I want to take Tanne with us, if he'll go. We can't leave home short-handed and, even though Aeval has stationed guards aplenty here, I don't trust them as much as I trust leaving ready hands here. Vanzir can't come, she summoned him out to Talamh Lonrach Oll tonight so she doesn't intend for him to go along with me. We need Menolly, Smoky, and Shade here. Trillian and Roz are traipsing off in Otherworld. I don't like the odds of just me, Morio, and you against Morgaine, Mordred, Arturo, and Bran, because honestly? I don't trust any of them. And Derisa told me I could bring three others with me. That leaves one opening."

Delilah made a face and motioned for me to follow her into the parlor where we could talk privately. She closed the door, as I took my seat on the sofa and pulled a throw over my lap. The parlor was always chilly compared to the rest of the house. Actually, the old Victorian was pretty drafty as a whole.

"First, what the hell does Aeval want with Vanzir?" She sat down next to me, crossing her right leg over her left knee. Her boots were new, and as I stared at the tread that looked like it could surface a tire, I thought once again that Delilah had become a formidable foe. She could kick the crap out of just about anybody.

"I don't know what's going on. But . . . here's something I never told you or Menolly. While I can't tell you much, because I'm sworn to oath, the night that Aeval initiated me into the Priesthood? Vanzir was there, Kitten. I saw him on the shore. And . . . well, as I said, I can't reveal the rest, but he was part of my initiation, though I never could figure out just why Aeval had called him in. He played a small, but significant part in it." Even saying that much felt almost like a betrayal, but I wasn't breaking oath, so much as skirting the borders of doing so.

Delilah's expression was priceless. After a moment, she shook her head, as if trying to ascertain whether she'd heard me correctly. "Say what? You're kidding. He was part of your initiation? After what happened?"

I nodded. "I think perhaps because of what happened with him and me. Somehow, during that encounter, when we were trying to get away from the ghosts, we formed an odd bond—don't even go there. I don't mean sexually, even though we ended up fucking. It was when he was in my head."

"Not like Menolly and Morio were bound when she gave him her blood to heal?" Now, my sister did look freaked. "Smoky really *will* kill Vanzir if that's true."

"No, no. Not like that. Vanzir's been . . . well, as much of a gentleman as Vanzir can be, since then. But some sort of connection formed."

I tried not to dwell on that night. It had been horrible, with Morio wounded so bad he almost died, and the ghosts attacking us from every direction. What had happened between Vanzir and me had set off numerous repercussions, but there was no changing the past and I didn't regret what I did.

A dream-chaser demon feeds on life-energy, and can burrow inside of thoughts. Vanzir had been unable to help himself. Having him in my head had been far worse than offering myself to him to distract him. The sex had been my choice. And, though it had brought Smoky close to killing him and sent me unwittingly into Hyto's clutches, I still didn't regret my decision. And I didn't blame Vanzir. That night had been desperate and terrifying and so hyped with energy we'd all been teetering on the edge.

"So you have no idea what the Triple Threat wants from him?"

I grinned. The Triple Threat was my nickname for the three Earthside Fae Queens. They knew what I called them, and so far there hadn't been any fallout from it except for a disgruntled look here and there.

Shrugging, I held up my hands. "I don't know, but I suspect that Aeval is behind him getting his powers back, along with the new abilities. He's changing, and she's at the end of his path. I just feel it, in my gut. Instinct, I guess."

Slowly nodding, Delilah leaned forward and rested her elbows on her knees. "Well, your instinct is usually right, so let's trust it for now. As to taking Tanne with us, if he's willing to go, I'm for it. I like him."

"He is rather fun to pal around with, isn't he? And I'm fascinated by his magic." I grinned at her. "I wish I could do some of the things he does."

"Just don't get *too* fascinated. But back to our traveling ensemble, I trust Morgaine even less than you do. And I've seen the way Bran looks at you. Like a raven eying a shiny object, but I don't think . . . I don't know. He's dangerous, Camille. And for some reason he's fascinated by you, in a not-so-good way. I don't think it's just because you killed his father. After all, the Black Unicorn wanted you to sacrifice him. It wasn't like an assassination."

I nodded. I'd felt the same thing myself. "Raven Mother has always been jealous of the Moon Mother, and I don't know why, but I trust her more than her son. Several times she's approached me about joining her in Darkynwyrd. I know she approached several other members of the Coterie, too. It's almost like she wants to *be* the Moon Mother."

"How very *Single White Female* of her." Delilah laughed, but then her smile fell away again. "Seriously, there's no way you can get out of taking them along with you?"

"No, Derisa was very specific. And you know that where Morgaine goes, she's going to drag that obnoxious nephew of hers. Mordred gives me the creeps. And of course, her silent helper Arturo will tag along, too. I don't consider him much of a threat, except that he does exactly what Morgaine tells him to."

"Who is he?"

I frowned. I'd thought over that question many times before. When we first met Morgaine, and found out that she was an ancestor of ours—essentially a cousin so many times removed we couldn't even begin to sort it out—she had introduced Mordred as her nephew.

And then, there was Arturo. I *thought* they were lovers but that had never been confirmed. Arturo was taciturn, quiet and soft-spoken, but she never seemed terribly solicitous of him. He was obviously devoted to her, and did whatever she said, but he always stayed in the background.

"You know, to be honest, he reminds me of Tom Lane—Tam Lin." Tam Lin, and yes—the Tam Lin of legend—had been Titania's lover when we first met. The Queen of Light and Morning had been in a pretty sad state then, but now she was restored to her former power, if not more so. She had fed her mortal lover the Nectar of Life so many times that he had begun to fade in and out, losing himself in other personalities as the eons rolled by. Tom Lane was the name we met him by, a confused, odd man.

"You're right. I wonder if Arturo is human? Morgaine has never really told us."

As the rain began to pour so hard outside we could hear it clatter against the windowpanes, I thought about Delilah's question. The truth was, I'd given little consideration to Arturo and Mordred, other than the fact that the latter was a pain in the ass, while the former seemed to fade into the woodwork. But now, I wondered. I'd always assumed Arturo was human. But was he truly? Mordred, on the other hand, was part Fae—no doubt about that. Like his aunt, he had delusions of grandeur and a thirst for power that led to unsavory behavior. He'd wound up with a permanent place on my shit list, that was for sure.

"We're stuck with them. And if Mordred and Bran band together . . ."

"There's bound to be trouble." Delilah stood up, then reached out a hand to pull me to my feet. "Ask Tanne. I think he'd be handy to have on our side. Because you know this is going to devolve into an 'us' and 'them' situation. And frankly, I don't want to see what would happen if 'they' end up on top. Not a good thing."

"Tanne, it is, then. I don't know if he'll want to come, but you know what? Can't hurt to ask." And so, pulling out my cell phone, I scrolled through my contacts till I found his name, and put in a call to him.

Tanne jumped at the chance to go along with us, and I had the feeling he was getting bored. His clan still hadn't set up complete operations here, and he seemed like a man used to action. He said he'd be right over as soon as he threw together his stuff. The man wasn't scared of a risk, that much was certain.

While we were waiting on him, and on Aeval and our dubious companions, Delilah, Morio, and I packed. Smoky sat beside me on the bed. I stared at the small backpack. We couldn't take much, and we didn't know how long this trip would take. What did one carry into the realm of the Elder Fae? Besides weaponry, that is.

I dressed in my spidersilk skirt and a leather bustier—it would be tougher armor than a shirt. I slipped a shirt, a second skirt, and spare panties and socks into the pack. I didn't want to take the unicorn cloak because the Elder Fae would be able to smell it a mile away and they'd be drawn to it. But the horn? The horn I would take. The power locked within just might save our lives. I zipped it inside my pocket, safe in its cushioned carrying case.

I also added toothpaste and a toothbrush, a compact pack of tissue, a roll of toilet paper, and facial wipes. Reluctantly, I left my makeup at home. Somehow, as much as I'd miss it, I didn't think I'd have much time to sit there putting on my face. The rest of the space would go to food and a blanket, in case we were caught in cooler climes. We might be facing snow or ice, or humid heat, for all I knew.

Morio was carrying a bigger pack than mine, and he would carry more food for the two of us. He made sure he had his skull in his bag—the youkai-kitsune had to carry a skull with them in order to change back into human form from both their demon and fox forms. They didn't have to touch it, but the skull must be within a certain radius. As he was pulling together his pack, I lifted the skull and looked at it. It was small and light, but so hard that it would take a tremendous force to crack it.

"When did you get this? Is this the only skull you've had?" I traced my fingers over the smooth bone of the very top. The rest of the skull was etched with runes—intricate, painstaking work. The magic resonated through my fingertips.

Morio glanced at it. "I was bonded to it when I was young. All my people are given skulls when we reach a certain age. The youkai have a high mortality rate. The skulls come from the children who die before they reach puberty."

That was a new one. Morio had never talked much about his kind. I knew bits and pieces of his childhood, and of his days before he met me, but he'd been reticent to discuss the subject and I'd left it alone, respecting his privacy. But since he was opening up . . .

"Do parents object to the use of their children's bodies?"

He shook his head. "No. It's part of our tradition. The children who die before puberty never achieve their demonic form. The first changing comes when the hormones hit, and you're then considered an adult, though still in need of supervision and training."

With a long look at me, he pushed aside his pack and

sat down beside me. "I have been very silent on my past, haven't I?"

I held the skull, wondering to whom it had belonged. What child had died and left this part of themselves behind?

"I know some of the story—about your father and what happened—but I don't know how much to ask without bringing up bad memories."

"We are a solitary people. Like the fox, we camouflage well and it's our nature to remain in the shadows. What do you want to know?"

"Do your parents know about us?"

"Of course they do. I've told them, and they want to meet you. They weren't happy, at first, that I married outside my people. But it has nothing to do with the fact that you are Fae, or half-human. It was solely that you weren't a youkai-kitsune. However, they've come to accept our marriage. One day, you'll meet them. I promise."

I wasn't sure how keen I was on that idea. Not with knowing that they'd been unhappy about his choice. But then again, Trillian's family was still upset over him marrying me. At least Vishana—Smoky's mother—graciously accepted me.

I glanced at the clock. While I wanted to ask more while the window was open, we needed to eat before we left. I slipped Morio's skull inside his bag.

"Should we take Rodney?" I hated the thought, but then again, the living nightmare had his uses.

Morio snorted. "You really want a twelve-inch bone golem mouthing off to an Elder Fae? You know it would happen."

Grimacing, I shook my head. "Forget it. Leave him here. That kind of trouble, we don't need." The doorbell rang as we gathered our bags and headed for the stairs.

Chapter 10

Tanne was at the door, backpack in hand. He'd been so quick on the uptake that I had the feeling he'd anticipated my call. While we waited for him and for Aeval and her crew, I slipped outside, down to the studio where Rozurial and Vanzir stayed. I knew where Roz kept his stash of weapons, and it occurred to me that it might not be a bad idea to raid his arsenal. Since he had gone off with Trillian, I figured what he didn't know about, he wouldn't miss. At least not till they returned home. And by then I'd either thank him for saving our asses, or I would have tucked the items back in the cabinet and nobody would be the wiser.

I slipped into his room and opened the armoire where I knew he kept his weaponry. Just as I'd hoped—a nice stash of the little red and white bombs that produced magical fire, and magical ice. I plundered five of each and tucked them in my pack. Buckling my pack shut, I returned to the house.

As I entered the kitchen, Hanna was finishing up a bag of sandwiches for us to take with us, along with fried chicken and yet more muffins and cookies. It all looked delicious, but my stomach was a tangle of knots.

The Elder Fae scared the fuck out of me, which was a good thing, because they were batshit crazy. They didn't play by *anybody's* rules. We had as little to do with them as possible. Ivana Krask—the Maiden of Karask—cozied up to us more than we were comfortable with, but there wasn't much we could do about it since she'd decided we were worth talking to. Having an Elder Fae angry at us? Far too dangerous. We'd already ticked off several of them. The scary thing was, Ivana was probably the least worrisome one we'd met so far, but I sure as hell wouldn't want to be alone in a locked room with her.

Ivana had a taste for "bright flesh." Meaning: babies. Plump, tender, succulent babies. We'd bargained with her several times and managed to push her into accepting prime beef and pork instead, but her routine was no act. If we ever raided an orphanage, she'd be quite happy with kinder-burgers. *And now,* a little voice inside whispered, *we're going to walk right into a realm full of the freakshows, all within the hour.*

"I guess it's about time." I glanced over at Vanzir. "You and Smoky and Shade keep an eye on things, okay?"

He cleared his throat, his kaleidoscopic eyes staring at me. "No worries there, chick. But you . . . don't forget us, okay? We need you here." And that was as close as he could come to saying he was worried about us.

I forced a smile to my lips. "Yeah, you'd never know what to do without Delilah and me bugging you." And then, because I was nervous and fretting, I slid my arms around his waist and gave him a quick hug. "Behave while we're gone," I whispered. "And watch out for everybody."

He didn't seem to know what to do at first, but then, he returned the hug and, with a glance to make sure Smoky wasn't around, planted a quick kiss on the top of my head before breaking away. "You'll be back, Camille. Don't ever think you won't."

As if on cue, Smoky peeked into the kitchen. "Camille?" He motioned to me to follow him. I gave Vanzir a little wave and followed Smoky through the living room, into the parlor, where he closed the door behind us and turned, taking my hands in his.

"My wife, listen to me. Don't forget our Soul Symbiont Ritual. If you or the fox get into trouble, both of you do your best to seek me through the connection and I will come. I hate letting you traipse off like this. Morio is strong, but even he cannot stand up against some enemies."

He wrapped his arms around me then, and I leaned into his embrace with a soft sigh. He smelled so good, musky and dark and strong.

"I wish we had more time. I wish we had some alone time for just us, like I had with Trillian. I love you, you know?" Pressing my hand against his chest, I looked up into those glacial eyes of his. He'd scared me so much when we first met, but now he was part of my world and I couldn't imagine not having him by my side.

"Oh, love." Smoky swept me up so I was facing him at eye level, holding me tight. I wrapped my arms around his neck and kissed him, his lips soft against mine. I wanted to hang on and not let go.

We'd been through so much loss lately, so much stress, and now Trillian was off into danger, too. And then, it hit me full force. While Otherworld was my home, it would never be the same. Even should we win this war, so many people had died already, including our father and friends, that returning would forever be bittersweet. The knowledge slammed into me that my sisters and I were effectively orphans. I shuddered, tears forming at the corners of my eyes, and buried my head against Smoky's neck.

"Don't ever leave me. Don't ever let go. I couldn't bear to lose someone else I love. I'm going to be worrying about Trillian until the day he sets foot back through the front door." I sniffled as he stroked my back, while tendrils of his hair rose to help brace me against him.

"Camille, my love. You are one of the bravest women I know. You daily face danger with steel nerves. I cannot begin to tell you how proud I am of you, and how much I admire you." He pushed me back a step, his voice dropping to a soft whisper. "You realize that I fell in love with a woman devoted to carrying out her duty? You *know* we'll weather this. We'll manage to walk through all of this. Trillian will return safe, and the four of us will live a long and happy life." He lifted my chin with another tendril of hair. "Now, breathe."

I inhaled a deep breath and then let it out slowly, the tension flowing from between my teeth. "You're right. Even though Father is dead, I will forever be a soldier's daughter. I'll buck up."

He hadn't been chiding me, but sometimes Smoky knew when I needed a reminder of why we were doing what we were doing. Of the fact that strength and courage weren't qualities we could afford to lose. He might want to sweep me away to hole me up in an ivory tower, but he knew all too well that I was needed on the front lines, so he'd stay with me, fighting beside us.

"I'm all right." I took another deep breath and shook my head, wiping my eyes and hoping my eye makeup hadn't smeared. "We'll get the job done, as we always do. And if anybody can rescue Darynal, it will be Trillian. They're oath brothers." I paused, then whispered, "I had to let him go." With a little hiccup, I added, "Right?"

Smoky set me down, kissing my nose. "Right. You had to let him go. I just wish you weren't heading off with Morgaine." He grimaced. Smoky didn't think much of the Fae Queens, and he didn't trust Morgaine at all.

When we first met, he and Titania had been at odds over his barrow out near Mount Rainier for years, until she finally gave up and focused on Talamh Lonrach Oll. Smoky had always maintained that the barrow was his until recently, when he'd admitted to Menolly that he had, indeed, taken it from Titania. Dragons were greedy by nature, so that didn't surprise me. But at least everybody was tolerating everybody else, so we were good for now.

The doorbell sounded. Aeval—it had to be her.

"It's time," I whispered.

He nodded. "Very well. Let's go out there and see what the Triple Threat has to say."

We returned to the living room, where Aeval was waiting. Behind her stood Morgaine, Bran, and as I had suspected—Mordred and Arturo. But next to them stood someone I hadn't expected to see—and who I really didn't *want* to see.

Voluptuous and wanton, Raven Mother waited beside her son. As Bran stared at her through cunning eyes, I could see the resemblance and it made me far more nervous than I'd been a few minutes before. I gave the five of them a nod and turned to the Queen of Shadow and Night. Technically, Morgaine was one of the Fae Queens, too, now. She was the Queen of Dusk and Twilight, but it was hard for me to acknowledge her as such.

I was about to say hello to the others when the floor suddenly rocked, lurching like the rug had just been literally yanked out from beneath our feet. I caught hold of Smoky as he planted himself firmly against the chair nearest us. Aeval barely blinked, and neither did Bran, but Morgaine stumbled and landed on her hands and knees. Arturo and Mordred staggered but managed to keep upright. Raven Mother stood as if nothing could shake her.

Delilah and Morio, who had been standing nearby, managed to keep on their feet, too. From the kitchen, Hanna let out a string of swear words I didn't even realize she knew as a clattering of pans hit the floor. A moment later, the swaying stopped.

Dizzy, I stepped away from Smoky. "Earthquake?"

The Seattle region was riddled with fault zones, highly prone to quakes. In fact, the area was long overdue for a major shake. And by *major*, we were talking eight points or better on the Richter scale. I hoped our house would stand whenever it came because it *was* going to happen, no question about it. The question was just *when*.

Raven Mother shook her head. "That was no earthquake. I know the heart of the earth, and the beat did not emanate from deep within her body."

As she spoke, once again I found myself falling down a deep well, and when I opened my eyes, I was staring into the glistening black eyes of Yvarr. He swished past me, the flames of his body coiling like snakes. Jumping back as one of the tendrils of fire nearly brushed against me, I looked for a way out but couldn't find one.

"You have the Raven near you. I smell her. Give her to me now and perhaps I will pass you by when I find the door out of my prison." Yvarr turned his terrible gaze on me, and swung his head around to hover in front of me.

I shook my head. "Raven Mother is not mine to give. I do not own her. Why would you think I do?"

Yvarr squinted. "You bear the mark of the Raven—you bear the smell of her. There is something . . ." And then his voice dropped even lower and took on an even more menacing tone. "But what is this? You are connected to the Black Beast. I knew you were—I can feel him on you. You are one of his chosen. You are a tricky one, and so is he. The Black Beast uses you as an arm into the other worlds."

Oh fuck. He must be able to sense the Black Unicorn horn. I had to throw him off track until I could figure out how to break this trance. "I have no idea what you're talking about. Maybe you smell dragon sweat on me. I'm married to a dragon, and he would kill any creature who bothered me." Might as well try a bluff, because I didn't seem to be leaving here in any great hurry.

Yvarr paused and then, leaning in closer so that his glowing black eyes filled my vision, sniffed at me. My skirt whipped up, as if I were standing in front of a giant vent, as he inhaled. When he exhaled, the material billowed around my legs and I felt like I was posing for a mockup of Marilyn's famous photo, only in some freakshow horror movie.

"You *do* smell of dragon. Perhaps that is what I sense. A very powerful dragon." Then, he laughed and reared back, like a snake coiling to strike. "But not so powerful as me. Not so ancient as me. I am old beyond counting, girl. Old beyond the oldest dragons! I am their ancestor. I am one of the mighty wyrms of history. Many of us still slumber under the mountains and in the clouds, waiting for the touch that will waken them."

I was about to say, "Sleeping Beauty, you aren't" but decided against it. For one thing, he probably wouldn't get the reference. For another, if he did, what good would it do to make him angry? Somehow, I didn't think my charms would work on him like they did Smoky.

But then, something he said intruded on my thoughts. I carefully returned his gaze. "Sleeping? You were sleeping? What woke you up?"

He paused, his calculating stare burning into me. "What wakes the ancients? What wakes the fathers and mothers of the dragons? There are creatures and gods who lurk in the depths, who slumber in a darksome sleep even deeper than mine. What wakes us all? A call. A summons. The waking of old gods and ancient enemies. The rise of those we fought in the before-times. Old Lords of your kind—your nonhuman self—imprisoned me. They went to sleep, too, but now they awake and so do I."

At that moment, before I could move, he blew a flame at me. There was no way to dodge it, so I steeled for the blast. But the moment before it engulfed me, I found myself on the floor, next to Smoky. Aeval was kneeling on one side of me, Raven Mother on the other.

"Holy fuck." I sat up, shaken. The two women helped me to my feet.

"Camille, what happened? Are you hurt?" Smoky jostled for a better position near me, with Morio hot on his heels. "Love, speak to me."

My pulse racing, I shook my head. "I was facing Yvarr again. I don't know how, but I barely escaped just as he breathed fire on me. Would his attack have killed me, seeing that I was out on the astral and not there physically?"

Aeval glanced over at Raven Mother, who pressed her lips together. Finally, the Queen of Shadow and Night stroked my cheek lightly. "Yes, he could have burnt your soul to a crisp. Yvarr is an ancient enemy and his flames sear more than flesh. Tell us what the wyrm said."

I told them, leaving out nothing. "He said ancient Fae Lords are waking and so he wakes, too. What was he talking about?" The appearance of Yvarr had to mean there was more to what was going on than we'd been told.

Raven Mother paced. After a moment, she stopped, folding her arms across her chest. "For the sake of the gods, Aeval. Tell her the whole story. If you do not, then I will."

"Tell me *what*? I'm not going anywhere until I know just what's going on. I'm done being a pawn." While it was a bluff and they probably knew it, right now I wasn't in any mood to be somebody's toy unless it involved sex.

Aeval scowled at Raven Mother. "I thought we agreed—"

"Oh, listen to the Raven. You wouldn't be *afraid* of telling my cousin the truth, would you?" Morgaine broke in. "You wouldn't fear she might change her loyalties? She might decide I was right? But then, you're the Queen of Shadow and Night. Of course, you aren't *afraid*."

Her voice oozed with honey, sweet and glomming. It set me on edge worse than anything Aeval had ever said, but I decided to let them duke it out. I wasn't about to get between two Fae Queens and an Elemental Lady, even if they were all supposedly on my side.

I held my breath as the three women stared at one another. Together, they were powerful enough to level not only our house, but quite probably the city if they had a mind to. I dreaded thinking of what the outcome of a war between them would be like.

Aeval stared at Morgaine, a hostile smile on her face. But she merely said, "The Dusk and Twilight presumes much, but since the bat is out of the belfry, so to speak, yes, *I* will tell her."

A smug look slid across Morgaine's face, but she quickly resumed her aloof, detached air. "Good, then I will not have to explain on our journey."

Raven Mother let out a cackle. Her bloodred lips were vibrant, sexual to the point of being overwhelming. Her hair was bluish black, dark as ink, dark as night, and she was wearing an Elvira dress, her breasts voluptuous and round, threatening to burst from the bodice at any moment. Raven Mother was chaos incarnate, she was a trickster, an Elemental who lived by her rules, and her rules only. She was alluring and yet lurid.

"Oh do let me, Aeval." Before the Fae Queen could

answer, Raven Mother turned to me. "During the days leading to the Great Divide, the Great Fae Lords managed to ally themselves with the wyrms of the Earth. Together, they ripped apart the worlds. And then, before the Fae Lords moved to Otherworld, they imprisoned both their enemies and their allies."

"How do you imprison the forerunner of a dragon?" I held her gaze. She wasn't embellishing—that much I could tell. This wasn't hyperbole.

"You lock them away behind magical gates and throw away the key. They were imprisoned rather than killed, not because of charity, but because arrogant men—these mighty Fae Lords—thought they might, again, one day need to harness the wyrms' powers."

"They put them in stasis, to use as weapons," Delilah whispered.

"Yes, very aptly put. So these noble and stalwart warriors harnessed the elements of Earth and Fire and Ice and Water and they locked away the giants of the world, keeping them like canned goods on a shelf, in case they might one day need them again. Slavery of the worst kind." She shook her head.

I blinked. Had the Great Fae Lords really done this? Had they not only engineered the Great Divide but locked away these creatures in stasis? Granted, the wyrms could be terribly destructive, but if you're going to destroy your allies after using them, death would have at least been a noble end for creatures of their power and might.

Smoky let out a rumble, low but audible. I glanced at him. "Is this true?"

He nodded, one short, quick inclination of his head. "Unfortunately, it is. The Fae Lords were—and are—arrogant in their assumptions. You think my kind egotistical, but the Great Fae Lords considered their magic infallible. They were mistaken. The fact that Yvarr is rising and able to shake the house from his prison on the astral plane means that he will break free. There is no question of this in my mind. It's simply a matter of *when*."

The blood drained from my face and I could feel myself

go cold. An earthquake of a very different sort, and possibly more deadly than the one I was thinking of earlier.

"And only the Merlin can fight him. But why don't the geniuses who engineered all of this clean up their own mess?" Delilah leaned against a chair, looking for all the world like she wanted to smack something—or someone. And she wasn't alone. I wasn't feeling particularly charitable myself.

"There are several of the Great Lords left, but they slumber, as well. Locked in stasis, locked in time." Raven Mother's smile never wavered, but now I could read the irony and disdain beneath the upturned lips. "They grew weary of their lives and went into hibernation."

"Like a vampire who walks into the sun when he's too tired to go on." My voice was soft but she still caught the words.

"Not quite—vampires choose to release their souls and move on. The Great Fae Lords fear death. They lived for so long that they dread finding out what the Land of Silver Falls is like. They're cowards, too tired to continue on, yet too fearful to die." Raven Mother turned to Aeval. "I know where two of them sleep even now. And the wyrm is correct—there have been portents that they might be waking." She frowned. "They are hiding deep within my woodland. For many eons, I did not know about them, but then, one day, one of my spies stumbled on their lair. We've been watching them ever since. I thought of killing them, but decided to wait and see what happened."

This was news to all of us, that much was apparent. Aeval let out a little *humph* and frowned. "You would be within your rights to destroy them, of course. There is little the Fae can do against your kind—but it might not be the wisest move."

"Yet, if they wake, what will they do?" Morgaine interjected, looking as nonplussed as the rest of us felt.

Confused, I cleared my throat. "I thought some of the Fae who divided the worlds still walked the back paths of Otherworld? Or was that all a children's story designed to make us behave?" I couldn't count the times our father had warned us to behave or he'd send us to the "great ones" for punishment.

"Yeah, were those just boogeyman stories? So to speak?" Delilah's eyes narrowed, almost to cat slits. She didn't look happy, and I realized that she was growing uncomfortable. I had the feeling that this trip wouldn't endear her to the Triple Threat any better. She already disliked them.

"Oh, the older ones do exist, but they were not the ones who created the Great Divide. And many of the ones who were born Earthside have become recluses, retired from the world. They seldom ever see the public. The majority of Otherworld Fae were born and bred there and have known no other life." Raven Mother let out a long sigh.

"They can stay there," Aeval said, her tone grumpy.

Raven Mother simply laughed. "Yes, well, I doubt that most of the Otherworld Fae long to cross over here. But we waste time discussing this. The fact is, if the Great Fae Lords wake, I doubt if they'd know what to do with the world the way it is—either Otherworld or Earthside. The problem lies simply with their waking. For when they wake, the enemies they imprisoned will feel it. And, like Yvarr, they will begin to shift and turn in their prisons. When you enslave someone magically, like they did the old wyrms, you risk forming a bond between yourself and that being. If you sleep, they tend to slumber. But if you wake . . ."

"They do, too. So, Yvarr's waking up is most likely connected to the Fae Lords beginning to rouse. Maybe we *should* just kill them and be done with it." I hated saying that—it sounded callous but it seemed like it might be the best route. If they never woke up, then maybe their enemies would stay asleep as well.

"Unfortunately, if we do that, we have no idea what will happen to their enemies. We have no clue how many of the ancient horrors they imprisoned and we don't know if they would wake and escape should the Great Fae Lords die. Do you know how much damage the wyrms and other monsters could do before they were noticed? Especially in lands cut off from the main passages of the world."

"Could the FBHs bring them down?"

"Perhaps. But with what weapons? Nuclear missiles? A hand grenade isn't going to do more than tickle a wyrm like

Yvarr. No, the cost of waiting till that became necessary would be tens of thousands of lives." Aeval shook her head. "We cannot chance it. If we rouse the Merlin, he will be able to tame Yvarr and make it easier to destroy him. He is the High Priest of the Druids, the High Priest of the Hunter. He is our best hope."

"What happens if Yvarr dies?" Delilah rubbed her temples, looking as tired as I felt from the discussion.

"Then . . . he dies. As far as we know, there will be no ramifications unless the other wyrms manage to free themselves as well." Aeval turned to me. "Do you understand why you must successfully manage this quest?"

I stared bleakly out the window, watching the rain slashing down into the evening hours. While I wasn't sure whether she was completely on track, Aeval was not one prone to hysterics, nor was she power hungry like Morgaine and Raven Mother. If she said there was danger in killing the Fae Lords, I tended to believe her. If she said there wouldn't be any fallout from killing Yvarr, I also believed her.

"I suppose we should get a move on, then." Reluctantly, I stretched and turned to Smoky. "Love, watch over the house for us. Tell Menolly we'll return as soon as we can."

"I will. Tonight we go to the Wayfarer and see what needs to be done still. The rebuilding is coming along quickly. She should be able to reopen in a few weeks." He stroked my cheek, then kissed me. "Meanwhile, Camille, I don't want you to worry about us. Focus on your journey. Finish the quest and come home as soon as possible."

"Easier said than done." I turned to Aeval. "We're ready."

"Who are you taking with you? And who . . . is he?" She nodded at Tanne.

I motioned for him to step forward. "He's going with me, along with Delilah and Morio. Tanne is a demon hunter from the Black Forest."

Tanne clicked his heels together and bowed to Aeval, his back perfectly straight. "Your highness."

"You may call me Aeval." She frowned, pursing her lips. "I don't believe we've met."

"We have not, Queen of Shadow and Night. But I have

heard of you, of course. I come from the Black Forest, from the Hunter's Glen Clan." At her look of surprise, the edge of his lip tipped up.

"Hunter's Glen? Your clan is still in existence, then? We thought your line had died out thousands of years ago." She blinked and I suddenly had the feeling we'd underestimated Tanne.

He tilted his head and a cunning smile spread across his face. "Oh, we are still strong. My mother and grandmother now seek to establish a subsidiary clan here, on this shore. I came to lay the foundation. My sister is here, too. We are setting up our base, and then will bring other members of the clan here. The monsters still outnumber the hunters by far too many on this continent."

Aeval regarded him silently for a moment, then with a quick breath, said, "When you return from this journey, I require you to appear at Talamh Lonrach Oll and register. We ask that any clan of such strength as yours be on our rolls." She turned to me. "I did not realize you were allied with the Hunter's Glen Clan."

Feeling slightly adrift in the conversation, I shrugged. "We . . . did not realize you'd want to know."

"Any time one of the ancient family clans sets up operations in our area, of course we want to know. Remember that for the future." At my silent nod, she continued. "Then, it is time. The realm will be teeming with Elder Fae and their creatures. Morgaine knows the history of many of them, and so does Bran. Share your knowledge and resources, the two of you. I do not want to hear any reports that *any* of you were uncooperative."

And with that, we shrugged into our outerwear and headed out through the kitchen, stopping to pick up the bag of food from Hanna, before piling into the backyard. I also took a moment to fetch the yew staff Aeval had given me.

The rain had paused for a moment, though the clouds were still thick, and by the look of the sky in the east, we were due for another soaking any moment.

We stopped by the portal. Derisa had shifted the destination, and the guards had been watching it closely in case any of the

Elder Fae tried to break through. The one thing in our favor was that the Elder Fae weren't numerous, not in the sense of, say, goblins, or humans, or even the Fae themselves.

They bred slowly, and every one—regardless of their parentage—was unique. While not all of them were malicious, they were all deadly and powerful. And it was impossible to tell the malign ones from the benign at first glance. Looks meant nothing in their world—in the world of the Fae, in general. The ugliest creature could be helpful, and the most beautiful deathly dangerous.

I turned to Smoky and Iris, who had joined us. Vanzir had stayed inside to help Hanna. Shade was standing by Delilah. Chase was back at Iris's house, watching the kids with Bruce.

"Well, here we are." I realized I was stalling, not wanting to face the moment when we walked into the portal. But procrastinating wouldn't get the job done. "Okay, if we're going to do this, let's get moving." Leaning up on tiptoe, I planted a kiss on Smoky's cheek.

He sucked in a deep breath and let it out slowly. "Take care of yourself, for me and for everybody who loves you."

I nodded, realizing this was his way of telling me he understood why I needed to go. "You got it. I'll be back, love. I'll be back before you know it."

"If you aren't, I'll come looking. You know that, right? I'll always come looking for you if something goes wrong. I'll never let you down." He buried his nose in my neck and his breath was hot against my skin. "I'll never let you down again."

"Don't make promises that you might not be able to keep. Just promise to love me and be here for me?" I stroked his hair away from his face and the tendril reached up to coil around my wrist, gently holding on.

"That, I promise, my love. Always." And then, he let go, though I could tell he didn't want to.

I turned to the others, steeling myself for the next move. "Delilah, Morio, Tanne . . . you ready?"

They murmured their ascent.

To my surprise and relief, Raven Mother kissed Bran on

the forehead but stepped back. "Be cautious, my son. Be brave."

"You aren't going with us?" I held my breath, hoping she'd say no. To my relief, she shook her head.

"No, I have much to attend to back in Darkynwyrd. I simply wanted to come talk to you before you left, and to bid my son farewell."

Thinking swiftly, I walked over to her. "Will you grant me a moment of your time, alone?" Maybe I could get to the bottom of why Bran was such an ass to me.

Raven Mother's eyes glittered. "Of course."

As we walked away from the others, I glanced back, making sure they were out of earshot. "I wanted to ask you something about Bran. He seems to hate me, and I get the feeling it's for killing his father. But it wasn't my choice—I was destined to do so, and the Black Unicorn reincarnated immediately."

Raven Mother's smile was cool, but her eyes twinkled. "My son is stubborn. He is also greedy at times and I admit, he takes after me. He is jealous of you, not angry. You were given a gift of something he covets—and when his father died, he thought sure he'd be given the horn and hide like the ones you possess. But my Lord, the Black Unicorn, chose to sequester them away for someone not yet born. Bran was furious. He hasn't forgiven his father, and he can't forgive you for bearing the tokens he longs for."

Great. So Bran was a child of the entitlement mentality—which meant he was just about like every other spoiled powerful being I'd ever met.

"How can I get him off my back?" I didn't mean to sound so blunt but the words just spilled out in a rush.

Raven Mother, however, just laughed. "I'd have a talk with him but that would make matters worse. You know how children are when their parents push them to play nice. Bran also has the misfortune of a promise I made him some time ago. I made it in haste, and so far, have not been able to fulfill it." As she gazed meaningfully at me, I flashed back to my last meeting with her.

Oh hell. I was right. She had hinted to me last time we

met that she'd promised me to Bran, if she could woo me to join her in Darkynwyrd. And that wasn't happening.

"Yeah. Not a chance. But you need to be aware that if he pushes me too far, I'm pushing back. I don't care if he's your son or not. I won't put up with bad behavior." Doing my best to appear stern, I turned my back on her—a dangerous move in itself—and started back toward the others.

"Camille." Raven Mother's voice was soft, singsonging the words. "Do not be surprised, do not, if my son oversteps his bounds. He is beyond my control. Bran the Raven Master is destined for great things. I would walk warily if I were you."

And with that, she vanished, whirling in on herself like a vortex spinning. I watched as she transformed into a great raven and flew away. Turning back to the others, I noticed that Bran was staring at me, and I returned his gaze. I couldn't let him see that I was intimidated by him. Whether his mother would mention our conversation, I had no clue. Raven Mother was tricky and she bent the truth to her own use. But for now, until they met again, he would have to just wonder what we'd been talking about.

As I returned to Morio's side, I nodded to Aeval. Her lips pressed into a thin smile, she inclined her head slightly, and handed me the silver-knobbed yew staff that she'd given me some time before. It resonated in my hand, ringing with the energy of death and rebirth, of transformation and the night.

"I think . . . we're ready."

Morgaine took the lead, since she had the best idea of where we were headed. "Then let's waste no more time." She plunged through the portal, vanishing.

Without another word, Bran, Mordred, and Arturo followed her. I raised my hand, holding it steady, and stared at Smoky. His forehead creasing, he did the same to me, and then, followed by Delilah, Morio, and Tanne, I stepped through the vortex, into the realm of Elder Fae.

Chapter 11

❧❀❧

The portal into the realm of the Elder Fae was one of the strongest and weirdest I'd ever experienced. Usually, it was bizarre enough—the feeling that you're being pulled into a million tiny pieces and then flung back together again somewhere else—but this time, add to that the sensation of sticking your finger into a light socket. Every inch of my body was quivering and I felt like I'd bathed in some sort of sparkling effervescent water.

As I stepped through the vortex, immediately moving to my left to allow the others room to come through, I took in as much of my surroundings as possible. Morgaine and her cronies were standing to the right, doing the same.

The landscape here was vivid, almost video-game bright. Every color seemed heightened, every line seemed to stand out more. The sky was a deep indigo with brilliant stars shimmering, and the temperature, hovering in the low 40s, a lot like Seattle's. A moist chill skirted the edges, as if there had been rain earlier, leaving the ground refreshed and the evening cool.

We were in a small glade, surrounded by a thick stand of

birch and alder. Through an opening to my left, a path was visible. The glade was enclosed, and as I tried to get my bearings, I could sense eyes watching us from behind the trees and the dark silhouettes of bushes that thickly shrouded the trunks.

Overhead, I searched for any sign of the moon. There she was, closing on to full and beautiful, blotting out the stars in the surrounding area. Surprised to see her, a sense of comfort descended. Otherworld matched Earthside's pace with the seasons and moon phases, but here—in the realm of the Elder Fae—I had no clue how things worked. Every dimension was different, every step away from our own world had its variations. And yet, all of these planes were connected by the portals, by the web that made up the very nature of the world.

I glanced over at Morgaine. She was staring at me. For once, she didn't look angry. In fact, she looked about as lost as I felt. She flashed me a tentative smile—I could see her teeth gleam in the flux of lights emanating from the portal— as Delilah appeared. She immediately moved to stand beside me as Morio and Tanne came through. We were all here, all intact.

"I hope we're done soon. Remember? Full moon? Me, tabby cat?" Delilah nudged me.

"Oh, hell, you're right. And I'll be swept up in the Hunt." I frowned. "Well, we'll have to muddle through the best we can. I'll tell Morio to keep watch over you if we're still here."

A fragrance drifted through the air—reminding me of the forests surrounding Seattle. I inhaled deeply, breathing in the scent of mildew and moss, of toadstools and decaying leaves and rain tinged with tree sap. Suddenly wishing we were back home, I slowly exhaled.

"So, what next? Where do we go from here?" I turned to Morgaine. "You're in charge, apparently. I certainly have no clue where the Merlin is located."

She frowned. "I know the tales of where he's imprisoned. Meher told me the story, and he seldom told anybody anything. I doubt if he took many others into his confidence. That was before he . . ." Pausing, she shook her head. "Never mind. The fact is, the Merlin was imprisoned at the same time as Aeval and Titania, during the Great Divide."

It was my turn to frown. We were here because of stories about where the Merlin *might* be? Had Aeval missed the mark this time?

"So, you never trained under the Merlin, then?" Morio knelt to examine the dirt. He lifted a handful to his nose and inhaled. "Tangy, and imbued with magic. This realm is magical to the core—don't let down your guard."

As Morio spoke, I realized that, as long as we'd known Morgaine, we really hadn't gotten to *know* her at all. She was dangerous and chaotic, and as a result, we had shied away from her, an oversight we might come to regret.

But Morgaine seemed inclined to talk. "Not Myrddin, no. But I trained under Meher. As I said, he was the acting Merlin at the time, but forgotten by history. He trained me well enough, though we had our issues and parted badly. Meher did have a deep regard for the earth and the water, and he could command their powers. He taught me how to charm the lakes and rivers, and the deep caverns of the world."

For a moment, through the dark greed that twisted her nature, I caught a glimpse of raw power—the ability to move stone and river—and the love for those elements. Morgaine might be hungry and rapacious, but she was able to sense and honor the powers of the earth, and they lent their secrets to her. But then, a black cloud washed across her face and she shivered and shook her head.

Tanne cocked his head. "In the Black Forest, we have our great wizards and witches, too. My clan follows a goddess who is a great sorceress. Holda leads the Wild Hunt, much like Odin."

"As long as she isn't Baba Yaga, we're fine and dandy." I had heard of Holda, but seldom encountered anybody who followed her. "Your goddess and mine have much in common—including leading the Hunt and being the patroness of witches. I wonder if they both answer to Pentangle, the Mistress of Magic. I met Pentangle not all that long ago, in my quest to vanquish a god."

Morgaine gave me a crafty look. "Pentangle is dangerous.

It isn't wise to attract her attention. Just because you and your companions managed to subdue Gulakah, doesn't mean he's gone forever." She laughed, her voice rough.

At my look, she added, "Oh, don't play surprised with me. Of course, I know what happened. You think the Court of the Three Queens doesn't keep tight tabs on you and what is transpiring?" Here, she paused, glancing at Bran. Then, her lips set, she fell silent once again. I had the feeling she wanted to say more, but that something about the Raven Master had stilled her tongue.

Mordred, however, wasn't quite so reticent. "You may tackle a god, but I doubt if you could tackle the Merlin." He sounded bitter.

I sensed a deep undercurrent of waves here, and as I glanced from Morgaine to her nephew, I almost could see the argument brewing between the two. My gaze flickered to Arturo. He, too, seemed unsettled but he wasn't paying much attention to the pair and I had no clue what was setting him off.

Tanne cleared his throat. "So, where do we go from here?"

Grateful he'd chosen to change the subject, I jumped on his question. "Yes. Morgaine, which way do we go?"

She held my gaze for a moment, but this time, it wasn't a challenge. She turned away and held out her arms. Closing her eyes, she sent out one low, lingering note to hover in the air a moment before the breeze snatched it away. A moment later, a note echoed back from the right.

"We take the path and follow the yellow brick road." Grinning, she slung her pack over her shoulder. "Let's get a move on, because frankly, I'd rather not just stand around. Stationary targets get noticed. We have no clue what might be nearby and with the portal activating, it's bound to attract some attention."

I moved forward to her side. "Morio and I will walk beside you, if you don't mind. Tanne, will you and Delilah bring up the rear?" I wanted players from our side in back, just in case Mordred and Bran got it into their heads to try something.

Again, an odd look from Morgaine but she inclined her

head and we formed our marching order. I took the center, so Morio and I could grasp hands for whenever our magic was needed. The odds against us were too high and once again, this was a matter of when, not if.

As we approached the edge of the glade, I shivered. The watchers in the woods had sent word ahead. In my heart I knew it, and it made sense. We had to be ready for any attack. We emerged from the enclosed circle of trees, and found ourselves on the edge of a vast plain. It was too dark to see very far ahead, but in the distance, lights flickered.

Oh, fuck. Deadly globes, dancing in the night.

Will-o'-the-wisps. The deadly, feral Fae. They were more alluring than sirens, at least for FBHs. Thank gods we didn't have Chase with us—a couple years before, he'd been lured in by them when we were on the trail of a Rākṣasa.

Also known as Corpse Candles, the will-o'-the-wisps devoured life energy, and that included magical power. And they would come running with spoon and fork in hand, just the minute they sensed our party.

Whether having Morgaine with us would make a difference, I didn't know. I could only hope that the fact that she was a Fae Queen would chase them off. But there was no way to know for sure unless they descended on us. And considering the Maiden of Karask had told us that they didn't fear either Younger or Elder Fae, chances were the freakish little buggers would pounce on us and try to turn us into magical juice boxes.

I tapped Morgaine on the arm. "Trouble ahead. Last time we fought them, we had the help of an Elder Fae. I've never been hurt by one yet, but I know they can be dangerous when they smell magic in the wind."

She nodded. "They are more dangerous than you think. Do you know what they are?" By her tone, I took it to mean that she did.

"Nobody does . . . or at least, that's what I've always been told."

"Wrong, child. I know, because the Merlin, or Meher rather, told me their secret. Only the Druids know, but with the demise of their order, the knowledge was lost. The modern

Druids—the FBH order—have no clue. They are a pale shadow of what their kind once was, but when we find the Merlin and wake him, all that might change."

The Druids knew what the will-o'-the-wisps were? Interesting. And if Morgaine was willing to tell me, that was one more piece of information that might serve us in the future. I waited, attentive.

She seemed to be mulling over something, but after a moment, she let out a sigh. "I have not even told Aeval this, mind you. I'm sure she knows, but you are not to tell her where you received the information. She doesn't like me usurping her instruction, even though I am supposed to be your trainer. Her bite is worse than her bark."

I nodded. "I know only too well." What I was thinking was, *that goes for you, too*, but I wasn't about to say it aloud. Morgaine was a snake, capricious and subject to whim. Even though she was taking me into her confidence, I still didn't trust her.

"The will-o'-the-wisps are spawned from the souls of dead Fae who were killed in the woods, on the moors and fields."

"Murdered souls?"

"No, regardless of how that death occurred—be it natural or murder or war. There is a fungus that only grows in the woodlands and fields. When one of the Fae dies near that fungus, the toadstool drains the energy as the soul leaves the body. Using that, the toadstool releases a number of tiny will-o'-the-wisps. They do *not* carry the consciousness of the departed—that part of the soul goes on to the Land of the Silver Falls. But the energy that is released upon dying? Feeds the birth of the will-o'-the-wisps. It's a symbiotic relationship."

I stared at her. It sounded bizarre, but then again—compared to some of the things we'd seen over the years, maybe not so much. But that meant . . .

"So each Fae who dies in the woodland, if they are near one of these toadstools, creates multiple will-o'-the-wisps. Not just one, but a number of them."

"Correct. In a sense, the corpse—or rather the dying victim—is like a midwife."

"That means that back in Otherworld . . ." I thought of the Elfin lands. They were wild and wooded, vast swaths of forest and grassland. "Does this fungus exist over in Otherworld too?"

Morgaine nodded. "Of course. And yes, this means your Elfin friends better steel themselves for a vast flood of will-o'-the-wisps, given the number of elves who died there. And unfortunately, will-o'-the-wisps are continually hungry. They not only drain life force from humans, but magic from the Fae. The rumors of them being pests are a myth. If you're stuck in a swarm of them, they will attack like piranha seething around a body in the water."

"Then we've been lucky, so far . . ." I thought of the amount of misinformation, even among my own people, regarding the dancing orbs of light. "That means they aren't a form of the eye catchers we have over in Otherworld."

"Right again. Even your home world has its urban legends. And now, we have to decide what to do about that group. So far we've escaped their notice, but unless we turn the other way, we're not going to remain so lucky. And quite frankly, we don't have the leeway to do so. It would be very easy to get lost here, and while I know the general direction in which we need to go, if we get off track, we're going to be in a lot of trouble." Morgaine moved closer to me, her voice dropping. "Regardless of our differences, we must work together on this journey because I don't fancy being lost in this realm."

The fact that she was nervous made me even more cautious. Morgaine had a hyperactive ego. When *she* expressed doubts, it meant that we were facing a task far more dangerous than I was comfortable with. For not the first time, I wished Derisa had chosen somebody else for this journey. I'd rather take my chances in the Shadow Lands with Trillian than be out here.

Delilah cleared her throat. "Whatever we're going to do, we'd better do it fast, because I think our grace period is

over." She pointed toward the will-o'-the-wisps. Sure enough,
they were moving in our direction.

"They eat magical energy. Are there any spells that will
disrupt them rather than feed them? Morio and I can wield
death magic." I motioned for him to move toward me. He
was already starting to draw in energy, I could feel it grow
and swirl—a vast current of violet light sweeping out from
deep within him. That was one thing about working with the
death magic. It came from deep in our core rather than outside of us. Regardless of the environment, if magic could be
worked, we could summon it.

Morgaine set her pack on the ground. "There are several
spells that can disrupt them, but death magic is not one of
them. So stand your ground, Fox. They can be attacked physically, but only with iron weapons, and none of us are geared
for that. They can be attacked more readily on the astral
plane. But again, plane shifting here would be dangerous."

"Then what do we do?"

She pointed at my staff. "Yew, correct?"

I nodded. "Yes. Aeval gave it to me."

"The wood can disrupt them." She pulled a wand out of
her pack. "I have a yew wand. Yew and elder are the two
woods that will affect them. Touch them with the wood and
it will disrupt their energy and send them packing."

"You mean we can actually kill them?"

"No, but we *can* buy enough time to hightail it out of
here."

Bran fumbled through his pack. "I have an elder mallet."
He brought out a small, hand-sized hammer. It barely looked
capable of driving a nail into wood, let alone fighting off
will-o'-the-wisps, but then I caught a whiff of the energy.

"Oh yeah, babe." I couldn't help it. I wanted to touch his
hammer. It sang to my yew staff and I realized that the
woods helped exacerbate one another.

Beside me, Morio shivered. "I can feel it, too."

Bran let out a snort. "Elder, like yew, is a wood of death.
It channels the energy. I suggest, when you find the opportunity, you look into making yourself a weapon out of the tree,

youkai. It fits your nature, deathly fox." He paused, then nodded. "Get ready. We've got company."

Morio whirled around, eyes blazing, as the will-o'-the-wisps descended and we were inundated by the creatures. They swarmed like ants boiling off of a hill. There were easily four dozen of them, and they zipped around us, darting like fireflies. Only these fireflies had stingers, and they were nasty.

One landed on my shoulder and jolted me. My shoulder burning, I whipped around, bringing my staff to bear. The glowing globe pulled away, but I managed to hit another one of them with it and—with a sizzle—the will-o'-the-wisp vanished, popping like a soap bubble. I tried to keep in mind that I hadn't killed it, just sent it packing.

Delilah let out a growl as she began to shift form. The will-o'-the-wisps were swarming her, too, and as she transformed into her panther shape, they pulled back. She lunged at one, catching it in her mouth. To my surprise, the creature let out a little shriek and disappeared. Delilah let out a satisfied grunt and went after another batch of them.

Beside me, Morio was shifting into his youkai form. In his demonic form, he stood eight feet high, a bizarre hybrid of fox and human and demon, with human hands ending in black claws, and he could make a horse envious with the way it was hanging.

He swiped his way through the mass of lights attacking us, and a few of them vanished. Whether they feared him, or whether his touch disrupted them, I didn't know, but it didn't matter. It was working, and we were slowly fending our way through them.

Bran and Morgaine were swinging right and left with their wand and hammer, popping the lights as they went. Another one landed on my other shoulder. The sting was fierce—like that of a giant hornet. I could feel it trying to siphon off my energy.

"Fuck you, too!" I jumped aside and swung my staff at it, managing to hit it square on. The creature vanished. A song behind me stopped me cold. I whirled around, as did Morgaine and Bran.

Tanne was standing, arms out, as he held a long note that echoed through the night. The music rolled like a wave, so tangible I could see it oozing forward. Unstoppable, it rolled through the lights and over us. I braced myself but the notes ran through me like mist.

When the wave of sound hit the will-o'-the-wisps, the creatures let out a collective shriek and began to deflate, like gas escaping from a bunch of balloons. A stiff breeze sprang up, catching the colored vapor, and swept it away, and we were suddenly alone, standing there in the dark of the night, with only the stars and the ground around us.

"How did you do that?" I turned to Tanne, as Delilah shifted back into her normal shape. "What was that?"

"I told you, I'm a spell singer and a demon hunter. Will-o'-the-wisps are common in the Black Forest and we've had to come up with a way of dealing with them. A witch I know named Liesel discovered what frequency they use to take physical shape. She was able to devise a spell that disrupts their energy enough to actually destroy them before they can vanish."

"Can you teach me that?" I cocked my head, wondering what it would require to learn how to be a spell singer.

Tanne frowned. "I doubt it—it's a natural talent, like your Moon Magic. Only members of my Fae clan have the power. We're widespread across Europe, but it's a hereditary gift."

"That figures." I grinned. I hadn't really expected him to say yes. "It was worth a shot, though."

Morgaine cleared her throat. "Well, that was impressive. I haven't seen quite such a display since my years spent in the forests of Britain."

Her tone was light, but I could practically see the wheels turning. She was always, always on the lookout for ways to increase her personal advantage, but Tanne could take care of himself.

"Well, that solves our first problem. If we're lucky, maybe we'll avoid anything worse." Delilah might be ever optimistic, but even she sounded like she didn't believe her own words.

"Yeah, that's not going to happen. You know it. I know it.

Let's not even kid ourselves." I snorted. "I'm thinking we're bound to run into something nasty over here. I just hope it's not Yannie Fin Diver again, or that freakshow spider-Fae that caught Chase."

Delilah shuddered. "Yannie Fin Diver is terrifying. In fact, he wins my 'never-want-to-see-again' award."

Yannie Fin Diver was as good as a god for the Meré—and the merfolk were a vicious race. He had come after us when we'd inadvertently entered what I realized now was this same realm. We'd just stumbled in from a different entrance point. Yannie had been all too intent on grabbing my unicorn horn and then eating us. At least, I had hoped the latter was his intent—anything else was too terrifying to contemplate.

Morgaine motioned for Morio and me to join her again at the front. "We have a couple days of hiking from here. We'd best get moving. I suggest we continue till midnight, then hole up for a few hours. We're roughing it, so I hope you all brought soft blankets. There aren't any hotels on the route we're taking."

Hotels were the least of my worries. Silently, we set off into the night, trying to keep to the path. Once again, I was center front, with Morgaine on my left and Morio on my right. I wanted to drop back and talk to Delilah but this was neither the time nor place—too many things could go wrong here, and we needed all eyes alert. Talking would distract us.

The scent of moss filtered past, but in the dark we couldn't see where it was coming from. The air was chilly, and I pulled my cape tighter around my shoulders. I'd decided against bringing the black unicorn cloak—too many chances to be noticed. As it was, I'd had to think long and hard about the horn, but in the end, I decided that the need for it might outweigh the danger of attracting unwanted attention. I just hoped that I wouldn't have to use it. Bran's greed was strong, and I had no idea how the trickster's son might react when a bright sparkly dangled in front of him.

There was moisture in the air, and wisps of clouds were crossing the moon. The sounds of night here were different than in Earthside or Otherworld. Scuttling from the bushes could be anything. And, below the night songs, I could hear a thrum that registered almost at the bottom of my hearing. A cadence, a beat that sounded like the patter of many feet on muffled ground. Was it the nature of this realm? Or some creature? Or was it just the sound of my thoughts?

Morgaine had fallen into an uneasy silence. She paused every now and then, as if taking stock of where we were, then would nod for us to start up again.

At one point, a loud shriek reverberated through the air, chilling me to the bone. Echoing, it pierced my thoughts, and I broke out into a cold sweat. It took every ounce of nerve I had to keep myself from racing off into the undergrowth. Morio slid his arm around my waist. Behind me, I could hear Delilah gasp and Tanne whisper something under his breath. Another moment, and the cry drifted off.

"What . . ." Delilah started to ask.

Tanne answered before she could get the rest of the question out. "*Bean Sidhe.* Hunting down the family she's bound to, no doubt. They usually scream twice. Once when they begin their journey, once when they reach their destination. We have similar creatures in the Black Forest. The *Erlkönig.* The Alder Kings ride to announce death for the families to which they are bound."

I let out a shaky breath. Bean Sidhe would have been my guess, had Tanne not beat me to it. Delilah caught my gaze in a moonbeam and her eyes went wide, shimmering with a swirl of sparks. The crescent tattoo on her forehead flared to life and I caught my breath.

"The Autumn Lord . . ." I whispered.

She nodded. "I responded to the Bean Sidhe's call. The more I walk under the reign of the Autumn Lord, the more I am drawn to his realm. I noticed . . . when we were in Elqaneve and the storm hit, I could feel something shifting. I'm evolving . . . and I'm not sure what he's planning for me right now, but something's on the move."

I could feel the swirl around her—bonfires and crisp autumn leaves.

Death magic . . . the energy surrounding her is very

*much akin to our death magic. I think Delilah is headed for
a very shadowy world soon.*

At first I thought *I* had thought the words, but then Morio
gave my hand a squeeze and I realized that somehow he had
entered my mind and whispered to me in a voice so low that
no one else seemed to catch it. I nodded, just enough for him
to see. Delilah's training with the Death Maidens had
changed her—for the better, in my opinion. But once Morio
mentioned it, I could sense change looming in front of her.
And whatever it was would not be easy but it would be worth
the challenge.

Returning my attention to Morgaine, I steeled my nerves.
"You say we have a couple of days of travel ahead? Where
are we going?"

Morgaine was short—very petite. We looked a lot alike,
although she definitely had some age wearing on her. In
some ways, it seemed like we were walking a similar path,
only hers had started a thousand years ago or so, while mine
was still in its infancy.

"We seek the Veiled Mountains. The Merlin was last
rumored to be sleeping there. The Fae Lords hid him away
very carefully. They did not want him waking."

"What part did he play in the war?" Delilah asked.

"The Merlin was their mightiest enemy when the argu-
ments were waging over the Great Divide. He led Titania and
Aeval and their armies against the Fae Lords who drove the
juggernaut along. The wars raged, vicious and cunning,
before their side won and ours lay in ruins. But the victory
was costly to everyone. Before there could be any counter
measures, the Fae Lords imprisoned the Fae Queens, and the
Merlin. And they imprisoned their allies as well. And when
they had accomplished their goal, they imprisoned both their
enemies and their allies. They turned on their monstrous
friends, and cast them deep into sleep. When they, in turn,
decided to withdraw and slumber, they rigged spells to prevent their new enemies from waking until they did."

"It wasn't worth it, was it?" I tried to block out thoughts
of the devastation.

"What?"

"I love Otherworld. But the destruction that was wrought while separating the worlds . . . it wasn't worth it. We were taught all our lives how noble the lords were, and how the Divide had happened solely to keep the demons at bay. Now, I wonder how true any of that was."

Morgaine started to speak, but stopped when Tanne let out a soft "Look" and pointed. We followed his direction. There, seeming to appear out of nowhere, was a large two-story building. It had a green man plaque hanging from it, and for all the world, it looked to be an inn. But where had it come from, and who the hell was running it?

Chapter 12

❧❦❧

Bran let out a relieved sigh. "Finally. I was not looking forward to sleeping on the ground, I'll tell you that."

I stared at him. He couldn't be serious? It struck me that Bran might be on the spoiled side. "You realize that none of us are looking forward to camping out, but I think it's safer than just traipsing into an inn that just appeared out of nowhere."

"There is no safety in this realm, regardless of where we sleep. And if someone bothers us, we can handle them." He sounded so cocky that it scared me. Why the hell had Derisa and Aeval insisted he come along? At least Morgaine seemed to have a level head about this trip. She knew it was dangerous, and she wasn't taking chances.

As if reading my thoughts, Morgaine shook her head. "We are all weary and the trip is only going to become harder, but we don't dare chance the inn. Just keep on moving. We aren't far from a wooded glade, and there we will find shelter in the trees just off the path."

Morio cleared his throat. "For once, I'm inclined to agree with you. This is not a realm to be taken lightly, and while we

have a fair amount of power at our fingertips, there are creatures far stronger and more deadly than we are."

Bran's eyes narrowed to slits as he stared at Morgaine.
"Do you forget what we discussed before we left? Do I have
to remind you?"

Okay, this was a new one. I glanced at Morgaine, who
flinched. She pressed her lips together and stared back at
him. Anger rolled off of her in a wave, so palpable I could
almost feel it.

She let out a short huff. "You might want to keep your
mouth shut, Raven Master. Use up your tokens now and you
won't have any for later. A promise can only be leveraged so
far, you realize?"

What the hell could Bran be holding over Morgaine's
head that would make her cave? And the more important
question: Did Aeval know about this little matter when she
ordered him to accompany us?

I glanced over at Arturo and Mordred. Arturo looked
unfazed as usual. He was a rough read, that one. But Mordred looked pissed. As he gazed at Bran, a sneer flickered on
his lips.

I shivered. The three of them made for a dangerous triangle, and whatever stakes they played for were far too high for
my comfort level.

Delilah nudged my elbow and I gave her a surreptitious
nod before leaning against my staff and whistling.

"Listen up. I have no clue what's going down between you
two, but whatever the issue is, we're not part of it. You can
do what you want, but the rest of us will take our chances in
the woods ahead. We're not going into that inn. If it showed
up out of nowhere, it can vanish just as easily."

Bran didn't even bother looking at me, but continued to
stare at Morgaine. "Moon Witch, you are under orders to the
Queen of Dusk. Your desires and thoughts have no place or
say here."

Morgaine's gaze flickered to meet mine and for the first
time in a long while, I saw a glimmer of fear behind that
cool exterior. "Play your cards wisely, Bran. Your hold on

me is more tenuous than you like to think. I've met more dangerous players than you in my life and lived to see them enter the grave. Now, do you insist on chancing the inn?"

Bran flashed her a shrewd smile. "Check and mate. We will sleep in the forest. But Morgaine, don't forget who holds the upper hand."

Before anyone could say another word, the inn shivered and vanished. I stared at the barren space where it had stood. Everything in the realm of the Elder Fae seemed deadly and nebulous, and now that we knew Bran had some hold over Morgaine, I was even more nervous.

Morgaine let out a snort. "Sleep in the inn. Yes, what a *wonderful* idea." Then, without another word, she turned and motioned toward the path. "Let's get settled for the night. We need rest."

The thicket was rife with deciduous trees, barren and sparse in the winter night. A thin veil of frost was beginning to form and it would be downright cold by morning.

Morio struck up a foxfire spell and the glowing ball gave us enough light to see our way behind a patch of ferns, their fronds waving a good five feet high. The trees were thick here. Among the alder and birch and oak, there also stood some fir and cedar. A dry, flat patch of ground beneath one of the giant conifers was large enough for us to spread out, and we gathered beneath the tree in a circle, resting on the ground.

I pulled out my blanket from my pack—spidersilk and thin, but warm. As I settled between Morio and Delilah, Tanne set up his gear on her other side.

Morgaine, Mordred, Arturo, and Bran set up their camp opposite us. I wanted to light a fire. Crackling flames would make everything seem so much better, but I didn't even broach the idea. Too many creatures out there in the darkness. Too many chances to be seen by unwelcome eyes.

Bran said little, but instead covered himself with a blanket and turned over. I wasn't sure if he was asleep, but it was a relief to feel like we weren't under his constant scrutiny.

Arturo silently went about setting out a snack for the three of them. Mordred leaned against one of the trees, his blanket wrapped around his shoulders.

I was tired, but hungry, so we dug through Hanna's sack of sandwiches and chicken. She'd also included water in reusable plastic bottles, and cookies. Delilah stared at Bran's prone figure, then tapped me on the shoulder and motioned for me to follow her. Tucking my cloak tightly around me, I did.

When we were far enough away from camp, back near the main road, she whispered. "What the hell is going on with Bran and Morgaine?"

"I don't know, but I feel like we walked in a demilitarized zone, and any moment, we could step over the wire. I'd like to throttle Morgaine, though, for not warning us that Bran's up to something. And I'd like to ask Aeval what the hell she knows about this and get a straight answer. She *can't* be blind to their feud. She's the one who brought Bran over to lead the Talamh Lonrach Oll Warriors. In fact, now that I remember, Morgaine was furious. I think she was doing her best to secure Mordred in that position."

Delilah cocked her head. "But why would that give Bran power over her?"

"I don't know, but when Morio was made my priest, during that rite, Morgaine acted like she hated my guts. Now she's . . . well, she's not friendly but she certainly seems to have transferred her anger for me to Bran." I wanted to get to the bottom of all this, but the potential for upsetting the applecart was more than I wanted to risk—at least until we returned home.

"This whole off-to-find-the-Merlin thing reeks of intrigue." Delilah sat down on a large rock. "I think I prefer dealing with the war in Otherworld. How can you stand the power plays going on out at the Triple Threat's compound?"

I nudged her to scoot over so that I could sit beside her. The moon was visible between the clouds drifting by, and it felt like I could reach up and touch her. "I guess this is all part of where my life is headed. I'm supposed to be the first High Priestess over Earthside for the Moon Mother. That's why Aeval is training me. But . . . there's something bigger coming, I think."

"That's kind of how I feel with my training for the Autumn Lord." Delilah let out a soft chuckle. "I mean, I know that one day I'm destined to bear his child, and that Shade will be the father by proxy . . . I guess that in itself is scary enough. At least, with that destiny, I can't help but feel I'll manage to survive. I can't very well give birth if I'm dead."

I let out a snicker and realized I could see my breath in front of me. "Well, that's one way to look at it. Damn, it's getting chilly."

She nodded. "Yeah, the frost is already forming."

"I wish that Aeval and Titania would . . ." Pausing, I glanced around to make sure nobody had followed us. No need for prying ears to hear what I was about to say. "I wish they would strip Morgaine of her powers."

A shuffle in the brush stilled my words. Delilah heard it, too, and we froze, waiting to see what fresh horror was going to leap out at us. Another rustle and then the huckleberry bush parted and out flew a familiar figure.

"Mistletoe!" I jumped up. The pixie darted over toward us. Even though pixies tended to look a lot alike, we knew Mistletoe well enough to tell him from the rest. "What are you doing here?"

He tipped his hat—a tiny green affair formed from a leaf, with a dashing yellow feather in it—and hovered in front of me. "I bring you news from Feddrah-Dahns." He spoke in Melosealfôr, the high language of the Cryptos, used also by Moon witches such as myself.

Mistletoe was about twelve inches tall, and he was nearly translucent, with flecks of light sparkling through his body. In addition to the hat, he wore a pair of burlap trousers tied with a belt made of ivy vine, and he had a brown leather bag slung over his shoulder.

Unlike the pixies we had fought earlier, Mistletoe was a good sort, and he was also the messenger of the crown prince of the Dahns Unicorns.

"It's been far too long since we heard from you and Feddrah! How are you faring?" I held out my hand and he flew down to settle on it. I brought him down to my knee and he made himself at home.

"As I said, Lady Camille, I have a message for you."

I frowned. "Feddrah-Dahns knows I'm here in the realm of the Elder Fae? And please, speak in the common tongue—Delilah doesn't know Melosealfôr." If the unicorn prince knew where I was, that begged the question: Who else had that information, and was I in danger?

"He does. Word travels fast and rumors, still faster."

"Damned Raven Mother. *Why* did she open her big mouth? She knows how important this trip is." I let out an exasperated sigh. Aeval sure knew how to pick our traveling companions.

But Mistletoe shook his head, his wings fluttering with the movement. "No, it was not her. She has been absent from Darkynwyrd for several weeks. The Black Unicorn summoned Feddrah-Dahns to the woodland yesterday. The rumors are thick, but we haven't been able to track their source yet. We have scouts looking into matters."

"If it wasn't Raven Mother, then there has to be a leak in Talamh Lonrach Oll, or in the Grove of the Moon Mother. Because *I* didn't even know I'd be making this trip until a couple days ago." I glanced over at Delilah and she shook her head. "Anyway, what news do you bring?"

"Feddrah-Dahns is concerned. With Elqaneve devastated, and the war spreading, he wanted to make this journey himself, but he is needed in Dahnsburg. The king has put him in charge of coordinating war efforts on behalf of all the Cryptos volunteering for service." The pixie scowled. "Telazhar . . . his name is as good a curse."

"I'm glad to hear your master is safe. We miss him." The unicorn might not be as stern as his father, King Uppala-Dahns, but he was noble and honest, and funny in his own way.

"Feddrah-Dahns bade me tell you this: There is reason to believe that danger heads your way. Questions have been asked around Dahnsburg about you . . . and about the Black Unicorn horn. We fear someone means to steal the horn. The prince asked me to find you and caution you to watch your back."

I sucked in a deep breath, once again regretting that I'd ever been gifted with the horn and hide. It made me a walking target and right now I had a big red bull's-eye painted on my back.

But if Raven Mother hadn't been at the roots of the rumors, then who? Bran? But if Bran wanted the horn, he wouldn't be spreading rumors around that I had it. He'd just find a way to take it, and being the son of an Elemental, I wouldn't be able to stop him. No, there had to be something else . . .

"Thank the prince for me. I wish I had some answer to all this. Wait, maybe you know something." I hesitated, not wanting to spread more rumors myself but maybe . . . just maybe . . .

"If I can be of service, you have only to ask." For a pixie, Mistletoe was incredibly polite. I wondered again, just how he'd gotten his job and why he was so unlike the rest of his race. He could be an annoying little twit, but he came through when it counted.

I glanced around again, to make certain none of Morgaine's crew was nearby. Delilah noticed and skirted the area, then returned.

"We're alone."

"Thanks. Mistletoe, if you don't know the answer, will you ask Feddrah-Dahns for me? But don't tell anybody else what I've asked, please. There's a lot riding on this."

He held up his hand. "I swear by my wings. What do you want to know?"

"Bran—Raven Mother's son. What can you tell me about him? Do you know what secrets he might be holding over Morgaine's head as blackmail? Do they have any history together other than out at Talamh Lonrach Oll? I'm stuck in the middle of what seems to be a conflict between the two."

Mistletoe let out a low whistle. "When you ask a question, you ask a question all right." He shifted, crossing his right leg over his left. The movement tickled me—he was so light that it felt like a butterfly was on my knee.

"Some history you might not know and that I have a feeling Morgaine might choose to keep you from knowing. When she was young, she crossed over to Otherworld for a time. She met Bran, who was younger than he is now, but still an adult. He wanted her. She didn't want him. She was in love with Arturo."

"Where did Arturo come from? He's human, isn't he? He drank the Nectar of Life, didn't he?"

Mistletoe stared at me. "You don't know who he is?"

I glanced at Delilah, who shrugged. "Not really."

"He is the Wounded King. He came out from the mists of Avalon with Morgaine after she sequestered him there to heal." Mistletoe slapped his knee. "You really aren't up on your history, are you?"

"History of Otherworld, yes—Earthside, not so much." And then I realized what he was saying. "Arturo is . . . *Arthur*? As in *King Arthur*? There really was a King Arthur? You've got to be kidding me! Why doesn't he remember who he is?" And then, another realization. "The Nectar of Life. She fed him the Nectar of Life and over the centuries, he's forgotten. Like Tam Lin."

Mistletoe nodded. "He was gravely wounded, and his son saved him. The stories and poems miss the mark. They were written long after the fact, like so much of history. Morgaine spirited him away when he was dying, but Avalon is a tricky place, and it's easy to lose memory there if you are of human origin."

"And Morgaine is half-Fae so she wouldn't have that problem. Nor would she have the same problem taking the Nectar of Life. Fae side wins out there. Always has." Just like it would win out when Delilah and I made the choice to drink. Our mother's blood would not cause a problem because of our father's heritage.

"Precisely." Mistletoe shifted again, his wings fluttering in the light breeze that had cropped up. The temperature was dropping again and I shivered under my cloak, wishing I'd brought my blanket.

"So she brought Arturo to Otherworld? Mordred, too?"

Delilah interrupted, though. "Wait—Mordred. He's Arturo's son? Was he the one who tried to kill Arthur?"

"Yes, and no. He is Arturo's son, but he did not try to kill him. That part of the story is wrong. In fact, Mordred saved his father's life by killing the man who went up against him. Lancelot and Arthur fought over Gwenyfar. She was married off to Arthur without her permission. She and Lancelot were already in love. They got it on, were caught, and the result was a bloody nightmare of a battle. Mordred wanted his father's throne, yes, but he loves Arthur, regardless of all his hunger for power."

"So what does that have to do with Bran?"

"Mordred noticed Bran's attraction to Morgaine while they were in Otherworld. She wasn't interested. Bran pushed. Mordred got pissed off and he swore that if Bran didn't back off, he'd fight him."

"Well, that would have been suicide, fighting an Elemental." Elementals were immortal—the only *true* Immortals. They couldn't die, not permanently. Even the Black Unicorn had been reborn, but he was like the phoenix.

"Then what could Bran be holding over Morgaine?"

"That, I do not know. I'm simply telling you what I know of their history. If it can give you an insight, then I'm hoping I have helped."

Mistletoe paused, then added, "I can tell you this: Raven Mother fears her son. I don't know why, but after you sacrificed her consort, Lady Camille, Raven Mother threw Bran out of Darkynwyrd for a period of time. He had barely returned home when he was called over Earthside. And that is all I know—" He stopped as a noise rustled the bushes behind us.

I pressed my fingers to my lips and nodded to the nearest fern. Mistletoe immediately dove for cover. The next moment, Mordred was standing there, staring at Delilah and me.

"Are you quite all right?" Animosity oozed from every pore.

"Fine. Thank you." I wasn't about to offer him an explanation. What Delilah and I were talking about was none of his business. I sat there, cold but unwilling to move because he so obviously was waiting for us to stand up and follow him back to the camp.

After a moment, he let out a snort. "You should sleep. Morning will come early and my aunt says the going will be rough. We have a mountain to climb. I should think you want all your strength about you."

I glanced at Delilah. He wasn't going to leave without us, and he did have a point. "True that. We'll be along in a moment."

As Mordred turned, I slid my hand behind me and wiggled my fingers in the direction of Mistletoe's fern. A quick poke in my backside told me he'd seen me and was saying good-bye in the only way he could without being noticed.

As we returned to the campsite, I glanced over at Arturo's sleeping form. So we had a king in our midst. A king who had forgotten his name. The *Wounded King*, at that.

A sudden sadness swept over me. The great humans of history died so quickly. Or, if they managed to get hold of the Nectar of Life, it seemed to stretch them beyond their ability to retain their sense of self.

Which made me wonder . . . what would happen to Chase? He'd been given a thousand more years to live. It had been that or let him die. Now, he was wrestling with the concept of a life in which everyone he knew—among the FBH community—would be dead long before him.

Add to that, the Nectar of Life had brought to the surface some latent psychic powers and that he had recently found out he had a little sprinkling of elf in his far distant past, and he must feel like he was on a roller coaster. Would Sharah and his daughter be able to keep him from fading like Arturo or Tam Lin? Would Chase manage to cling to who he was?

All these thoughts raced through my mind as I stared at the sleeping lord who followed Morgaine like a lapdog. He was Mordred's father, but did he even remember that? Did he remember his battle with Lancelot? Did he remember Gwenyfar? She must have been part Fae herself. Did he remember leading his people? Or was it all lost in the fog of centuries?

Delilah touched me on the shoulder and I looked up to

see Mordred eyeing me. He had followed my gaze, and now was looking at me with speculation in his eyes. I stared at him, challenging him to ask.

But then a strange thing happened. A shadow crossed his face and his expression fell into sorrow. And for the first time, the cockiness and brashness seemed to fall away, and he wiped his sleeve across his eyes and turned away.

I watched him as he returned to his bed. Mistletoe had given us so much to think about. Including the fact that there might be sorcerers after me—or bounty hunters. If rumors were filtering through the streets that I was here, and if someone had leaked the fact that I had one of the horns, then they might be on our heels even now.

Morio was sitting up, on a fallen log. "I'm taking watch. Tanne will take second. I don't trust that lot while we're all sleeping." He kept his voice low, but even so I saw Mordred cast a look our way before pulling his blanket tightly around his shoulders and rolling over.

I nodded, wanting to tell him what we'd learned from Mistletoe, but this wasn't the place. However, in lieu of that conversation, I settled for saying, "Good idea. We may have someone on our trail, looking for my . . . toy." I motioned toward my pocket. His gaze flickered and he nodded. "Will tell you more later, but it looks like someone planted a trail of breadcrumbs."

"Understood. Go to sleep. I'll keep watch in my demonic form. The best defense is a good offense." And with that, he stood and shifted into his demonic form. The transformation always sent me into an awestruck silence—it was like watching someone you loved grow into a monster who could tear you limb from limb. I felt the same way when Smoky changed into his dragon form. They became so much *more* . . .

As Delilah and I once again curled up on the ground, wrapping ourselves in our blankets, the silence of the night descended. I closed my eyes, trying not to think about how far away from home we were, or what might wait out in the darkness to come after us. We had survived the devastation of Elqaneve. Surely we could make it through the next few days.

Chapter 13

꧁ ✦ ꧂

By the time I woke up, it was morning and I felt just as tired—if not more—than when I'd laid down. I sat up, blinking. My body ached from the cold ground, and I felt like I'd been out on the astral but couldn't remember anything. But I knew I wasn't used to sleeping on the hard dirt, exposed to the cold, and that, plus being in a strange realm, was enough to interfere with a good night's sleep. As I rolled to a sitting position, I let out a groan at a stitch that caught my side.

Morio, who was just waking up, squinted and rolled over.

Delilah had been setting out food for our breakfast, and now she hurried over. "You all right?"

I winced. "Just a slight muscle spasm. I think the cold got into me."

Tanne, who was examining a nearby bush, reached out to offer me a hand up. I gratefully accepted his help and he pulled me to my feet. Delilah glanced over at Morgaine's side of the camp. Mordred and Bran were nowhere to be seen, but our cousin was staring at me. She turned, though, back to Arturo, as he handed her something to eat.

I gazed at the sky. Something was coming. I could feel it

in my bones and whatever it was made me both melancholy and hesitant. I brushed my hand across my eyes, feeling like I wanted to cry, but I didn't know why.

"What's wrong? Camille, are you all right?" Morio sounded worried, which just irritated me even more. Tanne lightly kissed my hand—pure politeness—and returned to examining the shrub.

"Sorry, I just feel short-tempered, and I don't like sleeping outside. I have a premonition, but I can't for the life of me tell you what's up. I have a feeling . . ." But just as an elusive image crossed my thoughts, it was gone again. I shook my head. "I think I can feel the Hunt rising."

"That means full moon isn't far away. Morio, when I change, you'll need to corral me in because Camille will be off on the Hunt." Delilah frowned. "Why the hell didn't they wait until afterward to send us?"

"Apparently the Fae Queens have their reasons, but yes, I wish they'd fucking tell us." I paused, letting my words sink in.

"Well, there's not much we can do now." Morio motioned to the pack. "We need to eat. Whatever is nagging at you will have to wait."

Delilah followed me over to a deadfall that was near where we had slept and sat beside me, handing me a sandwich and a bottle of water. I bit into the peanut butter and jelly, scarcely able to taste it.

"Do you want to talk? Maybe we can figure out what's bothering you." For once, someone else was asking the hard questions. I was usually the one reaching out.

I let out a long sigh, then took another bite of sandwich. It was a little stale but it was food, and right now, hunger won out over taste. "Everything just seems so mired in layer after layer of subterfuge. I don't know who to trust anymore. This trip, Morgaine has been oddly . . . sane? I find myself trusting her lead and that, alone, scares the hell out of me."

"Yeah, but look who else is along for the ride. Morgaine is the sanest of that bunch of nut jobs." She handed me the water.

I took a long swig to wash down the crumbs of my

sandwich. "I'm having a hard time reconciling what we were taught about the Great Divide with what we're finding out now. We've got demons over Earthside and a demon's pet over in Otherworld. Add to that, Yvarr and his kind emerging from the shadows." Pausing, I mused over a question that had been needling me. "Who do you think is worse, Telazhar or Shadow Wing?"

"Shadow Wing, because he's orchestrating it all." Delilah leaned forward, wiping the crumbs off her hands onto her jeans. "Two years ago . . . even a year ago, I would have had trouble facing all this. I've changed, you know? And Queen Asteria's death changed me even more. It was the first time I had to escort someone I loved through the veils. I think it hardened me."

I shook my head. "No, it didn't harden you. You toughened up, and lost what was left of that naïve little girl, but it didn't make you hard. You're still our Kitten. You still love your catnip mice and fleece toys and playing with string, and for that, I'm grateful." I leaned against her shoulder. "Thank you for coming with me. I don't think I could have dealt with Morgaine and her crew without at least one of my sisters here."

Delilah smiled and wrapped her arm around my shoulders. "We've *all* changed, Camille. You're tougher than you were, and stronger. We're all growing into whatever the future is holding for us, but we'll *always* be sisters, and we'll always be there for one another."

I nodded, wiping a thin veil of mist from my eyes. "Damn it, I don't need to be getting all sentimental here. We have a Druid to find." I let out a long sigh. "I guess we'd better get moving. I just wish I felt less like a walking target."

"Safety doesn't exist in our world anymore. And you know what? I don't know if it ever did." She took my hand, swinging it as we walked back to camp.

"Safety is an illusion." I picked up my blanket and rolled it up, noticing that Bran and Mordred had returned. "You can die in your bed if the ceiling caves in. Or the shower, or the garden . . ." The premonition still hovered in the back of my mind, but I was able to push it back for now. Because whatever it was, I knew it would find us sooner rather than later.

"Are you ready?" Morgaine approached. "We should head out. We've got a hard day's walking ahead of us."

I nodded. "We're just about packed up. Five minutes and we'll be set." I hadn't wanted to bring it up, but it occurred to me that the fact that someone might be following me would also put our mission in danger. I decided that I had to tell her. "I need to talk to you alone, but I want your word—on your honor—you won't mention this to Bran or Mordred or Arturo unless it becomes absolutely necessary."

She gave me a puzzled look. "All right. Come, they won't hear us over here."

We sequestered ourselves below a large cedar tree, and there, I told her the bare bones. I didn't tell her how I knew, but only that I'd heard rumors were filtering around that I was in the realm of the Elder Fae with the unicorn horn.

Her eyes glistened. Of course she knew I had the horn, but as far as I remembered, she'd never seen it, and I didn't fancy showing her now. Morgaine craved power. The horn promised far too much of that for someone with her greed.

But she surprised me—she didn't even ask to see it. "Then we must be even more cautious. If the Elder Fae catch wind of it, then we're in far more danger than anybody tracking you."

"True, that. Yannie Fin Diver sensed it and came after me. We barely escaped from him. But . . . there are those closer who wouldn't mind having this artifact." I was talking about Bran, but Morgaine's nostrils flared and she looked like I'd insulted her.

"Don't worry yourself. I'm not going to steal your toy from you, girl. I may envy you, and I find your lack of foresight distressing, but I will never steal what is rightfully yours. I have, at least, *that* much honor." The words rang true, even with the speculative look she gave me.

Deciding that, given the confrontation between Morgaine and Bran, she might prove more ally than hindrance, I decided to set her straight. "I wasn't talking about you. Bran envies me. He is angry that his father has never seen fit to gift him with the horn and the hide."

Morgaine let out a loud snort. "The Black Beast knows what he's doing. Bran, given one of the horns? We would all regret that mistake. Do not trust him. Do not believe him. He twists words, uses truth as a weapon, and is not above using secrets as fodder for blackmail."

I started to ask her what he had on her, but then decided it was neither the time nor the place. I didn't want to push her buttons, especially when we were forging an uneasy truce.

"I don't think there's much danger of me trusting him any farther than I can throw him. We'd better get back. I just wanted to warn you." And with that, we returned for the others, and headed out on the path.

We'd walked for a good three hours along the never-ending woodland, keenly aware of every sound and movement that rustled from within the forest. Every time we flushed a bird out of the bushes, one of us jumped. By the time we came to another open field, I was happy to leave the forest behind. Too many chances for ambush, too many places for the enemy to hide.

Bran had kept mostly to himself, which was a blessing. Better he ignore us than shower us with his dubious attention. Mostly, I kept close to Morgaine and Morio. At one point, I realized that I was traveling with three people whose names started with *M-o-r*. Laughing aloud, I startled the others.

"Something funny?" Morio grinned at me.

I cleared my throat, realizing that if I told him what I was thinking, it would sound totally lame. "Just my mind wandering off on its own."

The sky was rippling with the faint glow of sunlight behind the clouds. We had started off at the first hint of dawn. Now, the breaking light showed us the vast swath of grassland that we were in. But the grass was darker here, and the land felt more menacing. Maybe it was that we were farther into the realm of Fae, or just that I was noticing the energy more.

I paused, motioning for the others to stop and closed my

eyes. There was something on the wind. Something was coming our way. I reached out to see if I could discover what it was.

Cloaked in a swarm of bees and the stinging of wasps, it was big and vicious. Hive mentality ruled, and the over-mind was looking for an outlet for its anger. Whatever it was, it had been riled up and was out to vent its irritation on somebody.

"We've got company coming. I think it's a swarm . . . and yet . . . more. There's a cunning intelligence behind what-ever it is. One creature with many bodies. Something that can swarm and sting."

Morgaine raised her hands and closed her eyes. A moment later, she nodded. "You're right, and it's coming in fast."

Tanne pushed forward. "I've dealt with creatures like this in the Black Forest. They're deadly, and you're right that they have a hive mind."

Lovely. Just what we needed. But we still weren't sure exactly what we were dealing with. Hornets? Bees? Some other insect? While it was well-known that animals swarm-ing together exhibited much more complex behavior than individuals, this was something else.

"How do we fight this? Is there a way to disrupt the magic that brought them together as a creature?" If we could scat-ter them, maybe we'd have a better chance of avoiding a mass attack.

Tanne frowned. "Well, if they've been magically bound together, my Spell of Unraveling might work. I can't guaran-tee it, of course. But the trouble is, I need to be close to the creature to cast it. And if the spell doesn't work, I'll be prime target for its attack. I'm not sure I want that dubious honor."

"We need a giant can of Raid." Delilah shaded her eyes as she walked to the edge of the path. "I can't see anything, but that means squat."

"Fire." Bran stepped up beside her. "Fire will always drop a hive. The smoke. But we'll have to build a damn big one, and lure that thing into it. Either that or we resort to carrying torches till we're well away from it."

"Fire isn't such a bad idea, actually." I would have been happier if anybody but Bran had thought of it, but now was not the time to begrudge the message, regardless of how much I disliked the messenger.

"We need to move fast," Morgaine said. "I can feel the buzzing in my bones and there are tens of thousands of . . . wasps . . . yes—wasps—in the hive-monster."

"Grab whatever you can that will burn. Does anybody have any magic that produces flame?" I had the firebombs I'd stolen from Roz, but it seemed smarter to keep them for later, if somebody else could ignite the fire. Magical flame burned hotter than regular fire and worked against enchanted creatures better.

Tanne shook his head. "Not me. I don't work with the element much."

Morgaine and Bran both dissented, too. Mordred didn't even open his mouth and I realized that, although he was part Fae, he didn't work with magic like his aunt. He was more pretty-boy brawn.

Delilah pulled out a lighter. "I guess we go with a BIC."

Firebombs it was, then.

"No, I've got something. I was planning on keeping it in reserve, but I think we need it now. Gather all the kindling you can." I stopped, shading my eyes. "There's the creature!"

What had seemed to be a shadow on the horizon was now rapidly approaching. From where we stood, it looked like it was a swirling mass of color, but was actually tens of thousands of wasps creating the bipedal form.

That spurred everybody on. Mordred, Morio, and Bran quickly began gathering all the sticks and branches they could find. "We need dry wood or it won't burn!" Mordred said.

"Not to worry. What I have will burn even damp foliage. Just gather as much wood as you possibly can. We need to lure it near. When it's close enough to get caught in the smoke, I'll light the fire. Which means we need bait."

"I'll volunteer." Tanne moved out in front. "I'm fast enough to dodge it, as long as you can slow it down."

I shrugged off my pack and opened it, digging through.

Delilah knelt beside me, her voice low. "Are you going to use the Unicorn Horn?"

"No," I murmured. "I'm keeping that under strict wraps unless we absolutely have to use it. Before we left, I borrowed a few things from Roz." I grinned at her as I held out two of the firebombs. "I think two should do it, don't you? Or maybe I should get out a third just in case."

She stared at the reddish orbs in my hand, then peeked in my pack to see the other bombs I had tucked in there. "Good gods, you really did rifle through his stash, didn't you? He's going to be pissed."

"Too bad. He was gone, so I couldn't ask him. He never wants to let me play with his toys anyway." Grinning at her, I closed my pack again. "Now, how does he ignite them?"

"I think he just tosses them and they explode on impact. Which means you shouldn't get too close to the pile of brush. Can you aim right?" She shrugged at my stare. "Hey, I know you aren't that athletic. Even though you've been hitting the gym, your aim with a ball was never accurate. I remember— you gave me a black eye once."

I groaned. She *would* remember that. I hadn't meant to hurt her, but when we had been playing stickball, I'd ended up landing her a good one on her right eye. Father had lit into me for that, but it wasn't my fault. Truth was, I *wasn't* particularly good with throwing things, let alone a bomb that needed to land in a precise location. And I needed to just accept that fact.

Reluctantly, I handed them over. "Fine, but I never get to play with the cool stuff." Grumbling, I watched as she cautiously pocketed them.

The men had built quite the pile of combustibles. The creature was speeding up, oozing fury and the desire to attack. Whatever had pissed this thing off had done a damned good job of it.

By now, we could see it clearly and the swarming mass of wasps was a terrible sight. My skin crawled. Swarms always bothered me, and it seemed there were a number of Elder Fae who worked with them. The spider-Fae who had captured Chase had a swarm of horrible critters that covered her house.

Tanne calmly walked toward the creature. He paused till it noticed him, then, as it made a beeline for him, he began to back up quickly toward the impromptu bonfire-in-waiting. The men had been able to gather quite a few branches from the forest, and had piled the mound of brush and sticks a good five feet high.

Delilah motioned for Morgaine and Arturo to back up. Mordred and Bran took a clue and also moved to the side.

As Tanne neared the brush pile, he suddenly dove to the side as the hive-monster sped up, charging for him. The sound of the buzzing made my skin crawl and I shuddered, forcing myself to hold my ground.

Up close, the creature was a nightmare of whirling, buzzing wasps. They formed the vague shape of a giant, seven feet tall at least. A few of the insects broke off from the hive, probably reconnaissance, scouting ahead for new prey. Wasps were carnivorous, which told me that the hive-monster most likely ate its kills.

As Tanne dove to the side, Delilah tossed the first fire-bomb into the bonfire. It exploded on impact, and the branches burst into flame. The hive-monster began to rampage—a number of wasps shooting out from the thick of it. Delilah threw another bomb on the flames and the fire flared, smoke pouring out over the creature. She tossed the third one for good measure and the resulting explosion released a massive plume of smoke.

Tanne stepped forward, not close enough to be a target, but close enough to start singing what I now recognized as the Spell of Unraveling.

The wasps raged. For the most part, they seemed to be trapped within the construct of the magical body. But, as Tanne's spell began to work, the framework holding the wasps together dissipated. The cluster began to separate, chaotic masses of the insects swarming off. Several of the clumps fell to the ground, the smoke killing them. Still others scattered, the wasps drunkenly careening toward the forest.

We backed away. If we could get out of here without being stung, so much the better. Skirting the scene slowly but steadily, after a few minutes we were far enough away to chance stopping for a look back.

The fire was still burning brightly but we couldn't see any sign of the massive hive. Whatever magic had went into keeping the wasps together was gone, destroyed by the smoke and the spell.

"Good luck, you little freaks." Even though I hated wasps—they were mean suckers—they deserved to be free, answering to their queen, not whoever had enslaved them.

Another ten minutes and there was no sign of any wasps. Hopefully, they had a happier future ahead, and we'd gotten off easy. If I hadn't brought those firebombs, this could have gone drastically wrong. That many stings—if they'd attacked us—could easily kill us. And hitting a wasp with a sword or a dagger? Not so effective.

"We lucked out on that one." I stared back along the path. "We may not be so fortunate in the future."

"Was that one of the Elder Fae?" Delilah asked.

I shook my head. "No, it was a golem, made of wasps. So much could have gone wrong."

"Which leads us to the question: Who created it? And are they near here?" Morio glanced around, as if expecting to see the creator of the insect-creature standing near a tree or ahead on the road. But the grassland around us looked empty.

"I have no idea, but I hope not." I shaded my eyes, staring into the distance. The clouds were coming in thicker now.

"I wish there were a way to reach our destination without traveling on the open path. We just set ourselves up as a target that way." Morio turned to Morgaine. "Is there a back route?"

She shook her head. "It won't matter for long. Another few miles and we turn off the path, toward the foothills. We'll reach them by early afternoon, and then we start to climb. From there, we'll be out of sight or mind of anybody walking down the main drag. I hope you brought sturdy shoes. You're going to need them."

I'd worn my boots from when I lived in Otherworld—small heels, knee-high leather that resisted bites, scrapes, or scratches. While I wore a skirt and a leather bustier over a spidersilk shirt, everything was strong and warm. I was about as geared up as I was going to get.

A glance at the sky showed we were halfway till noon, with heavy clouds coming in from the east. We were headed north, and the wind was hitting us at an angle.

"How steep are the Veiled Mountains?" I hated heights but had managed to subjugate my fear into some form of submission. At least I was able to handle looking down without my stomach lurching.

"The cave we're headed to is about halfway up the hill, hidden within a narrow passage. The rocks on either side are dangerous. The potential for landslides along the way is pretty high, so be ready to jump out of the way—if you can. They form a narrow channel with little in the way of protection on either side."

For someone who had been searching for the Merlin for years, Morgaine seemed to have an intimate knowledge on how to find him.

She must have read into my expression, because she let out a bark of laughter. "Don't be so surprised. I have known *where* to look for centuries. It was a portal to the realm of the Elder Fae that has eluded me. Derisa and Aeval have provided the gateway in."

And with that, we moved out. It took us about an hour more on the path before we reached an area where a creek cut across the trail. A small footbridge crossed the stream, but as soon as we were on the other side of it, Morgaine held up her hand.

"Here we go off trail, to the east." She glanced at the sky. "The storm is moving down from the mountains and we will be headed directly into it."

Overhead, the clouds were gathering, dark and filled with moisture. The temperature had already dropped at least ten degrees and the wind was rising, whipping the grass as it billowed over the plains, setting up a rippling ocean of green.

I closed my eyes. The crackling off the clouds was so vibrant I could almost reach out and touch it. If I summoned the Moon Mother's power here, now, the lightning would be at my beck and call. The Moon Mother controlled the lightning and storms, as much as any god of thunder, even as she controlled the vivid halo that bled off the silver moon and the dark rings of the black moon.

"We should press on as soon as possible. The storm is dangerous—I can feel it coming in, with snow and sleet in its wake." Morgaine shaded her eyes, staring to the east.

"We're walking right into it. There's no way to go around?"

Morgaine glanced to the left, then right. Finally, she shook her head. "No. We cannot find the Merlin without journeying through the ravines into the mountains. As I said, the path is buttressed on both sides by jagged rockfall. We have to travel straight into the face of the storm. I'm sorry." And for once, she truly did sound sorry. She turned to face Delilah and me. "I know what you went through over in Otherworld, with the sentient storm. I am not heartless, but we have no choice."

I gripped my staff. "Then let's move out before it gets worse."

Waiting would only make it worse. And frankly, I didn't need any more tension and stress right now—I'd reached my quota some time back. I tied my hair back into a ponytail to keep the wind from whipping it around my face. Morio did the same, and Bran also. Mordred followed suit. Morgaine pushed her locks back, covering her head with her hood and fastening it firmly beneath her chin.

"Are we ready?" She gave us each a long look and we nodded in turn. "Then off we go." She stepped off the path, onto the grass, with Morio and I by her side. The long sweeping blades were knee high and with the wind whistling through them, they were as hard to navigate as water, and they could be as sharp. Almost immediately, a blade whipped against my hand, slicing me like a paper cut.

Sucking the side of my thumb where the blade had left a long, red weal, I tried to focus on keeping my footing. The grass hid a multitude of bumps and stones and burrows, so that within minutes, we were all silent, focused on making it through the plain without any major accidents. The wind picked up again, and now it was a steady resistance, forcing us to work even harder.

On we moved toward the foothills, which jutted out of the

ground. Atop their peaks, towering crags and spires of stone thrust into the sky. A trickle of moisture began to fall—first a light mist, and then sleet. I pulled my hood up and shrugged my cloak more tightly around my shoulders.

Morio leaned close to me. "How are you doing?"

"Fine. Just chilled and hoping we make it there without any problems."

Delilah sped her pace till she was right beside us. "Is it all grassland like this until we reach the mountains?"

Morgaine's eye twitched. "Unfortunately, we will shortly be coming to a boggy area. In fact, you should start taking more care now, because quicksand can appear without warning, hidden in the depths of the grass, and it's not that easy to spot the marshy areas given the darkness of the sky."

"Quicksand." Delilah grimaced. "I remember being caught in quicksand and it was in this realm that it happened." She tapped me on the shoulder. "Remember when we attracted Yannie Fin Diver's notice and I got caught in the bog?"

"All too well."

"Just be careful, since you're in the front row."

"I will." I began to use my staff to probe every few steps as we went along. We were about an hour or so from the mountains when the tip of my staff hit a soggy patch, sinking a good three feet before it rested on the bottom. I immediately stopped.

Beside me, Morgaine and Morio halted quickly. I glanced over at Morgaine, and she used her own staff to prod the ground in front. Bog. Morio used his blade. More bog.

"Okay, so where do we go from here?" I started to ask, but a noise put an end to that, as a group of creatures began to rise from the swamp ahead of us. They were covered in detritus and streaming with mud that—once it hit the air—developed a nasty odor, and they didn't look friendly.

Chapter 14

❧〜❧

"Mud men." Mordred whispered behind us. "They are dangerous—think kelpies of a vastly uglier nature, except they aren't independent. Like the hive-monster, all of the mud men are simply arms of the parent. They do their best to drag you into their bog with them, where the parent creature will absorb you."

That didn't sound like fun at all. A quick count told me there were about a dozen of them on the way. "What are their attacks?"

Mordred didn't bother with pettiness, thank gods. He answered quickly and decisively. "They're strong. They can drown you with their kiss—they'll fill your lungs with mud that they vomit into your mouth."

"Oh, no they won't!" Delilah held up her dagger. "Are they Fae, or enchanted like the wasps?"

Mordred glanced at her. "Fae. The parent creature is sentient. The mud men aren't enslaved beings. Think of them like tentacles. You can cut them off but they'll regenerate. And bog creatures are smart, and they're always hungry."

I wondered how Mordred knew so much about this thing,

but decided it wasn't the best time to ask. "How do you kill them? *It?*"

"The creature should be around seven feet deep and three feet wide," Tanne spoke up. At my look, he winked. "I've fought one or two of these in my lifetime. Anyway, if you are pulled into the creature—the bog—there's a heart the size of a bowling ball inside. You have to stab the heart to destroy it. There's not much else that will do any damage."

I stared at the mud men. "What about them? How do we fight them off?"

"If you cut them up enough, they will return to the bog creature and reform. But at least you'll be free of them while they're out of the way. The only ways the creature itself can harm you is either through the mud men, or if you get dragged in or fall into the bog." Tanne frowned. "So it's really a matter of staving off the branches, so to speak, while you destroy the root. Somebody has to rope up and go in there."

The mud men were advancing. I grimaced. No way in hell was I about to volunteer for the job. Swimming in mud? *Not* my strong suit. I'd end up putting everybody else in danger and I knew it.

Delilah let out a sigh. "I've been in quicksand before. I can deal with mud. Especially if there's a bottom to the pit."

Tanne said, "I've never heard of one being more than eight feet deep. They can't move, so they lie in wait for their victims. But we'd better get to work on these mud men before they get too close. Remember: they can drown you with their kiss—don't let them grapple you."

Delilah pulled me aside. "While the others keep the mud men busy, you and Morgaine tie a rope around me. You're both strong enough to pull me back up." She shrugged off her backpack and her coat, then started to strip while I grabbed a length of rope out of my pack. We'd learned never to leave home on a mission without some sort of rope. If we didn't have any, that would guarantee our need for it.

She was standing there, shivering in her underwear. "No way in hell am I letting that thing get my clothes filthy."

"Makes sense." I quickly tied it in a secure bowline around

her waist. If we'd had more time, I would have fashioned a harness, but this would have to do.

We skirted around the side of the mud men, who were intent on the men. Tapping our way along a narrow patch of grass, we wound through the marsh, until we located the actual bog monster. Unlike normal areas of marsh—patchy water spots along the thick grass—the bog monster actually *looked* like a bog monster. Or, rather, a big patch o' mud smack in the middle of the wet grassy wasteland, looking gray and oozy and . . . *oh fuck*.

Two more mud men emerged from the pit o' doom, and they were focused on us. The bog monster must have sensed us approach. Of course, that made sense—it could probably feel our footsteps vibrating through the ground. Grumbling, I decided to see if magic could disrupt the walking mud-pies.

I sucked in a deep breath and raised my arms. As the energy of the storm began to channel into my body, the mud men suddenly stopped, turned, and hightailed it as fast as they could move back to the bog.

"What the hell . . ." I stared after them, all amped up with nobody to blast.

Morgaine shook her head. "Can you feel it? The storm is rising."

"Feel what?" But I stopped and listened to the currents of energy. She was right. Entangled among the prickles and tingles of the energy I was channeling, something huge was sweeping across the bog.

"Everything's gone silent." Delilah glanced around. "Not a bird chirping, nothing—just the sound of the wind."

I closed my eyes. She was right. The thriving marshland, the birds and insects, were now still as death. The only noise we could hear was the whipping wind.

"Look." Tanne pointed to the bog creature. It was huddling, tendrils of mud pulling grass in around its edges to try and hide. That alone scared me more than anything else. If the bog monster was afraid of whatever was coming . . . I left the thought unfinished as my stomach flipped.

Trying to rein in the energy I'd gathered, I realized that it was too late to shake it off—I was abuzz with the lightning. I moved back, attempting to focus on keeping my footing and not slipping off the grassy strip between the bog creature and the watery marsh. I turned, Morgaine and Delilah following me, trying to safely navigate over to Morio and the others.

Morio reached out but I shook my head. If he touched me, I'd shock him—I wouldn't be able to help it, so much static had built up in my body. I needed to release it, needed to send it somewhere, but I was afraid if I just shot off an energy blast in some random direction, it would catch the attention of whatever it was that was barreling toward us.

Maybe it wouldn't matter—chances are, it knew we were here anyway. But then again, if it was so huge, maybe it would pass us by without blinking. I was beginning to panic, unable to think. My hands began to shake.

Delilah let out a whimper, and before I could do anything, she shifted into her panther form, growling toward the open space in front of us. Morgaine jumped as Delilah transformed, backing away from her with wide eyes. Mordred and Arturo hurried to flank her, but then, they, too, slowly turned toward the vast, open swamp and stared, glassy-eyed.

Tanne tapped me on the shoulder. "Camille, Camille— come here." He grimaced as a spark from my aura lashed out at him, burning his fingers. "Crap! I'm sorry."

"Sorry, sorry—can't help it." I glanced at Morio. "Watch Delilah." Morio shifted into his demonic form at that moment, nodding to me.

Tanne and I backed up to stand next to Bran, who was staring ahead without any fear on his face. Wary, yes, but not afraid. I wanted to know why, but Tanne was vying for my attention.

"What is it?" I swung around to the woodland Fae.

"Look!" He pointed toward the marsh. A flurry had sprung up, covering grass and bog alike. The sudden storm was fierce, and it felt driven by whatever force was headed our way.

"Holy hell and snow on a shingle."

"I should have known. The storm from the east, and it

being winter. I know what's coming our way." Tanne turned his wide, glacial gaze on me. "It's Beira. The Cailleach."

Oh, fuck. He was right. I closed my eyes and reached out. Sure enough, the energy coming toward us was so powerful, so forceful, it could only be a god. Or, in this case, an Elemental Lord. *Lady*, if you wanted to be gender-specific.

"Beira. Well, this is going to be unpleasant." Bran swallowed, his expression shifting as the storm grew fiercer. Elementals could go up against the gods and win. The gods were finite. But Bran was a lesser Elemental Lord, while Beira was far more powerful.

Beira was queen of winter, an avatar of the snow and ice, embodied in form and thought. She was also the mother of the *bean nighe*, the washer-women. She was the original Washer at the Ford. As such, her very appearance was a portent of doom.

I held my breath, hoping she'd pass by. If she stopped to pull out her tartan and washed it in the water where we could see, then one of us was in trouble. Her cloth remained plaid from Imbolc—February second—until she washed it on Samhain Eve—October thirty-first—when it turned white. It was then that Beira ushered in the winter months. But she would also wash it to indicate impending death.

And we'd had quite enough death for the present, thank you very much.

Morio had hold of Delilah's collar and at his yank, she slunk to his side, still growling, but obeying his subtle order. Morgaine backed up to stand beside me. Arturo and Mordred followed her.

"You know who that is, don't you?" Her eyes were wide.

I nodded. "Beira, the mother of the *bean nighe*."

"Yes. She is wily and dangerous and she bears no mercy, child, so watch your tongue and pray she doesn't ask you any questions." And then, Morgaine did something totally out of character: She wrapped her arm around my waist and leaned against me. "Aeval will have my head if you're hurt or worse on this trip. She threatened to burn me to a crisp if anything happens to you, so be cautious."

So Aeval had made Morgaine responsible for my safety?

That was why she had resisted going in the inn—she'd known that it would be dangerous and didn't want to risk my neck. Whatever Bran was holding over her had forced her into a difficult situation, for sure.

I resisted smiling, even though the image of Aeval towering over Morgaine, pissed out of her mind, gave me a Schadenfreude sense of glee. I particularly didn't want to encourage it, since the cause would be my own demise—or according damage. Besides, the fact that Beira was bearing down on us? *Not* news to smile about.

I simply gave her a nod and tried to ground the energy that, by now, was driving me nuts. It was as bad as being horny. There were days, well, especially before I'd met my men, where I just wanted to jump the next person walking by, regardless of who they were. Only this—this was my entire body, not just certain tasty bits.

Tanne noticed my discomfort. He leaned close enough to whisper, without touching me. "Ground it into your staff. I'll bet the weapon soaks it right up."

I stared at him. "That's a good idea. I'll try it."

My staff was sentient, or would be once she fully woke up. Surely she could take a jolt of energy without damage. I clutched the yew between my hands, and focused the energy into the staff. It met the aura of the yew with a bizarre kaleidoscopic mix. A flash blinded me, and then the staff began to siphon off my energy, greedily sucking it in. As I watched, a veil of faerie lights began to shine around it.

What the hell . . . ? But there was no mistaking it. A web of tiny, flickering eye catchers glowed from within my staff.

Relieved, feeling calmer, though by no means safer, I caught a deep breath. Now, I wouldn't risk the magic backfiring on anybody if I jostled them. Though what my staff was going to do with it, only the gods knew.

A swirl of snow stopped by the bog monster. We were clear of the creature now, but still too close for comfort. The wind beat a steady hail of sleet as snow mixed with the rain. The grassland beyond—marshy as it was—was covered with a thick layer of white.

The air began to shimmer, at the edge of the snow field, and then, slowly, a woman appeared out of the mist.

Beira. She wore a flowing white satin skirt that trailed behind her, the train blending into the snow that followed in her wake. An over-jacket of silver lace with a sweetheart neck—a wide keyhole cutout, fastened at her throat with a sparkling jewel. Over her clothes trailed a fur cloak that flowed along the train of her dress. The fur was silver—fox, perhaps, with a pale bluish tinge to it.

Beira's hair fell to her knees, pure white—reminding me of Pentangle, the Mistress of Magic. But when she looked at us, her eyes were the black void, with a single sparkling diamond in place of a pupil, and her skin was the color of milk.

A headdress rose from her brow, a complex web of thin ice pearls linking together to form a knotwork that looped and spiraled into the air, with trailing chains that draped like diamonds. The light—that odd color that always precipitates a winter storm—caught Beria. She sparkled like a giant prism, casting rainbows over the now-frozen ground. Everything about her shimmered softly, and she made the cold inviting. I wanted to snuggle at her feet and sleep for a decade.

The Mistress of Winter glanced down at the bog monster and lightly tapped it with her staff—a tall spiral of ice, carved with intricate knotwork. The bog monster let out a thundering moan and froze over. Though I wasn't close enough to see, I knew she'd just killed it with her chill touch.

Beira looked us up and down, her gaze fastening on Bran for a long moment. Raising her hand, she pointed at him and he suddenly jerked forward, his expression angry and resentful. Even from where I stood, I could tell he was under her control. He stumbled to his knees at her feet, head bowed.

With a pale smirk—her lips were the palest pink they could be—she raised her hand, yanking him to his feet. By her expression, she seemed to be enjoying this little game. Just what kind of Elemental were we dealing with? The Autumn Lord was aloof and frightening, but he seemed fair. Pentangle had been personable, though she left me breathless with her power. But Beira had a calculating and cruel look on her face.

I shifted, wishing we were in the mountains, away from this place.

Bran staggered forward, awkwardly bowing. His eyes smoldered. The son of Raven Mother didn't like answering to anyone or anything, and according to Morgaine, not even his mother could make him toe the mark. But here was Beira, yanking him around like a puppet on a string.

"Aren't you going to pay homage?" Her words startled me—everything had been so quiet except for the storm. "Lick my feet? Grovel at my side? I thought the son of Raven Mother played the toad when he was ordered. Or so it runs through the grapevine."

"Beira, what brings you down from your lofty mountain peaks? You manage to yank those stone spires out of your ass yet?" Bran's voice was ragged and forced, as if he were struggling to even open his mouth.

I cringed. He was playing a dangerous game, and he was playing it for all of us. And yet, seeing him held there, I felt an odd sympathy. Hyto had controlled me, forced me to grovel at his feet. I knew how much it cost the ego to kneel when the last thing in the world you want to do is show your enemy respect.

Beira seemed oblivious to the rest of us. She closed her hand and he scrabbled, his hands clutching his throat. Another moment and she laughed, then opened her fist. Bran fell to the ground, convulsing.

"You forgot, perhaps, a payment for which you are indebted? Perhaps it merely slipped your mind and you aren't trying to sneak out of our bet?" The words might have sounded cajoling, like Raven Mother's, if it weren't for the icy overtone that made them an outright threat.

"I haven't forgotten. I just don't have your payment yet." He glared at her, still breathing hard.

"You have until the Solstice, O Master of Ravens. Should you fail, winter will descend upon Darkynwyrd with a fierce and cruel nature, and your mother will know what you've been up to. I would not want to be in your place should that happen." With one last thrust of the hand, she sent Bran skidding and rolling over the grass back in our direction.

As he came to a stop, he rolled to his hands and knees and, with a shaky look over his shoulder, scrambled away.

Ignoring him, Beira turned to look at the rest of us. She caught my gaze and I felt as though I were looking into the depths of the ice and snow embodied. But there was no recognition there, no sense of acknowledgment, and she shifted her attention. I watched her. She gazed at every one of us, even Delilah in her panther form. Then she came to Arturo, and there was something there—a flicker. Morgaine saw it, too, and raised her hand to her heart but said nothing.

When she had made the rounds, Beira held up her tartan and walked over to the edge of the marsh, where the grass ceased to grow on solid ground and, instead, covered the dangerous watery swamp. She knelt and plunged her tartan into the icy water, then held it up. The white wool was streaked with blood. Beira stood, shook the cloth in the wind and it dried immediately. She held it up and turned toward us.

I had the impulse to ask her who, but then stopped. It wasn't fair to the others. I knew it wasn't me. In fact, I knew exactly who she had predicted—it had been obvious as sin when she held Arturo's gaze for so long.

Beira folded her cloth, then tucked it beneath her fur cloak once again. She gave Bran one last look. "Winter Solstice. This time, remember, or you will experience a winter you will never forget and your mother will pay for your ineptitude." And with that, the whirl of snow covered her and she began to walk forward, and vanished into the storm.

Silence descended on us again, except for the howling of the storm.

Morgaine spoke first, her voice shaky. "We head for the mountains *now*. We must reach there before night." Saying nothing about Beira, looking neither right nor left, she swept forward. I hurried to her side as Delilah shifted back into her two-legged form. Morio caught up with me. Mordred, Bran, and Arturo resumed their place in the middle of the pack, and Delilah and Tanne stepped in behind them.

It would be tricky going through the marsh now that the

snow was covering the grass. It would be harder to stick to the solid areas and avoid taking a nosedive into the water. We'd need to make good use of our staves. As I eyed the narrow strip, it struck me that we'd be lucky to get two abreast, let alone three.

Morgaine must have been reading my thoughts because she spoke up. "We really should travel single file. As much as I dislike the idea, I think it will be far safer in order to avoid the quicksand and bog."

"You're right." Morio didn't sound happy with the idea, but I was glad he'd been the first to speak up. I felt like I had somehow become Morgaine's *rah-rah* girl, and I just didn't have the cheerleader mentality.

We reorganized. Morgaine took the lead, then, in order: me, Morio, Mordred, Bran, Delilah, Arturo, with Tanne last. Before setting out, we made certain everybody had a stick of wood or long sword with which to prod the ground.

The storm had set in, in earnest. A parting gift from Beira, no doubt. Though the ground had only about an inch of snow so far, with the rate it was falling, we could easily see a foot by morning.

As we marched along, silent among the softly falling flakes, I thought about home and Smoky, and how everybody was doing. It had been a little under a year since my time in the Northlands. The months had flown by. And now, here I was again, off in a different world, once again fighting against the winter.

My thoughts wandered to Trillian. The Shadow Lands were deadly. If I faced the truth, he was in worse danger than we were. I didn't like thinking about it, because there was nothing I could do to help him. In the silence of our journey, his fate—and Rozurial's—weighed heavy on my mind.

I'd followed my conscience in telling him to go. He'd done what he felt necessary. So why did I feel so horrible about making what I knew was the right choice? I whispered a soft prayer to the Moon Mother that my worry was just that, and not a premonition.

The afternoon wore on. The temperature felt like it was hovering around thirty, and though my cloak and my spidersilk skirt and shirt were warm, I still felt the bite of the wind on my face. I'd already pulled out my long gloves and tucked them on, and I took down my ponytail so my hair covered my ears, then draped a scarf over my head and wound it around my neck, covering my mouth and nose. Morgaine had layered up, too, and I didn't have to turn around to know that everybody else had been digging through their packs.

For some reason, I hadn't expected it to be snowing here in the realm of Elder Fae. Or even winter, for that matter. When I thought about it, the expectation made no sense but then, not all of my ideas were one-up on the game.

Morgaine prodded the ground with every step she took. Now and then she'd shift direction—swing to the left or the right, and as we passed by where our path would have taken us, I'd look down and see water glistening below the snowy surface. Luckily, as the day wore on, we saw no more creatures. If there were more bog monsters, they were either frozen or dead. Now and then a bird would flutter past, looking for shelter, and once I thought I saw some sort of fox race through the undergrowth, but the plains seemed barren as far as fauna went, and the snow dissuaded the insects from making pests of themselves. Summer would be horrible here, with the bog and marsh—mosquito heaven.

Every hour brought us that much closer to the foothills and by midafternoon, they were looming close, their rocky crags a nerve-racking portent of what the mountains beyond them must be. As the end of the grassland came into sight, leading onto soil and low-growing forest ringing the hill, I leaned forward.

"Have you been here before?"

Morgaine shook her head. "No, as I said, I've been searching for an entry into this realm for centuries. When we first met, I told you I was in search of the Merlin. But when we discovered Aeval in the crystal cave, and Titania woke from her drunken slumber, everything changed. The Merlin didn't seem as important, once I'd met the Queens of Summer and Winter."

"Well, no longer Summer and Winter. Now they rule the cycle of the day, along with you." I had to give Morgaine her due, if only to appease the ego that I had begun to suspect was born out of insecurity.

She shrugged. "You and I both know that they keep me around for reasons only they can fathom. I'm very aware that I'm dispensable, from their point of view, which is why I keep my options open. I didn't survive this long without always putting myself and my loved ones first."

Darting a quick look over her shoulder—and over mine— she lowered her voice. "Arturo would not survive without me. Surely you can tell that much. And Mordred . . . he is blood kin."

"Well, he *is* your nephew . . ." The thought that Arturo might be Morgaine's half brother hit me like a ton of bricks. For some reason, I'd always thought that she was his aunt on his mother's side, but surely she hadn't been Gwenyfar's sister. If she was Arturo's sister, that put a whole new spin on the matter, but I didn't want to pry—and I couldn't, not without letting on I knew that Arturo was Arthur.

"Blood doesn't always make for good relations, Camille."

I let out a sigh. "I know that only too well. Back in Otherworld, Father's relatives ignored us as best as they could because of our mixed blood. You take care of both of them."

"I keep them out of trouble, if that's what you mean. And I keep food in their stomachs and clothes on their back. I do what I must." She let out a snort. "I know precisely what you and your sisters think of me. And well you should be cautious. I would not value your lives over those of my Mordred and Arturo. However, you're wrong in thinking that I am jealous of you." She tapped the ground beside her and nodded for me to move up to walk at her side.

"Then what is it? Why do you look at me like you do when we're together at Talamh Lonrach Oll?" Maybe she would tell me the truth. Yesterday, I wouldn't have laid odds on the idea, but today? Maybe. Just . . . maybe.

Morgaine inhaled a long breath and held it, then slowly let it whistle between her teeth. "Girl, you remind me of myself, so long ago I cannot count. I fear for you. You're being used. You're being used by Aeval. By Derisa. Asteria used you before her death. You're a pawn in a game far larger than you believe is under play. Just as I was—though for vastly different reasons."

I bit my tongue. My initial reaction was to wax on about my duty, about doing what needed to be done even if I didn't want to. But curiosity got the better of any self-righteous soapboxes onto which I normally climbed.

"What do you mean? How were you used? And who used you?"

Morgaine wiped a light drift of snow off her shoulders. The flakes were thicker, sticking to our cloaks, hair, and scarves. After a moment, she let out a long breath and turned to face me.

"Meher used me to stir up trouble. I was young and had no idea what he was up to. He had goals, you see. He wanted to become *the* Merlin—the High Priest in all forms. He was only acting for Myrddin, who had long vanished from sight. But until the Hunter gave call, there would be no chance for him to take the antlered crest. The Hunter—like the Moon Mother—decides who his High Priest will be."

"And the Hunter wasn't handing him the title."

"No. So Meher got a bee in his bonnet and he set in motion a series of events that changed history. But plans went awry and Meher hung me out to dry. He used me, he used my heart and then played me for a fool. In the end, I was saddled with a destiny I never would have accepted had I realized what was going on. You see, I was destined to be the Lady of the Lake in Avalon, but when Meher got done with messing with my life, I was lucky they let me leave alive."

The bitterness in her words hit my heart. There was so much truth in them, so much anger and loss, that my suspicion of her crumbled enough for me to see beyond my preconceptions. The woman beside me had been hurt, seriously wounded in her heart. She had been stripped of the promise of a destiny she had wanted and worked for. And now, she wandered the world, alone with two men as mysterious as the sorceress herself.

"Why have you been searching for the Merlin—the real one? Myrddin? What can he do for you?" I wanted to reach out, to make her understand that I heard her pain. But I knew she wasn't one for consolation and so kept myself from resting my hand on her arm.

Morgaine paused. We were at the edge of the grassland. She took one last look at the fields behind us—at the marsh and the swamp, and the blowing snow.

"What can he do for me? I don't know, to be honest. I want my name back. If I can't have my station back, I want to know the ways of the dark forest. I want to retreat deep into the woodland. I want . . . peace of mind. Do you think that is so much to ask, Camille?"

With a heavy heart, hoping that the Merlin wouldn't turn out to be like the Great and Powerful Oz—a con artist and huckster—I shook my head. "No, cousin. It's not too much to ask. And I hope, for your happiness, that he can give you what you seek."

She smiled sadly. "We shall see. But Camille, be wary. Don't let yourself end up following in my footsteps. Make sure you know what's going on. Don't trade in your heart for illusions. You have three men you love dearly and a family who cares about you. Above all, don't trade any of them for shiny titles. And make certain you know who the other players in the game really are."

And with that advice, she turned toward the foothill, and motioned for us to take shelter beneath the nearest outcropping. "We need to stop for food. By tonight, with luck, we will find our way to the Merlin. As to waking him, whether that be good fortune or not remains to be seen."

Chapter 15

As we rested, trying to keep out the of brunt of the storm, I realized we'd finished off most of our supplies. We might not have enough to make it home on. But a day or two of going hungry wouldn't hurt any of us, and we weren't that far from the mouth of the portal.

I leaned my head back against the rock wall behind me. We were under a large ledge, but if I peeked around it, the cliff face soared so far into the sky that I couldn't see the top. The Veiled Mountains were no slackers when it came to the geology department. What Morgaine had called a foothill was a substantial mountain—even compared to the dizzying heights of the Cascades that divided the state of Washington in half.

The mountains here, though, weren't volcanic. I couldn't feel the throb of the lava below the surface, like I could at home when we headed out to Mount Rainier, where Smoky's barrow was. No, these were older, weathered beyond time. They had existed before the dinosaurs. Before any living creature walked on the planet. They were rife with magic, like the Southern Wastes, and yet this magic was natural—innate within the molecules of the rock.

I turned to Morgaine. "This realm . . . it wasn't created at the same time that the Great Divide took place, was it?"

She licked something off her fingers—it looked like honey—and shook her head. "No. This realm existed long before the Great Divide. The Elder Fae have always been more detached from humans than the Sidhe and the Unseelie have. They are the parents of the twin Courts, and yet, they are as far distanced as . . . as . . ."

"As Yvarr is from Smoky's kin. They're our Titans, aren't they? Our forerunners." I was beginning to understand. There had been several great races through history, the Elder Fae, the Wyrms, the Titans . . . and from them, the more modern species and races had been born. A thought occurred to me. "Did humans . . . do they have their own version of forebears other than what's known?"

Morgaine nodded. "Yes, actually. They were known as the giants. But even with humans, there's so much about history we don't know. There was a time when the world was vastly different. When the Fae and humans coexisted in a tenuous peace, before recorded history. Then, the humans descended into a dark age and everything from that time is pretty much lost. They emerged again back around Sumer, and then later in Egypt."

She paused, holding up one hand. "The wind is picking up. We have to move."

And with that, our break was over. The path leading up into the ravine was narrow and, just as we had wound our way through the marsh-ridden, snow-covered grass, here we spread out single file, in the same order with Morgaine in the lead. I gripped my staff tightly—it still tingled from the magic I'd infused into it earlier.

As we left the shelter of the overhang, the wind hit us full force, channeling down through the ravine. It funneled through the narrow passage, gusting against us as if we were in a wind tunnel. The snow was still falling, and the weather had shifted for the worse with the passage of Beira. At the front, Morgaine was taking the brunt of the storm, but she was sturdier than I'd expected, braving the wind without a flinch.

The passage was narrow—if I stretched my arms out, I could run my hands along both sides of the channel. With a grade that was at least twenty percent, the going was steep and I was grateful for my staff. While we could manage it without too many problems, too long and we'd be off our guard with weariness. The climb was taxing, but the weather on top of it made everything treacherous.

Granite walls hemmed us in as we ascended, and I began to feel a lumbering sense of claustrophobia. The only thing we could see beyond the path in front of us and the walls to either side was the open sky, a churning mass of clouds and falling snow. The world had closed in around us, and as vast as the marshland and plains had been, this felt narrow and funneled and cramped.

I tried to focus on my feet instead of the never-ending trail. After all, we weren't underground. We weren't clinging to the side of a ravine, trying not to fall. We were headed toward our destination and we had to come out sometime. I thought about talking to Morio, but the wind was too loud and the howl of it would steal away my voice before my words ever reached him.

Perhaps that was what was the worst of it—the yammering winds. They raged and roared, blustering by, whipping up our cloaks and capes and anything not firmly anchored to our bodies. I had done my best to tie my cloak together in front to keep the wind from tossing my skirt into a frenzy, but that just made it more difficult, cutting down on the aerodynamics of my outfit. I felt like I was wearing a mushroom that billowed around me, making it difficult to walk without getting some layer or other caught between my legs.

On we went, as the day darkened. The snowstorm kept the sky from going pitch-dark. That silvery-green light that accompanied winter storms glimmered against the clouds, providing an eerie illumination. Vague snippets from our fights with zombies and ghouls cropped up—they took on that same eerie color, or they did once they'd been dead for a while before the necromancer reanimated them.

But that line of thought brought to mind too many gory fights, too much stress, and so I did my best to shake away the thoughts. Forcing myself to focus on thoughts of home and of Maggie, and Iris and all things that I loved the best, I brought my attention back to the path, and concentrated on putting one foot in front of the other as we marched along the mountain trail.

I wasn't sure how much time had passed, but I suddenly realized it was a great deal darker than it had been last time I'd paid attention, and my calves were beginning to ache. At that moment, Morgaine called a halt to our traveling. She motioned to a turnoff about twenty yards ahead, then pointed behind me to the others. I nodded.

Turning to Morio, I motioned for him to lean close to me. As soon as he had, I shouted over the wind. "There's a turnoff ahead. We're heading there. Tell the others to be ready. We don't know what will be in there." And he, in turn, began to pass the information on. As soon as everybody had their weapons ready, Morio gave me the thumbs-up and I turned back to Morgaine.

"We're ready to go."

She began to move. As we closed in on the turnoff, a shiver raced up my spine. What if there was something waiting in there? Would Morgaine be able to get out of the way in time? I was second in line and I had to be prepared to help her should anything come out swinging.

I readied the staff. As I gripped it tightly, I sensed something emanating from it. A sentience, of some sort. I jerked, but managed to keep my footing. I wanted to explore the feeling further but Morgaine's movements caught my attention again. I didn't have time to figure out what had just happened—I had to be on my guard. I hurried to catch up with her.

The turnoff was just wide enough so that I could swing in by her side. She gave me a hesitant smile from beneath the massive hood of her cloak, and we stepped into what I realized was an actual cavern.

Instantly, the wind died, rushing down through the path

rather than into the cave. I let out a long sigh, realizing how tense the weather had been making me, but I didn't let myself relax—not till we knew we were safe.

The walls and ceiling of the cave were covered with a myriad of crystals—long spikes of quartz and amethyst and citrine. And from within those spikes, a faint light sparkled, so that the entire cave was lit up with a soft glow reminding me of Christmas lights.

"It's beautiful," I whispered, not even realizing I was speaking aloud.

But Morgaine nodded. "The Merlin was locked within a crystal cavern, much like Aeval. Do you know the reason for that?"

I shook my head. "No. Why?"

"Because the crystals amplified the spells, making it that much harder for them to escape. There was always the fear that their powers were strong enough for them to break the spells and free themselves. And there is some truth to that— the Fae Queen and the Merlin—well, the great Fae Lords may have been powerful but they only won the war by enslaving the wyrms and creatures of the earth to their side. They would not have stood a chance against their enemies if they had gone up against them on their own. Aeval is proba-bly the most powerful sorceress who has ever lived here on Earthside, eclipsed only by the Merlin, and only by the fact that she is not pledged to the Moon Mother, while he is backed by the power of the Hunter."

I pondered this thought. "Aeval is more powerful than Titania, then?"

"Yes."

"The Merlin, if he and Aeval joined forces . . . "

"Trust me," Morgaine said. "There was good reason the Great Fae Lords feared Aeval, Titania, and the Merlin. Their powers combined? An almost unstoppable force." She laughed, and this time, I sensed no bitterness, but an actual joy. "I wish they had been more arrogant and not realized the strength of their adversaries. It would have made things so much simpler." She sounded nostalgic, almost wistful, but then stopped.

Pointing to one corner, she said, "Look—others have been here."

A pile of scattered bones were lying there. They looked weathered and old, like they'd been there well over a hundred years. There were three skulls that we could see, so there had been at least three victims.

I knelt by the bones. Too much time had gone by to tell why they had died—at least without a forensics team in tow.

"Either they took shelter from a storm and were trapped, or perhaps, something in the cave killed them. It's impossible to tell—the skeletons were torn to pieces years ago." One way or another, it was a warning.

The others were in the cave by now. As soon as we secured the immediate area, we could rest. The cavern went so far back that we stopped at an area where the crystals formed a line across the floor. The row of spikes looked like a border.

Not wanting to test what might be on the other side, we decided that we'd gone far enough for the moment. While we rested, we could keep watch on the boundary line.

We sorted through our food supplies, and combined all our reserves. We had enough food for two days for everyone if we rationed it out. We wouldn't go hungry, but there were no second helpings, either.

Water was running low, but we could gather snow from the path outside and melt it. Delilah and Tanne brought in a big mound of snow on one of the plastic tarps, and we spread it out, trying to warm it so it would melt and we could siphon it off into the bottles. After about fifteen minutes, we'd managed to fill up seven of the empty containers and decided to give it a rest.

I pulled out my blanket and wrapped it around me, trying to warm up. "So, where to do we go from here? Is this the entrance you were looking for?"

Morgaine nodded. "I think so. And I believe that line of crystals is masking an illusion. What looks like empty cavern will disappear, if my information is correct."

"What will show in its place?" Tanne asked, stretching out his long legs.

She shrugged. "That, my friend, I do not know. I suppose we shall find out, don't you? But first, we rest for a few hours. We used up a lot of energy and we should sleep for a while. Who will take first watch? We can't take any chances. There are guards and watchers, and traps here. They did not imprison the Merlin just to leave his prison open for anybody to stumble over."

The thought of sleep, after the long, chill march, sounded divine. I just wished we could light a fire. But again, advertising our presence wasn't in our best interests. At least we were out of the elements, and while it was still cold, the wind wasn't eating into our bones.

We paired off in watches of two hours each. A good six hours of sleep would do us all a world of good, and if we set four posts, that meant everybody would have time to recharge. Unfortunately, because of the animosity between our two groups, I ended up being paired with Mordred for third watch. As long as I could keep him out of arm's reach, I should be okay. I trusted Bran more than Mordred. Bran was openly hostile; Mordred was a little weasel.

Morgaine and Tanne took the first watch, Bran and Delilah the second. When Delilah woke me up, she told me that Bran hadn't said a single word during the watch. Instead, he'd fixed his stare on the line of crystals and never wavered, seeming to sink into a deep meditation with his eyes open.

"Which was just fine with me. If Mordred lays a hand on you, you scream bloody murder. You hear me?" She arched an eyebrow to let me know she was serious.

I nodded. "You got it. I doubt he'll cause trouble, given the situation, but you never know. I hope he'll just pass out and leave me to keep watch on my own. I can handle that. Four hours of sleep helped a lot, though I'm looking forward to the last two. Pray nothing happens before we're all awake and into the depths of the cavern."

As she settled down under her blanket and pulled it tightly around her, I peeked outside. The storm was still blowing and the snow was piling up, but the wind still channeled through the pass rather than into the cave. Unless Beira returned in a fury, it shouldn't do more than slow us down when we made the return trip home, which I hoped would be tomorrow at some point.

Mordred was perched on a rock, his blanket around his shoulders. I shook my own blanket out, then wrapped it around me snuggly, and sat near Delilah and Morio, watching the line of crystals. I did my best not to catch Mordred's attention. The last thing I wanted to do was invite conversation.

From this angle, the crystals along the floor looked like creatures—like scorpions, actually. The light within them flickered, glowing softly against the cavern floor. They were about four feet long and thirty inches tall, and I found myself entranced by the shimmer radiating off of them. Was this what Bran had been watching? Had he, too, been magnetized by their sparkling prisms?

Ten minutes into our watch, Delilah and Bran both had fallen asleep. I really didn't relish two hours spent in my thoughts. The more I settled into them, the harder it was to dig my way out. Only movement could bring me out of the depths—sex, or dancing. Magic and music helped, too.

I had a pocket watch with me to keep time. I couldn't wear Earthside watches. Something about the magical energy I ran stopped them. Actually, I knew several FBHs who had the same problem and almost all of them were either psychic, or actively worked with magic. Lindsey Cartridge, the director of the Green Goddess Women's Shelter, was one of them. She also was High Priestess of an ES neo-pagan coven. The magic of full-blooded humans was far different from my own, but it had its own power and beauty, and when practiced by those who had perfected their craft, it could be surprisingly strong.

"So, what do you think we'll find?" Mordred's question was soft enough not to wake the others, but clear enough to intrude into my thoughts.

I frowned, wandering if I could get away with pretending I hadn't heard him, but finally decided that would just lead to an altercation. And I wasn't in the mood to rumble.

"I don't know, to be honest. I hope we find the Merlin." After a pause, I couldn't help but add, "I think."

The look on his face told me he was on the same page. He

narrowed his eyes and tilted his head to the side, as if thinking. "You know, I wonder if the powers that be realize just how dangerous the Merlin might be. Who's to say what the old boy might decide he wants to do when he's woken up? He might very well decline to fight this wyrm. Or he might choose to fight on the side of Telazhar. If I had my way, I'd forget this and just prepare to battle it out when Yvarr breaks out of his prison."

I stared at the crystals, thinking over what he had said. "Unfortunately, I have my orders. As does your aunt. We have no choice. We're bound by our duty."

"Didn't the ES soldiers say that during the great wars?" Mordred turned a snarky grin on me and once again, I felt squirmy, in a bad way, like someone had just bathed me in slime. "But then, I suppose none of us have any choice. My aunt saved my father—don't look surprised. I know you know who he really is."

"But he . . . doesn't . . ."

"No, and I'm not going to tell him. Why shake him up? He's happy enough to be with us, though I find it disturbing that he seems to have a crush on my aunt. She's his *sister*, for the sake of the gods. But I know she wouldn't act on it."

His sister . . . So Morgaine was Arturo's sister after all. That answered one question.

"She humors him. Consider it Alzheimer's, brought on by the Nectar of Life." He sighed, staring down at the floor then. "I love my father. You don't like me, and I don't like you very much. But never doubt that I love him, and I'd die to protect him. I almost did, once. And history vilified me and turned me into a traitor."

I didn't want to like him—didn't want to feel sorry for him—but I could hear the pain in his voice. I could also hear the pride when he spoke of protecting his father, and I realized that it had to have been hard, spending century after century being looked on as a villain when you actually had been a hero.

I resisted my knee-jerk reaction. "I imagine it's been hell. But your aunt believes in you, and it's obvious your father is fond of you, even if he doesn't remember who you are." I tried to think of something else to say, but truth was, I had no clue what to talk about. I had no intention of getting into a discussion about the war. I didn't know if Mordred knew about the spirit seals, and it wasn't a good idea to dangle candy in front of someone with a sweet tooth.

"I'm sorry about your father's death." The words sounded forced, but they didn't feel false. He glanced over at me. "At least I still have mine, even if he's daft and lives in his own foggy world."

And . . . back to reality. I suddenly felt tired.

"Thanks," I mumbled, and huddled more tightly under my blanket. There wasn't much else I could say. Our father had died when the palace in Elqaneve had been destroyed, buried under a pillar that fell on him. His remains sat at home, in an urn. We'd had to change our entire tradition of interring the dead given the battles raging back in Otherworld, and nothing felt settled.

The memories of trying to escape that night through the war-torn countryside, with bodies on every side and the smell of blood clogging my nose . . . it was still too close. I bit my lip, forcing the tears down. Most days, Delilah and I did okay. We'd both been through the storm that had torn the country apart. The sound of lightning still startled me, and flashes—images from that night—would suddenly take over my thoughts and send me into a panic. Delilah was suffering, too. PTSD, the FBHs called it.

I slowly began touching my thumbs to my index fingers, then middle fingers, then ring fingers, and lastly, my little fingers. Speeding up, I counted as I went, until my breathing softened and the upswell of panic subsided. Then, taking a deep breath, I held it to the count of five, and slowly exhaled. Shaking my head, I opened my eyes, to see Mordred staring at me, looking perplexed.

He opened his mouth, as if to say something, but then closed it and leaned back, staring at the entrance to the cavern. "I'll watch that way. You watch the crystals. Good by you?"

Relieved that he wasn't going to try to extend the conversation, I nodded and fell into a comfortable, if melancholy, silence. Time ticked on, and at last, the alarm on my pocket watch let out a little ring, and we woke Morio and Arturo to take over our watches. I settled down on the ground next to Delilah and Tanne, but then, sat up again.

"Night, Mordred." I didn't really expect an answer, but was surprised when a soft "Night, Camille" came in return. Settling down again, I closed my eyes and fell into deep sleep for the last two hours, and thankfully, my dreams were so deep and distant, that I didn't remember them when I woke.

By the time we woke, it was very early morning. The storm was still blowing outside, and the snow was about a foot deep on the path. Our journey back to the portal would be more problematic, but if we managed to get back on the road by afternoon, we should be okay.

We'd be out of food by tonight but that wouldn't be an issue unless this trip dragged on for another day. As I slipped outside to take care of personal business—a dauntingly cold but necessary duty—I whispered a brief prayer to the Moon Mother that we find the Merlin, wake him up, and be done with it.

We finished a skimpy breakfast and then Morgaine led Morio, Tanne, and me over to examine the crystals. They were in perfect alignment and that right there told us they weren't natural. Nature didn't usually create straight lines. We stopped about two yards away. I closed my eyes, as did Morgaine.

At first, I heard nothing out of the ordinary but then, I could sense it. A deep vibration running the length of the chamber. I slowly let out my breath and tried to lower myself into the energy. At first, it resisted, but then, as I probed gently at it, it opened up and I found myself sinking into the brilliant neon glow.

A swirl of lights swarmed up, but they weren't like the will-o'-the-wisps, nor were they like eye catchers. I had never really encountered anything like them before. They did have a sentience—there was intelligence there, and cunning, but it felt alien and without malice or good will. I reached out to touch one and the shock reverberated through my body.

"What the fuck?" I shook myself out of my trance and glanced at my fingers. They were singed, and several small blisters began to raise on my index finger. "But I was in trance—I wasn't on the astral." I told them what I'd seen.

Morgaine cocked her head. "I don't know. I don't like this. I saw the same thing but I didn't try to touch it." She gave me a little smirk and the Morgaine I knew suddenly returned.

I rolled my eyes. "Of course you didn't. And of course, I did. But that's just who I am. So what do we do with this? It's a border. You said last night the crystals are masking a hidden entrance? Do we just step over them?" I gazed warily at the crystalline sculptures. Now that I knew they could bite, so to speak, they didn't seem quite so pretty.

Tanne cleared his throat. "I think it's best to try to dispel the illusion first."

"Well, Morio can do that. Can't you, love?" One of Morio's abilities—one he didn't get a chance to use very often—was the ability to dispel some illusions. Iris had the same power, but she was a long, long way away.

Morio nodded, kneeling down to get a closer look at the crystals. He held his hand close, without actually touching them. "I'll give it a try, but without knowing exactly what they are, I'm not sure how well this will work. I suggest the rest of you move back."

"How far?" Tanne grinned at him. "There's only so much space in this cavern."

Morio returned the smile, chuckling. "True, but I'd still feel better if you guys weren't within spitting distance."

As we stepped back, the blisters on my thumb were stinging. It felt like I'd been burned. I didn't trust the lights—whatever they were.

The others were watching us closely as Morio stood. He brought his hands out in front of him, palms aimed toward the crystal statues. As he lowered his head, whispering an incantation, a prickle of energy raced through the air. Morgaine shivered and so did I—my body responding to Morio. We'd worked magic together so much and for so long now, that it felt odd not to be at his side, not to be part of what he was doing.

A shimmer raced along the row of crystals, and the faintest of movements caught my eye as the air rippled behind them. A wall of rock began to materialize. But the movement wasn't limited to the dissolving illusion. The crystals themselves began to shift. I realized that they'd looked all too much like scorpions the night before because they were just that.

With legs and pincers formed from crystal spikes, and a central faceted body, the sculptures came to life, standing and turning our way. A massive crystal tail curved over their back, with an angular stinger. They turned, at attention, with front pincers aimed toward us. The ends were sharp and glinted with a dangerous edge.

"Oh, fuck." Morio leaped back as the nearest one scuttled forward, moving with a soft *clinking* sound.

Not sure how these creatures defended themselves, or if they were able to use magic, I quickly ran through the possibilities. Crystals could amplify electricity, and when I thought about calling down the lightning, something inside whispered, *Don't do it—they'll be able to feed on it.*

I grasped my staff firmly as the entire line of creatures began to edge forward. Delilah and the others readied their weapons.

"Does anybody know what the fuck these are?" It would help to know what it was we were fighting.

"Not a clue." Mordred's voice was actually a little shaky and for once he didn't seem quite so cocky.

"No idea." Bran had less to worry about, but even he sounded cautious. The Elementals and their children were true Immortals. But that didn't mean he couldn't suffer pain or damage.

Morgaine and Delilah moved to flank my sides. Delilah was staring at the crystal creatures with a puzzled look, while Morgaine just looked pissed.

"I don't think it matters whether we know *what* they are, the only thing we have to figure out is *how* to fight them." Tanne glanced back at me. He'd moved up to Morio's side and had his sword out. "I can tell you my Spell of Unraveling isn't going to work on these—they're actual creatures. They may have been in stasis, but they aren't golems. That much I can tell."

"Lovely, which is probably why Morio's spell to dispel illusion brought them out from their frozen state. The trap was a spell that kept the wall invisible, and kept them at a standstill. The spell's gone and so is their immobility." I groaned. "The Fae Lords really had it all planned out, didn't they?"

"Clever, very clever." Morgaine cocked her head, eyeing the creatures. "They didn't do anything by halves, did they?"

"Well, the creatures are made of rock—crystal, but still . . . rock. What can destroy rock?"

"Paper covers rock." Delilah tried for a joke but it fell flat, even in her voice.

I thought for a moment, then realized that I did have one weapon that could disrupt them. And if we needed it, I wouldn't hesitate to use it. But first I wanted to see if we could put a stop to them without me dragging out the horn.

I glanced around. There wasn't that much room in which to back up now, and as I sucked in a deep breath, the storm broke, and they scuttled forward again, and this time, the fight was on.

Chapter 16

⤖⤖⤖

"Incoming!" Delilah called out. She held out Lysanthra, her dagger. But the look on her face indicated that she knew just how ineffective a long knife was going to be against a creature made of stone and crystal.

I quickly counted the number of our opponents. Thirteen. There was no way we could take them on and, even if they just used their tails to stab at us—even barring any venom— they constituted a deadly force. Fuck it. We needed to be in top form for whatever waited in the passage beyond them.

Reaching into my pocket, I tugged at the zipper and fumbled for the horn. As I pulled it out, both Bran and Morgaine gasped and I realized that neither had seen me wield it before now. Or, at least I didn't think so. Bran—definitely not. Morgaine? Shaking my head—it didn't matter right now who the fuck had seen me with it—I thrust it into the air and held it tightly as I closed my eyes, thrusting my consciousness inside the horn.

Time stopped—or rather, I stepped outside of time. I was inside the horn, standing in the middle of a room flanked by four giant mirrors that were a lot like display windows. A simple table and two chairs were centered in the small room, and a man sat in one of the chairs. He was seven feet tall, at least this time, with olive skin and long dark hair caught back in a ponytail.

"Eriskel, thank gods you're here." I was relieved to see him. We hadn't spoken in a while, but he rose immediately.

Eriskel was the guardian of the horn. He was a jindasel, spun off from the soul of the Black Unicorn and yet a separate entity in his own right. Eriskel was quite capable of destroying anybody who attempted to use the horn if he decided they weren't worthy. Which was the one saving grace if it should ever be stolen, except that I'd probably end up dead either way. Thieves after major artifacts didn't tend to have much in the way of consciences.

"Camille—what do you need?" He wasn't one for small talk.

"I need the Lady of the Land. We're facing some sort of crystal creatures and I don't think we have the means to fight them. We don't even know what they *are*." I glanced anxiously at the mirrors and they began to shimmer, the reflective surfaces fading.

To the east, I now saw rocky crags, high in the air, and clouds swirled around the peaks. A man dressed in pale leather flew in on a gust of air, flaxen-haired and tall, carrying a sword polished to a high sheen. Lightning crackled around him. He landed on the rock and bowed to me. I nodded back. The Master of Winds.

Turning to the south, I recognized the Mistress of Flames as she emerged from a rolling river of lava. Her hair, the jet black of hardened obsidian, flowed into the current of molten rock that formed her dress. Her eyes flashed neon white, surrounded by an orange ring of flame. She knelt in the billowing torrent that spewed from the center of the world, a feral smile crossing her face.

Again, I nodded.

To the west, the Lord of the Depths rose out of a rippling sea. His skin glimmered with an azure tint against a fading sunset, and he carried a bronze trident. He rose up so that I could see his torso. His scaled tail remained hidden beneath the waves. He laughed when he saw me and hoisted the tri-dent overhead in greeting.

Once more, I acknowledged his presence, then turned to the north. Here would be the help I sought.

A woman with skin as dark as the soil sat on a rock amidst a verdant grove. Her hair was the yellow of fresh corn, and her eyes mirrored the same color. She wore a gown formed from leaves and vines, and carried an intricately carved wand. The protective energy of the oak spread through the mirror to surround me with a stable and secure feeling.

"Lady of the Land, I come seeking your help. I need you." I didn't have to say another word. She stood and raised her wand.

Behind me, Eriskel whispered, "Don't use all of the horn's energy on this. There's no need for a maul when a tack hammer will do."

And with that, I was back, holding the horn aloft, and I thrust it forward toward the advancing line of crystal crea-tures. A rumble sounded, beginning in the horn but rippling out to shake the cavern. Another moment and the vibration increased, setting the teeth in my head to hurting.

The others groaned. At least I was somewhat protected because I was wielding the horn. As the frequency shot up another notch, Delilah dropped to her knees, covering her ears, and so did the others, except for Bran, who was staring at me with a mixture of envy and fear.

"Shatter!" The word came ripping out of my throat, and it hung for a second, echoing before it swept in a rolling wave across the floor of the cavern, turning it into an ocean of rock and soil as it enveloped the crystal scorpions. They began to vibrate, darting back and forth.

The tremors crescendoed at an almost unbearable pitch, and the scorpions began to shatter, bursting apart in a flurry of powered quartz. The shards flew wild, but even as the oth-ers dove for cover, I held my ground. It was imperative I keep the momentum going, or it would end too soon and the energy would run wild, causing who knew what sort of damage.

Fragments of the breaking crystal pelted me, a number of the shards impaling my skin, but I forced myself to stay put. Fuck, though, the needle sting of the glass hurt. Last time I'd been through this, our opponent—a nasty-tempered sorcerer—had rolled me over a pile of broken glass. This was just a lovely reminder of what it felt like to be a pincushion.

At last, the shaking slowed, and the energy of the horn began to recede. I whispered a soft *thank you* to the Lady of the Land and slid the horn back in its secret pocket, zipping it up. I had used probably a third of the horn's force, so we still had a powerful weapon if needed. But I felt wrung out, desperately wanting to nose-dive onto a sofa and rest.

Morio scrambled to his feet, but Bran was quicker to reach me. He eyed me up and down. "You okay?"

I glanced down. My cloak had deflected a number of the shards, but some had made it through. I gingerly unfastened the brooch as Delilah and Morio descended on me. She silently took my cloak over to one side and began to shake the glass off of it, while Morio examined me. I held out my arms. My hands—especially the one that had been holding the horn—were bleeding like a stuck pig. At least a dozen needles of glass were stuck in the skin.

A drop of blood dripped into my eye, startling me. As I blinked it away, I realized that my hair was filled with shards, too. And judging by the sting, several had landed on my cheeks and forehead.

"I could use some help." I spoke cautiously, uncertain whether any glass had landed on my lips. The last thing I needed was to swallow something sharp.

Morio began to pluck pieces off of my face. "There are only a few here—but you are bleeding. Heads and hands always bleed heavier." While he occupied himself with keeping the glass out of my mouth and eyes, Morgaine went around behind me and began combing through my hair.

"Bran, you and Mordred watch the entrance. We don't want to be taken by surprise while we fix up Camille." Morio went back to wiping the blood off my face with a handkerchief.

I didn't ask if it was clean—at this point, I didn't care. I just wanted to stop feeling like a store window in a bad part of town during a riot. I flinched as Tanne began to pluck glass from my hands and my fingers. Grimacing, I forced myself not to whine. I could snivel later when all the little scars were scabbing over and beginning to itch.

Finally I was denuded of crystal guts, and able to put my cloak back on, but all I could think of was how much I wanted a shower to wash away anything still clinging to me. Nothing had come through from the passage, and I was both relieved and a little worried over this fact. But then again, how many creatures could have withstood the onslaught of the quartz guardians? If there were further traps waiting for us, they weren't likely to be right inside the doorway, so to speak.

Taking a deep breath, I turned to the others. "I hate to say this, but I really need food. I know we're low on supplies, but I'm a little shaky. Not to mention bloody." Though I had managed to avoid being pulverized by the shattering glass, I was streaked with the quickly drying blood. There wasn't water enough to wash with, unless I wanted to use snow, and the thought of chilling myself after the magical exertion the horn had put me through didn't seem like a good idea.

Morio dug into his pack and handed me half a sandwich. "Here, eat this. I also have a candy bar."

Between the roast beef and the Snickers, the shakes started to subside. I was tired, though, and dreaded the thought of having to face anything stronger along the way. "Okay, we've cleared the path," I said after a moment. "Now what?"

Morgaine gave me a mirthless smile. "We head into the dark."

I wiped my fingers, took a swig of water, and stood. "Okay then, we don't really have a lot of time to waste. Let's get moving."

And with that, we fell into our battle order and headed into the narrow passage in the newly revealed rock wall.

Unlike the outer passage, this one led down into the depths of the mountain. It was narrow and low, which didn't lend well to my dislike of small enclosed spaces. Maybe we'd fought one too many battles in the dark, or maybe I just didn't like feeling hemmed in—either way, the descent into the tunnel was anything but fun. At least the walls were lit with the same sort of jutting crystals that had lined the walls of the cavern.

"I wish this was more like Underground Seattle," Delilah said.

"I was thinking just about the same thing. At least there the passages are wide enough to feel like you're actually walking in what used to be a city street. This . . . all I can say is watch for viro-mortis slimes along the wall. This would be the perfect place for them to hang out."

It was Delilah's turn to let out a muttered "ick." She hated the oozing jellies that mimicked the Blob, right down to trying to absorb the hosts they latched on to. They might be prettier than Steve McQueen's black amorphous menace, but they were no less deadly, if a little slower on the uptake.

"Yeah, and we don't have Smoky or Iris here to freeze them, either." Delilah's words echoed against the rock and she flinched and lowered her voice again. "Sorry."

"It's loud, isn't it? Do you hear that dripping noise?" I could hear a faint *plink plink plink*, as if a faucet were dripping somewhere in the distance.

Morgaine, still leading the way, answered. "I hear it, yes. I'm not sure of what it is but do you notice how damp the air is getting?"

I sniffed. Sure enough, the air was laden with moisture. It was cold and damp, and I realized that I was getting a chill. There was nothing I could do about it unless I wanted to pull out my blanket and drape it over my shoulders, and I didn't want it getting shredded if we ended up in another fight.

"Do you think we're nearing an underground stream or something?"

"I don't know, but . . . hold on." She held up a hand and I stopped, motioning for the others behind me to follow suit. A moment later, she turned. "I sense . . . I can feel an energy that I haven't encountered for a very long time." She turned back to the tunnel and began to hurry forward.

Hoping she wasn't possessed or under a spell—she was

almost running down the descending corridor—I followed at a good pace. Not twenty more yards and the floor began to level out as up ahead the tunnel ended, leading to an entrance into . . . well . . . I didn't know what. But it definitely opened into something else. Selfishly, I hoped it wasn't just another passageway. I was getting tired of being underground.

As I reached Morgaine, who was anxiously waiting by the archway, she turned to me, an excited look on her face. I'd never seen her expression so animated. "We're here. I think we're here."

"Where? Do you mean we've found the Merlin?"

She was practically vibrating. "I think . . . we have. And I think we've also found a door into one of the byways that leads to Avalon." With that, she turned to plunge through the arch, and vanished from sight in a flash of light.

"Oh fuck! What the hell? Where did she go?" My first impulse was to rush forward, but I stopped myself, tentatively sticking the end of my staff through the arch. It crackled, and the energy raced up the staff to tingle through my fingers. But it didn't feel dangerous. Instead, it felt inviting and warm.

I turned to look at Morio. "What should we do? I have no clue where she went other than through that doorway."

Tanne pushed his way to the front. "Let me go find out. Tie a rope around me so you can pull me back if need be."

But at that moment, Morgaine's head popped back through, seeming almost disembodied. "It's a hidden entrance. Veiled, but not dangerous. Come on." She vanished again.

Still not trusting what I saw, I looked at Tanne. "You willing to go through?"

He nodded. "I'll tell you what, hold on to me and I'll poke my head through. If . . . well . . . if something happens, contact my family."

Morio took hold of his arm and Tanne edged his head through the archway, then a few seconds later, withdrew. "She's right. She's also lucky. That could have been anything, but it appears to be a veil that covers the entrance. It may well lead into a different realm, but it didn't try to prevent my return. I think we can go through. There's no way to explain what the hell I'm seeing on the other side. You have to see it for yourselves."

Hesitantly, I agreed. One by one, we crossed through the portal, into the unknown.

As I stepped through, following Tanne, the scent of lilacs and wisteria descended to fill my nose. I inhaled a deep breath and cool, clear air filled my lungs, imbued with the fragrance of the flowers. The chill and the gloom vanished and I found myself facing a blazing cavern filled with brightly illuminated walls. Whether it was crystals or eye catchers or faerie fire, I wasn't sure, but everything sparkled and glowed here.

The chamber was so vast I couldn't see the end of it, and while there were no trees or vines in sight to account for the scent of the flowers, what I did see was a placid lake filling the center of the vast chamber.

In the center of the lake, we could see a small island. It was large enough to house a building that reminded me of a large temple.

The floor in front of us was still stone, but as we approached the lake, the stone changed to solid dirt, and then to pebbles. Albino grasses waved in a light breeze, growing by the edge of the water, along with reeds as tall as I was. A boat rocked lightly on the waves, tethered to a mooring stump anchored firmly in the rock next to the lakeshore.

The temperature had warmed by at least thirty degrees. It was still chilly, but compared to what we'd been through, it felt positively balmy. My body began to relax, the tension flowing out of my shoulders.

Slightly alarmed by my reaction, I turned to the others. "Can you sense anything? Any spells or charms in the area?"

Tanne shook his head. "I've already been searching, but no, I can feel no sense of danger here. That in itself may be the result of a spell. But as far as I can tell, I'm not picking up on anything untoward."

"I almost wish you did." Dangers that were out in the open were far easier to deal with than hidden treachery. And

I couldn't quite bring myself to believe that the crystal guardians had been the only obstacles in our path.

"I suppose we just keep alert." Delilah stared at the water. "I don't want to go on that boat."

Ever the cat, my sister had an innate distrust of water, which had pretty much developed into a phobia. She hardly ever relented to taking a full bath—preferring short, frequent showers. She had never voluntarily been swimming a day in her life, and she refused to even own a bathing suit.

"We have to go on it. We have to get across the water to that building." Morgaine frowned. "That's where the Merlin is."

Delilah's eyes flashed but she kept her mouth shut, for which I was grateful. We didn't have time for personal fears to interfere. My own fears had been ever present with me during this journey but I'd managed to push them aside. After a moment, my sister just nodded, tight-lipped but acceding.

"Will we all fit? There are eight of us." I stared at the long boat, mentally calculating the space and number of seats. Yeah, we'd fit, but it would be snug. "Can it carry all of us, weight-wise?"

"If there are eight seats, the boat will carry eight people. Unless we're hiding a giant somewhere." Tanne winked at me, and I laughed. "No? Didn't think so. Who else knows how to row? There are four oars here. I can man one of them."

Mordred spoke up. "I know how to man a boat." Arturo volunteer to take a third and—to my surprise—Morgaine the fourth.

"Before we shove off, can we find out if the water's safe to touch? And if it is, I want to wash my hands and face." I was tired of feeling grungy and the dried blood had only added to that feeling.

Morgaine dipped her finger into the pond, held it to her nose, and waited. A moment later, nothing had happened. "I think you should be okay, but if there are any hidden dangers—any bacteria—do you really want to wash open wounds with it?"

Grumbling, I shook my head. "Never mind. Good point. At least we know it's not battery acid, though."

Morio and Tanne had been examining the boat and they

deemed it water-worthy, so we climbed in. Delilah clutched the edge of her seat tightly, whispering a prayer to Bast that we didn't capsize. I, myself, was praying we didn't run into any sirens along the way. The last thing we needed was a gaggle of gorgeous women luring us out of the boat to a watery death. The boat glided smoothly over the water, though, and we landed on the shore of the island without incident.

Relieved, I scrambled out, but I couldn't beat Delilah in her desire to get her land legs under her again. Mordred tied the boat securely against the mooring pole so it couldn't drift away. The island was small, pretty much big enough to hold the building and not much else but the small swath of land around it. It truly did look like a temple, single story—at least aboveground—and was about the size of a large gymnasium. The walls were white marble veined with gray, and the structure was covered with a ghostly web of albino ivy. Columns buttressed the sides, evenly spaced and carved with intricate Celtic knotwork. A wide door in front was the only visible entrance.

The island itself was covered with a plush layer of moss, pale and luminous. A narrow walkway led through the moss from the mooring to the door of the building. Morgaine paused at the edge of the path, her caution getting the better of her excitement. She stared at the building, then turned back to me.

"Whatever wards there are, they'll be at the door or beyond. Do you see?"

"See what?" I squinted, trying to get a better vantage point.

"By the door—on the ground. Look closer, child." She pointed to the left of the door.

I tried to focus—the light wasn't very bright here and I wasn't sure at first what I was looking at but then I saw. Skeletons. Several of them, piled by the foot of the door. They were bleached, weathered, indicating they'd been here some time. Whether age or animals had picked them dry, it was hard to tell.

It could have been anything—gas or poison, magic . . . there were no signs anywhere of guards hiding, but then again, they might come out from the inside of the building and we weren't close enough yet to get a better look. I tried to gauge how the skeletons were arranged, which might give us an idea of how they'd died, but we were too far away for me to make out much.

"The trap is by the door, then."

"Not so fast." Tanne squinted, then shook his head. "Something seems off. Look how neat the path is—the moss hasn't overgrown it at all, and moss takes over. You know how invasive it is."

He was right. Whether above- or belowground, moss spreads and spreads quickly. It could take over a lawn within a few months, if let go, and that included sidewalks and decks and anything else just hanging around. In fact, a good share of the lawns in and around Seattle were quite happily covered with moss. It cut down on mowing, for one thing.

"The path looks like dirt—not stone. But even if it were stone, the moss should have covered it by now." I studied the winding trail. It was untouched. "Notice something else? The path is also clear of any other type of foliage. It looks meticulously groomed."

Bran went up to the edge of the trail, without setting foot on it. He leaned down, and cocked his head to the side as he examined it. Then, he got down on his hands and knees and leaned forward, sniffing the dirt. A moment later he reared back, a startled look on his face.

"There's something on that dirt. I don't know what it is, but it's dangerous. If I was mortal, I might be unconscious now." He leaned out and touched his finger to the dirt, yanking it back. He held out his hand to show us the blistering that spread across his fingertip.

"That tells us one thing—the path is poisoned." He pulled a leather pouch out of his backpack and, fitting it over his hand, touched it to the soil. Another moment and he removed it.

"I didn't feel anything on my palm, but look." He turned the pouch inside out. An oily stain spread across it. We waited for another moment and it soaked through the top layer. "You can walk along the path if you have shoes on and not feel it. But by the time you reach the door, it will have saturated the soles of your shoes. My guess is that by then, it will not only be eating into your feet, but infecting the blood. And if you *can* die, you will."

I knelt beside him, eyeing the leather. "All of the skeletons are by the door. That means it must be quick acting but not instantaneous. It shouldn't take more than a few minutes to reach the temple. Okay, so we stay off the path. What about the moss? Surely somebody else figured this out before us? Or, are those the only four who have ever made it down here?"

"We'll never know, but it really doesn't matter." Morio frowned. "Bran, I hate to presume on you, but you're the one that can't be affected by the poison. Can you check out the moss?"

Bran moved over to the pale mulch that covered the rest of the island. He took his other hand and placed it on the moss, then after a moment lifted it. "Nothing. I'll try the leather." Again, he repeated the experiment with the bag. And again, nothing.

"Then we should be able to walk across the moss without a problem." Morio was frowning, though. "It still feels too simple, but maybe I'm over-thinking matters. We don't know how the skeletons in the cave died, but I can't understand how this group could have gotten past the crystal scorpions— the spell hadn't been triggered."

"Unless somebody reset it. Another mystery we'll never figure out." I sighed, looking around. "Well, we can't stand here forever," I was getting antsy.

"I'll go. I can cross the moss, and if there's nothing on my shoes by the time I get over there, just follow in my footsteps. I'll scrape through it with my sword so you can follow the path." Bran stood up and dusted his hands on his pants. "I'm going to move fast though—there's no sense in giving whoever built this hellhole any more of a chance to destroy us than they already have."

He calculated the distance to the door, then moved away from the path a little more. After one more check of the moss, he took off, running through the moss, dragging his sword behind him to leave a trail that we could follow. A moment later, he stood by the door, examining the soles of his boots. Another minute and he waved for us to join him. I sucked in a deep breath and moved up to the trail he'd left.

"I'm going next. Hurry. We don't want to be separated in case anything comes creeping out of those doors." And, hiking my cloak and skirts so they weren't trailing on the ground, I turned to Delilah. "Can you carry my staff for me? I'm not the best athlete and running with this is bound to get a little iffy for me."

She laughed and nodded, taking it from me. "Be careful. Don't fall down."

And with that advice ringing in my ears, I took off, racing along the trail made by Bran's sword. The distance seemed immense, even though it really was only a matter of fifty yards or so. It passed by in a blur of pale luminosity from the faint glow of the moss.

Shaking, I managed to reach the other side. Bran made me sit down and he looked at the soles of my boots. Nothing but regular dirt and a few embedded pebbles. He motioned to the others. One by one, they joined us and, one by one, we looked at their shoes. No sign of the poison.

I took my staff back from Delilah and wandered over to the skeletons, not really wanting to examine them but feeling we should. As I knelt, making sure they weren't bonewalkers—we didn't need any bones-on-the-hoof attacking us—I saw that the bottoms of their feet were pitted, the bone looking terribly porous, like pahoehoe lava.

"The poison. They did come across the dirt—and whatever is in it ate through their boots and into their feet. So I guess—regardless of where they came from—they never made it inside." I slowly reached out to run my hand over the door. A deep knell reverberated through my fingers and hit my stomach like a gong, almost keeling me over.

Morgaine whirled around. "What was that?"

"I don't know! I just touched the door." But something had happened—I could feel it all through my body. I'd woken something up with my touch and now . . . now we would have to face whatever it was. I just prayed I hadn't inadvertently set Yvarr loose from his prison.

As I stood there, frozen by the energy that clamored through me, the door softly opened, crushing the bones as it swept them aside. A low murmur echoed from deep within the chamber and I thought I could hear my name on the wind that rushed out. I knew then—knew in my gut, in the depths of my soul. The Merlin was in there, sleeping. And it was time to wake him up.

Morgaine stepped up to my side. She glanced over at me. "We have to go. You know that. You can feel it." It was a statement, not a question.

I nodded. "Yes, I feel him waiting for us." Without pausing to decide whether it was a good idea or a stupid one, my cousin and I stepped over the threshold and into the chamber. Mordred followed us, and then the others. The moment we all entered the building, the door slammed shut behind us. We were trapped, alone in a tomb as old as the hills. And by the sound of a low rustling skirting the perimeters of whatever room we were in, we weren't alone.

Chapter 17

❧❦❧

"What the hell is that?" When the door slammed shut on us, the room was plunged into pitch black. I could hear the rustle of something swirling around the room, like wings brushing against fabric. But there was no sound of breath or voice or anything to give us a clue of what was locked in the room with us.

I had to do something. My fear seemed to translate into my staff and it jolted my hand enough for me to realize that I was still carrying it. With a sudden hunch, I struck the end of it against the floor, hitting it hard as I shouted, "Light!"

The energy I had basically downloaded into it from the lightning flared, and the crystal orb on the end blazed to life, shining like I'd just turned on the light switch. It glowed, sparkling with a clear lilac-colored light, illuminating the room enough for us to see where we were.

I immediately looked for whatever it was that had been making the rustling noise and there, to one side, I saw it— whatever *it* was. Tucked back against a corner, shying from the light, was a ghostly shape of a long, narrow serpent. But as we watched, it peered out, its head bobbing and weaving as it gazed at us. The form was translucent, but unmistakably sea green. Pale blue undertones blended through it, a lot like tie-dye. It was then that I noticed the vestigial wings.

"Is that . . . a dragon?" It couldn't be—it looked like no dragon I'd ever seen. Not even Yvarr.

Morgaine let out a soft gasp. "Yes—but it's a baby."

As she spoke, she held out her hand and the creature slowly moved forward. Once it was out in the light, I could see she was correct. The baby dragon was pretty, almost cute, even though I knew it was probably older than everybody in this room. With wide eyes the color of toffee, it let out a soft sound that hovered somewhere between a mew and a growl, and it hiccupped, breathing out a puff of smoke from each nostril. By now, I recognized a lot of the Dragonkin, but this one . . . I had no real clue what class it belonged to and Smoky wasn't here to tell me. At first I thought it might be a blue dragon, but the energy felt more grounded than the water beasts.

"What kind? I don't recognize it—"

But Morgaine knew. "She, and I believe it *is* a girl, is a cross between blue and green. Water and earth. The elements of the Merlin." She motioned toward the center of the room. "Look."

In the center of the room rested a long crystal coffin, carved from flawless green glass. In the coffin, stretched out in repose, lay the body of a man. He might be dead, or he might be sleeping, but he was holding a staff and antlers rose from the headdress he wore. I stepped in for a closer look and the room began to hum. The dragon swirled around excitedly, accidentally knocking against me when she sped by. I stumbled, but caught myself before I went sprawling.

Morgaine stepped forward, but the dragon whirled with a flourish and nose-dived into her, driving her back. The creature growled then, baring her teeth. Even though she was a baby, she was bigger than we were. Morgaine tried to step around her, but the dragon had had enough, and this time, she bowled into Morgaine and knocked her off her feet.

Mordred moved to help his aunt, but the dragon growled again and he backed away. Morgaine scrambled back, fear on her face. Once again, the dragon turned to me again, ignoring her.

"Stay back," I told the others. "Don't interfere."

Morio held Delilah back. We were linked enough for him to know I meant what I said. Tanne was keeping an eye on Bran and Arturo. Morgaine seemed to grasp that she wasn't welcome. She and Mordred moved back with the others.

I waited, wondering what was going to happen next. It didn't take long to find out. The dragon rustled through the air, like a fish through water, and stopped close enough for me to feel her breath on my neck. She leaned in, her brilliant yellow eyes swirling, and then gently reached forward and nose-bumped me. I stumbled toward the coffin. When I was leaning against the glass, the baby let out a muffled sound. Not sure what she wanted me to do, I turned around to gaze through the glass at the man inside.

He was the Merlin. I knew it in my heart. I knew it in my soul. His energy emanated from the casket even though he was still sleeping. He was beautiful—in a way—and terrifying. Great spiraling horns rose from his headdress, and from this position, I could see they were attached to the skull plate of an ancient elk.

Myrddin's face was long and angular, not gaunt by any means but definitely British, with thick, full lips that beckoned me in a way I'd never quite felt before. His eyes were open—limpid and warm as liquid caramel.

As I stared at him, mesmerized, it was as though I could see the ages passing by in his silent gaze. He showed no sign that he saw me, but somehow, I felt he knew I was here. His chin was strong but not boxy, and a thin stubble of hair covered it—red sprinkled with a little gray. His hair curled down his bare chest, the locks the same deep burgundy as his beard. His chest was muscled and strong. He wore a cloak, open and fallen to the side, of green and brown, and trousers that looked like a brown suede.

As I gazed at him, the dragon began to circle the coffin, and me. Faster she moved, as if doing laps, her body streaming by in a smooth flowing cadence. She moved widdershins—counterclockwise—and my stomach began to knot as the

floor swayed beneath my feet. And yet, I could not look away.
There he lay, the most beautiful sorcerer of all time: the High
Priest of the Hunter himself, locked within a crystal casket.

I clutched my staff. The echo of a drum reverberated in the
background and, startled, I glanced to the side. A shadowy figure sat on the floor next to the foot of the coffin. He was playing
a silver dumbak, with a stretched hide head. Around the base,
embossed knotwork circled the drum. Cloaked in the shadows,
the drummer focused on his task, and I closed my eyes as the
voice of the drum began to sing to me.

The spirit of the music swirled, beckoning me to join her
dance as she raced through my body. I shivered, for a
moment unsure of whether she was actually in my body, or
whether I was in hers. Swaying to the beat, I allowed her to
guide me on the journey.

Another spirit filtered out of the drum, and this one
entered my staff—the ethereal shape slithering like a snake
into the base of the yew and up to the crystal orb on top. I
began to tap the staff's butt on the floor and the orb sparkled
with the colors of faerie fire, the colors of the magic deep
within the ancient woodland.

Images began to flash through my mind as I journeyed
back through the mists. They unfolded in my mind like a
movie.

*A line of drummers, keeping perfect synch with their
rhythm as people circled around a huge bonfire. Men
dressed in hides and antlers told stories with their dance, as
others beat together bones, keeping up a rhythm with the
drummers. Women joined in the ritual—some in long woven
tunics, some bare-breasted with skirts—all the clothing
adorned with intricate vining designs.*

There was a hush, as I hovered, suspended over the scene,
and then as I watched the dancers gave way, moving back.

*A woman, pale as the night in skin, with hair as dark as the
sky, entered the circle. She wore a black cloak over a gossa-
mer dress that was pale violet with silver embroidery. She
began to dance in front of one of the drums. As she danced,
another figure bathed in shadows came into the scene.*

Gasping, I pulled back, trying to shake myself out of the

vision. Something was coming, something huge and wild and feral, and fear built in the pit of my stomach. But the dragon pushed me forward again, nudging against me, and I recovered the scene.

The figure emerged from the shadows. It was the Merlin, with his huge antlered headdress riding high, the rack thrusting into the air, tines sharpened and stately. He wore a long green cloak, and it fell open, revealing his chiseled and defined stomach, and below that, the perfect V leading to his erect cock—long and rigid, lined with veins that pulsed with desire.

He had eyes only for his lady, and as he moved toward her, she swept off her cloak. The sheer material of her dress parted in the center, and she swept it back, the thatch of her hair dark against her mound. She reached down to stroke herself, then raised her fingers to her lips and slowly licked them. At that, the Merlin moved in, stalking her as she began to tease him around the circle.

I caught my breath, feeling the fire rise as my hunger grew. The dragon stopped her circling, and I knew what I had to do.

I whirled, motioning to Morio. "Get over here. Now."

He slipped into the circle and the dragon resumed her spinning, but now a wall of mist began to form around the coffin, cutting us off from the rest. I slid off my cloak, oblivious to the cold, and then shrugged out of my clothes. Morio asked no questions. One glance at the coffin and he seemed to understand exactly what we needed to do. He stripped, his chest glistening in the ghostly illumination of the pale green mist. I tapped the staff and the beating of the drums grew stronger. Morio began to sway to their rhythm and the bond between us—the Soul Symbiont bond—told me he could hear them through our connection.

I gasped as he stood naked before me. His long dark hair gleamed, a curtain of black against his skin. The slant of his eyes, the tint of his skin, the smooth, lithe muscled body, never failed to make me hunger. He reached out and gripped his cock firmly in one hand as his gaze never left my face. I couldn't take my eyes off his hand as he roughly stroked himself, the look on his face hungry and demanding.

Like the priestess in my vision, I set aside my staff and began to circle the coffin, beckoning my priest to follow me.

Morio danced forward, the dance of the Hunter, the dance of the predator following his prey. He stalked me, deliberate and cunning, as I danced widdershins around the coffin. I began to clap to the drumbeat, then, using my body, I drummed on my thighs and my butt, teasing him, turning so he could see my ass, waiting till he was almost within reach and then darting away.

Around we went, the Hunter and the Priestess, weaving the magic with our bodies, with our passion, building the energy with our offering. The dragon circled still faster as Morio leaped toward me. I turned to run, leaving a wave of faerie fire in my wake. He inhaled deeply, sucking in the magic with his breath, and the haze of magic now sparkled from his eyes. And then—the energy was so strong that I couldn't move. I froze, arms stretched wide to my sides, legs spread.

Morio dropped to his knees by my feet. He gazed up at me, longing and hunger, fire and passion all rolled into one look. "Honored Priestess, may I worship at your temple?"

The mood shifted and I closed my eyes, the energy crackling through my body like lightning incarnate. The scene from long ago faded, and now the only thing that existed in the world was my priest, myself, and the coffin beside us. And there was one way to wake up the ancient one who needed to be walking among us.

"You may."

Morio kissed the tops of my feet. "Blessed are the feet of the Priestess, that she might walk the path of the Moon Mother."

My feet began to tingle as his lips touched my skin, and I was running through the night, with the Hunt, wild and feral. The Moon Mother shrieked and her cry pierced me with longing and spurred me on, as I swept through the night.

Morio kissed my knees. "Blessed are the knees of the Priestess, that she might kneel at the sacred altars."

My knees began to tingle, and I was kneeling before a bonfire that raged out of control, mirroring my lust and desire for the consort of the goddess—the Hunter was coming in from beyond the great mountains, from the ancient forests and deep woods, and he was driving a host before him.

Morio kissed below my belly button. "Blessed is the womb of the Priestess, that she might embody the passion of the Moon Mother."

The drumming grew louder, and a lone, sinuous flute began to weave through the pounding rhythm. I began to breathe heavily, my body aching for release, hungry for touch. I wanted to fuck, to fuck the priest of the god and by doing so, fuck the God incarnate.

Morio stood. He faced me, then leaned down to kiss my breasts. "Blessed are the breasts of the Priestess, that the love of the Moon Mother might shine through her."

A cold fire raced through me. Love—honest love, tough love, the love that both created and destroyed when it was time—blossomed forth. I wanted to embrace the world with my love and both destroy and create it anew.

Morio leaned in, and kissed my lips. He barely pulled away to whisper, "Blessed are the lips of the Priestess, that she might speak the words of the Moon Mother."

"Take me." The Moon Mother spoke through me to the Hunter, as I spoke to my priest.

And then, slowly, his gaze fixed to mine, he leaned in again and roughly fastened his lips to mine, his tongue gently darting between my lips. I lowered my arms, enfolding him in my embrace, my hands sliding across the smooth skin of his back. Morio moaned, low and muffled, his mouth pressed against mine.

Sliding my hand down to cup his perfect, tight, ass, I caught my breath as his cock pressed against my stomach, erect and rigid. As I shifted my hips, he broke away from the kiss, his eyes flaring with desire.

He picked me up and swung me on top of the casket. I braced my feet against the smooth crystal, spreading my knees. Morio let out a hungry laugh and crawled between my legs, his cock primed. Whimpering, I pulled him down, and he drove himself into me, as he filled me up to the hilt. I was wet, slick, and he slid in with a soft sound, stretching me wide, yet that did nothing to relieve the tension, but just merely stoked the fire.

As he began to thrust, my breasts rubbed against his chest and he leaned down, lowing his lips to my right nipple, tugging it with his teeth, teasing me as he held still, deep within me, forcing me still. Impaled on his cock, I shifted my hips, begging him to move, to drive himself into me, but he held fast, building the heat between us, and reached down to stroke my clit.

I whimpered, wanting to be driven over that edge, to soothe the itch and growing pressure. I tightened my pussy around his cock, squeezing to firmly hold him inside me. That pushed him into action, and he drew back, then drove himself in me for all he was worth, ramming his cock deep before sliding out for another thrust.

Drunk with lust, I met his pace, fucking him with every ounce of energy I had, pouring all the pent-up hunger and desire into the mix. The dragon picked up her pace, whirling around us, whipping our passion into a cloud of mist that covered the circle we were in.

Another moment, and I suddenly felt myself on the edge, teetering on the rocks, and then nothing could stop me and I fell, bucking as I came. I screamed out the name "Myrddin" and a flash filled the circle, blinding me as I orgasmed. Morio climaxed, pumping with one, final thrust as he cried out. The energy we had built spiraled into a cone, and then, swirling, dove down again and disappeared into the coffin.

We froze for a moment—a lifetime?—and then, he slowly relaxed into my arms as I went limp, all the energy dissipating.

The dragon slowed her circling, and an inner nudge pushed me to sit up. Morio climbed off the coffin and helped me down. As we turned, I wasn't surprised to see that the mist now also filled the casket.

"We have to get it open. Quickly." I shrugged into my clothes as fast as I could. The cold had returned and whatever altered space we'd been in had just vanished.

Morio hurried to dress, a goofy smile on his face. He was a loving and passionate partner, and when magic entered our sex, it was mind-blowing. While he finished putting on his boots, I hurried over to the coffin and looked for a way to open it. There, on the side, I found a recess. I slid my fingers inside and felt a button.

"Hurry—we need to open this now."

As Morio fastened his belt, I pressed the button and a soft sigh issued from inside the casket. The mist began to swirl out. Morio joined me, helping me swing the lid open. The hinges were strong and kept it from bouncing against the floor.

The last whiffs of the mist wafted away, and the dragon slowed her circling as the rest of the room came back into focus. Delilah and Tanne had pulled out flashlights and the cool beams lit up the room. Morgaine, Mordred, and Arturo began to edge forward. Bran was keeping his distance, and Delilah and Tanne were keeping an eye on everyone.

I turned back to the casket, as did Morio. Now, I could see the man lying within had coiling blue snakes tattooed around both forearms. As we watched, his open eyes, blinked, and he slowly turned his head.

"Where am I?"

The Merlin had woken up.

Out of the coffin, Myrddin was even more beautiful than he was in it. His hair was shoulder length, and the burgundy locks tumbled around his shoulders in a cascade of curls. The scruff on his chin gave him a rugged look, and he stood with authority. I don't think there was a person in the room—including Bran—who wasn't at least a little in awe. Morgaine stared at him with shining eyes, and I'd never seen her look so happy.

Myrddin let out a slow breath, and as he did so, the dragon wound herself around him in a sinuous hug. He reached out and lightly stroked her head.

"Áine, my love." Affection filled his voice, and he lightly kissed his fingers and pressed them to her forehead. "You are still with me."

The dragon—apparently named Áine—let out a soft

croon and went back to circling the room, but at a slower pace. She seemed at peace now, almost comforted. As I watched her, memories of the woman in the vision filtered back and then I knew who Áine was.

She'd been the priestess—the Merlin's consort and partner. I hung my head, wondering how long she'd waited for his return. Had she always been a dragon-shifter? A young one, she'd had to have been when they were first together, if she'd watched over him for thousands of years. But then, Smoky was a young dragon and he had lived before the Great Divide.

"Welcome back, Lord Myrddin," I finally said, not knowing exactly how to approach him. I had no clue what title he preferred, or if he had any idea what year he was now in.

Myrddin turned to me, and then glanced over the group. "You have the advantage. You know who I am, but I have no clue who any of you are. Or . . . even *when* I am. Introductions, if you would, and tell me what year is this?"

His English was impeccable. How the hell he adapted to our language without even hearing us talk confounded me, but then I glanced over at the dragon. She tilted her head and I could have sworn she winked at me. Somehow, she'd played a part in it. I wasn't sure how, but women had a way of letting other women know their secrets.

I curtseyed. I was used to curtseying before those I considered royalty and the practice felt as natural as breathing. "My name is Camille. I'm a Priestess of the Moon Mother. This is my sister Delilah, a Death Maiden for the Autumn Lord. Morio, one of my husbands. And these"—I turned to gesture to each in turn—"Morgaine, the Queen of Dusk and Twilight. Her nephew Mordred, and . . . Arturo." I wondered if Myrddin would even have a clue who they were—he'd been imprisoned before any of them had been born. It had been Meher who had played the Merlin to Arturo's Arthur.

But Myrddin walked over to Morgaine and gazed down at her—he was close to six feet without his headdress, and Morgaine was short. "You remind me of someone." He turned back to me. "You, too. The both of you remind me of my Áine when she took her human form." His expression fell, and I had the feeling there was something we didn't quite know about the dragon-shifter. He must have seen the question in my eyes. "Do you know . . . of the battle that took place—"

"The Great Divide, when the Fae Lords separated the worlds into their own realms?"

He nodded.

"Yes . . . we were taught in our history courses about it. Well, over in Otherworld. You are Earthside, by the way." I wasn't sure how much information to pile on him at once.

But Myrddin merely nodded. "I thought as much. I rather doubted they would imprison me over in the new realm. When we stood at trial—Aeval and Titania, Áine, and I— they chose to imprison the Fae Queens and me. But Áine was young, and they took pity. They laid a spell on her, forcing her to forever be locked within her dragon form."

That was so many shades of wrong. The more I was hearing, the more pissed off I was at the Fae Lords. "Couldn't they just let her return to the Dragon Realms?"

Áine silently glided up, bumping lightly into the Merlin's arm. She rubbed her giant head against him and he laughed, stroking it. "My love . . . I begged her to, but she wouldn't leave my side. They locked her here as a guardian for me. She's been alone all this time, watching over my body."

Morgaine's eyes narrowed. "There are reasons that many of the Fae stayed Earthside."

"But what year is this? And how did you find me to wake me up? Dreams have come and gone, and so many visions that I have no clue what might be real and what isn't. I have my memories, now that I'm awake, but there are some images that haunt me, and I do not know if they were actual, or if they were simply paintings on my mind's canvas." Myrddin was soft-spoken but the authority behind his voice echoed through the chamber.

I sucked in a long breath and told him what year it was, watching his eyes widen. "Morgaine knew how to find you thanks to Meher, the acting Merlin who trained her." Standing back, I had the feeling that Myrddin would have some questions for her.

And that, he did. "Meher? I do not remember him."

Morgaine curtseyed, as deep and gracious as I had, which surprised me. She didn't look in the least like she was trying to be a smartass with him, and I realized she was afraid. The Merlin had her scared spitless. Either that or she was running mega-fangirl.

"My lord, Meher took the title from the ashes of your reign, some five hundred years after you were imprisoned, I believe. I wasn't around at that time. There was a period in which the great Fae Lords prevented anyone from acting in your stance, and only then did they enthrone someone they could control. Meher was firmly in Otherworld's pockets, until he got greedy and struck out on his own."

Myrddin didn't look very happy. "Only the Hunter may choose his High Priest. This Meher had no authority to act in my stead and the Fae Lords had no right to appoint him to the task." He drew himself up, straightening his shoulders. "Is he still holding office?"

Morgaine shook her head. "I think there may be someone else in charge now, but I have no idea. There is no strength to the post any longer."

Áine fluttered around Myrddin in a dizzying spiral. She then gently nudged Morgaine, and then, me. I wasn't sure what she was doing. I knew better than to lose any respect for her, but I realized that I no longer feared her. Oh, she would be deadly if roused, but there was a gentleness to her, a softness that was both vulnerable and terribly strong at the same time. I shivered, thinking of how she'd been trapped in here, all that time, protecting her lover's body as he slept.

Reaching out, I hesitantly held my hand up to her cheek. She purred like a cat and rubbed the feather-like scales along my fingers. I stroked her lightly, reveling in how smooth and warm her cheek was. She hiccupped then, a puff of smoke emerging from her nostrils to make me cough, and I laughed.

"She likes you." Myrddin glanced at me. "She needs a friend. She's been alone for so long." He turned back to Morgaine, and then his gaze fell on Arturo. He beckoned him forward. Morgaine looked wary, but there was no way she could contradict the Merlin. Only Titania or Aeval would have the power to do that, and even they might be hesitant in going up against him.

"You are so lost . . ." Myrddin reached out to touch Arturo's hand. He swiftly raised his gaze, staring into the Wounded King's eyes. "You are lost and everything seems as if it's in a dream." With a wave of his hand, he swept his fingers lightly across Arturo's temples. "Wake, old man, and remember your greatness. Wake, and remember your destiny."

As Morgaine realized what he was doing, she let out a faint cry. Mordred sprang forth, but before he could reach them, Myrddin slapped his palm against Arturo's forehead and the fog in the man's eyes cleared. As we watched, he came to life once more, understanding flickering into his eyes. He woke, from centuries of lethargy, to Myrddin's touch and as he did so, his shoulders straightened and his aura flared.

Arturo turned to see Mordred running toward him and he opened his arms. "*My son.* You *are* here. I've thought . . . I thought you existed only in my memories and even those were fading into distant songs and glimpses of the past." And then, whirling, he saw Morgaine and the expression on his face crumpled into one of pain and loss. "You—what are *you* doing here?"

For a moment, Morgaine stared at him, uncertainty and fear crossing her face. "I saved your life when Lancelot would have taken it. I've kept you going all these years. *That's* what I'm doing here." Anger replaced anguish. "I took care of you, and fed you, and kept you out of trouble."

Mordred fell into the mix looking confused. "Why are you mad at Aunt Morgaine? She tells the truth—she's taken care of you."

"I will not let her have you back! She would turn you to her side to spite me. I asked you for nothing, Morgaine—I wanted *nothing* from you!" Arturo's pale and complacent look had taken on a sanguine, defiant expression. "And what do you mean, you saved my life? Mordred saved me."

"He fought off Lancelot, but you were bleeding out. I did the only thing I could to save your ass. I fed you the Nectar of Life and took you back to Avalon at my own risk." Morgaine was crying now. I'd never seen her so distraught and my first impulse was to take her side, but Morio held me back.

"What for? Did you think it would change my feelings? Did you think you could make me love you by saving my life? Did you think I'd give Mordred back to you just because you did your duty and saved your king?" Arturo was raging now, and in that moment, I realized that the villain here wasn't Morgaine, and it wasn't Mordred, but instead—ignorance and anger and denial.

"Why are you yelling at her?" Mordred tugged at his arm, looking terribly confused. "Father—your sister saved your life. You should be grateful."

Arturo petulantly waved him off. "*Sister*? You still believe she is your aunt. You mean you did not tell him all of this time?" He turned a cold eye on Morgaine. "Then perhaps you didn't care as much as you protested."

Without moving a muscle, without letting Morgaine out of his gaze, Arturo dropped the bomb. "Morgaine is your *mother*, Mordred. She's the sister of my half brother. She's not of my blood. In a drunken fit, I spent a night with her and she gave birth to you. I took you in order to give you the upbringing you deserved—after all, you are the son of a king. Morgaine . . ." He turned to her, a snide look filling his eyes. "Morgaine made the mistake of falling in love with me, though I told her it was futile. And . . . apparently, she's dragged me around the world like a dog on a leash all these years."

Mordred froze. He turned from Arturo to Morgaine. "Is he telling the truth? Are you my real mother and not Gwenyfyr?"

Morgaine stretched out one hand. "Mordred—how could I tell you when you grew up believing I was your aunt? Arthur refused to let me tell you as you grew up. Didn't you ever wonder where you got your Fae heritage from?"

"I thought Gwenyfyr had it in her bloodline." His face cold and devoid of reason, Mordred turned on Arturo. "You took me from my mother to give to another woman? You turned me against her and then let me throw my life on the line for you? And yet you denied me a place in line for the throne? Lancelot was right—you have no honor! Everything I believed about you was a lie." He drew his sword, fury surrounding him like a cloak.

"Stop—you have to stop now!" Delilah jumped forward, but Tanne grabbed her arm, pulling her out of the way.

"This is between them," he said.

I had no clue what to do. I whirled on one heel to face Myrddin. "You started this. What do you intend to do about it?"

The High Priest of the Hunter shook his head, an imperturbable look on his face. "This was frozen in time for too long. It must be reconciled for destiny to move forward. I can—and will—do nothing to stop whatever will be."

Morio slid his arm around me, and I turned to him, feeling helpless. Even Bran, standing next to me, looked alarmed.

Crying, Morgaine crumpled to the floor, her hands pressed against her face. Arturo stared at his son. Mordred was standing tall, his hair streaming back. He held his sword out, waiting.

"Well, then, now you fight for your *mother's* honor?" Arturo lifted his own sword. "How quickly your allegiance changes. I meet your challenge."

Mordred hesitated, and the world seemed to pause with him. Then, with one quick thrust, he lunged toward Arturo, who dropped his sword and opened his arms to the blade. Taken by surprise at the sudden surrender, Mordred couldn't stop. His sword sliced neatly through Arturo's stomach, emerging from the back.

As Morgaine let out a scream, the blood began to pour, running a river to pool at Arturo's feet. Mordred stumbled back, leaving his sword embedded in Arturo's gut. He began to stutter, then turned to Morgaine, who crouched weeping and broken like the stem of a reed. Mordred stuttered out a garbled word that we couldn't understand as the door of the tomb crashed open, slamming against the back wall. He turned and raced outside.

Arturo stared down at the blade piercing his gut, then, with a look of wonder, let out a croak of laughter, and dropped where he stood. Morgaine scrambled on her hands and knees to hover over him, frantically feeling for a pulse. But there would be no heartbeat. Not even Nectar of Life could heal an attack so deadly. She looked over to the door and whispered, "Mordred," and then fainted. Outside, the light of the cavern never wavered.

Chapter 18

Bran hurried over to the door, but shook his head. "I don't see him anywhere."

"The boat!" If he took the boat we were in trouble.

Bran vanished out the door, Tanne following. Delilah crouched beside Morgaine, but she was out cold. With Morio's help, my sister moved her out of the way so Arturo's blood wouldn't stain her clothing. That would just make everything so much worse.

I turned to the Merlin. "So *this* is your idea of letting destiny unfold?"

He shrugged. "I don't make destiny, I just help enable it." With a soft voice, he added, "I don't enjoy seeing people hurt, but sometimes there are no winners."

I was about to ask if he could help Morgaine like he had Arturo, but he held up his hand.

"There's nothing I can do for her," Myrddin said. "Her wound is emotional, not physical. I can help heal physical problems, but injuries of the heart are not my forte."

I knelt beside Morgaine and brushed her hair away from her face. For all of her faults, she didn't deserve this. Losing the man she had loved and taken care of all these years, and losing her son in the same moment? Not fair.

As I glanced over at Arturo, I realized I now despised him instead of pitying him. Myrddin should have left him in his fog. He'd been happy and Morgaine had—in her own way—been content with the life she'd carved out. But then again, she'd been seeking the Merlin herself, looking for answers. Now, she had them, even if they weren't the ones she'd hoped for.

She was still unconscious and I had the feeling she'd remain so for a while. I turned back to Myrddin. He was standing, watching the scene impassively.

"We need your help. We tracked you down for a reason." I wasn't entirely sure that we were making the right move, but there was no help for it now. He was awake, and we'd already seen fallout from his return.

"What do you want?"

"An ancient wyrm is waking. Yvarr. The Fae Lords imprisoned their allies as well as their enemies. It's only a matter of time before he breaks out of his prison. Can you help?" I didn't ask *will you* . . . he might choose to say no, but I wasn't going to offer up the choice. If he wanted to be the bad guy, it would be on his own head.

But he surprised me. "I can. And I *will*." His smile suggested he'd either read my expression or my thoughts, and I sincerely hoped it was the former. Either way, though, at least this gods-awful trip had some positive results.

"We still have daylight with us, so we'd better get moving, before it gets too late. We're nearly out of food, though, so I hope you don't get too hungry before we're out of here." I told him where we were—in the realm of the Elder Fae— and he at least had the courtesy to look alarmed.

"I concur. The sooner we leave this place, the better. The Elder Fae have always been capricious, and I doubt they have mellowed any in the time I've been asleep." Myrddin motioned to Áine and she flowed up beside him. "But with my lovely by our side, I doubt if many will bother us on the return trip."

By then, Morgaine was beginning to wake up, but she wasn't all there, and could barely speak. Instead, she let us lead her, and I realized she'd be no use in navigating back the way we'd come. I'd have to take over.

"Delilah, please watch her? Tanne, cover our butt. Myrddin, you and Áine take your place right before Tanne please. Morio, follow me. And Delilah can follow Morio, bringing Morgaine." I turned to Bran. As much as I didn't want to interact with him, now was not the time to be choosy. "You—up front with me, please."

He, too, seemed quiet. With a long look at Morgaine, he fell in beside me. We made sure we had all our gear. We'd plundered Arturo's body for what we could salvage, feeling guilty with everything we took. But he wouldn't need his things now, and there was nothing to be gained by forfeiting them.

Since there was no way to take his body back with us, we placed him in the crystal coffin and gently shut the lid. Morgaine stared at it mutely, then pressed her lips to the cool crystal and hung her head as Delilah led her away.

"What about Mordred?" Tanne asked.

"We can't go chasing after him. We don't know where he went, and we don't have the resources to find him. It would be too easy to get lost in this place." I shook my head. "We have no choice. We have to leave him behind."

Myrddin spoke. "His destiny lies elsewhere, I fear." He opened his mouth to say something else. Afraid of what might be coming, I shook my head.

"Shut the fuck up, please." I nodded toward Morgaine. "Have some pity."

With a shrug, he closed his mouth and, crooking his finger to Áine, he fell in line and we set off. By the time we got to the shore, Mordred was nowhere to be seen, but the boat was there. If he was still on the island, he had to have found some sort of cover we couldn't see. If he'd chanced swimming, then he was dead. It was simply too cold for human or Fae to make it across the lake. Silently, we took our places in the boat. This time, Bran, Tanne, Delilah, and Morio rowed while I looked after Morgaine. Áine swept along beside us as we traversed the water, the only sound the swish of our oars.

Returning through the tunnel was worse than heading in, primarily because we were tired and hungry. Morgaine refused to eat the last of the food that we tried to give to her, and rather than throw it away—it would go bad if we left it any longer—I handed it to Myrddin. He hadn't eaten in several thousand years. We'd see what he thought of a sandwich. Apparently, he didn't think it too bad, because he wolfed it down with no comment.

By the time we reached the cavern again, I was exhausted. A glance outside told me it was near nightfall.

"We need to rest. We have two days walk back to the entrance." The thought of going that long without food didn't sit well. It wouldn't hurt us, though we'd all be wolfish by then, but it sure as hell wasn't going to make for happy campers. At least not Delilah and me.

"I can try to hunt along the way," Tanne offered, but I nixed the idea.

"We're down on manpower. We're in a hurry. We don't want to light a fire to attract any unsavory types. And it's still snowing, thanks to Beira, who left us this lovely present of winter weather. I think we'll just push on as hard and quickly as we can. As it is, we need to melt a lot of snow tonight so we'll have water for traveling."

Having said that, Delilah and I gathered all the water bottles and slipped outside the cavern, into the blowing storm. Again, we took one of the plastic tarps and heaped a mound of snow on it, then brought it in. The men tied the corners to four stalagmites. Áine swept in, took one look at the snow, and breathed warm smoke on it. The resulting melt was quick enough for us to not only fill our water bottles, but to drink deep, go for seconds, and refill them again. By the time we bedded down that night, all our water bottles were full.

Áine and Morio took the first watch. Tanne and Delilah volunteered for the second, and I took the third with Bran. I still didn't trust Myrddin enough to leave him up watching over our sleeping selves. We settled for four solid hours of sleep each, and broke camp while it was still dark. But at least we knew which way we were going, and though the snow was a bitch, we weren't afraid of falling over the edge, given the tall rock face that sheltered us from the drop to the side.

The journey down was rough, plowing through the snow, but it wasn't as difficult as the climb and to my surprise, we made it down with a distinct time advantage. But, staring across the marsh, I realized crossing the bog was going to be hell. The snow was deeper, and it was impossible to see the way we'd come.

"This is a mess. How the hell do we cross this in one piece?" I explained the problem to Myrddin.

He grinned. "Not so much of a problem. Áine is a cross between water and earth in the Dragon Realm, so she can seek out the path and guide us over. Would you like me to take the lead since I can talk to her?"

I wavered. I was still unsure, but if I said no, then we'd be slogging through here far longer than we could afford to. I didn't want to be caught on the marsh any longer than we had to be. Myrddin might not be our ally—we couldn't be sure yet—but he wasn't going to be inclined to take a nose-dive into the icy water either. Morio agreed when I pulled him aside to ask his opinion.

But Morgaine worried me. She still hadn't spoken—the last word she'd said was to call after Mordred, and we'd seen no sign of him. I had a suspicion he might have flung himself into the lake, but we couldn't know. We might never know.

I slipped my arm around her, and she gave me a blank look. "Cousin? Can you hear me?" Her eyes flickered but she made no reply. "Morgaine, please say something. I know you're hurting, I know this was a horrible thing for you, but you have to say something." Still nada. Finally, I brushed her bangs back and the look in her eyes shifted—she was pleading with me, but I didn't know what she wanted. Then, as quickly as the light had come, it faded and she went back to staring straight ahead.

I motioned to Delilah. "We're going to have to just take her back to Aeval and see what they can do."

Myrddin whistled. "We'd best go. Áine says there's a dark force on the horizon. It will be here within the hour, so let's be off before it crosses our path."

The last thing we needed was another encounter, so we headed out, following Áine and Myrddin, silently crossing the marsh. Nobody felt like talking, and it was well toward night when we reached the other side. I glanced up at the sky. Even though we couldn't see her, the Moon Mother would be full tonight, which meant even more trouble for Delilah and me. And . . . Morgaine.

"Delilah, you need to stay near Morio. He's going to have to keep you from wandering off tonight. We aren't going to make it out of here without spending a full moon under the skies."

She frowned. "I hate to say it but you might want to use this. I brought it, just in case we needed it." Fishing through her pack, she frowned as she handed over a leather harness, tabby-cat size.

Morio grinned. "I think it would be a good idea if you changed now, before the moon rises and sends you into a frenzy. That way we can harness you into this and I'll carry you on the rest of the walk.

She rolled her eyes but agreed. Handing her pack to Tanne, she exhaled slowly, shifting with an even, smooth transition. The moment she was in tabby form, I snatched her up before she could change her mind and—together with Morio—managed to get her harness on. She put up a lazy fight but seemed to be doing her best to cooperate. He tucked her into his arms and we headed off again.

Everybody was tired, but I was grateful to Áine for leading us through the marsh. It had saved us hours of indecision. I was really beginning to like the dragon and wished she could shift into human form so we could have a chat.

We passed the dead bog monster, and by the time midnight

neared were back onto the grassland, and headed toward the path to the stream. I was done in. We'd been walking through snow and cold for hours without a break, and I still had to look forward to the Hunt tonight. I could feel the pull.

I turned to look at Morgaine, who was staring at the sky. With a long sigh, I turned back to Tanne. "I have no clue what's going to happen to Morgaine when the Hunt comes riding past, but when we stop for the night, watch her, would you?"

All I wanted was some downtime. We had no food, and we were cold and tired. But one more hour and we'd reach the path again, where we'd crossed the bridge and turned off into the grassland. We might as well drag our sorry butts that far before setting up camp.

By the time we came to the rushing stream, we'd had all we could take. There was no shelter here from the cold, but we did our best, huddling together with the blankets tight around us. We had Arturo's blanket, which we gave to Myrddin. He whispered something to Áine and she began gently circling us, slowly. Her bulk kept most of the wind from blasting right past us, and she began a thrumming that sounded almost like the purr of a cat. Whatever she was doing raised the temperature around us by a few degrees—enough to take the worst of the bite off.

"She'll keep watch till morning." Myrddin held my gaze. "Trust me enough to rest. If anything comes near, we'll know in advance."

Exhausted and cold, and still heartsore over a journey in which we'd lost two of our party and yet a third was traumatized beyond counting, I gave in and accepted the offer. Myrddin offered to take first watch, to guard Morgaine, making sure she was comfortable. Tanne and Bran laid down near them and quickly were snoring away. Even Delilah wasn't up to her usual moon-play. She curled up next to Morio, who fixed her leash so she couldn't get away while he slept.

I pulled my blanket around my shoulders and looked up at the cloud-covered sky. She was up there, my Lady, waiting for me. Too tired to resist, I leaned against Morio's back, and closed my eyes.

I found myself walking out under the sky, the moon rounded and full. Bright overhead, she was singing to me. I gazed up at her, my heart swelling with love. She was my lady, my goddess, my all. She was my reason for living and from her I drew my power and strength.

As I looked around, the grassy field seemed to stretch as far as the eye could see, and there were no mountains here. No trees. No place to hide. Reaching up toward her, I tried to touch the shimmering light, but she was too far away, and I could only hear her whispering.

As I turned, I realized I was waiting for the Hunt, but I wasn't in my usual place where I leaped into the passing cavalcade. Which meant there was something to be learned here, first. Some lesson the Moon Mother had in store for me. Lucid dreaming, much like wandering the astral, usually led me to some piece of knowledge that I needed to hear.

I waited, and then, like a freight train rumbling, the world fell into shards.

As I watched, a horde of goblins and ogres came racing across the field toward me, waving their weapons and singing battle songs. To my left, men in robes were marching—wands and staves in their hands. And at their helm a bearded man that I recognized as Telazhar. The sorcerers were marching.

To my right, a legion of soldiers wearing the colors of Svartalfheim rallied to meet them. At their helm, was my cousin Shamas. We'd been in love when we were younger—long before I met Trillian—but his pride and our families had interfered. Marrying cousins was commonplace in Otherworld, but marrying a half-breed? Not so acceptable. He couldn't bring himself to break tradition.

His jaw was set, a grim look on his face. Fear began to work its way into my heart. They were headed on a direct course to intercept the goblins. But there wasn't a thing I could do. Once again, I turned to see, behind me, another army appear. The colors of Y'Elestrial flew high, and as the four armies approached the center, I floated up, to watch from above.

So this must be what Menolly feels when she hovers up to the ceiling, I thought. And then, once again, my attention was riveted to the scene below. As the armies met, the soldiers began to fight and the blood was flying. Bodies fell, and in that moment, I found myself standing up on the astral, at the helm of the Moon Mother's Hunt. She was there, with her silver bow and her gleaming eyes, and she handed me my yew staff.

I reluctantly accepted it. All of a sudden, I wasn't dreaming—I *was* on the astral, in full physical form, and the moon was dazzling and brilliant, commanding me with her presence. We were above a real battlefield, and though I couldn't recognize the exact land, I knew we were in Otherworld.

"My Lady, what is this?"

The Moon Mother leaned down to stroke my cheek. "The Hunt rides tonight. The Hunt rides where it is called. The Hunt rides under the shining moon but this evening, we face a dark duty. And you walk under the dark shadow, my sweet one. There is death on the battlefield and we have soldiers' souls to gather tonight."

Chilled now, I realized what we were about to do. The Wild Hunts—there were many, from many cultures—gathered up the soldiers who fell in battle. The Hunt called to it the animals and the beasts of the world, and the wild, feral witches who served the gods of the chase.

With a shriek, the Moon Mother leaped forward and I found myself racing in her wake. We dove through the moonbeams, and ran on the astral winds, mighty gusts blowing in our wake, storms rising from our footsteps.

"Run, my loves, run and gather. Catch them up—for the moon heralds a bloody harvest tonight!" The Moon Mother spiraled down toward the battle and we followed.

Soldiers were thick in the slaughter, blood streaming as they used knife and sword, arrow and bow, hammer and mace, spear and dagger to kill the enemy. Screams right and left led us to the fallen. The enemies—the goblins and ogres—were not our affair. We paid no attention to their dead, but swept past them.

A soldier lay in my path, his heart no longer beating. But his soul was there, looking confused. A wild hunger filled my heart as I laughed, throaty and deep, and swept past him, catching him up in my wake.

"Run with me! Come to the Hunt—you are chosen!" And he fell in, racing behind me, leaving his physical life behind.

We passed by more men, and as we did, I caught their souls in my snare. "The Moon Mother commands you—join the Hunt, valiant one." As I touched each one, a single tap, they, too, joined the pack.

The Hunt stretched for miles—it was ever growing and had been since the very first night the Moon Mother had raced across the sky, calling to the dead. On most full moons, she ran for the love of it—she led the Hunt in a triumphant charge. But tonight, she was deadly serious. We were here to gather. Here to increase the pack. To sweep up the dead. We were the carrion of the skies, we were the vultures waiting for the fallen. We were fur and fang, flesh and bone, and gleaming magic.

And then, I saw who was next in line. He was standing next to his body, and looking confused as hell. And I skidded to a halt, the bloodlust high but my heart screaming, *"No!"*

"No. No . . . please, no."

But the Moon Mother urged me on. "This is what it means to be my priestess. This is what it means to serve the gods."

I wanted to cry. My stomach knotted but the pressure to run, to touch, to call to the pack remained. I bit my lips as I stared at the soldier. He was a sorcerer, but he was on our side. And at that moment, he saw me and a smile formed on his lips.

"Camille . . . how did you get here? The fighting—you have to leave!"

"No . . . oh, no. Oh, Great Mother. I didn't expect this. I didn't want this to happen. Why did you come back here? Why didn't you stay with us?" I wanted to smack him, to hurt him. But it was too late. He'd made his choice and I hadn't been around to stop him. And damn it, Menolly hadn't tried to talk him out of it. Furious at her, furious at Shamas, I stuttered out his name.

Shamas looked down and saw his body lying by his side. His face crumpled, slowly, and he hung his head. "I didn't make it . . . did I?"

Tears choking my throat, I shook my head. "Why did you leave? Why did you go? You're our cousin—we *needed* you."

He let out a soft laugh. "No. You didn't need me. Not really. Camille, you could never need me the way I needed you to. Not since our youth, when I was too stupid and too vain to stand up for us. And you don't need me now. You love more than anyone I've ever known. You have more love in your heart than is good for a person."

I was crying in earnest now. Shamas, our cousin, had returned to Otherworld, and now I knew the reason, even though Menolly hadn't told me the truth. He'd still been in love with me, but it was too late. When we had a chance, he'd caved to family prejudice. He was full-blooded Fae, and I was half-blooded. And our father's relatives hadn't been able to accept it.

"Shamas . . ."

"It's okay, Camille. Really, it is. I've made too many mistakes in my life. I caused too much pain, too much harm. I hurt you in so many ways. The truth is, I'm tired. I think I was just waiting around for something to happen. At least, here at the end, I did something worthwhile. My death means something here."

The pull was too strong. I wanted to hug him, to kiss him, to take him home and put him in bed and tuck him in. But it was too late. It would forever be too late. I nodded as I reached out, shaking.

"I'll tell Aunt Rythwar. I'll tell her you died defending our lands."

"Thanks. And Camille—remember me next Samhain? Don't forget me. Please? Go and be happy. Defeat our enemies. Live free, in a way I never could." He smiled, and the radiance of his love filled his face.

"Good night, sweet Shamas. When you reach the Land of the Silver Falls, tell my mother and father we miss them. On Samhain . . . forever . . . you'll be in my heart." Unable to say another word, I took hold of his wrist, and yanked him into the pack, and we were off again, running through the battlefields.

And there, I spent the night gathering the dead who fell in the face of our enemy. And all the while, Shamas ran by my side, never again saying another word to me. But he looked happy, and at peace.

Chapter 19

Waking up was hard, made harder because I had to tell the others what had happened. At least, I had to tell Delilah and Morio—they were the only ones who would really care.

As we rolled up our blankets, I laid out what had happened. "I didn't see Morgaine there, but she might have been. But . . . Shamas was there. He's dead."

Delilah let out a little cry.

"There were four armies," I continued. "One from Svartalfheim. Shamas was part of their forces. Another was from Y'Elestrial. Together they fought goblin hordes, and Telazhar's sorcerers. I have no idea how many there were. Thousands. And so many dead. We swept up the soldiers who could see us. Cousin Shamas . . . he said good-bye. He told me . . ." I couldn't go on. I wanted to sink to my knees, wanted to cry. We'd lost our Father. We'd lost friends—Queen Asteria for one. We'd lost so many people. And now our cousin. A man I had once loved with all my heart.

Morio leaned forward and kissed my forehead. "Remember who you are."

His words were precisely what I needed to hear, especially

with where we were and who our companions were. I wiped my eyes and looked up at Delilah. Her face was a mask of loss and vague anger, but she waited and I realized she was going to take her cue from me.

"We go on. We go home. We tell them what happened. There's nothing we can do now, except remember that he tried to do something to make the world a better place." Pushing my grief into a dark little corner until I had time and energy to face it, I wiped my nose again and pulled Morgaine aside to help her attend to her toilette before we headed out again, hungry and aching.

It was early dawn, and so far, we'd seen no other creatures. The storm must have been keeping them at bay because the isolation continued as we numbly slogged along the path and through the woodland. And then, before I realized it, we were at the portal.

I just about kissed Tanne when he pointed it out, I was so freaking glad to get the fuck out of there. The realm of the Elder Fae was wild and windswept and incredibly dangerous. By our accounts, we'd been gone since Saturday late afternoon, and if my counting was right, it was now Tuesday, around noon.

As we approached the portal, I turned to Myrddin. "Are you ready to see just what's happened to the world in the millennia you've been asleep?"

He gave a short chuckle and nodded. "If I'm not, I can always come back here, I suppose. All right, Lady Camille. Lead on, and show me the wonders of your world."

The yard never looked so much like paradise. The guards sprang into position, but seeing me, they relaxed but waited at attention until we'd all come through. All but Mordred and Arturo, that is. If they noticed the absence, they kept it to themselves, saluting Bran as he nodded to them. As leader of the Talamh Lonrach Oll Warriors, the guards—all from the sovereign nation—owed him their allegiance.

Delilah tucked her arm around my shoulder and gave me a squeeze. "We're home."

I nodded, wishing I felt more excited. I was happy, but we'd had so many shocks and the trip had been harder than we thought it would. All I wanted was a warm bath and to sleep for days.

The kitchen door opened and Smoky and Shade burst out, down the steps. Shade swung Delilah into his arms, while Smoky grabbed me around the waist and kissed me deeply. Both of them stopped suddenly as Áine appeared, walking behind the Merlin. They stared at her, and she suddenly swirled up and around in what I could swear was a happy dance.

"Who is this?" Smoky asked softly.

"Her name is Áine and she's under a curse. She can't shift into human shape. She's been stuck guarding Myrddin since the Fae Lords imprisoned him. Not so much of a fun time. We think she's a baby."

"Baby is relative. She is young, but not like a child per se. She's younger than I am by far, but an adult as far as her human form goes. I've never met a blue-green mix." He looked intrigued, as did Shade.

"Well, she's Myrddin's lover. Or, was, before they were sentenced to an eternity in that gods-forsaken cavern." I let out a long sigh and turned to see how Morgaine was doing. She was still silent, staring at the sky as the rain poured down on her face. "We have another problem. Arturo woke up, remembered he was King Arthur, Mordred found out that Morgaine is actually his mother and that Arturo is a prick."

Shade let out a disgruntled noise. "That figures. Delilah would manage to get involved in a Jerry Springer moment. So what happened to Arturo and Mordred?"

"Mordred killed Arturo in a frenzy, then he ran off when he realized what he'd done. We had to leave Arturo's body there and, since we couldn't find Mordred anywhere, we had to leave him behind, too. Morgaine is in bad shape. She hasn't spoken since it happened and we can't seem to bring her out of the fugue into which she's retreated. We couldn't get her to eat, either. And none of us have eaten in over twenty-four hours." My stomach rumbled.

"Let's get you inside. I don't know if Áine will fit . . ."

Smoky looked hesitantly at the dragon. "She's small as dragons go, but . . ."

"But she'd probably knock over a buttload of things and piss off Hanna." I turned to Myrddin. "I'm sorry, but Áine needs to stay outside. We can't fit her in the house."

He frowned, but nodded. "Let me speak to her. She can at least stretch and get some fresh air here. She's been down in that cavern—that tomb—for so long that she'll probably welcome the chance to fly."

Smoky gave the High Priest a quick smile. "Let me talk to her." He moved toward the dragon and whispered something to her. She squirmed, wriggling like a happy puppy. A twenty-foot-long, round-as-a-barrel happy puppy. But then, she shot up in the air and flew toward the woods.

When he returned, Smoky was laughing. "I told her Shade and I would come out later and go flying with her. And we'll do whatever research we can to see if there's a way to reverse the curse that she's under."

Myrddin let out a grateful sigh. "Thank you. I . . . it's been so long for her, but a frozen moment in time for me. I remember watching them curse her and wanting nothing more than to destroy every last one of them, but there was nothing I could do. They'd bound me in a place where I could do no magic, and then . . . then they came for me and that was all I clearly remember until Camille and Morio woke me up." He grinned. "I woke up to see a very interesting sight on top of the casket, that's for sure."

Smoky frowned but before he could ask, I moved us all inside.

Delilah and I took Morgaine up to my bedroom to change. We gently removed her clothing—she neither protested nor helped, just let us move her around like a rag doll.

After she was naked, I ran a warm lavender bath. The herb soothed and healed. Delilah guided her into the bathroom and, between the two of us, we managed to get her into the tub. I gently washed her back, and lathered up her hair. Her eyes were vacant, as if she'd packed up and left home.

As we cleaned her up, Morgaine's body relaxed, but she still wasn't talking and I had my doubts that she even knew we were actually there. It was beginning to feel eerie, like the lights were on but nobody was home inside. But when I thought about how long she'd been in love with Arthur, how long she'd taken care of him and how long she'd hidden her true relationship with her son, the fact that she was shell-shocked shouldn't really come as a surprise. PTSD, plain and simple.

We guided her out of the tub, dried her off, and wrapped her in a bathrobe. Then, while I pulled out my blow-dryer and dried her hair, gently brushing it smooth, Delilah went downstairs to get the parlor ready. Morgaine needed to rest. Until we could return her to Talamh Lonrach Oll, we'd keep her in there. I braided her hair and then led her down to the living room.

Nerissa was there, surprising me since it was a weekday. But Delilah said, "I called her and asked her if she could come home to keep an eye on Morgaine while we bathe and change clothes and eat."

Grateful, I turned over care of our cousin to our sister-in-law and then headed toward the stairs again, this time to take care of my own needs. The smell of grilling meat stopped me, though, and my stomach rumbled so loud that I blushed. Smoky, who was behind me, slapped me on the butt.

"Get up there, and I'll bring you something to tide you over, woman." He laughed and headed toward the kitchen.

Morio had already gone ahead and by the time I got upstairs, he'd taken a shower and was sprawled on the bed, just enjoying the feel of the mattress beneath his back. I started the water again, and added vanilla bubble bath, then went back to the bedroom to undress.

"I'm taking a bath. Wake me when the apocalypse is over, would you?" I grinned at him, tossing my underwear in the clothes hamper, followed by my skirt. Smoky entered the room, stopping to stare at my naked body. "Don't even think it," I cautioned him, waggling a finger his way. "Not till I've rested, eaten, and bathed. And not in that order."

"You take all the fun out of ogling, woman." But he handed me a protein bar and a glass of milk. "Eat before you bathe."

I stared at the milk. "Who do you think I am, Delilah? I want caffeine."

"Caffeine won't sustain you. Now do as I say or I'll spank you." He meant it. Smoky had a real thing for spanking. Because he respected my safe word and would stop if I asked him to, I had no objections when he was in the mood. Besides, getting spanked by the *right* man could be a real turn-on.

I drank the milk in one long gulp, and carried the protein bar in with me to the bathroom, where the tub was full. Turning off the faucets, I dipped one toe in the hot water and winced. Almost too hot, but after a moment, I adapted, and then, inch by inch, I lowered myself into the tub. As I leaned back and let out a long sigh, my muscles briefly complained, and then shut the fuck up as the heat of the water began to work its way into the knots, undoing the tension.

The protein bar was chocolate and peanut butter and within three bites, I had gobbled it down. My stomach gurgled, complaining that there wasn't more where that came from, and I willed it to be quiet as I languidly ran the washcloth over my skin. I was tired and chilled, but as I flashed back to the hours after I'd been rescued from the Northlands—from the ordeal Hyto had put me through—I stilled my complaints. *This?* Was uncomfortable. *That* had truly been hell.

Twenty minutes later, my stomach was raising hell and I finally hauled my ass out of the water and dried off. Most of the bubbles were gone, anyway. I dressed in a cozy knit skirt and top, and then dried my hair. After a five-minute makeup application, I finally felt almost back to myself.

Smoky and Morio had already headed downstairs. As I set foot on the first step, the house rumbled and began to shake. I grabbed hold of the banister, trying to prevent the quake from propelling me down the steps. As I managed to pull myself back up on the landing and crawl away from both railing and steps alike, the floor rolled again and a shriek announced Delilah, landing on her back at the foot of the steps leading down from the third floor to my suite of rooms.

"Kitten! Are you all right?" I gauged whether I could stand up, decided that the quaking was too strong, and crawled over to her.

She winced, but managed to sit up. "Yeah, I think so. Nothing broken that I can feel but I bruised my butt, that's for sure. What's going on?"

"Yvarr—it has to be Yvarr! And since I'm not being pulled into trance, I have a really bad feeling that this is far worse than last time." Yvarr had been waking up. He'd been trying to break out of his astral prison. And now, I had the feeling he'd managed it.

Pictures began to fall off the walls, and we scrambled out of the way as a large framed painting of a bowl of fruit hit the floor, the frame splintering. One of our friends had painted it—I couldn't remember who at the moment—but now it was a twisted mess.

"So much for that." Delilah nervously glanced overhead, looking to see if there was anything that could fall on us. Luckily, the light fixtures were still firmly in place and there were no chandeliers up here to come crashing down.

"You know, given that we came through the siege on Elqaneve, I think we've weathered too much in the earth-quake department. It's time for something new," I grumbled. "We don't need any sentient storms here."

The rumbling slowly ground to a halt.

She stared at me. "Don't even joke. Not about that."

We waited, but there were no aftershocks, and so we scrambled to our feet and hurried downstairs before the quaking could start again. In the kitchen, Hanna was staring at a plate of overturned hamburgers and a large tureen of soup that hadn't quite made it to the table. I felt unaccountably angry at whoever had been doing the shaking. Damn it, I was hungry!

Nerissa led Morgaine in from the parlor, and Shade brought Myrddin in from Hanna's room where the high priest had showered and was now wearing a pair of Chase's jeans and a turtleneck. He looked oddly out of place without his antlered headdress. His hair, though, shone brilliantly red under the lights now that it was washed. Yeah, I thought as I ran my gaze over him. The Merlin cleaned up *quite* nicely.

"Where's Bran?" I looked around.

"He stayed outside to talk to his men, then he was going to return to Talamh Lonrach Oll. But I think he's still here."

I sucked in a deep breath. "I didn't have the psychic contact this time with Yvarr, but ten to one, it's him."

"You think so?" Smoky looked worried. "Even my kind hesitate to take on the ancient wyrms. Not only are they dangerous and crafty, but they are our forebears. Some among the Dragon Reaches think it heresy to even speak of fighting them." He paused at my look, then blinked. "I will, of course. Make no mistake about that, my wife."

That *Smoky* sounded so cowed made me want to break out in laughter, but I quickly sobered. This was no laughing matter. "Good, because we're going to need every hand on deck. How do we find out if he truly escaped his prison?"

"I can answer that." A voice from the front door startled us. The wards hadn't gone off so it couldn't be anybody meaning us ill will, but most of our friends were well-mannered enough to knock before entering. But the answer to that came when Raven Mother followed her words into the kitchen.

"I can tell you, yes I can, that Yvarr has escaped from his prison so tight. The two Fae Lords I spoke of? They have woken, and when they woke, their spell holding him was broken, and he comes now, to your house, to fight you."

"Fucking hell, why not go after the Fae Lords who imprisoned him in the first place?" I wasn't feeling particularly charitable, and I was getting tired of being the target of every creature with road rage. "And what the hell are the freaks doing, now that they decided to emerge from their self-imposed nap?"

"I have . . . taken them into protective custody, you might say. They are in my territory, I have a right to restrain them until we decide what to do with them. There is no need for others to know they've woken. But to Yvarr . . . destiny involves herself in this matter, Camille. You and the Moon Mother have much you have not discussed, and there are so many milestones that wait for you. But there is more—Yvarr sensed the unicorn horn. He comes to destroy you and take it."

"But Eriskel will booby-trap it. He won't be able to use

it—that's what these sorcerers don't understand! The Black Unicorn gifts the horn. If it's stolen, the spirit of the horn can prevent its use." But even as I said the words, I knew that anybody looking to steal it wouldn't believe me. They'd think I was trying to throw them off track. Which brought me back to Mistletoe's warning. I needed to keep my eyes open because I had a gut feeling that I hadn't seen the fallout from those rumors yet. Or, if I had, I hadn't recognized the danger yet.

"Why does Yvarr hate the Black Unicorn so much? And you? Why is he after you?"

Raven Mother's eyes grew darker and her lips curled into a luxurious, sensual smile. "It is true. Yvarr has a special hatred for the Black Unicorn. They fought, one time long ago. I have been hunting down information, I have. And I discovered that my love fought in the Great Divide on the side of the Fae Lords, and he helped to rip the worlds apart."

"The Fae Lords in Darkynwyrd—did the Black Unicorn help them imprison Yvarr?" Things were becoming clearer now.

"Yes, that he did. Much to my dismay. I would have kept the worlds together but since I can travel between them, it matters not in the long run. But yes, he did, my love. He did . . . and Yvarr has held a grudge. And he holds a grudge against me because he believes that I helped the Black Beast. He smelled me on you, and he smelled the horn. So now he believes you are in league with us. The friend of my enemy is also my enemy."

"So he's coming here to avenge himself on us because he thinks we're all cozy with you. And he thinks we hang out together. But where is he right now? How far away is he? We don't dare let him enter Seattle."

"He flies toward the Sovereign Nation. They will not be able to fight him on their own. You must hurry if you are to catch him. I will wing my way there and warn them. Bring the ancient one." She nodded to Myrddin. "He has the magic needed to battle the great beast."

And with that, she vanished out the back door and a huge black raven went flying off. I stared at the others. "You heard her. We have to get out to Talamh Lonrach Oll before Yvarr does. Because if he ends up *here*, he'll destroy Seattle in one happy fireball."

Hanna pulled out the bread and meat. "I'll make sand-wiches while you get ready." She knew the drill. And so did we.

We headed out the door, food in hand, fully equipped. For this, we took everybody we could spare and left the guards to watch over the house. It was either stop Yvarr, or have no home to return to.

I brought Morgaine with us—we needed to get her back to Talamh Lonrach Oll anyway. I had no clue how Aeval and Titania would be able to help her, but there was nothing more we could do for her.

Iris had come up to the house to be with Hanna. The Duchess was still in town for another week. "I would help you, but I think I need to sit out this fight." The house sprite gave me a tired smile.

"No, you stay here. If we don't call by afternoon, take the children and get away from here. I've called Chase and told him what's going down. He can't leave, not if the city is in any sort of danger. So if things go south, take Astrid with you. He knows I'm telling you this."

Nerissa cleared her throat. "I'll make sure Iris, Hanna, and Maggie get to safety if it comes to that. I can't take Menolly out of her lair, but if Yvarr breaks through and attacks the house, she should be okay in the basement, given the steel reinforcements to keep fire from burning through." The look on her face told me how hard it was for her to vol-unteer to leave Menolly behind, to make sure the others were safe.

We'd fought demon lords, a dragon, and even a god, but we'd never yet tried to fight something quite like Yvarr. While he was from the dragon family, Smoky had warned us he was bigger, stronger, and far less connected to humanity than most of the Dragonkin. The wyrms were giants even among their kind.

"If it comes down to it and we don't make it back, you

know what to tell Menolly. We couldn't wait for her to wake up and we love her, and did what we had to do. We have to go now." I hated what I was saying, but we'd lost so many that I couldn't bring myself to pretend everything was peachy-keen. The words barely came out of my throat, but I was able to add, "Tell her that Shamas is dead. I met him on the astral. He was fighting for King Vodox."

Nerissa pulled me in for a hug. "I'll tell her everything you need me to tell her, but it's *not* going to come to that. You're going to kick this wyrm's ass to hell and gone. And then you're going to come back here and eat dinner and go to bed and sleep for a week. After that, we're having one fucking huge party for Yule. Do you hear me?" She gazed down at me, her limpid eyes catching the light. She really was gorgeous, and she loved my sister with all her heart.

"Yeah, I hear you. And we'll start in earnest, teaching you how to fight. You can hold your own as a puma, but . . . it's time we brought you into the family business, so to speak." I laughed then. "We have to be able to turn you loose without worrying about you. Menolly would rather protect you. She's like Smoky is with me—if she could, she'd set you up in an ivory tower and bring you presents every day. But Smoky's learning—and Menolly has to learn—life's not like that."

I wasn't sure why I said that, but it seemed appropriate, and Nerissa ducked her head, smiling.

"I've been telling her that for a while now. Thanks, sis. With you and Delilah on my side, she'll have to listen."

"Camille, get a move on!" Morio's voice echoed from the foyer.

"I have to go. One more thing . . . if . . . if it goes wrong, find a way to get word to Trillian for me? Take the Whispering Mirror with you if you have to go. Menolly can use it. I'll see you in a while. Wish us luck." And with that, I gave Nerissa a quick kiss on the cheek and headed out.

Chapter 20

The drive to Talamh Lonrach Oll took half an hour in a storm. While it was raining heavily, the temperature was just high enough so that it hadn't iced over, and our cars ate up the miles on the freeway. Rush hour hadn't set in yet, but it was growing dark. Here in western Washington, with the cloud cover ever-present except for sixty-odd days a year, it was always gloomy. Add in to it that we were still three weeks out from the longest night of the year and sunrise took her time, and sunset came early.

The freeway was relatively clear at 3 P.M. though. Another hour and it wouldn't be, but now we hurried to the exit that would lead us onto the winding road into the Cascade foothills.

We couldn't all fit in my Lexus, so Morio volunteered to drive his SUV. I called shotgun; in the second seat were Myrddin, Morgaine, and Tanne. Smoky was hunched in the back. Delilah, in her Jeep, ferried Bran, Shade, and Vanzir, who we'd managed to dig up from where he was holed up in the studio. Áine followed overhead—dragons could cloak up when they didn't want to be seen, but she wasn't all that proficient and now and then I caught a glimpse of her, shimmering over the car.

I wanted to ask if there'd been any news of Trillian, but decided to wait. If he'd been hurt, I didn't want to know right now—not going into battle. And if there had been no news, I didn't want to worry even more than I was.

"At some point, my wife, you need to get a bigger car." Smoky's head grazed the ceiling in back. He wasn't that thrilled to be stuffed in the back of an SUV, and he was also constantly grumbling about the height of my car.

"Buy me one for Yule." I glanced over my shoulder, flashing him a smile.

"What kind do you want?" He was dead serious.

I snorted. "Right now, I'm focusing on how the hell we're going to fight Yvarr. We'll talk cars after we're done. So, what can you tell us about the wyrms? Do you know anything that might be of any use? And the others should know, too, so put in a call to them and tell them to put you on speaker."

Smoky sighed and pulled out a smart phone. He'd objected when I asked him to get one, but finally gave in because he knew I wasn't going to give up on it. And when I chose to nag someone, I was a master at it.

He punched Shade's number—Delilah and I had taken a united stand on the matter—and quickly told him what we were doing. When everybody was set, Smoky let out a grumbling sigh and spoke loudly enough so that everybody in the SUV as well as Delilah's Jeep could hear him.

"Wyrms. We are taught about them when we are children, of course, but that isn't saying much. Even among Dragonkin, they're almost considered legends. I do know they are all fire-breathers, in a big way. They aren't divided the way Dragonkin evolved—while they may have different colorings, they all have much of the same abilities. They're more fighters than magic-users, though it's said they can charm with their voices."

"If Yvarr is the gold standard, his charm comes through fear—he's mesmerizing, but in a terrifying way. And he's huge." I shuddered, flashing back on his up close and personal face. He wasn't lecherous in the way of Smoky's father, but he was greedy for power and revenge.

"Yes, they are huge. Their scales are stronger than those of the Dragonkin. Their fire is hotter, and their tempers are worse than even those of the whites and the reds." Smoky seemed to hesitate for a moment.

Shade's voice came crackling over the phone. "We have to tell them, Smoky."

"Yes, of course, you're right. This goes against all my teaching—but the Wing Liege will understand." Smoky looked up at us. "There is a way to get them to tell you their true name. The Dragonkin bred that out of our strain, but it will work on the ancient wyrms. But . . . Myrddin, only you or the Fae Queens can do this. Only you have the innate powers needed to charm them."

Myrddin let out a long breath. "The Spell of Naming."

Tanne jerked his head up. "I know of that spell. Our greatest bards—our heroes—used that to gain power over the forces of the world. We have remnants of the incantation but no one alive has the complete reference to it."

"Correction: Smoky speaks the truth. I know the spell. I do not know if either Titania or Aeval remembers the incantation. *But I do*." Myrddin's voice was soft. "It takes a great toll on the caster, and will not subdue the creature for long. You will have a short window in which to attack Yvarr after I cast it. And I won't get a second chance. By the time I recoup my energy, he will have toasted me alive."

"Then that's our way to defeat him. You cast the spell, the rest of us pile on and rip him to pieces. What works against his hide? Smoky, you said his scales are far stronger than yours or that of other dragons?"

Shade interjected at that point. "Magical weaponry should work. Regular swords and daggers will probably just bounce off, his hide is going to be so strong. Fire won't affect him, and neither will most magic, except for lightning. Death magic *might* have an effect, so you and Morio could prepare your most powerful spell and try it out, but have your weapons ready. Smoky and I can attack in our natural forms. Vanzir, don't try to suck out his life energy—that won't work on him and will just get you one hell of a headache."

"Shade's right." Smoky glanced around the car. "Delilah, your dagger won't be of much use unless you come in from behind. Tanne, what do you have in your repertoire?"

"I have no magical weapons, but I am Woodland Fae. I might be able to use my spell-singing to coax the forest to help us."

"I doubt it," I broke in. "Considering the entire area is under the dominion of the Fae Queens, I'm pretty sure it's warded against outside influence. Just keep an eye out for what you can do to help the rest of us. I do have one weapon still. The horn is still two-thirds charged. And this is the time to use it. You said fire won't work, but I can call the Master of Winds to call down the lightning. That's going to pack one hell of a wallop."

There was a brief silence, then Shade laughed. "Yeah, that will. Let Myrddin cast his spell and then use it while Yvarr is under his control. That way he won't be able to deflect it. In fact, Myrddin, if you can get him to roll over and expose his belly, the underside is more vulnerable than his back."

"Then we have a plan." I glanced out the window. The rain pelted down in earnest, the afternoon shadows growing. I began to see a few flakes of snow mixed in. "We're going to face a cold, gloomy battle. Our exit's coming up."

The exit ramp diverged onto a two-lane highway. We were northeast of Seattle, and here the forest crowded thick on either side of the road. Morio slowed down as the road grew narrower and bumpier. With the trees so flush on either side, it was darker than the freeway had been. Now, the rain fully turned to snow but it wasn't sticking yet.

Another ten minutes and we approached the gates leading into Talamh Lonrach Oll. The Court of the Three Queens had been granted permission to create a sovereign nation within the state. They had originally bought one thousand acres, but recently had increased it by two thousand more. The government had set a limit—for now—on the size of the reservation at five thousand acres.

The land was covered with fir and cedar, vining maple and birch and cottonwood. In the past couple of years since they had purchased the land, they had worked ceaselessly to create a home for Fae who wanted to live among their own kind. No electricity was allowed here, but magic ran fast and thick, and the population had been steadily growing. The Talamh Lonrach Oll Warriors were headed up by Bran, and as much as I still didn't trust him, I had to admit he did a good job of training them.

As we slowed, turning onto the road that led to a pair of ten-foot-tall, silver-plated gates, the energy crackled around us.

Myrddin shifted. "They have not forgotten their origins, that much I will say." He glanced out the window. He'd adapted quickly to the car, after a couple of minutes, and I had a feeling that little could jar this man. He had to be able to hold his post in the most frenzied of battles. Something as simple as an automobile? No challenge. Though I wouldn't want to see him try to drive one without practice.

The guards were waiting. There were at least twenty of them at the gate, and they were in full leather with weapons at the ready. As Delilah pulled in behind us, easing to a stop, Bran hopped out of the car and hurried forward to talk to his men. He said something. Apparently, one of the guards tried to contradict him, because the next minute we heard a storm of cussing. The guard immediately saluted and stood back, and the gates opened wide. Bran came back to our car and motioned for me to roll down the window.

"Normally you'd have to leave the cars here and go by buggy but we don't have time for that. I've sent one of the men ahead to the barrow palace to let them know we're on the way. Drive on through. The paths are wide enough to maneuver. Try not to take out the statues though, if you would. I don't want Aeval hounding my hide for broken bric-a-brac."

Before I could say a word, he hurried back to Delilah's Jeep and hopped back in. Morio eased through the gates and jumped the curb at the parking area, following the cobblestone path. One of the guards had commandeered a horse from the stall where horses and carts waited, and he galloped ahead to clear the way and lead us in. By buggy it would take us twenty minutes to traverse the road to the palaces. By car, we could make it in five.

The houses along the path were single story, cottage-like and covered with moss roofs. Eye catchers shimmered, lighting the paths that intersected and crisscrossed. Along the route, we saw the Fae hurrying every which way, and loud alarms were sounding. At least they hadn't been caught unaware.

The palace came into view as we entered the cobblestoned courtyard. The giant barrow mounds held three courts—Aeval's, Titania's, and Morgaine's. The grass covering the mounds was rich and green, but a scattering of snow was beginning to accumulate, giving the barrows a shimmery look.

Morio put the SUV in park and turned off the ignition. We all piled out, except Morgaine, who sat there until I took her hand and drew her out with us. Delilah's Jeep was right behind us, and they did the same, parking in back of my Lexus.

At that moment, Aeval and Titania appeared, both in battle gear. I'd never seen either of them wearing anything but gorgeous dresses, so to see them in full trousers and leather armor was disconcerting. But the leather—Titania's was green, Aeval's was black as night—was finely crafted and embellished with intricate designs. I would have thought the runes ornamental if I wasn't tuned into magic, but even from a distance, I could tell the enhancements gave them extra protection and other abilities.

Behind them, Raven Mother stood ready. Her presence on the land was proof enough as to how serious the threat was. Aeval didn't like Raven Mother, and the feeling was mutual.

I gave them all a quick curtsey, but there was no time for chatter. "Obviously you know Yvarr escaped and is on the way here?"

They nodded, then Titania looked over at Morgaine and Myrddin. "Myrddin!" Her shout rebounded through the courtyard. "You found him!" The Queen of Light and Morning practically bounced over to Myrddin, hugging him with a brilliant smile on her face. Titania was as effusive in her emotions as Aeval was reserved.

Aeval moved forward, nodding to the High Druid. "Welcome back to the land of the living. I wish we could have time to sit and talk before heading into war, but alas, we have no such luxury." Then, her gaze fell on Morgaine. "What happened?"

I joined them. "Short version? Myrddin woke Arthur up. Arthur told Mordred the truth. Mordred killed Arthur, then ran off when he realized what he did. We had to leave them both—Arturo's body, and Mordred—in the realm of the Elder Fae. Morgaine hasn't spoken since she watched her son kill his father. We've tried everything we could to bring her out of it, but . . ." I looked into Aeval's eyes, and for the first time, saw pity in them.

"And so it plays out," she said softly, motioning for a guard to take Morgaine away. "Take her to my chambers. Tell them to tuck her into bed. Guard her well." After he left, taking the Queen of Dusk and Twilight with him, Aeval turned back to me. "Yvarr will be here any moment."

"We've asked Myrddin to use the Spell of Naming on him."

Aeval turned to Myrddin. "I remember part of the spell. But I'm not sure I remember all that goes with it."

"No worries. After this battle is over, I'll refresh your and Titania's memory on it." He gave Titania a quick hug, like he might hug a sister, but his gaze landed on Aeval with respect and a touch of fear.

Aeval glanced overhead. "Áine lives, then?" There was a catch in her voice and I could swear a saw a tear in the corner of her eye.

Myrddin smiled at her then, ducking his head. "Aye. Your foster daughter lives. But she is under a curse. After you were imprisoned, they cursed her and took away her ability to shift form."

I whirled to Aeval. *"Foster daughter?"*

"Áine was commended into my care after she met the Merlin and fell in love with him. The Wing Liege assigned to me to watch over her. I tried to send her home when the great wars began, but she would not go. Before I could contact her kin in the Dragon Realms, the Fae Lords caught me and locked me within the crystal cave."

She shuddered. "But we have no time to reminisce. He is within ten minutes of here. You have a plan, then? We have all our warriors ready, but a wyrm such as Yvarr will decimate the land before we can make a dent in him. As I said, I've been struggling to remember the Spell of Naming the past few days, and so has Titania, but neither of us was able to recall the complete incantation."

"Myrddin will cast the spell on Yvarr, and I'm going to use the horn to make the initial wound. Then the others will attack and between everything, we hope to be able to kill him. I'd better prep the horn." I moved to the side while the others continued discussing strategy.

As I pulled the horn out of my pocket, the energy quickened rapidly. The energy of Talamh Lonrach Oll must be causing a chain reaction because I slid into trance without any difficulties. Once again, I faced Eriskel in the center of the horn. He was looking particularly solemn.

"You know what's going on, don't you? I need the Master of Winds. I need him to call down the lightning for me." I turned toward the mirror that looked into the Eastern realm.

Eriskel walked over to stand beside me. "You know that killing a wyrm will set off repercussions you can't even begin to dream of?"

"I know that if we don't kill Yvarr, many innocents will die as he ravages the country. The government will call out their own weapons to try to destroy him and things will escalate to an end none of us want to see." I turned to face the jindasel. "I was given the horn for a reason. I've never used it lightly. Trust me?"

"I have no choice. You are the mistress of the horn and I'm your servant. Just remember, there will be repercussions down the line, and not from using the horn. Kill one, and it will waken others." He stood back, and the Master of Winds appeared in the mirror, looking down from his rocky crag high in the mountains. The wind blew through his hair and he saluted me, arm held high.

"Master of Winds, I need your lightning. Sky Lord, I need all the lightning you can bring to bear."

He grinned. "You have my full force, Lady Camille. As much power as is left in the horn will be charged with the force of the sky."

And, just like that, I found myself back in my body, holding the horn, which now felt amped up by the force of over a billion volts of energy just waiting to be discharged. It set my teeth to chattering and I was suddenly terribly afraid of accidentally triggering it in the wrong direction. Not only did I have the force of one fucking strong-assed lightning bolt in my hands, but it was also magically enhanced, so it would not only strike, but it would strike and keep hold.

"Look—there he is!" The cry came from behind me and I hurried over to Myrddin's side. I had to know what he was doing, and when he was doing it, so I could play my part. Smoky and Shade had both moved back into large clear areas and now they transformed, taking their natural shapes— Smoky, a great white and silver dragon, and Shade—a skeletal dragon with bones that were the color of the earth.

Morio shifted shape, too, into his youkai form. Delilah, Tanne, and the Fae Queens waited back of Myrddin and me. Bran was marching into position, leading the warriors, but he waited to bring them into the arena. If Yvarr let loose with a blast of flame, no point in having all targets on hand. Vanzir had vanished but I knew he was somewhere around, probably waiting in the Ionyc Seas so he could come in for a sneak attack.

Raven Mother moved forward then, and at first I wanted to shout for her to get out of the way, but I realized she was luring him in. He wanted her, he wanted revenge, and he was blustery enough to talk it up before trying to kill her.

She read him right. Yvarr appeared over the trees, huge and serpentine, reminding me of Áine but far, far older and more dangerous. He glimmered against the light of the storm, his terrible claws polished to a high sheen. At least half-again as big as Smoky, Yvarr was a horrible beast, beautiful and deadly and circling to strike. He spiraled down, aiming toward Raven Mother, and she let out a laugh that echoed through the air, amplified by magic.

"Yvarr—enemy of my love! Come down here, you coward, and face me!" The wind was streaming through her hair and she stretched her arms wide, inviting him to attack.

I had to remind myself that she was an Elemental. She could be hurt, but she was one of the true Immortals and there was no way Yvarr could kill her. Whether he knew that was another matter.

Yvarr spiraled down, landing on the ground in front of her so hard that he shook the land. "The Raven! I have waited long to repay you for my imprisonment."

He really *was* under the misassumption that Raven Mother had played an integral part in locking him up. I wondered what part the Fae Lords had played in encouraging the idea. By now, I wasn't putting anything past them.

"Wily one, how did you escape?" Raven Mother circled, moving his attention away from Myrddin and myself. She was giving us the opportunity to do what we needed to do.

"You forgot to destroy the key. Something seems to have opened my cage door, cunning one." Yvarr's skin glistened, the sheen of the scales illuminated by the glow of the clouds. "I see you have brought two wretched descendants of my kind to help you. They are puny in the face of my power." And then, without warning, he turned on Smoky, breathing out a long breath of fire.

Smoky immediately launched himself into the air, bellowing as the flames scorched his wings. I braced myself to keep from screaming, but instead, followed Myrddin as he raced into the clearing, holding his staff up high. He was wearing his headdress and robes, and as a brilliant flash emanated from the staff, Yvarr jerked around, his sinuous neck writhing like a serpent.

"What is this? *The Merlin!* You cannot be alive!" There was a look in the wyrm's eye—a flicker of fear.

I stood back, letting Myrddin do his thing.

Myrddin began to incant the Spell of Naming, and as he did, the energy in his words was so strong and so ancient, that it sent a shock wave through my body. If he controlled *this* much power, just what else could he do?

> *Ancient one of bone and flesh, of scale and hide and fire,*
> *I seek your name, the truest word, force you to my desire,*
> *This spell I weave, to seek the name, to hunt the key,*
> *Through rock and bone and history,*
> *Through air and wind and gale and breeze,*
> *Through wave and ocean, lake and sea,*
> *Through flame and ember and spark I seek,*
> *Your name I call, Your name I sing,*
> *This spell to me, your name will bring!*

Everything fell silent, including Yvarr, and then a single bird—a raven—flew in and landed on the Merlin's shoulder, cawing once. Myrddin laughed and shouted, "Yvancian Lucern Tregastius! Hear me and obey!"

Yvarr froze, and in that moment, I could see the spell winding around him like a silver net of sparkling wire. Smoky landed next to Shade and I could feel both sorrow and relief through our bond. He was mourning for Yvarr, even though he understood the need to do this.

"Show your most vulnerable area." Myrddin was harsh and commanding, his demand held no mercy. He reminded me of Aeval in that moment, and I realized that as soft-spoken as he might be, I hoped we never had to tangle with the Merlin, because chances were, he'd come out on top.

Yvarr rolled over, showing his belly. Myrddin turned to me. "You have only moments. Hurry!"

I brought the horn to bear and yelled, "Hit the deck!"

Everyone scrambled, including Raven Mother.

I wanted to close my eyes. I didn't want to see the damage I was about to inflict, but then I stopped. If I was going to attack a creature as powerful and magnificent as Yvarr, I owed him the respect of watching the results.

"Master of the Winds, I call down the lightning!" A bolt shot out from the horn, over a billion volts of energy, brilliant and neon hot. A single, flame-blue fork seared its way into Yvarr's stomach, and the ancient wyrm let out a scream so loud it deafened me. He writhed, his serpentine body flailing, as the lightning exploded against him. It crisped the skin as he convulsed, the chain of lightning hopping and skipping around him, holding him in its fiery blue embrace.

A moment later, and Yvarr lay on the ground, still writhing, but hoarse from his screams. At that moment, Smoky and Shade moved in and as we watched, they finished the job, talons and great jaws flashing bloody as they ripped Yvarr in half.

The carnage turned my stomach. And yet, if we hadn't gone in for the kill, if we'd hesitated, Yvarr would be ripping up the compound even now, and then moving on to Seattle.

I didn't realize tears were running down my cheek until Myrddin turned back to me and gently reached out to wipe them away from my face.

"Little witch, this is the nature of life. These creatures . . . they may be beautiful, but beauty does not preclude deadly force."

I nodded. I knew this all too well but still, the power we had over life and death never ceased to affect me. And Yvarr, as greedy and grasping as he might be, had been used and abused by my father's ancestors.

I turned to Delilah, who sheathed her dagger. "I'm stick-a-fork-in-me done."

She smiled grimly. "I have to say, I'm grateful I didn't have to run into the mix. If we hadn't been able to control him? We'd all be running for our lives now." She wrapped her arm around me. "You okay?"

I let out a long, slow breath. "Yeah, I'm fine. Just . . . sometimes the energy can overwhelm me. How many of these creatures still exist in the world? Eriskel told me that Yvarr's death would wake others. Whether he meant wyrms or other creatures from before the Great Divide, I don't know."

"What happened to your hand?" Delilah grabbed my hand up. I was still clutching the unicorn horn and as I looked down, I saw a row of blisters covering my palm. The pain was barely beginning to register.

"Fuck. Must have been residue from the heat of the discharge." At that point, Raven Mother walked up and I stuffed the horn in my pocket. "Thank you. You distracted him enough for us to attack."

She shrugged. "It would seem we're in this all together, now wouldn't it? Besides, my son told me about your journey, he did. You are too bright, my Camille, too beautiful for so much darkness. And yet, you would walk under the dark of the moon. It bodes well to incur your favor, young Priestess, yes it does, considering that which has been set in motion. But the deed is done, and I am off again. Do not forget—Raven Mother was helpful, was she not?" And in that singsong way of hers, she tilted her head and then, in a flash of light, transformed into a large raven and flew off.

In silence, we watched her leave.

Then, Myrddin stated the obvious. "You owe her a favor now, and so do I. We would do well to not forget that fact."

I nodded. "Yeah, I'm aware of that."

As the cheers rang out from the warriors and I ran over to make certain Smoky was all right, I caught sight of Aeval. She was looking at Myrddin, then she turned to stare at me. Her gaze was not unfriendly, but contemplative, and I flashed back to what she had said when she had looked at Morgaine. *"And so it plays out . . ."* and then, Raven Mother saying, *"It bodes well to incur your favor, young Priestess, yes it does, considering that which has been set in motion."* Something had happened, and I didn't have a clue what.

But I pushed the thoughts to the back of my mind as Smoky and Shade resumed their forms. Smoky was okay—he looked mildly singed, which was the most I'd ever seen him damaged, but he swung me into his arms, laughing. Beside me, Shade opened his arms to Delilah.

"We need to let Nerissa know everything's okay," I said.

"We will—no worries." Smoky turned to look at Yvarr, and again, I saw the sorrow in his face. "He is one of the ancestors. One of our Titans. It seems such a pity to kill so magnificent a beast. But no worries, my love." He kissed the top of my head. "I know why it had to happen."

Aeval and Titania joined us. "The Merlin will stay with us, here in Talamh Lonrach Oll, until he decides what he wishes to do. I would not be surprised if he journeys to his old country and reestablishes the ancient groves. I have a feeling Stonehenge may be reclaimed from their government before long."

I laughed, but then sobered. How much would the human governments put up with our coming out of the closet? How far could we push the issue? But then, the cheering began anew as one of Bran's warriors shouted, "Armor!" as he held up one of the wyrm's scales.

Yes, we were building a whole new world, and the more that happened, the more Earthside felt like home. I wrapped my arm around Smoky's waist and he kissed me on the forehead.

"You saved the day, my love. You went up against the wyrm and you saved the day." He sounded so proud that I laughed.

"No, I didn't. Don't you see? We *all* saved the day. We each had our part to play, and we each did what we were called to do. We're all in this together, Smoky. We're all equally in danger. We all fight . . . and we all either lose . . . or triumph." But inside, I realized that sometimes, someone got lost along the way while the rest of us kept moving. Arturo left us this round, and most likely, Mordred. And Morgaine . . . who was still lost within her mind somewhere. Whether she would return to us remained to be seen. I decided to keep quiet, though. No use dwelling on the collateral damage we'd already faced.

He laughed then. "Very well . . . *we* saved the day. Again."

I nodded, my thoughts drifting to Trillian. Maybe, if we were lucky, there would be news of him when we got home. And with that melancholy thought, I decided to shake off all of the scattered thoughts and worries, and try to enjoy the victory. Just a little bit, at least.

Chapter 21

YULE—THE WINTER SOLSTICE

Back home, everything was decked out, waiting for us to return from the ritual. The presents were under the trees, the food was waiting in the kitchen. But for now, in this moment, we were all here to celebrate the turn of the Wheel. It was Winter Solstice and, once again, we were gathered down at Birchwater Pond. Eye catchers dappled the snow-covered woodland, and we were dressed in warm, festive clothes. Music echoed from the speakers—Damh the Bard, Spiral Dance, Woodland, Faun, Gypsy—all FBH musicians who had tapped into their pagan roots and put their feelings and beliefs into song.

The moon shone overhead—the Moon Mother watching over us through her waxing eyes, sparkling in the chill night air. The sky was clear and the temperature settled around freezing, but in the center of the Circle, the bonfire burned brightly, a beacon of hope in the darkened night. Vanzir and Rozurial were minding the fire, keeping it stoked. Roz had forgiven me for stealing his firebombs, especially when he found out how they'd helped keep us alive.

Menolly stood by the water, her arm around Nerissa as they watched the moon glisten on the surface of the waves. Delilah and Shade snuggled in the shade of a cedar tree, cuddling on a bench together as they held Maggie, playing with her. Maggie was wearing a scarf Hanna had crocheted for her, and a Santa hat, looking cute as a button.

Chase was helping Hanna decorate one last tree near the pond with giant silver and gold ornaments and cranberry garland. We'd bedecked the entire grove and now everything sparkled. The babies were tucked warmly in their carriages, as Bruce guarded over them. We'd invited Tanne to join us, but he was celebrating with his own clan, as was fitting.

Around the Circle, Smoky, Shade, and Trillian finished setting up the candles and final touches for the ritual. Trillian had made it home safely, but without Darynal, and he was heartbroken about it.

We didn't know whether Darynal lived or not, and Trillian had no idea where to find his soul statue. After an ambush, Trillian and Rozurial had managed to escape and had made their way back to Ceredream, and from there, home. I knew Trillian felt he had failed, but there wasn't much else we could do. So we would hope and pray, and keep asking Trenyth for updates, and Trillian intended to try again when there was anything new to go on.

As I took in the scene, I smiled softly. Family and friends— that's what mattered most. Money made a difference, yes, but it couldn't buy back a life. All the treasure in the world wouldn't bring back our father, or Shamas, or Queen Asteria, or Chrysandra. All the fortunes combined couldn't bribe the Lady of Ice to loosen her grasp on the dead.

And *so many* were missing or dead. Or they were among the walking wounded. Morgaine was still wandering in the shadows of her mind. Aeval had fully taken over my training. She said very little of the Queen of Dusk and Twilight, save that the shock had been more than our cousin could handle, but she would not tell me if Morgaine would recover. And there had been no sign of Mordred. Whatever fate awaited him was clouded from our view.

Morio motioned to me. "It's time. Let's begin."

Since we'd returned, he'd been spending time with the Merlin, and what they discussed, he wouldn't tell me. But Aeval had warned me to let it alone. All I knew is that Morio had become integral to my magic—not only the death magic we practiced but my Moon Magic. I was paired with a priest who was my match now, and while Morio always acceded the primary role to me, he took part in most of my rituals.

Iris joined us at the altar. As the others took their place in Circle, Morio, Iris, and I joined hands. We called on the spirit of Winter. We petitioned Beira to go easy on the land. We invoked the Holly King, and Undutar. We embraced the depths of the snow and ice.

I glanced up at the shining Moon, wondering what she had waiting for me next. And what was in store for all of us? The war against Shadow Wing had settled into a long fight, yes. But I had the feeling that our individual destinies were also beginning to play out in our lives. Something was brewing—a witch's brew of intrigue and shifting power and rising tides that the world had not seen in many ages. The Merlin was back, and the world would never be the same.

As I sang out to the Moon Mother, she flared, brilliant and silver overhead, and a moonbeam shot down, bathing me in her magic. I could hear her laugh, distant and tinkling, like chimes on the wind.

"Are you ready, Camille? Are you ready to embrace your destiny? Are you ready to step up to the task?"

I caught my breath, as I looked up to meet her gaze as she stared down at me from among the stars. Wild she was, and feral, but also beautiful and as fragile as glass on a cold night. One wrong movement and the web we were weaving would shatter. But follow the threads, and the web was strong as steel.

"I'm ready, Lady. I'm willing to do whatever you ask of me."

"The way is long and difficult, but you are my Priestess. And you will lead the path for those who are lost and seeking their star. But Camille, watch close to your back. Enemies come from all sides, seeking the horn, seeking the seals. Even now, Shadow Wing sends new envoys to your

city. The vultures are gathering. The lions are hunting. Keep alert. Be ready." And then, she vanished and I was back in Circle.

Shaking, yet feeling stronger than I had in a long time, I looked at the faces surrounding me. The faces of those I loved. And they beamed their love back at me. Yes, events were brewing in this, the longest night. But I would meet them, chin up and face forward.

I was a priestess of the Moon Mother. And *that* made me strong. Whatever new threats were coming our way next, my sisters and I, and our lovers and friends, would stand against the enemy together. Where there was darkness, we would shine light. Where there was danger, we would remain strong. Because this was our home, and we would defend it till the very end.

CAST OF MAJOR CHARACTERS

The D'Artigo Family

Arial Lianan te Maria: Delilah's twin who died at birth. Half-Fae, half-human.

Camille Sepharial te Maria, aka Camille D'Artigo: The oldest sister; a Moon Witch and Priestess. Half-Fae, half-human.

Daniel George Fredericks: The D'Artigo sisters' half cousin; FBH.

Delilah Maria te Maria, aka Delilah D'Artigo: The middle sister; a werecat.

Hester Lou Fredericks: The D'Artigo sisters' half cousin; FBH.

Maria D'Artigo: The D'Artigo sisters' mother. Human. Deceased.

Menolly Rosabelle te Maria, aka Menolly D'Artigo: The youngest sister; a vampire and jian-tu: extraordinary acrobat. Half-Fae, half-human.

Sephreh ob Tanu: The D'Artigo sisters' father. Full Fae. Deceased.

Shamas ob Olanda: The D'Artigo sisters' cousin. Full Fae. Deceased.

The D'Artigo Sisters' Lovers & Close Friends

Astrid (Johnson): Chase and Sharah's baby daughter.

Bruce O'Shea: Iris's husband. Leprechaun.

Carter: Leader of the Demonica Vacana Society, a group that watches and records the interactions of Demonkin and human through the ages. Carter is half demon and half Titan—his father was Hyperion, one of the Greek Titans.

Chase Garden Johnson: Detective, director of the Faerie-Human Crime Scene Investigation (FH-CSI) team. Human who has taken the Nectar of Life, which extends his life span beyond that of any ordinary mortal, and has opened up his psychic abilities.

Chrysandra: Waitress at the Wayfarer Bar & Grill. Human. Deceased.

Derrick Means: Bartender at the Wayfarer Bar & Grill. Werebadger.

Erin Mathews: Former president of the Faerie Watchers Club and former owner of the Scarlet Harlot Boutique. Turned into a vampire by Menolly, her sire, moments before her death. Human.

Greta: Leader of the Death Maidens; Delilah's tutor.

Iris (Kuusi) O'Shea: Friend and companion of the girls. Priestess of Undutar. Talon-haltija (Finnish house sprite).

Lindsey Katharine Cartridge: Director of the Green Goddess Women's Shelter. Pagan and witch. Human.

Luke: Former bartender at the Wayfarer Bar & Grill. Werewolf. One of the Keraastar Knights.

Maria O'Shea: Iris and Bruce's baby daughter.

Marion Vespa: Coyote shifter; owner of the Supe-Urban Café.

Morio Kuroyama: One of Camille's lovers and husbands. Essentially the grandson of Grandmother Coyote. Youkai-kitsune (roughly translated: Japanese fox demon).

Neely Reed: Founding member of the United Worlds Church. FBH.

Nerissa Shale: Menolly's wife. Worked for Department of Social and Health Services. Now working for Chase Johnson as a victims-rights counselor for the FH-CSI. Werepuma and member of the Rainier Puma Pride.

Roman: Ancient vampire; son of Blood Wyne, Queen of the Crimson Veil. Menolly's official consort in the Vampire Nation and her new sire.

Queen Asteria: The former Elfin Queen. Deceased.

Queen Sharah: Was an Elfin medic, now the new Elfin Queen; Chase's girlfriend.

Rozurial, aka Roz: Mercenary. Menolly's secondary lover. Incubus who used to be Fae before Zeus and Hera destroyed his marriage.

Shade: Delilah's fiancé. Part Stradolan, part black (shadow) dragon.

Siobhan Morgan: One of the sisters' friends. Selkie (wereseal); member of the Puget Sound Harbor Seal Pod.

Smoky: One of Camille's lovers and husbands. Half-white, half-silver dragon.

Tanne Baum: One of the Black Forest Woodland Fae. A member of the Hunter's Glen Clan.

Tavah: Guardian of the portal at the Wayfarer Bar & Grill. Vampire (full Fae).

Tim Winthrop, aka Cleo Blanco: Computer student/genius, female impersonator. FBH. Now owns the Scarlet Harlot.

Trillian: Mercenary. Camille's alpha lover and one of her three husbands. Svartan (one of the Charming Fae).

Ukkonen O'Shea: Iris and Bruce's baby son.

Vanzir: Was indentured slave to the sisters, by his own choice. Dream-chaser demon who lost his powers and now is regaining new ones.

Venus the Moon Child: Former shaman of the Rainier Puma Pride. Werepuma. One of the Keraastar Knights.

Wade Stevens: President of Vampires Anonymous. Vampire (human).

Zachary Lyonnesse: Former member of the Rainier Puma Pride Council of Elders. Werepuma living in Otherworld.

GLOSSARY

Black Unicorn/Black Beast: Father of the Dahns Unicorns, a magical unicorn that is reborn like the phoenix and lives in Darkynwyrd and Thistlewyd Deep. Raven Mother is his consort, and he is more a force of nature than a unicorn.

Calouk: The rough, common dialect used by a number of Otherworld inhabitants.

Court and Crown: "Crown" refers to the Queen of Y'Elestrial. "Court" refers to the nobility and military personnel that surround the queen. "Court and Crown" together refer to the entire government of Y'Elestrial.

Court of the Three Queens: The newly risen Court of the three Earthside Fae Queens: Titania, the Fae Queen of Light and Morning; Morgaine, the half-Fae Queen of Dusk and Twilight ; and Aeval, the Fae Queen of Shadow and Night.

Crypto: One of the Cryptozoid races. Cryptos include creatures out of legend that are not technically of the Fae races: gargoyles, unicorns, gryphons, chimeras, and so on. Most primarily inhabit Otherworld, but some have Earthside cousins.

Demon Gate: A gate through which demons may be summoned by a powerful sorcerer or necromancer.

Dreyerie: A dragon lair.

Earthside/ES: Everything that exists on the Earth side of the portals.

Elemental Lords: The elemental beings—both male and female—who, along with the Hags of Fate and the Harvestmen, are the only true Immortals. They are avatars of various elements and energies, and they inhabit all realms. They do as they will and seldom concern themselves with humankind or Fae unless summoned. If asked for help, they often exact steep prices in return. The Elemental Lords are not concerned with balance like the Hags of Fate.

Elqaneve: The capital Elfin city in Otherworld, located in Kelvashan—the Elfin lands.

FBH: Full-Blooded Human (usually refers to Earthside humans).

FH-CSI: The Faerie-Human Crime Scene Investigation team. The brainchild of Detective Chase Johnson, it was first formed as a collaboration between the OIA and the Seattle police department. Other FH-CSI units have been created around the country, based on the Seattle prototype. The FH-CSI takes care of both medical and criminal emergencies involving visitors from Otherworld.

Great Divide: A time of immense turmoil when the Elemental Lords and some of the High Court of Fae decided to rip apart the worlds. Until then, the Fae existed primarily on Earth, their lives and worlds mingling with those of humans. The Great Divide tore everything asunder, splitting off another dimension, which became Otherworld. At that time, the Twin Courts of Fae were disbanded and their queens and the Merlin were stripped of power. This was the time during which the Spirit Seal was formed and broken in order to seal off the realms from each other. Some Fae chose to stay Earthside, others moved to the realm of Otherworld, and the demons were—for the most part—sealed in the Subterranean Realms.

Guard Des'Estar: The military of Y'Elestrial.

Hags of Fates: The women of destiny who keep the balance righted. Neither good nor evil, they observe the flow of destiny. When events get too far out of balance, they step in and take action, usually using humans, Fae, Supes, and other creatures as pawns to bring the path of destiny back into line.

Harvestmen: The lords of death—a few cross over and are also Elemental Lords. The Harvestmen, along with their followers (the Valkyries and the Death Maidens, for example), reap the souls of the dead.

Haseofon: The abode of the Death Maidens—where they stay and where they train.

Ionyc Lands: The astral, etheric, and spirit realms, along with several other lesser-known noncorporeal dimensions, form the Ionyc Lands. These realms are separated by the Ionyc Seas, a current of energy that prevents the Ionyc Lands from colliding, thereby sparking off an explosion of universal proportions.

Ionyc Seas: The currents of energy that separate the Ionyc Lands. Certain creatures, especially those connected with the elemental energies of ice, snow, and wind, can travel through the Ionyc Seas without protection.

Kelvashan: The lands of the elves.

Koyanni: The coyote shifters who took an evil path away from the Great Coyote; followers of Nukpana.

Melosealfôr: A rare Crypto dialect learned by powerful Cryptos and all Moon Witches.

The Nectar of Life: An elixir that can extend the life span of humans to nearly the length of a Fae's years. Highly prized and cautiously used. Can drive someone insane if he or she doesn't have the emotional capacity to handle the changes incurred.

Oblition: The act of a Death Maiden sucking the soul out of one of their targets.

OIA: The Otherworld Intelligence Agency; the "brains" behind the Guard Des'Estar. Earthside Division now run by Camille, Menolly, and Delilah.

Otherworld/OW: The human term for the "United Nations" of Faerie Land. A dimension apart from ours that contains creatures from legend and lore, pathways to the gods, and various other places, such as Olympus. Otherworld's actual name varies among the differing dialects of the many races of Cryptos and Fae.

Portal/Portals: The interdimensional gates that connect the different realms. Some were created during the Great Divide; others open up randomly.

Seelie Court: The Earthside Fae Court of Light and Summer, disbanded during the Great Divide. Titania was the Seelie Queen.

Soul Statues: In Otherworld, small figurines created for the Fae of certain races and magically linked with the baby. These figurines reside in family shrines and when one of the Fae dies, their soul statue shatters. In Menolly's case, when she was reborn as a vampire, her soul statue re-formed, although twisted. If a family member disappears, his or her family can always tell if their loved one is alive or dead if they have access to the soul statue.

Spirit Seals: A magical crystal artifact, the Spirit Seal was created during the Great Divide. When the portals were sealed, the Spirit Seal was broken into nine gems and each piece was given to an Elemental Lord or Lady. These gems each have varying powers. Even possessing one of the spirit seals can allow the wielder to weaken the portals that divide Otherworld, Earthside, and the Subterranean Realms. If all of the seals are joined together again, then all of the portals will open.

Stradolan: A being who can walk between worlds, who can walk through the shadows, using them as a method of transportation.

Supe/Supes: Short for Supernaturals. Refers to Earthside supernatural beings who are not of Fae nature. Refers to Weres, especially.

Talamh Lonrach Oll: The name for the Earthside Sovereign Fae Nation.

Triple Threat: Camille's nickname for the newly risen three Earthside Queens of Fae.

Unseelie Court: The Earthside Fae Court of Shadow and Winter, disbanded during the Great Divide. Aeval was the Unseelie Queen.

VA/Vampires Anonymous: The Earthside group started by Wade Stevens, a vampire who was a psychiatrist during life.

The group is focused on helping newly born vampires adjust to their new state of existence, and to encourage vampires to avoid harming the innocent as much as possible. The VA is vying for control. Their goal is to rule the vampires of the United States and to set up an internal policing agency.

Whispering Mirror: A magical communications device that links Otherworld and Earthside. Think magical video phone.

Y'Eírialiastar: The Sidhe/Fae name for Otherworld.

Y'Elestrial: The city-state in Otherworld where the D'Artigo sisters were born and raised. A Fae city, recently embroiled in a civil war between the drug-crazed tyrannical Queen Lethesanar and her more level-headed sister Tanaquar, who managed to claim the throne for herself. The civil war has ended and Tanaquar is restoring order to the land.

Youkai: Loosely (very loosely) translated as Japanese demon/nature spirit. For the purposes of this series, the youkai have three shapes: the animal form, the human form, and the true demon form. Unlike the demons of the Subterranean Realms, youkai are not necessarily evil by nature.

PLAYLIST FOR *PRIESTESS DREAMING*

I write to music a good share of the time, and so I always put my playlists in the back of each book so you can see which artists/songs I listened to during the writing. Here's the play-list for *Priestess Dreaming*:

AJ Roach: "Devil May Dance"

Air: "Moon Fever," "Napalm Love," "Surfing on a Rocket," "Playground Love"

Amethystium: "Shadow to Light," "Enchantment," "Fairyland"

Android Lust: "Saint Over," "Here and Now," "God in the Hole"

Awolnation: "Sail"

The Black Angels: "The Return," "You on the Run," "Evil Things," "Black Isn't Black," "Young Men Dead," "Manipulation," "Phosphene Dream"

Black Rebel Motorcycle Club: "Feel It Now"

The Bravery: "Believe"

Broken Bells: "The Ghost Inside," "The High Road"

Bryan Adams: "Run to You," "Heat of the Night"

Crazy Town: "Butterfly"

The Cure: "From the Edge of the Deep Green Sea," "The Hanging Garden"

Death Cab for Cutie: "I Will Possess Your Heart"

Eastern Sun: "Beautiful Being"

Eels: "Souljacker Part 1"

Faun: "Iduna," "Hymn to Pan," "Arcadia," "Sieben," "Rad"

The Feeling: "Sewn"

Foster the People: "Pumped Up Kicks"

Garbage: "Queer," "1 Crush," "I Think I'm Paranoid"

Gary Numan: "I Am Dust," "Here in the Black," "Everything Comes Down to This," "A Shadow Falls on Me," "Splinter," "Haunted," "Melt," "Cars (re-mix)," "Petals"

Godsmack: "Voodoo"

Hanni El Khatib: "Come Alive"

In Strict Confidence: "Silver Bullets," "Snow White," "Tiefer," "Silver Tongues"

Kyuss: "Space Cadet"

Lady Gaga: "Teeth," "I Like It Rough," "Paparazzi"

Ladytron: "Destroy Everything You Touch," "I'm Not Scared," "Ghosts"

Lord of the Lost: "Sex on Legs"

Loreena McKennitt: "The Mummer's Dance"

Marilyn Manson: "Arma-Goddamn-Motherfuckin-Geddon," "Tainted Love," "Personal Jesus"

Mark Lanegan: "Methamphetamine Blues," "Phantasmagoria Blues," "Gravedigger's Song," "Riot in My House," "Black Pudding," "Pentacostal"

Morcheeba: "Even Though"

Nick Cave and the Bad Seeds: "Red Right Hand," "Ain't Gonna Rain Anymore"

Orgy: "Blue Monday," "Social Enemies"

Peaches: "Boys Wanna Be Her"

Pussycat Dolls: "Buttons," "Don't Cha"

REM: "Drive"

Rob Zombie: "Living Dead Girl," "American Witch," "Mars Needs Women," "Never Gonna Stop"

Scorpions: "The Zoo"

Screaming Trees: "Where the Twain Shall Meet," "Dime Western," "Gospel Plow"

Stone Temple Pilots: "Sour Girl," "Atlanta"

Tamaryn: "While You're Sleeping, I'm Dreaming," "Violet's in a Pool," "The Waves," "Afterlight," "Transcendent Blue"

Thompson Twins: "The Gap," "Love on Your Side," "All Fall Out," "Watching," "Doctor! Doctor!"

Tom Petty: "Mary Jane's Last Dance"

Transplants: "Diamonds and Guns"

The Verve: "Bittersweet Symphony"

Warchild: "Ash"

Zero 7: "In the Waiting Line"

Turn the page to read an excerpt
from the next book in the Otherworld series

Panther Prowling

Coming February 2015 from Jove Books

"Do you think she knows what we're up to?" Menolly fretted. She hiked herself up onto the counter of the newly renovated Wayfarer Bar & Grill and began swinging her legs. It had been rebuilt, revamped, and revitalized, and tonight we were going to rock the block with a grand reopening party, welcoming back—we hoped—all the regulars who had made the Wayfarer their local watering hole. The doors opened in twenty minutes and we were just killing time as the staff finished last-minute touches, which included a massive number of balloons for Camille's birthday, which also happened to be today.

I sat on one of barstools, absently flipping through a book I'd picked up at the pet store: *How To Take Care of Your Mouse*. I had no plans on getting pet mice any time soon—that idea could too easily turn into a disaster. No, my friend Misha, a mouse who had helped me out in a sticky situation, had just died. I wanted to look after her children . . . and her children's children. The micelings were still frightened of me, but I'd managed to keep my promise to her and never once had chased after her extended family when I shifted into cat form.

"Probably. Camille makes it her business to know everything about everybody. She can't help it. It's the control freak in her. You know that by now."

Hunger pangs hit my stomach and I ran my tongue over my teeth. I'd just had them polished and the dentist had been a nervous wreck the entire time. Even though he was Supefriendly, my fangs were sharp, and while not overly large, they didn't retract. Slicing a finger open would be all too easy, and I could feel him tense up the entire time he was checking through my mouth.

Occasionally I cut my tongue on them, but I figured that was all part of being a werecat. What was really dicey were blow jobs. Shade and I had managed to work out a system so I didn't hurt him most of the time, but in the end, it was easier to focus our attentions on other forms of love play, given the risks.

"I'm hungry, you have any snacks in this joint?"

Menolly leaned over and flicked my nose. "Doofus. I'm surprised you aren't packing a candy bar. Go check near the birthday cake in the kitchen—we have plenty of cupcakes and one or two won't be missed. We won't be firing up the grill till its officially opening time, so if you want, grab yourself one . . . or some nuts from the bar." She smiled and let out a satisfied laugh. "Kitten, I can't tell you what a relief it is to actually *have* a decent grill to go with the name."

Before an arsonist had torched it, the Wayfarer Bar & Grill's kitchen was barely passable. The cook had managed a few simple things like fries and burgers, or grilled cheese, or cold sandwiches—standard dive food. It had been filling but nothing to write home about.

But during renovations, Menolly had consulted with the architect and they'd redesigned the entire joint. She had commandeered the upper floor and ditched her attempts to turn into a bed-and-breakfast. Instead, they'd relocated the kitchen upstairs, added an elevator, and revamped the staircase to make it user-friendly. A dumbwaiter and intercom system completed the cooking arrangements. They'd gutted two of the bedrooms in order to create a large private meeting room, to be rented out as needed.

"Are you going to miss having a bed-and-breakfast?" I glanced around. While the outside of the building looked the same—red brick, old, and historic—inside, the Wayfarer had a far different feel than when we'd first came Earthside and Menolly had started working as a bartender for her cover job.

"No, I don't think so. I barely had one, anyway. The bar had its charms, but now it's *my* vision, through and through." She glanced around, a satisfied look on her face. "As painful as the fire was, at least I was able to rebuild and put my own stamp on it."

She bit her lip, drawing a drop of blood with her fangs. That they were showing told me she was stressed. Unlike me, vampires had retractable fangs. I knew she was thinking about the people who had been lost during the fire but I said nothing, no use scraping an open wound.

The walls were covered with postcards and wine labels, the bar was polished to a high sheen, as were the barstools. Two large tables that seated up to ten people each took center stage. The booths had been rebuilt, their upholstery now a supple black leather. All the tables on the floor were new, the wood was a deep mahogany, rich and warm.

Menolly had asked the contractor to build a dance floor and, to replace the antique jukebox, she'd installed satellite radio. Two large-screen televisions were mounted on the side wall of the bar itself for the sports freaks who occasionally came in—she kept the sound off, but they were continually running two different games.

But despite all of the Earthside trappings everywhere I looked, I could see touches from Otherworld, giving the Wayfarer an exotic feel. Star crystals from the mines of the Nebulveori Mountains. Woven lattice tapestries from the shores of Terial, the Eastern Port on the Mirami Ocean. And sandcast urns holding dried flowers, potted from the dunes of the Sandwhistle Desert. The Wayfarer Bar & Grill had become a beautiful hybrid between the two worlds.

"Well, I approve of the kitchen. I approve of anything to

do with food." I reached out and ran my hand along the red brick of the wall. There was a lot of red brick in this building and together with the warm wood and muted lighting, it gave the bar a cave-like feeling, but in a cozy, protected manner.

Menolly sobered. "To tell you the truth, I don't think that I could rebuild as a bed-and-breakfast, given the fire was set in one of the bedrooms. No matter how much people say the deaths weren't my fault, I'll never be able to forget." She gave a quick nod toward the new waitress. "I just hope she works out."

I followed her gaze. Jenny, an FBH—full-blooded human. Camille had met her at Broom Stix, a magic shop, and Jenny had taken Chrysandra's place as head waitress. She was a good worker, eager to learn, and just as eager to be out of her stepmother's store.

"She'll do a good job. She's sincere. But I'm surprised you hired another FBH, given Chrysandra . . ." I stopped at the stricken look on my sister's face. "I'm sorry . . . I didn't think." Great, I was just making things worse. I had a knack for opening mouth, inserting foot.

After a moment, Menolly shrugged. "What can I say? Her death will always weigh heavy on my shoulders. Especially, the end." She flinched. Chrysandra's end had been rough and Menolly had played a part in releasing her the only way she knew how. "But you're right, Jenny will do a good job. She's smart, personable, and sassy enough to handle the customers we get. The vamp crowd will love her." She glanced at the clock. "So when does the birthday girl arrive?"

"Camille and Smoky are supposed to be here in about ten minutes. Smoky said he'd have her here right before the opening. They'll come in the back, so the crowd out front doesn't swarm in behind them." I grinned. "You have a fan club waiting, you know." I jerked my finger toward the front of the building.

"I'm surprised anybody's showing up, considering how many people died during the fire. Final count . . . twenty-five deaths, including vampires." Again, the haunted look.

I wanted to wipe away the memory, wipe away the guilt I

knew Menolly felt, but there was nothing I could do. Only time would help her sort out everything that happened.

So, instead, I forced a bright smile. "*I'm* not surprised in the least. People love this place. And they love you." I reached out, patted her hand. The coldness of her skin had ceased to bother me. She was just my sister now, even if she was a vampire.

I wasn't lying. There *was* a crowd out front. A number of vamps—I assumed they were vampires by their pallor—had shown up to show their support for the Wayfarer and my sister. There were also a number of Weres and Fae out there. All in all, there must have been fifty people outside, waiting in the rain-soaked January evening.

But tonight was more than the reopening. Tonight, we'd planned a special surprise. It was also Camille's birthday. Smoky had volunteered to keep her occupied until we were ready for her, while the rest of us decked out the bar for both the reopening and her party.

"I'm not so sure about this, Delilah. You know Camille isn't much on surprises. You think we can pull this off without a hitch, given our track record?"

I wrinkled my nose. "I know our parties kind of suck, but at least this time nobody's hired a stripper."

It was sadly true. We seldom had people begging us to throw another shindig. But it was also true that, at least this time, there was no stripper in a fringed G-string for me to attack as my fluffy-butt tabby self. Although the balloons were mesmerizing, I could keep a handle on myself unless the ribbons were left dangling. Then all bets were off. Candy in front of the baby time.

Shade sidled up to me and slid one arm around my waist. He nuzzled my neck and I planted a kiss on his cheek. We were officially beyond the honeymoon stage, and had been together almost a year and a half by this point. But as I leaned my head against his side, the warmth of his musky scent quickened my pulse. I'd rapidly fallen in love with him—and it was the kind of love I'd never experienced before we met. He was loving and funny, and sexy in that easy, comfortable way.

Shade reached into his pocket for something, but at that moment, Jenny came scurrying out from the back.

"Your sister is here." Her eyes were wide. Camille had cowed her at one point, and she still seemed to be scared of her.

"Thanks, we'll take it from here. You go ahead and finish checking all the booths and tables to make sure everything is ready." Menolly jumped off the bar. She glanced around. "Everybody here?"

I counted. Trillian and Morio were in the corner— Camille's other husbands. She had three of them and they were all very happy together, if at times a little loud.

Vanzir—a dream-chaser demon—and Roz—an incubus— were playing darts together. We called them the demon twins. Hanna, our housekeeper from the Northlands, and Maggie, our baby calico gargoyle, were sitting at a table with Iris and Bruce.

Nerissa—Menolly's wife—carried the cake down from the kitchen. She set it on one of the large tables. Everybody was here tonight, including Erin, Menolly's middle-aged "daughter," Roman, the son of the vampire queen, and Chase, the FBH detective who had become part of our extended family. Even Mistletoe and Feddrah-Dahns had traveled over from Otherworld for the party, though having a unicorn at any function was always problematic.

"Yep, looks like we're good to go." I motioned to Jenny. "Ask Smoky to bring her in."

Whatever excuse the dragon had made for keeping our sister out of the way appeared to have worked. Menolly doused the lights and, a moment later, a rustle told us they'd entered the room. But as she flicked the lights on again and we all yelled "Surprise," we found ourselves shouting and throwing confetti at one very nervous toadsquatter.

"Ah, hell!" Menolly's fangs came down and she launched herself forward, but just then Camille and Smoky followed the creature through the door.

"Stop!" Camille grabbed the arm of the toadsquatter, yanking him out of the way. The squat goblin-like figure let out a shriek and hissed at her. "Shut up, you little weasel."

She swatted his nose as Smoky loomed up behind her, all six-foot-four of him.

"What the fuck?" Menolly pulled back. "What's *that* doing in my bar?"

A whiff of the toadsquatter's stench hit me and I grimaced. Lovely. Cross a patch of skunk cabbage with a lumberjack who's gone a week without showering and that's pretty much what the creature smelled like. My stomach shifted just enough to make me wish we were another three yards apart from each other.

Derrick Means, Menolly's bartender and a werebadger, stared at the thing with a horrified look on his face. He leaned over to me and asked, "What the hell is that? It looks like a goblin that's been squashed and deformed."

"Toadsquatter. From Otherworld. A mutant version of goblins. Goblins use them as slaves, and the toadsquatters hate them as much as we do. The little creeps aren't blameless though—they can be nasty-tempered, fickle, and they're all a pack of thieves." Which begged the question: Why was one of them standing in the bar, and why had Camille protected him from Menolly?

Derrick, whose pony tail was black streaked with white, shook his head. "Guess it's no worse than some of the things we have over here. I bet you have no clue how many strange beasties we have running around the woods."

"I'll bet you're right." I grinned at him. Derrick was usually pretty grumpy, but he was fair, honest, and respectful. And that was more than we got from a lot of the Earthside crowd, FBHs or Supes.

Camille was trying to calm the toadsquatter, who was—by now—disturbingly close to tears. "Don't upset him any more. He has important information for me, or so he says."

Menolly paused. "Information?"

"We think he may know the name of the sorcerer who is tracking Camille." Smoky glared at the toadsquatter, obviously not thrilled with this turn of events.

Camille knelt down by the creature. Toadsquatters were about four feet high, and squat. And butt-ugly. "Listen, calm down. I warned you people would react this way, so chill out. I promised you that if your info was worth it, I'd give you a reward, didn't I?"

He nodded and, in a halting variant of the common tongue from Otherworld, said, "Yes, yes . . . You promised. You have to promise they won't kill me, though." He jerked his finger toward us. I'd say *thumb*, but since he had six or seven digits I wasn't sure which stood in for what finger.

"I promise." Camille stared at the rest of us, and we slowly nodded our heads. None of us were too enthusiastic, though. While toadsquatters weren't inherently evil like their brother race of goblins, they *were* sneaky and reminiscent of cockroaches—they might not do anything to you, but they were so nasty you just kind of wanted to squash them.

She straightened up and looked around, her gaze falling on the cake. "Oh, hell—birthday party? For me?"

"Yeah, but you kind of blew that one out of the water." Menolly laughed. "Let's get drinks started, Derrick. Camille—take that . . . thing . . . to my office. I don't want my customers coming in here and finding him."

Camille grabbed the toadsquatter by the hand and started for the back.

Menolly turned back to us. "Delilah, carry the presents to my office, please. We don't want them to get stolen. It's time for me to unlock the doors. Luckily, I ordered a gigantic cake—big enough for my patrons. But Jenny, would you set it out of sight till we're done talking to that creature?"

And with that flurry of orders, Menolly headed over to unlock the doors. I gathered up the presents, then paused, watching her as she inserted the key, and unlocked the Wayfarer for the first time in over two months since it had been destroyed by an arsonist.

The crowds flooded in, swamping the staff. I headed for the back, presents safely in my arms, once it appeared that everything was going off without a hitch. Menolly motioned that she'd join us in a bit.

The office had been expanded, and now we all managed to fit in it, albeit a little snugly. I set the gifts on the desk, and Camille walked over, looking at them. Smoky was holding the toadsquatter in place, his hand firmly on the creature's head. The toadsquatter wasn't moving, but neither did he look like he wanted to be here, and I didn't blame him. He was in the middle of a group of people who could easily make mincemeat out of him and who wouldn't mind doing so. His gaze darted toward the door.

"Easy boy. You're not going anywhere. Not yet. So, what's your name?" Smoky asked.

Shifty-eyes thought for a moment, then sighed. "Rataam."

"Well, Rataam, you can give us the information we're looking for and leave here alive. *However*, if I discover that you've gone back to whoever you've been snooping for and ratted us out, I'll personally track down your family and there will be no more little Rataam babies in the world. Do I make myself clear?" When Smoky played hardball, he didn't hesitate to break heads.

The toadsquatter gulped and nodded.

Smoky let go of his head. "Tell us what you know, then. If it's worth it, we'll pay you for your knowledge."

Rataam ducked his squat head. He really did look very toad-like and for a moment I felt sorry for him. It was a scary thing to be surrounded by people who could pull you apart. I'd been there. But then, he let out a noise—I didn't know what it was and didn't want to—and his stench filled the room.

"Oh dude, that's nasty. Do you have to do that?" I blurted out the words before I could stop myself.

Rataam scowled, but ignored me. Instead, he turned to Camille. "The sorcerer following you is named Iyonah."

Iyonah . . . we'd had a run in with the woman recently—or rather, Camille had. But none of us realized she was anything other than a blip on the radar of "potential issues." That she was following Camille and out to kill her stepped up the whole game.

Camille blanched. "Oh, fuck. I knew there was something about her! How do you know this? How do you even know about me?"

"I only know about her because I was paid to find out. I never heard of you before my employer paid me to look into the matter." Ratam shifted, obviously uncomfortable.

I blinked. The fact that someone paid the toadsquatter to snoop into Camille's life was unnerving. Apparently, Camille thought so, too, because she knelt beside him, pale and looking worried.

"And *who* is your employer?" She took his hand in hers, unleashing her glamour, which immediately seemed to have a calming effect on the creature.

He let out a long breath. "Promise you won't tell them I told you?"

She held up her hand. "On the Moon Mother's honor."

Rataam scuffed his foot on the floor, then shrugged. "Raven Mother. She asked me to find out who was following you, and to warn you."

Startled, Camille withdrew her hand and stood up. Raven Mother could be bad news when she wanted to be. But for some reason, she'd decided to help us out. That didn't mean we could trust her, though. Raven Mother was wily and cunning, and she had so many hidden agendas that our enemies looked like simpletons compared to her.

Camille had been getting to know more about the Elemental than she ever wanted to know—she had no choice given the way events had been turning. As a result, Menolly and I'd been privy to a number of late-night conversations. Intrigue seemed to run rampant in the whole Raven Mother-Triple Threat-Moon Mother triangle that was going on.

"Did Raven Mother tell you *why* she wanted you to spy on me?" Camille's eyes flashed—they were a vivid shade of violet, and now silver flecks appeared. No, she wasn't happy, and her magic was rising.

Rataam shook his head. "No, but she made it clear it was important. She threatened to destroy my family if I didn't do what she asked." He sounded disheartened and I instantly felt guilty for being so uncharitable toward him.

Smoky and Camille looked at each other, and she slowly nodded. There was no real way of telling if he was lying, but odds were, Raven Mother hadn't told him *what* Iyonah wanted. Her motives might be questionable, but she wasn't stupid by any means.

Smoky let out a grumpy sigh. "All right, we will pay you

well, but only if you vow on your family's life to keep your mouth shut about everything that's happened. As long as you keep your bargain, we won't tell Raven Mother that you told us it was she who hired you." Smoky nodded to the door. "Come, I'll take you to a portal where you can return to Otherworld immediately."

Camille kept her mouth shut until Smoky escorted the creature out. Then she let out a slow whistle. "I should have known Iyonah was up to no good. I think I did, I just didn't realize she was after *me*."

Irritated that we had to focus on enemies, even on our birthdays, I shook my head and gave her a hug. "Well, we should be able to take care of the matter as long as she remains clueless to the fact that you know about her. We'll go over there tomorrow." I pointed to her presents. "Meanwhile, birthday party."

"You didn't hire a stripper, did you?" She stared at me, pointedly.

I blushed, but then swatted her playfully. "No, and I'm not going to turn into a cat and go lunging after the customers tonight, either. But, can you imagine Smoky walking into the room to find a guy jiggling his junk in your face?"

Trillian meandered over, laughing. "Oh, I'd *pay* to see that." He, Smoky, and Morio had a good-natured rivalry going on. While they were all married to Camille and she loved each of them with a passion, they still sparred at times. But when push came to shove, they had one anothers' backs, and together they surrounded her with a ring of protection that sometimes chafed at her. I knew because the three of us didn't have secrets.

Feddrah-Dahns spoke up. For a unicorn, his voice was simultaneously melodic and authoritative. "This Iyonah—I will send Mistletoe home right now to do research on her. Don't take her on until we've dug up everything we can. He'll return within forty-eight Earthside hours. I don't want you in any more danger than you already are. If she's truly a sorcerer, chances are she's fairly powerful. And powerful sorcerers are danger incarnate."

Before Camille could say a word, I interrupted. "She

promises. She'll be good and wait. Now, can we go join the party? This is Menolly's special night, and it's also special for Camille. We don't get many celebrations. Please, let's enjoy the ones we can." I pushed Camille toward the door and, for the moment, the issue was shelved.

The front was rocking, the music loud, and the bar crowded.

The two large center tables were reserved for our party, but most of the booths were full, as were the counter stools. Our friends were packing the joint, showing their support for Menolly.

In one corner, Marion Vespa—the owner of the Supe-Urban Café—and her husband were ordering drinks. Jonas and his werebear buddies had crowded into a booth and were eating burgers and fries, along with giant steins of beer. At a table near the door, Frank Willows, the leader of the Supe Militia, was holding court with three other werewolves.

And, of course, Roman, the son of the Vampire Queen, sat in the most luxurious booth, along with several of the higher-ups from the Seattle Vampire Nexus. Menolly was his official consort. She walked a tight wire between her wife, Nerissa, and Roman. Nerissa was her heart-mate. Roman offered her the chance to play hard when she needed to let herself go. Both were head over heels about my sister and skirted each other with varying degrees of respect and suspicion.

All in all, the bar was crowded, and it made me happy to see the look on Menolly's face. She'd expected people to ostracize her after what happened, but the truth was none of it was her fault. Maybe tonight would drive that through her thick skull.

As we gathered around the table, Jenny brought over the cake. Camille winked at her, and the girl, flustered, stuttered out a "Happy Birthday" and immediately left.

"Hey, I wanted to order—" Camille laughed. "I'm going to have to do something to put Jenny at ease, it seems." She stood up, looking over at the bar.

I motioned for her to sit down. "You're the birthday girl.

I'll get a waitress. What do you want to drink? Do you want anything to eat?"

"I want a Goblin Blaster and can you order me a grilled cheese and fries? We'll cut the cake while we're waiting for the food." She was eying the massive sheet cake like I eyed catnip. Normally Camille didn't go for sweets, but Earthside store-bought birthday cake had proven to be a weakness for her.

I motioned to a different waitress and gave her Camille's order, and my own. Grilled cheese sounded good, so I asked for two. As the others ordered, I pushed my way up to the bar. Derrick, along with Digger—the assistant bartender who was also a vamp—were mixing drinks as fast as they could.

Derrick winked at me. "What do you need?"

"Camille wants a Goblin Blaster. For me? A Kahlúa and cream, please." I didn't drink a lot, but when I did, I preferred my booze with something to soften the impact.

He raised an eyebrow. "She wants a Goblin Blaster? We don't get much call for those. They're an acquired taste, that's for sure." As he began mixing up the basil liqueur with orange juice and both light and dark rum, the drink took on an earthy, pungent smell. The drink almost glowed green, and I grimaced. I preferred my drinks sweet.

Derrick added a twist of orange to the glass, then whipped up my Kahlúa and cream, and slid both drinks across the counter. I started to thank him but he had already moved on to his next order.

I picked up the drinks and brought them back to the table, handing Camille's to her. She took a long sip and closed her eyes. Something about the basil and orange really appealed to her. Like me, she wasn't much of a drinker, but ever since Menolly had concocted the recipe, Camille had, for the most part, stuck to a standing order.

Over the past few weeks, Menolly had gotten so irritable without the Wayfarer to distract her that she'd turned her lair into a makeshift bar and had managed to get just about everyone in the house drunk at one point or another, experimenting with new recipes. The upside was the drink menu at the Wayfarer had increased by at least fifty percent.

While we waited for the food, Camille cut the cake. The frosting was an inch thick and my taste buds were doing a happy dance on my tongue. Camille's favorite flavors were strawberry and lemon, so the cake was strawberry with lemon icing. There were chocolate cupcakes for those whose tastes ran to the more traditional, but I wasn't picky. If it was cake, I'd eat it. And I did. Two pieces of cake and three cupcakes.

Menolly climbed on the counter and whistled to the bar. "Listen up! Tonight's not just the reopening of the Wayfarer, but it's also my sister Camille's birthday, as you may have surmised. We have a lot of cake here, so feel free to drop by our table for a slice. It's free till it's gone."

A general round of applause rang through the bar as I settled in beside Camille and Menolly with a sigh of satisfaction. Despite the toadsquatter, everything had gone off without a hitch.

A little voice in the back of my head kept whispering, *Don't let down your guard*, but I was tired of always being on alert, and I decided what the hell. I'd let down my hair for once. A giggle escaped. That was more than a cliché for once. I actually *could* let down my hair more than usual, because I'd started growing it back in. I was sporting a chin-length shag. Shade liked it, and while I wasn't sure I'd ever grow it long again, it was fun for a change.

I downed the Kahlúa and cream and got a second, then a third round of drinks for Camille and myself. A fourth followed shortly. The volume of noise was rising to a steady buzz now as more people crowded into the bar, and I blinked, realizing that I wasn't following any particular conversation, but instead, I just sat back, taking it all in.

Menolly was beaming. Another round of drinks later, and the party was growing louder.

Wild Cherry came over the speakers, singing "Play That Funky Music." Nerissa grabbed Menolly's hand and dragged her up to dance. Nerissa towered over Menolly in her tawny, werepuma glory, but the two could boogie it up good. In a

skintight hot pink minidress, with golden hair and gold sparkling heels that sent her over six feet tall, Nerissa was a
striking sight.

Camille and Trillian followed, spinning onto the dance
floor in all their fetish goth-glory. Dark and vampy, they
made one hell of a pair. I blinked. Trillian cut a damn fine
figure, now that I looked at him through my Kahlúa colored
eyes. The song shifted and it was retro city all over again,
with "Electric Avenue," followed by "She Blinded Me with
Science," then "Whip It," and of course "Safety Dance."

I polished off my drink and grabbed Shade's hand.
"Dance with me."

He blinked. I danced, but it wasn't a common request,
considering I preferred curling up on the sofa with television
and junk food.

"Are you sure, babe? You look a little flushed." His voice
sounded huskier than usual, and I wanted nothing more than
to press up against him.

I glanced down at the glasses on the table. Apparently, I'd
had seven rounds, not four like I thought. But though my
mind was a little fuzzy, more than anything, I wanted to
dance with my lover.

"Dance. *Now!*"

We whirled out on the dance floor, but I whirled a little
too enthusiastically and would have gone toppling to the
floor, except that Shade had a tight grip on my hand.

He pulled me back into his arms and we began shaking it
up to "Elevator Man" by Oingo Boingo.

But as Shade spun me around, I began to realize that
maybe I was a tad drunk. Booze hit my system overly fast
and I hadn't planned on having seven drinks, that was for
sure. Not entirely certain what I was doing, I just attempted
to stay on my feet. I probably should have asked Shade to
take me back to the table, but I was so light-headed I couldn't
seem to form the words.

The next minute, none of that mattered.

The door burst open and Daniel, our Earthside, FBH
cousin, darted inside, followed by what looked like a very
angry Viking. The muscle-bound man wearing the leather

breeches and tunic grabbed Daniel by the collar and lifted him over his head.

Shade let go of my hand and I was so startled that I tripped back into the crowd, taking down a couple of vampires who were dancing. We hit the floor as Daniel sailed across the room; the Viking tossed him like a Scotsman tossing a log in the Highland Games.

As Daniel landed in a shuddering heap by my side, Camille darted toward the northern intruder, but the man took one look at her, then at the rest of the bar, and vanished from sight, as if he'd never existed.

New York Times bestselling author **Yasmine Galenorn** writes urban fantasy, mystery, and metaphysical nonfiction. A graduate of Evergreen State College, she majored in theater and creative writing. Yasmine has been in the Craft for more than thirty-four years and is a shamanic witch. She describes her life as a blend of teacups and tattoos, and lives in the Seattle area with her husband, Samwise, and their cats. Yasmine can be reached at her website at galenorn.com, and via Twitter at twitter.com/yasminegalenorn, and via her publisher. If you send her snail mail, please enclose a self-addressed stamped envelope if you want a reply.

Don't miss *New York Times* bestselling author

YASMINE GALENORN'S

"addictive"* bestselling series!

NIGHT'S END

An Indigo Court Novel

Newly crowned Fae Queens Cicely and Rhiannon have embraced their destinies and claimed their thrones. But Myst is rising once more, and now, at the helm of her armies, she begins her final assault on the Golden Wood. As Fae, vampires, and magic-born alike fall under the tide of blood, Cicely and her friends must discover a way to destroy the spidery queen before they—and their people—face total annihilation.

Praise for the Indigo Court novels

"Filled with taut suspense, delicious intrigue, and dangerous antagonists."
—*Smexy Books*

"Galenorn has created a multifaceted world full of adventure and passion!"
—*RT Book Reviews*

galenorn.com
facebook.com/AuthorYasmineGalenorn
facebook.com/ProjectParanormalBooks
penguin.com

M1488T0414

FROM *NEW YORK TIMES* BESTSELLING AUTHOR
YASMINE GALENORN

Crimson Veil

An Otherworld Novel

Meet the D'Artigo sisters: savvy half-human, half-Fae
operatives for the Otherworld Intelligence Agency. With
a war in Otherworld and a daemon to stop in Seattle,
their enemies are closing in on all sides. And this time,
there's no place to hide...

PRAISE FOR THE OTHERWORLD NOVELS

"Yasmine Galenorn creates a world
I never want to leave."
—#1 *New York Times* bestselling author Sherrilyn Kenyon

"Spectacularly hot and supernaturally breathtaking."
—*New York Times* bestselling author Alyssa Day

galenorn.com
facebook.com/AuthorYasmineGalenorn
facebook.com/ProjectParanormalBooks
penguin.com